Darrell, E.

SCARLET SHADOWS

Author's Note

All aspiring authors long to see their work in print, so when a mainstream publisher asked to talk to me about two historical novels with a military background I'd submitted, I was thrilled. We faced each other across a pocket-handkerchief-sized table in a trendy London restaurant as she explained that she was presently having great success with big historical blockbusters. "So what I want you to do," she said, "is to take bits from both these stories, link them together, then add the Crimean War."

Before I knew it I heard myself say, "No, sorry."

We gazed at each other bemused. She because an unknown author had probably never before refused the kind of opportunity she was offering, and I because I was wondering how to tell my husband that I had thrown away my big chance to get published. Feeling miserable, yet knowing I wouldn't do as she suggested, I said desperately, "I could write you a new novel featuring the Crimean War, instead."

Scarlet Shadows is that novel. It not only started a long, successful career, but also prompted my ongoing fascination with the kind of men and women who endured war in those harsher days. Our ancestors. Our history.

And the other two novels? They were later extended and published under the titles *Beyond All Frontiers* and *Forget the Glory,* both soon to be reissued by Severn House.

© Elizabeth Darrell, June 2000.

Other titles by Elizabeth Darrell

SCARLET
SHADOWS

Elizabeth Darrell

severn
House

This first hardcover edition published in Great Britain 2000 by
SEVERN HOUSE PUBLISHERS LTD of
9–15 High Street, Sutton, Surrey SM1 1DF.
Originally published in Great Britain 1978 in paperback format
by Futura Publications, Ltd under the pseudonym *Emma Drummond.*
This first hardcover edition published in the USA 2000 by
SEVERN HOUSE PUBLISHERS INC of
595 Madison Avenue, New York, N.Y. 10022.
Previously published in paperback format by
Dell Publishing Co., Inc. under the pseudonym *Emma Drummond.*

British Library Cataloguing in Publication Data

Darrell, Elizabeth, 1931-
  Scarlet shadows
  1. Love stories
  I. Title
  823.9'14 [F]

ISBN 0-7278-5495-X

Printed and bound in Great Britain by MPG Books Ltd, Bodmin, Cornwall.

PART ONE

CHAPTER ONE

Whenever the Castledons gave a ball, it was Nanny's custom to indulge her young charges by allowing them to creep onto the gallery in their dressing gowns to see the scene in the hall below. This chilly night in late October 1852 was no exception; the two youngest Castledon children knelt side by side with their faces pressed through the carved wooden balustrade, unseen by guests who danced a lively quadrille.

The children saw nothing of the rich paneling of the walls, the paintings and framed diplomas that hung there, nor the elegant porcelain chandeliers highlighting the only room in the house large enough to allow dancing. Both pairs of eyes were glued to the changing kaleidoscope of color as crinoline swayed between gay scarlet, blue and gold: the boy and girl were intent on the opulently uniformed military men whose presence made the ballroom come alive.

A contingent of officers from the local garrison outside Brighton provided the brave scarlet tunics of foot regiments and the more dashing blue and gold of Hussar jackets with fur-trimmed slung pelisses designed with more thought of impressing the ladies than daunting the enemy. It was on these that the girl had her eyes as the officers took their partners through the dance with the panache for which they were famed, and her head became full of dreams and sighs. The boy stared at the infantrymen in scarlet and thought his own thoughts. For perhaps ten minutes they watched in silence until the girl could contain herself no longer.

"How handsome they are!" she breathed, shiny-eyed.

The boy's pudgy hands tightened their grip on the balustrade bars. *"Dancing!"* he exploded with the scorn of a ten-year-old male. "Soldiers are not for dancing, but for fighting wars. They are brave and strong. They fight on and on, even when the cannons are blowing them into little bits, or when they are chopped up by the enemy's swords."

The girl fell silent as his horrifying words burst into her dreams and broke them apart. Below her a young Hussar subaltern was laughing into the eyes of his partner, and, as she watched him, the little girl felt a knot form inside her stomach, an anguish she had never before felt and could not identify. With her eyes following the handsome lieutenant, she whispered, "*Really* into little bits?"

"Yes," came the unemotional answer. "Arms, legs and heads fly about all over the place. And bits of bodies, too," he added for effect. "It wouldn't be a real war otherwise."

It was too much for the girl's awakening womanhood. She turned to bury her face in Nanny's skirts, crying as if her heart would break, but the boy, having received a severe reprimand, stumped back to the nursery, unabashed.

"When I become a soldier, I shall go to war, not waste my time on dancing," he muttered to himself.

The Hussar subaltern who had caught the little girl's first romantic fancies was certainly far from thoughts of being cut to ribbons by enemy swords. England had been at peace for forty years—practically double his lifetime—and at this moment his head and heart were full of the painful knowledge that he would obey any command from his beautiful partner if, by doing so, she would think more generously of him.

Victoria Castledon, fresh from the schoolroom, had taken the military garrison by storm this summer. There was hardly a subaltern who was not head over ears in love with her and threatening to blow out his brains if she looked at any other man (although Miss Castledon had looked at a great many gentlemen throughout the summer months, without the strength of the garrison being tragically reduced). Admittedly, Captain Augustus Parchmore had broken his shoulder on the hunting field due, according to the gallant warrior, to his distress on being rebuffed by the young lady, but those who had seen him ride to hounds knew it was more likely a careless seat than a broken heart that had caused his fall.

The Castledon girls were fair and pink-cheeked, but this one, a cousin who had been orphaned as a child, blazed from their midst like a dark velvet rose amid frilly carnations. No fault could be found with her manners, but she had an unusual forthrightness that left matrons clucking and officers charmed. Some females uncharitably suggested that Miss Castledon cultivated this trait to gain favor with the more dashing members of the garrison, but the lovelorn officers could see only fresh innocence in their heroine's engaging ways.

Now, the summer flirtations, the tantalizing carriage rides, the carefully calculated chance meetings, the words that flattered or shattered, the sun-drenched picnics, the idyll, had ended. Major the Honorable Charles Stanford, heir to Lord Blythe, had finally fallen victim to one of the fair sex, albeit a child of not yet eighteen, and plainly meant to offer her his name and future title. The girl might be half her suitor's age, but none thought her likely to refuse such an advantageous offer on that count, and even if she had thoughts of doing so, her aunt must surely dissuade her from them. With four daughters of her own to settle advantageously, Almeira Castledon must regard Major Stanford's offer as a godsend—even if it meant the little cousin beat the two older Misses Castledon to the altar with a coronet, to boot.

Victoria became aware that her partner had grown strangely silent as they swung round in the last figure of the dance.

"If you spoke the truth when you claimed to have been counting the minutes until this quadrille, Mr. Edmunds, you have very soon tired of it. You have not spoken since the gallopade."

Harry Edmunds was jolted back to the present to meet laughing reproach in a pair of large brown eyes, but his reply held none of the banter with which she had spoken.

"You must know by now that the pleasure of your company makes many a fellow lost for words, Miss Castledon."

Victoria reveled in such speeches from young suitors. She had never wondered whether they were sincere. Flirting was a delightful game she had discovered—a game too new to be marred by thoughts of heartaches and shattered hopes. She could not resist tormenting him further.

"Dear me, if that is the case I must consider retiring, at once. It would never do for my aunt to have a completely silent company at her ball."

"Better that than have no company at all. For that is

what would happen if the loveliest creature present were to retire."

Victoria felt a small pang then, and the smile died on her lips. She had entertained foolish dreams of Harry Edmunds for one whole month in the summer, when his sweep of dark hair and merry blue eyes had filled her thoughts, but he was only a subaltern, and Aunt Almeira had very firmly put an end to his hopes and Victoria's youthful infatuation. Nevertheless, there was still an element about him that called to the young girl with disturbing persistence, and she looked up at him from her sweeping curtsy, feeling it quite strongly.

"How absurd you are, sometimes."

The young officer looked unhappier than ever and gazed down at her with an expression she did not recognize. "I beg you not to laugh at me. That would be the final blow."

She was dismayed. "I . . . I did not mean to . . . "

"If it is absurd to see only you in a room full of people, to listen only for the sound of your voice, to know the day will be empty unless you appear, then I am absurd," he went on huskily, taking her hand in both his gloved ones as she rose from her curtsy. "Miss Castledon . . . *Victoria* . . . tonight will see an end to my impossible hopes, but I swear I shall be your devoted slave as long as I live."

Thrown into complete bewilderment she had no idea why he was suddenly showing such excess of feeling in so public a place, but she was soft-hearted enough to know he was completely vulnerable to the slightest hurt if she did not treat him with kindness.

"I am very flattered and grateful," she told him, "but I do not see what tonight has to do with it that it will make our friendship in any way different."

For answer, he gripped her hand tighter. There was desperation in his voice. "I know they think the match brilliant—and I daresay it is—but it is more than a fellow can bear to see a sweet beautiful creature . . . " He broke off and tried to take hold of himself. "You will be out of my reach forever, but if there is ever any service I can perform for you, if ever you are desperate for someone to turn to, swear you will call on me wherever I am."

With her heart thudding against her bodice, Victoria suddenly became aware that retiring dancers had left them isolated in the center of the room, and eyes were watching the highly provocative scene they must be providing.

"*Please,*" she whispered urgently, "we are being observed." She tried to wrest her hand free of his, but he would not let her go. "Mr. Edmunds, I beg you to escort me from the floor."

Pale with emotion he went on. "Swear you will call on me if you ever need help," he insisted.

"Yes, yes, but I shall need help immediately if you do not take me to my aunt this minute."

Letting out a great sigh he obediently offered his arm for her gloved hand. "This has been the most wonderful and most painful night of my life. I shall never forget it."

Wishing the distance to her aunt shorter, Victoria walked beside her partner across a polished floor that looked immense now that she realized almost every eye in the room was upon her. Apart from the fact that Harry Edmunds had just behaved with immoderate ardor before the assembled company, it was surprisingly clear in a flash that there was an element of expectancy about the evening, after all. Had he been right to adopt an attitude that suggested he was never going to see her again and that she was about to be thrown into a state of great peril? Her legs became a little trembly, and did not improve when she saw the anger in Aunt Almeira's eyes, and the red spots in her cheeks.

"I had begun to think you had forgotten the direction of my chair, Mr. Edmunds," the matron said icily.

"My apologies, ma'am," the lieutenant began.

"I felt a little overcome after the exertions of the dance, Aunt," Victoria put in quickly, knowing the poor young man was unable to offer any excuse for his behavior. "Mr. Edmunds kindly supported me until I felt sufficiently recovered."

"Really?" Aunt Almeira was not appeased. "From here one would have thought Mr. Edmunds to have been under the greater affliction. You do not look at all well, young man," she told him. "I shall understand if you feel obliged to withdraw very shortly."

It was a directive to leave the ball from a very angry hostess—one that could not be ignored. Growing even paler, Harry Edmunds made his bows at the Castledon ladies with meticulous politeness. Then he turned to Victoria and said with an air of drama, "Goodbye, Miss Castledon."

She watched as he walked away, feeling a small shock because he had said *goodbye* instead of *good night*. She was very fond of him still, and the evening had become less enjoyable because of the incident. She turned to her aunt intending to ask why she had been so unkind to him. She did not have the chance to speak.

"How could you have allowed such a thing to happen?" hissed Aunt Almeira. "Was it your intention to make yourself the subject of gossip, and ruin all I have worked for? Right there in the middle of the room! I have seldom felt so mortified. What Major Stanford thought I dare not contemplate."

"Major Stanford?" echoed Victoria. "Why should Major Stanford be considered? It is usually the ladies who make a week-long topic of conversation from a small incident. Gentlemen are, fortunately, much more sensible."

Mrs. Castledon puffed herself up with indignation, then remembered that one should always appear as if nothing had happened under such circumstances, and smiled at Mrs. Ponsonby-Grayle before saying to her niece under her breath, "Gentlemen are not always so sensible when a matter concerns them very closely. And I advise you to mind your tongue, Victoria. It is not a delightful trait in a young female to find her putting forward comments that are distinctly argumentative. I earnestly recommend you to spend the next few minutes acquiring a more conciliatory manner. If the damage has not already been done you will need to present your most gentle and amiable face to the major when he comes to partner you in the supper dance. With the right response you might yet save the day, but I vow it will break my heart if this disgraceful affair with a young man I discouraged some months ago were to persuade the major to cry off. We should none of us be able to hold up our heads in society again, and your cousins would suffer, as a result."

In a flash, the answer to the puzzle confronted Victoria—why Harry Edmunds had bidden her a tragic farewell; why her aunt was so very put out; why tonight was different from any other. Harry had known, so had her aunt and all those watching her walk from the floor with the desperately unhappy lieutenant—everyone had known except herself that Major the Honorable Charles Stanford planned to declare himself tonight.

She did, indeed, mind her tongue, but not from any heed of her aunt's words. Feeling the breath in her lungs was not sufficient, she sat trying to cope with her discovery, young Harry Edmunds forgotten in thoughts of the man with whom her aunt could find no fault. When would he choose to speak? What would he say? How must she answer? It had come upon her so suddenly, it was impossible not to feel a heady sense of importance—an almost regal sensation. Looking around the ballroom she held her head just a little higher in an unconscious movement as she thought of being chosen from all the young females who were present by a man countless mamas had tried to snare for their daughters.

Tall, blond, handsome, and distinguished. She got that far in her mental description of the Honorable Charles Stanford, then paused. Add wealth and breeding to the list, and women like Aunt Almeira looked no further—but her aunt was not expected to marry him. Victoria knew so little about her suitor. He had beautiful manners—even if he appeared a little stiff after the high-spirited junior officers— and anticipated a lady's desires to perfection. A shady spot was always conveniently near on a picnic, a bouquet chosen in just the right color to match a dress or bonnet, a dinner was invariably selected to suit the most fastidious palate, and a box at the theater was always free from drafts.

Although he was not exactly amusing, one was never bored in Major Stanford's company, for he was an extremely cultured and well-traveled man, and Victoria realized that she liked him mainly because there was nothing to actually *dislike* about him. But there were two things about the future Lord Blythe that distinguished him from other gentlemen she liked. No one else had pursued her quite so relentlessly, and no other male acquaintance had behaved with such correctness yet had so filled her with such breathless timidity. To be truthful, she was slightly in awe of the man whom everyone expected to offer for her very shortly. There was something about the fleeting expressions in his pale blue eyes that set prickles of ice upon her skin whenever she thought about them.

"Victoria! Major Stanford is approaching. Pray iron out that awful frown and give some sign of the honor his attention affords you."

At her aunt's words the room sprang into color and shape, the genteel laughter and chatter that had faded on the wings of her daydream were around Victoria once more, and the warmth from the great log fire dispelled the momentary chill. An obedient reply sprang to her lips, but her thoughts were still wayward. For the first time this evening she looked at her aunt. She saw an elderly matron in maroon silk with an evening cap of ruched ribbons set upon gray sausage curls. She seemed quite sincere in her request. Could it be that Almeira Castledon had reached her vast age without discovering that a gentleman considered it an honor if a lady paid him attention, not the other way around? The simpering smile she had fixed upon her lips persuaded Victoria it must be so. Feeling a great deal wiser than her aunt, she turned to watch the major approach for the supper dance.

Charles Stanford was every inch a military aristocrat, from the proud set of his head to the assurance with which he crossed the room. A hundred or more speculating eyes turned in his direction might not have existed for all the notice he gave them, and Victoria attempted to match his nonchalance. Fighting the temptation to cast down her eyes, she even managed what she hoped was a cool smile. She would play the part to the full.

"You granted me the pleasure of the supper dance, Miss Castledon," he said with an elegant half-bow.

Victoria consulted her dance-card to suggest that she was not at all sure who was taking her to supper, then looked up wide-eyed.

"So I did, Major Stanford. I must confess I had not realized the time had passed so quickly. Can the evening really be half-flown?"

The major rose gallantly to the occasion. "On my part, the evening has only just begun." He favored Mrs. Castledon with a smile. "Not through any lack of entertainment, I assure you, ma'am."

Aunt Almeira glowed. "I perfectly understand, sir. When one is young, the success of the party does not always depend on what a hostess may provide."

A smile threatened to overcome Victoria's composure as she considered that her aunt was barely twelve years older than Charles Stanford. This assured, mature man standing before her in the elegant trappings of his profession could hardly suggest a lovelorn boy. Indeed, it was difficult to imagine his having emotions strong enough to make or mar his enjoyment of a party, apart from that indefinable hint in his eyes. It was there in double quantity as he offered her his arm. In that moment Victoria hesitated, as a strange feeling of feyness washed over her. Perhaps it was a late echo of Harry Edmunds's mood or the ghost of the future passing overhead. It lasted but a second before she rose and took his arm with characteristic determination.

Something of his composure passed to her, enabling her to walk beside him onto the floor with no thought of those watching, the slight sway of her lace crinoline over its many petticoats making her unconsciously tilt her head higher and straighten her back as if she were already Lady Blythe. A quick glance over her shoulder as they took their places gave her a gratifying view of the Castledon women dotted about the room, watching her avidly. Her cousins had tittered during the lecture she had just been given, but they were all looking rather jaundiced at the moment. A brief feeling of triumph faded beneath the generosity of her nature. It must be very upsetting for Lavinia and Charlotte, yet they had been more generous than could be expected of two older girls as yet unspoken for.

The music began the introduction. "You are in a thoughtful mood tonight, Miss Castledon," Major Stanford observed as he slipped his arm around her waist and began circling. "Might one inquire what occupies your mind so exclusively?"

"I beg your pardon. You must think me very rude, sir, but I could not help reflecting that my two older cousins have a generosity of nature one seldom finds."

Smothering a smile, her partner asked gravely what had prompted such a significant conclusion. Victoria flushed. Under the circumstances she could not enlighten him. "It was nothing of importance—just a silly fancy."

He nodded. "And I had a silly fancy that you knew quite well whose name was written in your card against the supper dance. Since it entails more than a waltz, a young lady does not normally take so little interest in who might claim it."

Victoria lowered her glance to the thick gold lacing covering the front of his jacket. "As to that, sir, can I truly believe that you were unaware that the party began some two hours ago?"

"Shall I amend my remark? The evening held no interest for me until now." He swung her around and around, guiding her across the paneled hall. "I believe I indicated something of the kind at our last meeting. Can it be that you did not understand my meaning?"

Her head came up, and she was about to return a teasing denial when it became clear he was steering her through the great arched entrance leading to the reception hall. Unequal to the situation, Victoria allowed him to waltz her across the marble floor until they reached the well beneath the broad curving staircase—a place much favored in games of hide-and-seek. Here, Charles Stanford brought their dance to a halt and gently placed her onto the ottoman Mrs. Castledon had put there because she could think of no other use for it.

The maneuver had been accomplished so smoothly and expertly that Victoria knew it was pointless to try to delay the moment. She waited with racing heartbeat for him to begin. He took a seat beside her and asked gently, "*Is* it possible you did not understand my meaning when I told you the supper dance would decide my enjoyment of the evening?" He continued without waiting for an answer. "You cannot have been unaware of my regard for you over these last few months. I sometimes feared I had been too particular in my attention. Of late, however, it seemed to me that you were not averse to the small gallantries I paid and were pleased with my flowers and other trifles which it gave me pleasure to present to you."

Victoria relaxed slightly. It was all quite proper, after all. Though she was finally alone with him, Charles Stanford showed no signs of doing any of the things chaperones hinted they were there to prevent. For one shameful moment she felt a sense of disappointment as she thought how differently Harry Edmunds would have behaved under the same circumstances, then she flushed for fear her thoughts had been read by the very honorable man beside her. To compensate for her shocking thoughts she put her hand on his sleeve and assured him his presents were highly treasured.

Before she could stop him, he seized her hand and held it tightly. "Miss Castledon . . . Victoria . . . your happiness has become increasingly important to me until I find I can think of nothing else. It would give me great joy to be the custodian of it for all time."

Victoria stared at him. She knew it was rude but she could think of nothing suitable to say. Should he not now go onto one knee and declare he could not live without her?

"Perhaps I express myself badly?" he suggested, remaining on the seat beside her. "It is my earnest hope that you should become my wife. Only tell me you would do me the honor of accepting my addresses and I will immediately seek your uncle's permission to pay them. I undertake to consider your every wish and provide all a female could desire of her husband. Life as an officer's lady can be very pleasant. There are always balls, dinners, races and military reviews to occupy the time and, should duty take me from your side, my brother officers would do all in their power to serve you. As to the future, you are already aware of my heritage and must know that my wife will become Lady Blythe on the sad demise of my father. Nothing would make me prouder than to bestow that title upon you."

The pause was so pregnant this time that Victoria felt obliged to fill it. "Major Stanford, you quite take my breath away with your words. I hardly know what to say."

He pressed her fingers with his own. "Say that I may approach your uncle. Say that I have not mistaken your feelings. Say the words that will end my uncertainty."

The strength of his grip was beginning to hurt her fingers. Alarm rose in her breast. Surely he had moved nearer . . . or was it that she had suddenly realized he was a great deal larger than she? There was no escape from a situation she had allowed to develop. An answer must be given, and it must be her consent. Having allowed him to go this far, she could not refuse his offer. Charles Stanford would be extremely angry, her uncle and aunt would never forgive her, and society would dub her witless.

"I . . . I cannot deny your wish to speak to Uncle

Garth if that is what you truly desire," she told him, her free hand pleating the lace of her skirt nervously.

"Then, you do return my regard?" he pressed.

"With someone so considerate and attentive it could hardly be otherwise," she faltered.

Her gloved hand was raised to his lips. "You have made me the happiest of men, my dear," he told her triumphantly. "I shall call upon Dr. Castledon in the morning." A quick glance across the hall told him the guests were drifting out to the conservatory where supper was laid, and he rose, offering her his arm with a smile. "Shall we rejoin the company?"

He stood waiting, and Victoria experienced an overwhelming sense of anticlimax. Was it over? He had not once vowed to put a pistol to his head if she should refuse him, nor had he declared he would enter a monastery if her heart were not his. In the novels she had read, gentlemen always said such things as they knelt at the feet of their beloved, and something told her that under similar circumstances Harry Edmunds would have done so. She rose and took his arm, wondering why a slightly leaden feeling had invaded her legs.

Without looking at her he said smoothly, "I apologize for young Edmunds's behavior after the quadrille. I shall deal with him in the morning in a way he will not soon forget. I will not have my future wife made the subject of embarrassment, believe me."

She leaped to his defense. "It was nothing. He is a friend . . ."

"*Was*, my dear. As a major's wife you will not be expected to associate with junior officers."

She looked up at him in dismay, but it vanished the minute they entered the conservatory and she became aware that all heads were turned toward them, every face reflected in the candleglow was expectant. Hands froze in outstretched positions; slices of ham dangled from forks; pies remained uncut; pheasant patties hung in the air between serving-tongs; chicken and asparagus mold trembled; a pig's head stared open-mouthed in their direction. The cessation of movement was but momentary, but it was enough to tell Victoria she had accomplished a victory tonight, and a smile turned up her lips. She was no longer the

orphaned niece of the Castledons, but the future Lady
Blythe. Surely, that was enough for any woman.

The following morning when the formalities were settled
and she was left alone with her betrothed, she discovered it
was not as simple a matter as she thought. Charles went to
her side immediately.

"I cannot tell you how happy I am at this moment." He
reached into his pocket and drew out a leather ring-box. "I
withdrew the family betrothal ring from the bank two days
ago in the hope of placing it on your finger. I shall have it
altered to fit as soon as I am able."

A dozen diamonds clustered around a sapphire that announced its own quality by the fire in its blue depths. He
slid it onto her finger and kept her hand in his.

"With that on your finger I know you are really mine," he
said in a low urgent tone, and began covering her wrist
with tiny practiced kisses. Her gasp of pleasure was smothered as she was drawn against him while his lips sought
hers. The strangeness of his proximity, his sudden relaxation of formality, and his warm mouth topped by blond
whiskers took her breath away and robbed her of words
when he released her. Somewhere deep inside, a small
movement—hardly pain, hardly shock—filled her with the
first exciting overtures to womanhood.

"Victoria, I do not know how I have waited for this. All
summer I have watched you and planned to win you
against all odds."

She smiled mistily at him. He had suddenly become
much more like Harry Edmunds. He was a Knight of the
Order of Chivalry, a searcher after truth and honor, a noble hero who lay his heart at her feet.

"I will send out the announcements immediately," he told
her. "There are so many people you must meet, and I shall
give a dinner party so that my brother officers can welcome you into the regiment. On the fifteenth of December
we shall travel to Wychbourne to spend the festival with
my parents."

"Christmas in your family home . . . there is nothing I
would like more!" she cried, filled with visions of blazing
logs, candles on a tall fir tree, and bright merry faces.

"My parents and aunt will make you feel at home, but I
doubt my brother will be able to join us. He is in Vienna."

"Oh, and I do so much wish to meet him after all I have heard of his prowess."

He smiled. "And so you shall—just as soon as he returns to England. I doubt the crazy fellow will ever tear himself away from the Austrians."

She studied his face. "You always speak of your brother as if he were a complete madcap. If that is the case, why was he sent to Vienna to represent the regiment?"

"He is not representing the regiment, my dear. Far from it."

"I do not understand."

He smiled. "I have no intention of discussing my wayward brother at a time like this."

She was even more intrigued now. "He is to be my brother, too. Should I not know a little about him? I know most of the other officers so well. I have heard he is very popular."

"Hugo cannot help drawing people to his side, but it was probably from the subalterns that you have heard the most enthusiasm for him. He has only just left their ranks, where he could be depended upon to lead their wilder escapades. He is a brilliant horseman and enthusiastic to the point of obsession over cavalry. But until he steadies up a bit I fear no one will take him seriously." He patted her hand. "Perhaps he should consider matrimony. In my present happiness I am prepared to suggest that course to everyone I know."

She smiled. "The time will not pass quickly enough until I set out for Buckinghamshire. I have not been to that part of England before. Even without your brother, Christmas is certain to be one of the happiest I have spent. Will there be parties and balls and visits to all your friends?"

His eyebrows rose slightly. "No doubt there will be the usual festive celebrations . . . but there is something more important to consider, my dear. The main reason for our visit to Wychbourne will be to discuss the wedding plans. The bridal veil has been worn by Stanford brides since the sixteenth century." He paused. "Is something amiss?"

She tried to give a careless laugh. "You are so full of plans. There is time enough to talk of bridal veils."

"You will not think so when you embark upon the complications of a large wedding. March will be upon us before we are aware of it."

"March?"

"The month upon which I have decided. Would you like a spring wedding?"

"Yes . . . but so soon?" Victoria was flustered. The engagement was enough to handle for the moment. Her thoughts had not gone beyond that. "March is only four months away. I had thought it would be longer."

Charles smiled. "Your aunt is a very capable lady, and you will find my mama well-versed in the requirements of a bride. She has been preparing long enough," he added with a caustic note that was lost on Victoria. She was too busy trying to cope with a situation that appeared to be carrying her along in a whirlwind.

"Does Uncle Garth know of this?" she asked, looking for a champion.

"Naturally. He understands the reason only too well. " He narrowed his eyes shrewdly. "Is it possible that you do not, my dearest?"

"The reason?" she repeated uneasily.

He drew her to a sofa and sat beside her with an arm along the back. With his other hand he turned her face to his while he explained something she had never considered.

"Victoria, there is some difference in our ages—twenty years, to be exact. I have always known it to be my duty to marry, but I am a man of definite tastes, and felt no inclination to do so until I was presented to you. My mind was made up immediately, but convention had to be observed in timing our betrothal. However, having disappointed my parents for so long by not providing an heir, I am under an obligation to do so as soon as possible now I have found a bride of my own choosing." He tried to look at her face that was now turned down to study her skirt. "It will give me the greatest of pleasure to do so," he said in a voice grown suddenly intimate. "Our son will be worthy of the Stanford name, and if there are more than one I swear there will be no finer boys in the whole of England." When she made no move he asked, "Do you see why the marriage must be soon?"

She nodded, not daring to look at him now the color had flooded her cheeks. The sapphire on her finger gave her no

more pleasure. It was merely a symbol to society that she had been chosen by a Stanford to provide the future upholder of their name and title. In a flash, he had fallen from his white charger. The knight, the searcher after truth, had vanished.

The chill that had filled her last night returned with a vengeance and remained until Charles took his leave of her some five minutes later. No sooner had he gone than Victoria was surrounded by her aunt and cousins, all laughing and hugging her—all, that is, except the youngest girl who had watched from the gallery the night before. On being told that her cousin was to marry a handsome Hussar, she ran sobbing to Nanny, where she buried her face in that lady's skirts and refused to be consoled.

The girl who traveled to her future home was more thoughtful than the one who had agreed to marry into the aristocracy so short a time before. The weeks since then had been filled with preparations for the visit, for Aunt Almeira was determined to send her niece to Lord and Lady Blythe with no reason to blush for her appearance.

There had been dinner parties, as well new people to meet, engagement gifts to be acknowledged, theater outings and a military review. There, Victoria had come face to face with Harry Edmunds, who had made a stiff bow and offered felicitations in a voice almost as cold as the pain that gripped Victoria. That sapphire on her finger removed her from the world of laughter and dalliance she had enjoyed all summer. It shone out like a warning light on a jagged rock, telling everyone that the Honorable Charles Stanford was about to fulfill his duty to his family and heritage. Even now, as they approached the gates, its cold glitter chilled her. Victoria's first view of Wychbourne House was enough to make her understand Charles's desire, for who would not display pride in such a place? A straight gravel approach led to a great house of gray stone, half in shadow, half washed in yellow light from branches of lanterns that flanked the entrance. Mullioned windows rose tall and perfectly balanced in the main part of the building and also in the two wings that protruded beyond the entrance to form a rectangular carriage approach. A spread of

autumn creeper, turned to flame by the lantern light, softened the austere lines, providing a welcoming touch.

Charles had met her at the station in the family carriage and thanked the matron who had kindly accompanied his bride-to-be on her long journey before going to see her own daughter, who lived in Aylesbury. The carriage covered the distance quickly and entered the approach to the house just as dusk was creeping across the sky. Victoria was enchanted as they passed along a driveway bordered by rhododendrons and neatly trimmed privet hedges that suggested dark sentinels on duty. The coachman brought the vehicle around to arrive at a precise alignment with the entrance arch.

Light flooded into the carriage as Charles said, "Welcome to your future home, my dearest."

"It is so *beautiful*," she breathed. "I cannot wait to see inside."

The next few minutes were all bustle as the doors were flung open and her luggage was unloaded into a vast hall. Victoria drank in the air of elegance and wealth that surrounded her and twirled around, gazing at the acquisitions of a long line of aristocrats and quite forgetting her apprehension at meeting Charles's parents. While she was admiring the vaulted ceiling, pillared alcoves and costly tapestries, Charles took her arm and introduced a woman in black he said was the housekeeper, Mrs. Trume.

"She will conduct you to your room, where you will wish to refresh yourself with some tea and to rest before dinner. I shall come to escort you to the withdrawing room a half hour before the dinner gong in order to introduce you to my parents." He took her gloved fingers and kissed them. "Until then, my dear."

In something of a state of shock Victoria glided up the staircase in the wake of a smiling housekeeper. So she was not to meet Lord and Lady Blythe until just before dinner! It was hardly the welcome she had expected. Her aunt and uncle never packed guests off to their rooms without greeting them warmly and inquiring after the comfort of their journey. Her spirits sank.

So many corridors without a soul about! Mrs. Trume smiled but said nothing. It did not occur to the girl that the housekeeper was trained to speak only when approached by her superiors: Victoria's own silence governed her behavior. The corridors were vast and silent. It seemed to Victoria they had been walking forever, and her heart grew heavier and heavier. Finally, the housekeeper paused before a door. Thank heaven Charles was to collect her, for she was certain to lose herself if she stepped outside her suite of rooms. It had never occurred to her that her future husband's home would be quite so splendid.

There was a little comfort to be gained when she was shown into a small set of rooms where a pretty young maid awaited her, blushing to discover her mistress no older than herself. The sitting room was pale blue and rose, with touches of ivory. A chaise longue, low round-seated chairs and two round vanity tables clustered before blazing logs in a fireplace that dominated one wall. The soft lighting, the warmth and the comforting youth of the maid brought a smile from Victoria as she hurried toward the fire, untying the ribbons of her bonnet.

Sipping tea and sitting on one of the low chairs before the fire, Victoria plied her maid with questions as she unpacked her mistress's luggage. The task took a long time, because the girl was forced to keep walking to the connecting doorway in order to answer more fully. At last, when Victoria could manage no more muffins and the warmth that had crept over her body was making her sleepy, she allowed Rosie to undress her and make her comfortable on the chaise longue with a soft rug to cover her.

But no sooner had the maid discreetly closed the connecting door and Victoria was left alone than she was wide awake, her mind racing on a course that robbed her of all serenity. As she went over the details of her arrival it occurred to her that she was doing just as she was told until her future parents-in-law were ready to meet her. A little flame sprang up in her breast, and she began to think over the other grievances she had felt.

Since Charles had been at great pains to leave her in no doubt of her important role in the continuation of the Stanfords, some acknowledgment of it should have been made on her arrival. After all, she thought pettishly, if she were to supply an heir to all this she should never have been packed off for muffins and a rest, like a child. As she dwelt on this, her anger swelled until she had persuaded herself

Charles's parents should be quite falling over themselves to please her. Why should they not? she asked herself crossly, bouncing into a more comfortable position on the padded brocade.

If she should decide *not* to have an heir, where would they be? Quite who decided the matter she was not sure, but gentlemen were always so surprised when their wives were in a delicate condition it must be supposed they had no say in it. How a female came to be in a delicate condition was a complete mystery to Victoria, except that she had an idea it was something to do with showing one's ankles. Since great insistence on never doing such a thing with gentlemen present was always made by matrons, young girls could only suppose something quite drastic would befall them if they did.

The thought of revealing her ankles to Charles brought an uncomfortable ache to her stomach, and she felt herself grow uncomfortably warm. Her cousin Charlotte had once whispered that the officers of the 44th Foot—or was it the 54th—often attended a theater in London where vulgar actresses displayed not only their ankles but even their knees! It seemed likely that cavalry officers also attended such places, in which case there was the possibility that Charles was among them. She bit her lip. He was so very proper with ladies it did not seem possible that he could do such a thing, but there were times when a strange intensity came into his eyes when he looked at her, and since their engagement he had alarmed her from time to time with embraces she would not like anyone to witness.

Forcing her mind from something that only caused her agitation, Victoria once more gave rein to her indignation against the Blythes. What kind of lady would allow her son's promised wife to arrive in her home without bustling out to welcome her? Her surprise that she had not been introduced to Charles's parents before he spoke for her was satisfied by Uncle Garth, who explained that a man of thirty-eight did not expect to have to ask his father's permission to marry, although Lord Blythe had been informed of Victoria's pedigree in advance and had approved the alliance. That small confidence had increased Victoria's chagrin, since it suggested that it did not matter about her appearance or manners so long as her blood was right.

She had been offhand with Charles for several days as a result, but no one could remain so for long. Hardly a week passed without some beautiful present arriving at her door; he never called upon her without bearing flowers or sweetmeats; and, most important, he seemed to worship her. He might have made it plain what her duty was to be, but, unlike his parents, he recognized her importance and doted on her.

This comforting fact might have lulled her anger had it not been for a note that had been delivered by Charles's valet into the hands of Rosie, the maid. Victoria opened it with great curiosity.

> *Dearest,*
> *I cannot wait to show you to my parents. It will be a proud moment for me.*

Victoria thought him charmingly absurd to write to tell her such a thing. But the next sentence added the finishing touches to her anger against her hosts.

> *I shall be pleased if you will wear your simplest gown. Mama has a great dislike of over-ornamentation. She also abhors unpunctuality, so I earnestly request you to be ready when I come at the half hour.*

Color flooded Victoria's cheeks as she crushed the sheet of crested notepaper and flung it into the fire just as Rosie tentatively asked which gown Miss Castledon wished to be laid out. In high dudgeon Miss Castledon marched to her wardrobe and indicated an extremely elaborate, silver-green satin dress, swathed with silver net caught up all around the skirt with bunches of artificial snowdrops. It had been intended for a party, but it would make its debut tonight. She would be ready on time, for punctuality was a matter of good manners, but Charles would see she had no intention of playing the good child any longer.

The withdrawing room was dark and impressive. Rich wood paneling hung with heavy portraits, carpeting of royal blue and crimson that offset deep red upholstery, and gigantic jars and platters of oriental design placed on cumbersome pedestals, all gave Victoria a feeling of drowning in splendor. The ceiling was high and vanished into shadows, the carpet went on forever and the three people already assembled there were marooned on chairs at all points of the compass, like strangers who occupied a small kingdom and ruled it in isolation.

Charles's arm held her firmly as he led his bride-to-be across the room. The glint was still in his eyes, but he had not said a word about her costume. Indeed, as he escorted her down the stairs, he had not said a single word at all. Now, they were marching across an endless expanse of carpet toward a matron in crimson taffeta whose proportions vanished into the matching upholstery so that Victoria could not tell if she was tall or short, slender or plump. That she had once been pink and pretty was still apparent, but the liveliness of youth had disappeared. Charles stopped before her and raised her hand to his lips.

"Mama, I have written to you of my deep regard for Miss Castledon, and she has been so anxious to be presented to you I could delay no longer in bringing her to Wychbourne."

Victoria sank into a deep curtsy that would have delighted Aunt Almeira with its gracefulness.

"Get up, child," said Lady Blythe in a faded voice. Close-set eyes raked Victoria up and down. "So you are my son's choice! Well, you are very pretty and, I suppose, have the winning ways that please gentlemen, but did no one advise you on your dress? Ah, of course, you are an *orphan*, are you not? Never mind, we can see to it before the nuptials . . . and before any harm is done. Augustus," she called to the occupant of a chair away to her right. "Here is Miss . . ." then louder, *"Augustus!"*

Lord Blythe looked up from a paper he was reading and rose quickly. "Bless my soul, I had not noticed you come in, Charles. Forgive me, Miss Castledon." He came across, a tall, elegant figure in the evening clothes that suited him and his son so well. "I have been awaiting this moment, yet was so deep in an account of land taxes that I must have appeared unforgivably rude. Welcome to Wychbourne, my dear. How do you find it?"

Victoria rose from another graceful curtsy. "Rather lonely, sir, when I find one is compelled to communicate by the sending of notes."

Charles reacted visibly, and she had the delight of knowing he was staring at her, nonplussed.

Lord Blythe laughed. "Yes, yes, well, one grows tired of trundling back and forth along all the corridors. Of course, the place has changed beyond recognition. Too many laws and statutes these days. Endless paperwork. Industry ruins anything rural, you know. Yes, it is all changing," he repeated, introspection glazing his blue eyes.

"I hope it does not alter too much, for what I saw on the way from the station was quite charming," Victoria told him.

He seemed to shake himself mentally. "Eh? Yes, yes, it is a fine part of England." A smile lit his face. "That is a dashed pretty dress, if I may say so. Very astute of you, Charles, to choose a wife with such looks."

"Thank you, sir." Charles's eyes still glared at the subject of the compliment.

"Well, I cannot agree," put in Lady Blythe waspishly. "The essence of good taste is simplicity. You will never find Charity Verewood in anything but the plainest styles."

"One cannot compare Miss Castledon with Miss Verewood," protested Lord Blythe. "Charity's personality is such that austereness better suits it."

Victoria was already beginning to regret her impulse to defy Charles. "I always consider Charles when selecting a gown," she put in, hoping to end the subject. "He has always admired individuality. Is that not so, Charles?" She looked up at him with wide eyes, but was not prepared for the burning intensity in his as he replied with difficulty, "Yes, Victoria."

"You will have the pleasure of meeting Miss Verewood before long," said Lady Blythe. "Her parents own the neighboring estate. Such a goodhearted girl. Now Charles has selected a bride of his *own* choice, the way is open for his brother. Hugo knows such a union would please me more than anything."

Charles gave his father a quick glance, then said, "I should not depend upon it, Mama."

"Am I *never* to meet this girl?" demanded a strident voice from the third chair. "You all imagine I have long since passed on, I know, but I will see the boy's bride. I insist upon it."

Charles put his hand beneath Victoria's elbow and said in a low voice, "My great-aunt Sophy is very deaf, but that is her only failing. She is very sharp in wits for a lady of eighty-nine."

The old lady wore a dark-green dress of Regency style and an enormous taffeta turban on her head, and she appeared to be smothered in ropes of pearls. Victoria soon discovered that Aunt Sophy was not only stone deaf but imagined everyone to whom she spoke suffered from the same affliction.

"Aunt, may I present Miss Castledon?" asked Charles after dutifully kissing the stick-like fingers she offered.

"I suppose this is Miss Castledon," she declared loudly, unable to hear the volume of her own voice. "Oh yes, I know the young lady's name. There is not much I miss. Well, you are very lovely, Miss Castledon, for which you must be congratulated. It is a woman's duty to look as beautiful as possible. You show excellent taste, despite the terrible bell shape that is so fashionable these days. One might suppose females had no legs . . . but if Her Majesty approves, one cannot condemn it." Her turbaned head turned, and she gave her great-nephew one of her completely audible asides. "She'll do, Charles. Youth is a great asset. You can depend on her bearing you many fine children."

Victoria flushed with rage. It was plain Charles was fighting a terrible battle against laughter. The moment was saved by the dinner gong. Lady Blythe rose with every sign of impatience, and Victoria was given an example of the lady's temperament.

"We shall be late if we do not go in immediately. Charles, you may take me and Miss Castleford on your arm. Your papa can bring Sophy. She is sure to take an age."

"It is Miss *Castledon*, Mama . . . Victoria, if you please."

"Do hurry, Augustus, the soup is sure to be cold if you keep us waiting."

Now that she was standing, it was revealed to Victoria that the lady was short and plump—the picture of motherly kindness in every way but for her manner. That was eccentric in the most hurtful way. Lord Blythe was charming, like his son, but appeared too greatly absorbed in the worries of the estate, which put a frown on his face when he was not taking part in the conversation.

They had settled around a table that obliged each person to sit at least six feet away from the other, when Lord Blythe said, "I trust you will not find life too dull at Wychbourne. We do not entertain overmuch, my dear, but I expect you young people will be going to parties and such like."

"Where is Hugo?" cried Aunt Sophy, making Victoria jump. No one took the slightest notice of her.

"The Verewoods are giving a ball, are they not, Charles?" Lady Blythe signaled for the soup plates to be removed the minute the last spoon was lowered.

"Yes, Mama. I hope it does not snow. Last year James Ferriston landed his gig in the ditch and had to walk home."

"I trust you do not encourage his acquaintance. I believe it was not so far back that a Ferriston tilled the land with his own hands. They try to hide it, of course, but everyone knows."

"I suppose he will arrive late, as usual," Aunt Sophy complained in her cracked voice. "Hugo is never dependable, but it will be a shockingly dull Christmas without him."

"I quite like old Ferriston," commented Lord Blythe as if the old lady had not spoken. "He gave me some excellent advice on vines once."

"Quite!" said Lady Blythe, attacking the turbot with enthusiasm. "That bears out my point. Nobody of any consequence is an expert on *plants.*"

"My uncle is an eminent physician, yet he can coax even the most stubborn plants to thrive," put in Victoria determinedly. "He says horticultural interest relaxes the nerves. I do not know how true it is."

Lady Blythe leaned forward and said across the table, "How long have you been orphaned, Miss . . . ?"

"Victoria," supplied Charles instantly. "Her parents died in India when she was an infant."

"Dear me . . . *India!* Well, of course, it is *such* a heathen country." She waved a hand at the butler. "Pray, do not stand there, Norton. We are waiting."

The fish was replaced by duck beneath Victoria's bemused eyes, but she could not begin to eat any of it. All at
once she felt weak with homesickness and longed for Aunt
Almeira, who now seemed the embodiment of loving ma-
ternity. Lady Blythe, on the other hand, appeared so unin-
terested in her successor as to forget her name . . . and it
was all too plain that the simply dressed Miss Verewood
had been the lady's choice for Charles.

Victoria was too young to have suffered much from deep
hurt, but this was the second occasion since her engagement that someone had drawn that knife edge across her
emotions. Harry Edmunds's rebuff at the regimental review
had been a cruel shock, but the young lieutenant was not
likely to cross her path too often. This was different. Not
having a mama of her own, Victoria had cherished a hope
that Lady Blythe might see her as the daughter with whom
she had never been blessed.

For a few moments Victoria feared she would succumb
to tears, but at the thought of her cousins, who had been
filled with envy at her good fortune, her head came up
again. She would not let herself be cast down by this ill-
mannered woman. If defying her preference for plain dressing was not enough to impress herself on Lady Blythe, she
would do something less easily forgotten. If she were expected to provide an heir for the noble Stanfords, she
would be recognized as someone of importance.

The conversation had turned to plans for the carol singing that took place in the grounds of Wychbourne each
year.

"I depend more and more on Charity to help me with
social tasks. I do hope Hugo will do his duty to me and to
her when he is next here." Lady Blythe turned to Victoria
in the most confiding way. "Hugo is greatly attached to
her, and it is no wonder, for her looks are only exceeded
by her wealth." Her glance shot across to her son. "Really,
an excellent match for any gentleman."

Victoria felt her color rising. "If we are to be sisters, I
trust it will not be long before I meet the delightful young
woman."

"You are certain to get on famously," put in Charles,
"for she has the sweetest of natures."

"And does your aunt also consider *she* will bear many fine children?"

It was out before she had known she was about to say such a thing, and Victoria's heart thudded against the silver-green bodice in the silence that followed.

Suddenly, Lord Blythe began to laugh until he was forced to wipe his eyes with his napkin. "Damme, if you have not chosen yourself a saucy little miss, Charles."

"Yes," he breathed. "Damme, if I have not!"

"Gentlemen!" wailed Lady Blythe. "I will not have such language at the dinner table. It has come to a pretty pass when I find coffeehouse manners in my own dining room. Silver spangles and unsuitable conversation! If these are town ways, I declare I want no part of them."

"Now, my dear, do not get into such a miff. Victoria has said no more than Sophy," said Lord Blythe, struggling to control his laughter.

"Sophy, sir, is half out of her wits."

"I suppose we shall have to suffer that milk-and-water miss from next door," cawed Aunt Sophy, right on cue. "She will never do for Hugo, but none of you has the wits to see it. This duck is unbearably greasy. I am not surprised none of you will eat it."

Victoria sat with her hands in her lap and her eyes on a scroll decorating the carpet. She followed the intricate pattern to its extremities several times as she wondered how best to return to Brighton without disgrace. She was considering an attack of measles when a footman entered and spoke to the butler, who then approached Lord Blythe and bent to his ear. The incident brought all conversation to a halt, except for Aunt Sophy's wondering aloud why the servant had interrupted a meal when he knew Lady Blythe disliked it so much.

The butler backed away, and Lord Blythe wagged his head slowly. "My dear, something most unfortunate has happened. I really do not know how to tell you without putting you in the greatest agitation."

"Then pray do not say a word until this duck has been removed," she told him sharply. "Agitation and duck do not marry well. I am sure to have unpleasant symptoms by morning."

"But, Agnes, in this case . . . "

"Please," she implored, clapping her hands at the butler. "Norton, take this away. I do not wish to see duck on my table again this side of Christmas."

"You look very serious, sir," said Charles. "Please explain what is amiss."

Lord Blythe cleared his throat. "It concerns Hugo."

"About time that duck was removed," shouted Aunt Sophy. "I told you it was disgustingly greasy."

"Agnes, kindly prevent your aunt from interrupting when I am trying to speak," complained Lord Blythe.

"How can I when she hears nothing I say? Really, I cannot bear any more upset this evening, or I shall have one of my spasms."

Victoria felt she could stand no more and put her finger to her lips as a signal to silence the old lady. With a glance at the expressions of discord on the faces surrounding her, the enormous turban nodded its thanks.

Charles bade his father proceed. "Hugo is all right, sir?"

"Hugo has just arrived at Wychbourne."

"How delightful. Has he had dinner?" asked Lady Blythe.

"He will dine upstairs, I believe. He will have to remain there for some days."

"Do not tell me he is in some fix that obliges him to retire from society!" cried Charles. "I felt that he would be well occupied in Vienna."

"He returned from Vienna last week, it appears. Brigadier Lord Murchison desired him to attend some military exercise at Chobham where his experience was earnestly required. Unfortunately, it has turned out to be a sad duty, for there has been an accident with explosives. The boy's eyes are damaged."

"Good God, sir," breathed Charles in shock.

"Charles, if you cannot control your tongue I shall be obliged if you will leave my presence," Lady Blythe said. "Have I not enough with which to contend?"

"I beg your pardon, Mama. It was concern for my brother that led me to forget myself. My father gives us terrible news." He turned back to his lordship. "Are you saying he is blinded?"

"For a short while they feared it would be permanent, but there is every chance that he will recover his sight. To aid his recovery he has been ordered complete rest, with bandages to cover his eyes until a specialist calls to see him in two weeks. His army servant has traveled with him and is, at this moment, putting him to bed. We must respect the medical advice and leave him to rest. We can do nothing for him except pray to the Lord."

"Poor boy. Oh, my poor boy. I shall make him the sole subject of my prayers," Lady Blythe sobbed theatrically. "When I awoke this morning I little dreamt what a day it would turn out to be. So much upset; so much agitation! And now *this*." She dabbed at her eyes with the corner of her handkerchief. "Really, it has been such a shock I cannot fancy the galantine. A tea tray will have to be brought to my room, although I doubt I shall be able to partake of any."

Aunt Sophy had been watching with inquisitive eyes, and when she saw the distress on all faces she asked, "What has happened to make everyone so upset?" And when no one took any heed, she added, "Do not tell me our dear Queen is ailing."

"Augustus, I cannot bear these constant questions when my head is in such a whirl," cried his wife. "I wish I had not said she could dine with us tonight. Such occasions are always exhausting."

"When Sophy cannot hear a word there seems little point in saying any," Lord Blythe said, rising and going to her chair. "Let me escort you to your room, my dear." He looked apologetically at the others. "Miss Castledon, I do ask you to forgive us. Such an unfortunate thing to happen on your first night with us. We are naturally upset."

"Of course," she said warmly. "I am so sorry about your son. Please give him my earnest wishes for his recovery."

"Thank you. When he is a little better I shall visit him and give him your message."

They went out, and Victoria turned to Charles in consternation. "Do they not intend going to him immediately?"

He went to stand by her. "Mama cannot face sickrooms. She has a delicate constitution."

"But . . . your papa," she protested.

"Complete rest means just that, Victoria. I shall call to inquire of his servant before I retire. He will give me all the details."

"But . . . "

"Dear me, I cannot bear to think what has happened," cried Aunt Sophy in her cracked voice. "The Queen must be upon her deathbed."

Victoria ran to the old lady and saw the real distress in her face. Impulsively she begged, "Could you not write down a mild account of the accident, Charles? It must be so dreadful to be cut off from the world in this way."

The major swung around and ordered writing materials to be produced immediately, then told Victoria he would escort her and his great aunt to their rooms. The wording of the note was such that the old lady was not too alarmed, and when they had delivered her into the hands of her maid, Victoria felt an impulse to kiss Aunt Sophy's cheek. Charles dropped a dutiful salute on the outstretched fingers, and she beamed at him.

"You have waited a long time, but it was worth it, my boy. Miss Castledon has a great capacity for affection. Do not abuse it . . . ever. Good night, and God bless you both."

Charles offered Victoria his arm, and they began walking slowly along the maze of corridors in the direction of her room.

"I cannot pray hard enough for your brother's safety," she began almost at once. "To lose one's sight would surely be an unendurable disaster. And he is a man with a life before him that promises greatness, you suggest. If such a person could never sit a horse again it would be a great loss to himself as well as to his profession. Do you truly plan to inquire after him tonight?"

He looked down at her and patted her hand. "Yes, of course, my love. Did you think I would not?"

"Then, promise you will send me a note on how he goes on. Please."

"Very well." They walked a few yards in silence. "I sent you one note this evening which you chose to ignore. Might I inquire why?"

She continued looking straight ahead, but the pulse in her throat began throbbing uncomfortably. "I was ready when you called, I believe."

"And I believe that the very beautiful gown you are wearing is possibly the most elaborate you have in your wardrobe. Why did you find it necessary to disregard my advice?"

She played for time. "It is late, and I am tired."

He halted at the foot of the stairs. "I mean to have an answer, Victoria, and we are liable to stand here a very long time unless you give me one."

There was that darkness in his eyes she was too immature to recognize, but he did not seem angry. "I quite believed you were pleased with my appearance and manners until I received that note. Then it seemed you were afraid I would not do for your mama. Are you no longer happy with the girl you knew at Brighton?"

He gripped her fingers until they hurt. "More than happy. You are my choice, and I have no wish to change a facet of that girl."

She gave him a reproachful look. "That is very strange talk, sir, after your note."

He raised her fingers to his lips. "I beg your pardon, Victoria. I see I made a mistake in trying to make things easier. Mama is . . . highly strung. Small things upset her. I had hoped to avoid any discord. That is all."

"I think you might have told me she wished you to marry Miss Verewood."

"My dearest, if I cared a fig for Mama's opinion I should not have made you mine without first consulting her. It is me you must please . . . and I find you most delightful tonight." His eyes narrowed shrewdly. "There is more troubling you than a mere request to wear a plain gown. It has been written in your behavior for some weeks." He drew her to a velvet alcove seat nearby and sat beside her, keeping her hands in his. "What is troubling you, dearest?"

Victoria saw there was nothing for it but to confess her hurt feelings at not being welcomed as a daughter on her arrival.

"You must not judge us by your town friends," he said gently. "Life in the country is quite different. It is the custom here to allow guests to rest after their long journey to Wychbourne."

"But I am not a guest," she cried, the hurt flooding back as she spoke of it. "Good gracious, the importance of my role has been made more than plain to me."

He smothered a smile. "I apologize for my aunt's forthright remarks. That you were angry was demonstrated by your repetition of them."

Victoria's eyes blazed. "You apologize, sir, yet you were the first to speak of it. No sooner had the ring been placed on my finger than I was told the reason for an early wedding. It is not pleasant to be regarded as a . . . as a . . ." She dissolved into the tears that had been threatening all evening.

Charles was full of concern, putting an arm around her shoulders and kissing away the tears. "Why have you not mentioned this to me before? I have been unhappy at your sudden reserve since our engagement."

After the chill of her treatment by Lady Blythe, his apparent gentleness and contrition opened a gulf of warmth in her. Clasping his hands in a youthful excess of gratitude she cried, "You are so kind. I do not deserve it after the way I have behaved. I will ask your mama's pardon in the morning and do as you suggest in the future. Only say you are not angry with me . . . that I am not in disgrace."

Immediately he pulled her to him. "Such disgrace that I am impelled to scold you."

The mouth that closed over hers became more and more insistent as he forced her to yield and arch backward. His left hand fastened around the curls on her shoulder so that her head was held back in a tilted position for him; the other arm was clamped around her waist. Victoria tried to pull away. She was frightened by his strength that turned him from a kindly refuge into a savage stranger.

At length, his arms slackened to allow him to cover her smooth brow and throat with searching lips, but that was as far as he got. She pulled away and gasped, "I hear someone approaching."

As Charles released her, she jumped to her feet. The embrace had scared, yet excited, her. That strange ache was back in the pit of her stomach and had extended to her thighs, making her feel she might collapse if she tried to walk. The alien smell of masculinity, the scratchiness of a thick mustache and the warm wetness of a mouth that seemed to engulf her own left her shivering and cold.

"You were mistaken. There is no one about," said Charles, taking her hands again and drawing her toward him, but her urge to flee was too strong.

"Please, Charles, I really would like to go to my room now. You were right. The journey to Wychbourne is a tiring one. I am quite overcome with fatigue." She turned quickly, and he was obliged to follow her.

Delivering her to the door, Charles merely kissed her fingers before leaving her a prey to a whirl of thoughts. Longing for her home in Brighton returned, although she knew Aunt Almeira would be shocked over all that had happened here today. Lady Blythe had *not* taken to her at all; she had been indelicate at the dinner table; and worst of all, she had allowed Charles to treat her cavalierly.

Tucked up in a bed enclosed by ivory curtains, she realized that her life had grown complicated since her betrothal. What Charles had demanded of her just now filled her with doubts. Should she have been angry with him? Why had he stopped being courteous to her? Could it have been her unforgivable reference to Miss Verewood bearing fine children? She had noticed a bright look appear in Lord Blythe's eyes as well as his son's. Had they thought her vulgar?

She knew in her heart that what had just happened was not something she could mention to her aunt—or even her cousins. To make matters worse, something inside her had seemed to melt and bring an ache that almost persuaded her she should not struggle against it. The ache was there still, and she turned with a groan to bury her face in the pillow. Why could the happy life with her cousins not have gone on forever? The next minute she was filled with remorse. Her selfish preoccupation with her own happiness had led her to forget that somewhere down these endless corridors a young man lay in darkness trying not to contemplate the possibility that the light would never come. Hastily slipping from the snug nest under the covers, Victoria knelt beside the bed and closed her eyes. Her bare feet sticking from beneath the self-embroidered nightgown grew colder and colder, for she kept adding postscripts to her prayers.

CHAPTER TWO

After two days, Victoria felt stifled and heavy with homesickness. Charles was constrained to spend the greater part of those first days with his father; as the heir, he must know what was being done with the estate. Using Hugo's accident as an excuse to indulge her own love of illness, Lady Blythe had retired to her room, emerging only at dinnertime, when she feigned frailness, Aunt Sophy had not put in another appearance at all.

The days dragged by with no one to keep her company but Rosie. She wrote long letters to her aunt and each of her cousins, entered her thoughts in a diary, put the finishing touches to a pair of embroidered slippers for Lord Blythe and taught Rosie how to make gauze water lilies, but by the third day she was at a loss to know how to occupy herself. At breakfast the problem was solved for her when she made her usual inquiry after Charles's brother.

The major sighed. "He was sunk into his boots when I put my head in this morning."

"It does not surprise me," said Victoria spiritedly. "He has been in his own company for three days. I should think lowness of spirits would impede his recovery more than a short period of quiet society. I would be perfectly willing to sit with him for a little while. I might read the newspaper, for the poor man cannot even do that to pass the time."

Charles tugged at his mustache and looked at his father. "What do you think, sir?"

Lord Blythe deliberated for a while, then shook his head. "I think not, Victoria. The medical instructions are that he must be kept quiet. Better to wait awhile."

Though she was disappointed in the hope of doing something useful, an idea nevertheless occurred to her.

"Christmas is only a little over a week away," she began, "and I have no present for the invalid since I did not know he would be here at Wychbourne. Should you have any objection to my setting up my easel in the conservatory, where the deer park can be seen to great advantage? A small water color might remind him of his home when he is away from it."

"A splendid idea," agreed Lord Blythe. "Hugo thinks there is nothing in life apart from horses. Your gift will persuade him otherwise, I am sure."

Charles was only too thankful Victoria would be occupied. "I beg you to put a shawl around your shoulders if you mean to sit in the conservatory. When the wind is in the east there are some uncomfortable drafts. Come, my dear, we shall collect your paints and easel."

"Thank you, Charles. I still find I cannot reach my destination without making a wrong turning."

"Then you must learn to do so" was the humorless reply. "If this is to be your home one day, you cannot be afraid of its size."

Stung by his remark, she could think of nothing to say, even when Lord Blythe called to her to be certain to show him the work as soon as it was completed. Charles's uncompromising mood remained as they journeyed to her room and back to the conservatory, so that when he informed her that his mama was feeling more herself and would be glad of help in the planning of decorations for the Great Hall, she told him she would keep it in mind and silently vowed to take all day over the picture.

The work went well. The bright, cold day gave sharp lines to the trees, icing the lake with gilded blue, and persuaded the deer into the open to pose obligingly, but unconsciously, for the artist. As Victoria struggled to capture the exact shades to give the reproduction reality, it crossed her mind that the recipient of her gift must have ridden across the park on countless joyful occasions. Then her hands dropped to her lap. How thoughtless she was. Hugo Stanford would be unable to see her present on Christmas Day, for his eyes would be bound in bandages. How could she present him with such a bitter reminder of his present blindness? A painting was a purely visual thing. Had she no sense at all?

Depressed and upset, she rose and left the conservatory where the easel and canvas still stood. In a daze, she turned up the nearest staircase, only to find at the top that she had lost her way again. Memory of Charles's annoyance at breakfast made her stamp her foot in vexation. She knew it must seem stupid to him, but the stairs were all similarly designed and she never could remember whether to turn up the right- or left-hand flight.

Hoping a landmark would present itself at the end of the corridor, she hurried along it, her kid slippers making no sound on the blue carpet. The deserted halls always gave her an eerie feeling, so when a door opened and a fierce-looking man stepped right into her path, it was impossible to keep back a small frightened cry.

The man had received a similar shock, for his bunched fists came up to chest height immediately. Then he took another look and gasped, "You ain't a ghost, miss, are you?"

"No . . . I assure you I am not," she replied with her hand at her throat and her heart thumping. "If I look pale it is because you startled me so."

The man scratched his head. "Well, I beg your pardon if I did. I didn't know nobody was coming along or I'd have announced meself." He looked hard at her. "Are you Miss Castledon?"

"Yes."

He straightened, flushing. "My real humble apologies, miss, but this corridor is always quiet, and the captain swears to me that there's ghosts come along here. A young girl, he says, with her head tucked under her arm."

Victoria laughed with high-pitched nervousness. "I certainly do not carry my head under my arm."

"*Stokes!*" roared a voice from inside the room.

The man turned with agitation. "Yessir?"

"With whom are you gossiping? Keep your eyes and your roving hands off the servants."

Stokes blushed crimson. "It ain't no servant, sir, it's a lady. Miss Castledon."

Enlightenment dawned on Victoria. "Are you Captain . . . ?"

The question was never completed because the voice from inside shouted, "Show her in, Stokes."

The soldier was still red from embarrassment. "You heard what he said, miss."

"Certainly I heard what he said, but I understand he is not allowed visitors."

"As to that, I don't rightly agree. All I know is, if he don't soon have someone to talk to, he'll do something drastic. I caught him walking out of this door this morning."

Victoria was aghast. "How very foolish. He could have fallen. Does Major Stanford know . . . or Lord Blythe?"

An emphatic shake of his head. "I dursn't tell them, miss. You don't know what he threatened to do if I bleated out the fact." He pulled the door to and said confidentially, "He don't show it, but I know the captain well enough to recognize when the end of his tether is reached. Go in and have a word with him, miss. He won't stand much more of his own company."

Victoria looked worried. "All right, but whatever he threatened you with applies to me also if you tell anyone of my visit."

Stokes grinned and smoothed his large black mustache. "Understood, miss . . . and thank you."

Victoria went through the door he held open for her and found herself in a room that did not appear to be part of Wychbourne House, for grandeur had been discarded for modern comfort. Large horsehair sofas stood about the room, which contained a sturdy table and some padded teak stools. A bookcase and a desk of immense size occupied one whole wall, and the other three were merely backgrounds for large numbers of pictures of equestrian subjects. Lamps stood on desk, table, mantleshelf and every spare space. A pile of logs crackled in the fireplace, throwing out welcome heat and sending leaping lights to dance on the gold-brocaded curtains and the row of silver trophies on the desk. She felt it must be a room that reflected the personality of its occupier, and so it proved.

"Miss Castledon, sir," announced Stokes.

The man who rose from one of the overstuffed chairs and stood rather uncertainly beside it inflicted a whole range of emotions on Victoria: surprise that he was so young, pleasure at the attractiveness of his smile, pain at the sight of a strong, healthy man so isolated behind the black blindfold.

As tall as Charles, his brother was the more physical in every way. His broad shoulders were more muscular and his neck sturdy upon them. The tight-fitting checked trou-

sers revealed legs that were well developed in the manner
of cavalrymen but never meant to perform in the ballroom
with any distinction. That the room was his was only too
plain, for he would look completely out of place on Lady
Blythe's spindly chairs.

He turned in the vague direction of the door. "At last. I
thought I was not to be allowed to offer my felicitations
until well after the event." He gave a slight bow. "I am
honored, dear lady, but full of apologies for my present
situation."

"Please sit down," begged Victoria. "I understand you
are to rest."

Hugo made a rueful face. "A nurse, I fear. It was my
hope that you would support my campaign for a little freedom. Everyone is acting as if I were at death's door, you
know."

"Well, I must say you do not look it," she said with a
giggle. "I doubt I have ever seen a patient so full of health.
Certainly I will rally to your cause, but it will be at the risk
of receiving a severe scold from all who are concerned
about you—not the least your brother."

He bowed again rather uncertainly. "I cannot allow you
to make such a sacrifice on my behalf. I will dutifully sit in
my chair and shake and moan to your complete satisfaction. Please make yourself comfortable if you have not already done so." He turned his head and shouted, "Stokes!"

"Yessir." The soldier was beside him.

"Dash it, man, I have told you to stop creeping up on
me," said Hugo, much aggrieved.

"Yessir." Stokes threw Victoria a see-what-I-mean look.

Hugo sat down carefully. "Bring some wine, man."

"Right away, Captain." The servant did a smart about-
face and started for an adjoining room. As soon as he
opened the door, two great masses of golden fur hurled
themselves in Victoria's direction. Next minute, she was
engulfed in paws, wet tongues, wagging tails and quivering
bodies.

"Oh," she cried from the depths of canine onslaught, and
Stokes came running over.

"Them dratted dogs," he cursed. "I forgot they was in
there."

"It is quite all right," Victoria gasped, laughing. "I adore dogs."

"*Down!*" ordered Hugo in a tone that made the girl and the soldier jump. The golden retrievers obeyed, recognizing his tone. "Forgive me, Hugo went on. "I hope they have not frightened you or spoiled your dress."

Victoria, busy fondling the silky heads, said fervently, "They certainly do not frighten me. I have always wished for a dog of my own, and if they had spoiled my dress, which they have not, I would not give a fig for it. What are their names?"

"Salamanca and Waterloo."

"I beg your pardon?"

"They are listed among the regiment's battle honors."

"Shame on you, sir, to dub these beautiful creatures with the names of battlegrounds."

"Nonsense," he told her calmly. "They do not know of the fact."

"No, they do not, but dogs should have more suitable names."

"Such as?" he parried quickly.

"Such as . . . well . . . such as . . ." She broke off, unable to think of anything.

"Nugget and Guinea, perhaps?" he suggested artfully.

"I did not mean . . . oh, you are just being foolish." She laughed. "I am quite defeated. You could call them Culloden and Hastings, I suppose. They are your dogs, after all."

Stokes appeared with the wine and glasses on a tray and offered some to Victoria.

"No, thank you," she declared. "I could not drink wine at this hour. Perhaps a small glass of lemonade."

"*Lemonade*, miss?" said Stokes, trying manfully to cope with the situation.

"Yes, lemonade," repeated Hugo with a perfectly straight face. "Fetch some of my lemonade at once."

"Yessir," growled Stokes, calling down mental curses on his officer's head as he walked out. But inspiration came in time for him to return and announce in a perfectly steady voice, "The lemonade is all run out, Captain Esterly."

"How very vexing. You really must keep a better eye on my cellar," Hugo remonstrated, struggling not to laugh.

"Miss Castledon, I cannot drink alone. Can I not persuade you to take a small glass of wine? I assure you it is very light."

Knowing a refusal meant he would be deprived of one small pleasure in which he could indulge, she agreed, casting aside any doubts on the advisibility of doing something she had never done before. When her glass had been half filled she told Stokes to stop pouring. Hugo raised his glass, not exactly in her direction but near enough to be effective. "To your future health and happiness . . . yours and my brother's."

They both drank. Victoria found the wine very pleasant and said so, then added curiously, "Stokes called you Captain Esterly."

Hugo smiled. "I have trained him to be polite."

"But . . . should it not be Captain Stanford?"

He seemed puzzled for a second or two, then said, "Can Charles have failed to mention that we are not blood brothers? Surely not. You are engaged to be married, are you not?"

"Not brothers? But Lord and Lady Blythe refer to you as their son, and the officers of the regiment called you Charles's brother. I do not understand."

"Poor Victoria . . . you are to be my sister, so I may call you that, mayn't I? Charles and I are brothers in every respect except that we have entirely different parents." His long fingers began caressing the head of one of the dogs that had wandered over to sit by his knees. The other animal remained by the visitor, enjoying having his ears fondled by soft hands. "Shall I tell you the story, or do you prefer to hear it from Charles?" Hugo asked.

"Please, tell me now. I am wholly intrigued." She sipped her wine and settled more comfortably against the cushions.

Hugo carefully felt for the small table beside him and set the glass down. The small action smote at Victoria's soft heart, and sympathy welled up for this young man who, it appeared, was not Charles's brother after all. The knowledge made her realize there was little similarity between the two men. Hugo's hair and smart cavalry mustache were a rich dark brown, and what little she could see of his features suggested that his face was broader than Charles's aristocratic lines. Here was a mystery indeed, and she could not wait to hear it unraveled.

"I trust you have several handkerchiefs about you," he began, "for it is a tragic story."

She hugged herself with amusement, for he was so entertaining. "Proceed, sir," she said in a dramatic voice that brought a broad smile from him.

"I am an orphan," he said with pathos. "At least, enough of an orphan to wring sympathy from you. My father was a sea captain and a great friend of Lord Blythe, who was the Honorable Augustus Stanford at that time. My mama was extremely beautiful, as you might guess after casting your eyes upon me."

Victoria giggled. "Of course."

"She was also the daughter of a French count . . . but her heart was cold and disloyal. Three months after I was born she ran away with an extraordinarily wealthy gentleman from America, leaving my remaining parent with a wrapped bundle at his feet."

Victoria must have sighed or given some sign of reaction, for he grinned and said, "Ah, the tears will begin any moment. What was a poor sea captain to do? He was due to set out on an expedition to China and had no family with whom to leave his baby son. The only solution was to leave him in the care of his very generous friend Augustus Stanford, little dreaming that the voyage to China would be the last he ever made." Suddenly he no longer seemed to be joking. "My father died of yellow fever, alone in the Orient, and I was dependent on my benefactors. They have been absolutely splendid to me. I regard them as my parents, as they think of me as their son."

Victoria was touched in spite of herself. "How fortunate we both are. My parents died in India when I was eight. I hardly remember them because my mama returned with me in my fifth year before going back to Delhi. I lived with my aunt and uncle then, and when the sad news reached them they took me on as another daughter . . . although I called them Uncle and Aunt, and my cousins have never called me sister. *I* have misled no one," she added pointedly.

"Do not accuse me, I beg you," said Hugo. "I have been in Vienna and quite unable to mislead you about anything.

The blame must be laid at my brother's . . . Charles's door," he amended. "The truth is I have lived my whole life as his brother, and what else could he call me? I am not a cousin. A *friend*? Hardly! We are brothers, and no one will persuade us we are not. There is no doubt I have been taken completely into the Stanford family, as we shall take you most willingly into our ranks."

She felt herself color, but it did not matter, for he could not see it. There was a strangely relaxing aspect about the situation—almost as if she were there in disguise. To see and not be seen gave one a tremendous feeling of confidence, and it was this that enabled her to cast aside mannered conversation and be strictly herself.

"Do you ride, Victoria?" he was asking now.

"Well enough . . . but you would not think so."

"Why so defensive?"

She leaned back with a laugh. "Oho! Do you think I have not heard of your brilliant horsemanship? Even if Charles had not sung your praises to the sky, every officer in the regiment has told me of your prowess. I shall not tell you what they said, for my aunt always impressed upon me that too much flattery turns one's head."

Hugo was growing every minute more delighted with her fresh and entertaining company. She must tie his self-assured brother in knots.

"Remember that in future, Stokes," he said. "It is bad for my nature to hear you congratulate me on winning a race."

"If you say so, sir, but I think the damage has already been done, if you don't mind me a-mentioning the fact."

"How foolish you are," said Victoria, blushing pink again; then to cover her confusion: "May I give Marston Moor and Agincourt a piece of this biscuit?"

"Salamanca and Waterloo, if you please," he replied sternly. "I suppose I must say yes or you will accuse me of being a monster." He sighed theatrically. "They are the most dreadful creatures at begging for tidbits. I seem unable to school them the way I school horses."

"I should think not," she said indignantly. "From what I hear, you have new ideas on schooling *men*. What were you doing in Vienna?"

He seemed surprised. "It is not the kind of thing a lady would understand."

"Of course she will not if it is never explained to her. When I am a lady of the regiment I intend becoming very knowledgeable on military matters. Think of the honor to the regiment if the next Lady Blythe should become its patroness."

Hugo sighed. Charles would hardly consider cavalry tactics a suitable subject for a lady—especially his own betrothed—yet she had a point. How often did a man dismiss a woman's interest by saying she would not understand? All the same, he hesitated.

"If you can find no more to say to me, I shall leave," she told him roundly.

He sighed again. "It is not easy to explain to a person who knows nothing of military maneuvers, so you must stop me if I grow boring."

"It will not be boring—too complicated, perhaps."

Stokes, seeing that Hugo was not likely to need his assistance for a while, went quietly out, and the young officer began on a subject dear to his heart.

"The present system we have for moving mounted troops from place to place is visually attractive and impressive during reviews and field days, but not a few cavalrymen think it too slow and cumbersome to be effective in war."

"But we are not going to war. Charles says the world has never been so peaceful."

"So it has not, but affairs in the East are very unsettled and there is a constant threat from Russia. The regiment was engaged in the Afghan war of '38, and we have been involved in putting down riots in the industrial cities more recently. There is no knowing when we might be sent to combat unrest anywhere in the world. A soldier's job is not merely to look splendid in ballrooms and opera houses. Soldiers are meant to fight."

"Even when there is no reason?" she put in.

"It is better when the world is at peace, naturally, but an army is useless if it is not taught to fight should the need arise."

Victoria was quite absorbed. "What has that to do with moving cavalrymen about?"

He leaned forward so that the reflection of flames glowed on his unruly brown hair. It was easy to imagine how desperately he wished to tear that black band from his eyes in order to make his point with more force.

"Since Waterloo, weapons have changed and improved. Guns are more effective and deadly. Cannon can be angled more quickly. Therefore, it is imperative to be able to change the direction of a body of mounted men instantly, without losing formation or effectiveness. Our present system does not do this."

"I see," she said slowly. "Do you mean that your new methods would turn the cavalry away before too many were lost?"

"Not turn them away," he said rather defensively. "Redirect their attack. It is senseless waste to send cavalry galloping into the mouths of cannon."

"No commander would do that, surely," she cried.

"If the guns are hidden in the jungle, as they were in the Sikh wars of '45 and '48, a regiment of cavalry might almost be upon them before they opened fire and betrayed their positions. In such a case, can you see how important it would be to maneuver quickly, without scattering?"

"Yes. Even a simpleton would see that."

He let out his breath in a long sigh. "Our generals do not, I fear. Correction. They see it but do not feel any need to do anything about it. Since there is no likelihood, at present, of going to war, they imagine there never will be. They have disbanded half the army and are thinking of going even further."

She considered that for a moment. "I suppose they can always recruit them again, should they be needed."

"Certainly. They can press-gang as many as they like, but they will be completely untrained and therefore useless. It takes a long time to train a good soldier."

"Does it? I thought recruiting sergeants accepted anyone who wished to take the shilling."

Suddenly he laughed and leaned back. "I have been riding my hobbyhorse, Victoria. You must forgive me."

She sensed that she had put a foot wrong and was anxious lest he felt she did not care about his ideas.

"Please go on. I may sound ignorant, but this is the first time anyone has spoken to me on the subject. I assure you I am most interested and am prepared to believe that if a horseman of your reputation says there should be changes, he must be right."

"Despite all the generals?"

"Despite any number of generals," she said decisively.

He bowed his head. "Thank you, ma'am—patroness of the Hussars."

At that moment the faint sound of a gong resounding through the house set her heart thumping. Waterloo or Salamanca was standing erect in a frenzy of barking as she swung her feet to the ground from the curled-up position she had unconsciously adopted.

"This is the luncheon gong. Charles is always so punctual I shall never be ready when he comes for me!"

Hugo stood up and held out a hand. "You sound panic-stricken. There is no need. Charles will not eat you. He is the most reasonable of men!"

"Is he, indeed?" she told him fiercely. "I shall be in dreadful disgrace for even setting foot inside your room against all advice. He will be furious."

"Then do not tell him."

She was taken aback. "I could not deceive him."

"I could—quite easily. For the sake of your good name," he added artfully. "It would be much easier to say nothing, would it not?"

"Ye-es," she agreed doubtfully, "but what shall we do when introduced as strangers?"

"Act like strangers." He shook his head. "My dear sister, it is plain you are not used to telling lies."

"I am not, sir. It is also plain you are an old hand at it."

He smiled. "I am also an old hand at telling tales. You have no notion of the tale I shall tell if you do not promise to come again tomorrow. I shall swear you were here the entire morning, spinning my head with your chatter and exhausting me with your energy. I shall moan and groan— I am excellent at that—and sit gasping as if my last breath were about to be drawn."

Perhaps it was the wine or maybe the warmth of his personality that contrasted with the other members of this household. Whatever it was, she laughed merrily.

"You are quite unscrupulous, sir."

"I know it," he replied calmly, "but you have no idea how lonely I have been these past days. Take pity on me," he begged, knowing no woman could resist such words from him, then added something unintentionally heart-stirring: "If you do as I ask I swear I will pretend when we are introduced that I have never set eyes . . . on you," he finished slowly, leaving a silence that was more telling than words.

"I will do my best," she said eventually, "but you must promise that you will make no more attempts to slip past Stokes and leave this room."

"Done!" he said with warmth. "Your visits will eliminate the need. *Stokes!*" he called, and the soldier appeared like magic from the other room. "Miss Castledon is leaving . . . but she will be coming to tea with me tomorrow."

"That is good news, miss." Stokes gave her a smile that turned up the ends of his mustache and escorted her to the door.

Victoria had almost left when she remembered the circumstances that had brought her there and turned back to the blindfolded man.

"You will think me quite stupid, but I do not know how to return to my room."

Hugo laughed. "If I were really unscrupulous I should refuse to help you, thereby ensuring myself company for luncheon. Where have they installed you?"

"I really cannot say. Charles always accompanies me. The furnishings are mostly pink, blue and ivory . . . and there is a superb oil of a sunset in my room."

"Ah, you are in the South Gallery." He frowned. "How thoughtless of Mama to situate you so far from the main rooms. However, you are in luck, for it is no great distance from here if you cross the Mirror Room. At the end of this corridor you will find a pair of doors leading to it. Cross there and you'll find yourself in the South Gallery." He grinned. "You are not likely to be spotted in your clandestine journey, for it avoids the main rooms."

She smiled back, then let the smile fade. What use to smile at a man who could not see her?

Hugo knew she had gone only when he heard the door close with a soft click he had never noticed until forced to concentrate on sounds rather than sights. He sagged back in his chair and told Stokes to pour him some more wine.

"And, Stokes, please do not let my stocks of lemonade dwindle so again."

Stokes sighed theatrically. "No, sir." He put the glass safely into his officer's hand. "About tea, sir."

"Find out Miss Castledon's preferences and ensure they are available, even if it means going into the village to purchase them."

"That's all very well, Captain Esterly, but I ain't exactly popular down in the kitchens, as you know. I've had another argument with Dawkins this morning."

"Good God, man, can you not make an effort to get along with him?"

Stokes drew himself up to his full height. "No, sir, that I can't do. I think you are well enough used to my ways to know I am not a person as likes to have enemies, but me and Dawkins is completely *incomperapatible*."

Hugo laughed and shook his head. "Not incompatible, just too full of your own importance. Dawkins has had his nose put out of joint by your presence and feels he should resume his personal service to me. You, on the other hand, sniff at him because he is too high-flown by military standards." He sighed. "But I depend on you, Stokes. God knows, I do. Dawkins would drive me to the devil at a time like this."

"My very words to him, Captain," put in the incorrigible Stokes. "Now, if you'll excuse me, sir, I'll be seeing about your luncheon and giving them dogs a bit of exercise. Sorry about letting them annoy the lady."

"That is all right. Miss Castledon does not appear to take umbrage over small things."

Stokes departed with the retrievers, and Hugo sat deep in thought until his restless spirit drove him to his feet. He felt his way to the window and stood before it. The sun was warm on his hands. He imagined it must be one of those glorious blue and gold days December exploded into from the usual grayness now and again. Outside, the shrubbery would be ablaze with scarlet holly berries and pyracanthas, contrasting with the yellow and gold of witch hazel and forsythia. The ivy rambling over the wall of the south aspect would be russet and crimson at this time of year, and just below his window two tall conifers must be sharply

divided into light-and dark-green by the slope of the sun's
rays over the roof.

Beyond the gardens he could visualize the lush spread of
the park encircling the tranquillity of blue water. The grass
would be dew-laden and shimmering, the air would fill a
man's lungs with sharp, cold purity, and a horse would go
like the wind, consumed by the same exultation as its rider.

He knew it so well: a lesson learned from boyhood. With
a good mare like Flame between his knees he could bend
low over her ears and feel the wind rushing past as the
long-striding beast took him across the park, through the
lower meadow, a leap to bridge the stream, up through the
copse and along Three-tree Ridge. Then a gentle trot past
the old granaries, slipping and sliding down the leaf-
covered bank, on past Mother Timmins' cottage and a long
easy ride back through the orchards to the home paddock.

For several minutes he stood with his head tilted back,
reliving every yard of that ride. Then his hand gripped the
gold-brocade curtain beside him and twisted it savagely.
Dear God, had he seen all that for the last time? His other
hand unconsciously tightened around the stem of his glass.
Why had he not looked more closely at those familiar land-
marks on his last visit? Why had he not appreciated it to
the fullest extent of his senses? Why had he not drunk the
wine of perfection in deep draughts against the possibility
of it being the last?

How could he live as a blind man? He was not cut out
for drawing-room existence. Always ill at ease in the company of intellectuals, Hugo was also bored to tears among
political figures. If he could not be a military man there
was nothing left for him. The possibility of buying a small
estate and becoming a squire was attractive to him, but
what use was a gentleman who could not ride over his
acres and superintend them?

A man who reveled in an active open-air life would be
stifled and caged by an infirmity such as he might have to
face. Dammit, he could not even see to his own dress and
ablutions. In time, the art of eating might be mastered sufficiently to allow him to accomplish the business without too
much mess, but he could never entertain guests in his own
house. As for the fair sex, even if he could find a trollop

willing to sell her favors to a blind man, he would have too much pride to go to her. Marriage would be out of the question. Even an angel of virtue like Charity Verewood would hardly relish tying herself to half a man.

In a sudden rush of fear and desperation he flung the wineglass as hard as he could and had the satisfaction of hearing it smash against the wall. Patience was not one of his virtues; ten more days of uncertainty would have him in an asylum.

Hugo waited for his visitors the following afternoon with a sense of anticipation. How would his new sister carry off the meeting? The news that there was to be one had come as a surprise, and he wondered if Victoria were responsible for his father's change of mind. It seemed likely that Charity Verewood had persuaded them it was not good for him to be left alone, for she could influence his parents more than anyone. His spirits dropped. Now that Charles had dashed their hopes, he knew his parents would wish him to make a match with the girl—but he was not yet ready to settle down. There was so much he wanted to do with his career before contemplating matrimony—so much that involved his entire days to that end. It was too soon to devote himself to home and family.

A knock fell on the door and he yelled, *"Stokes!"*

"Yessir," said a voice from a few yards away. "I bin listening for it, never fear."

"A minute, man, before you open the door. You are not to forget we have never met Miss Castledon."

"Oh, sir," said Stokes in his most hurt tone, "as if I'd give the young lady away! It's them dogs as might do it."

Hugo groped his way to his feet. "For God's sake keep them out of it. Miss Verewood does not care for their form of greeting."

"I see, sir."

Hugo could picture the look on his servant's face and knew the rough soldier had already decided the other lady was not of the same caliber as Victoria Castledon. The door was being opened, and there was Charles's voice greeting Stokes in friendly fashion and making him known to the ladies. He smothered a smile at the polite exchange between Stokes and Victoria. So far so good.

"Come in and make yourselves comfortable," he said, trying to judge whether they had come right up to him or still lingered in the doorway.

There was the rustle of silk shirts and the smell of fresh lavender. That would be Charity. Victoria had brought a scent of lemons and sweet hay yesterday that had reminded him of happy interludes with village maidens.

A hand took his elbow suddenly, making him start nervously, and his brother said in his ear, "Hugo, old fellow, you are very fortunate to have two charming ladies come to visit you. Miss Verewood has driven especially across to Wychbourne on hearing news of you this morning."

"You are the most considerate of friends," said Hugo, putting out his hand, praying he would not touch the girl's person in doing so.

She put cool fingers in his. "I would have come sooner, Captain Esterly, if I had thought it advisable. Dare I hope you are on the mend?"

"Yes, thank you. Please take a seat by the fire. I value your concern that brought you out on a cold day such as this. I'll feel very guilty if you should catch a chill because of it."

"There is no chance of that" was the reply as she moved away in a cloud of lavender perfume. "I have been across the hills to visit parishioners with the Reverend Meakins on worse days than this."

"Now, I have the honor and extreme pleasure to present you to my future wife," said Charles warmly. "Victoria, my dear, Hugo has been most anxious to meet you."

"Miss Castledon, it is most unkind of you to arrange your betrothal at a time when I am not fit to celebrate it," he said, putting out his hand for a second time and taking the warm fingers to his lips as he executed what he hoped was a graceful bow. "But I offer my sincere felicitations and promise to be all in one piece when I stand beside Charles at the wedding."

"It is my fervent hope that you will be" was the controlled reply. "I apologize for my atrocious mistiming, but you were also at fault, sir, for deserting your regiment at the beginning of the summer."

He smiled. "I stand rebuked, Miss Castledon."

"Please call me Victoria. I am to be your sister so very shortly."

He would have sworn she was smiling, for her voice had taken on a richer tone. Damnation! This continuous infernal darkness!

Charity expressed the hopes of the members of her family for his quick recovery, and he answered automatically. A clear mental picture sprang to mind when he heard that soft cool voice—perfect oval face unmarred by selfishness or indulgence, large blue eyes full of feminine appeal, corn-gold braids wound around her head in the manner of Teutonic opera singers and an attractive rounded body that she would insist on disguising with severely plain gowns. But as for the other voice, he had nothing to accompany it but blackness deeper than night.

There was no guide to tell him whether she was fair or dark, fat or thin, tall or short, pretty or plain. Did her nose tip up or was it long and pointed? Was her complexion cream and rose or sallow and spotty? Was her smile slow and beguiling? Surely it could not snap on and off like Dan Ferriday's sister's ghastly grin. No, he could not associate the *sound* of Victoria Castledon with any girl he knew. The ephemeral Victoria of yesterday had been full of gaiety, yet hauntingly uncertain of herself, and try as he might she would not take form in his mind.

"Miss Verewood has brought you some potted meat that has proved beneficial in other cases, Hugo," said Charles, breaking into his thoughts.

"How kind of you, Miss Verewood. Will it cure all ills?"

"It sustains one's constitution, Captain Esterly. It is not a medicament" came the slight reproach.

He pulled himself together and tried to concentrate on the conversation. "Foolish of me. I beg your pardon, Miss Verewood."

"Victoria has great regrets at being unable to bring a gift fit for an invalid but has suggested to me what I think might be an excellent scheme," said Charles after letting out a breath that told Hugo he had taken a seat. "She is very willing to devote a part of each day to reading to you. We have all discussed the matter and feel a short period of that nature would do you no harm and would keep you from brooding. Do you approve?"

"Heartily. Thank you, Victoria. I have been quite cut off without even a newspaper to keep me in touch with the world."

"You need not have been, for I wished to perform such a service several days ago."

"Perhaps it was all for the best," put in Charity soothingly. "There is sometimes nothing more taxing for a gentleman than the newspaper. My papa rages over some of the items he reads in them—not that I believe you are prone to rages, Captain Esterly, for you have always been exceedingly sweet-tempered when we have been together."

Hugo felt irritated. He did not wish to sit there being complimented on the sweetness of his nature—which it was not, however one looked at it. If people were permitted to visit him at last, let them tell him amusing stories and entertain him.

"You must have caught me when I was being particularly angelic," he said, and a merry laugh came from across the room.

"I think it likely to snow," said Charles heartily. Hugo was familiar enough with his brother to know he was being tactful. Dear Charles—so much better at drawing-room manners than he would ever be.

"It is very attractive visually, but it brings much hardship in its wake," said Charity. "Was there snow in Vienna, Captain Esterly?"

"Not in the city. I spent a weekend with a colonel of Lancers at his country home and the snow there was so deep I was prevented from returning until halfway through the following week. I was not the most popular officer in the mess when I did arrive, for the visiting Russian detachment was impatient to see a demonstration of my new cavalry drill and had been cooling their heels for longer than they cared to do."

"But they must have known you had made every effort," protested Miss Verewood.

"Yes. Was it not uncharitable of them?" agreed Hugo, choking back a chuckle, for he had not tried all that hard to return from the chateau. The colonel's daughter had had a governess who was extremely unresistant to British cavalry officers, and the small room at the top of the house had provided him with several more comfortable and satisfying nights than he would have spent in some isolated inn on the snowbound road to Vienna.

"Would you describe your new cavalry drill?" The light voice sailed across from his right like a sip of champagne after heavy mulled wine.

The chair squeaked as Charles moved again. "What a very odd thing to ask, my dear. Females should not concern themselves with such things."

"But if I am to become a patroness of the regiment in the future, I should understand what you do, Charles."

"Patroness of the . . . what nonsense is this, Victoria? You might well be a colonel's lady in time, but that does not mean you will have to train as a cavalryman." His indulgent laughter made Hugo clench his fists.

"I think it was not meant to be a joke, Charles," he said.

"Of course it was a joke, my dear fellow. Victoria can be very entertaining, as I know full well."

Hugo recognized the caressing note in his brother's voice. This child bride teased the maturity of the thirty-eight-year old major with her naïveté, but Hugo did not feel that Victoria was likely to be content as simply an amusing play thing for an experienced man. The naïveté was due purely to her lack of years, not to her lack of intelligence. Surely Charles could see that?

"I confess I do not understand the first detail of military life, but your ideas must be quite brilliant if gentlemen come from Russia just to witness them." Silk rustled and lavender wafted on the air in a delicate assault on his nostrils. "You have always been acknowledged as an outstanding horseman, Captain Esterly."

"Please do not flatter me too much, Miss Verewood. I am told it is extremely bad for me and might well turn my head."

God, how he longed to tear away the black band over his eyes to see the effect of his words on the girl who had quoted them to him only yesterday. Silence had descended. What were they all doing? Exchanging significant glances? Signaling that it was time to go and leave him isolated in his darkness again? Raising their eyebrows at his facetiousness?

"Will you take tea with me?" he asked in the urgent hope of keeping them there.

"I really feel . . . " Charity began, when Victoria cut across her refusal.

"That would be very pleasant. I am persuaded Miss Verewood must feel the benefit of some refreshment if she is to set forth in the December chill once more."

"Stokes!" Hugo called and listened for the door to open. "Yessir?"

"We would like tea as quickly as you can produce it."

"Right away, sir." The door closed again.

"There is something missing. Where are Badejos and Minden today?" asked Victoria in identifiable teasing, and Hugo knew she had dropped her guard.

He laughed. "You have heard about my dogs, have you? They are called Salamanca and Waterloo, in fact. It was probably Mama who told you of them, for she can never remember names correctly."

"Yes, it was your mama."

He could tell she realized how near she had come to betraying herself, for a little of the earlier warmth had gone from her merry tones.

"Are you not afraid to have two such boisterous creatures with you at this time? If they should leap at you?"

"They are intelligent beasts, Miss Verewood, who appear to know I cannot cope with their romping."

The laugh was lifeless in contrast with Victoria's. "You are always so loyal. I trust the animals appreciate their good fortune in having you for a master."

"They should, for I have impressed the fact upon them often enough."

"My brother has the same affinity with dogs that he has with horses." Charles's rich baritone revealed that he must be smiling. "He can persuade animals to do as he tells them immediately."

"Ah, Charles, I am glad you use the word *persuade*. Therein lies the secret. When one has a shy, frightened or sensitive creature in one's hands, force or anger only increases those tendencies."

"So you maintain, old fellow, and I am prepared to allow that you are right, since your results are so successful."

The tea appeared to loosen Charity's tongue and relax her stiffness with Victoria that puzzled Hugo so much. The girl from the neighboring estate was usually so very sociable and warmhearted. But Hugo was in for a more puzzling surprise when his guests rose to depart.

The lavender perfume rustled nearer until he could feel Charity's warmth beside him and her sweet breath on his neck.

"Goodbye, my dear Captain Esterly. My prayers will be for your complete recovery . . . as they have been since I first heard of the tragedy. But prayers alone will be useless. You must take very great care of yourself. Rest and quiet are essential in any illness, and I cannot approve of taxing you with the problems to be read in the newspapers these days. May I depart in the confidence that you will heed my advice?"

Charity's voice had altered in some subtle way. He was sufficiently familiar with women to recognize the preliminary sharpening of claws before battle, but why should this girl leap out of character over Charles's chosen bride? Having learned some hard lessons in tact where women were concerned, he smiled in what he hoped was the right direction and said, "Your concern is very comforting, dear friend. I promise to do nothing that would cause you to leave here with anxiety clouding your brow. Thank you for your visit . . . and the gift," he added hastily, not being more explicit because he could not remember what it was.

A hand was lightly laid on his arm. "I will come again and promise to inform you of the latest items of local interest so that you will not feel neglected."

"Whenever you decide to visit, Miss Verewood, I shall be happy to abandon what I am doing in order to accompany you," said a merry voice from the center of the room. "But I must ask you to choose your items of interest with care. We do not wish to tax Hugo with inconsequential nonsense, do we?"

Hugo fought a desperate battle against laughter. So Victoria had her claws out, too. What a delightful situation. If only he could *see* the confrontation. There was nothing more entertaining than two of the fair sex in skirmishing order.

"I think you need not worry, my dear. Miss Verewood has had a great deal of experience with invalids."

"But, Charles, your brother is not an invalid. I have seldom seen a gentleman in more splendid health. That he has been forbidden to use his eyes for a short while does not mean that he has a fever or will collapse with shock if he discovers yet another railway has been opened."

"I think you have had scant experience in the sickroom, Miss Castledon. I have invariably found the patient who resists the rules takes longer to recover. Captain Esterly might put on a brave face, but it is up to his friends to show an understanding of what he is suffering."

Good God, thought Hugo. She will have us all in tears before long! Attempting to put a strangled note into his voice, he said, "Forgive me if I remain standing no longer. One is apt to lose one's balance after a short while." To emphasize this he began to sway slightly.

There was an immediate rustling of skirts and sighs of concern from female throats. Charles manfully assured the ladies his brother had enjoyed their visit and was merely feeling a little tired, and they all departed, leaving Hugo free to explode with laughter as he manhandled Waterloo and Salamanca, who had been allowed in for a biscuit.

But Charles was soon back, as he had guessed he would be.

"By heaven, Hugo, that was the most infernal trick you have ever played, but it has done me more good than any of your capers so far." Charles collapsed into a chair with a heavy grunt of laughter. "I am now fully persuaded you have come to terms with your present situation. God, man, you have had me worried these past days with your introspection."

"It is easy to become introspective in one's own black company. I tried hard enough to impress you with the fact."

"Dammit, Hugo, the first time you *do* have visitors you stage that excruciating melodrama in order to be rid of them."

"Only one, Charles . . . only one. Charity Verewood is a sweet girl, but I swear her patients must cure themselves very hastily in order to avoid a second visit from her."

Charles laughed again, and Hugo heard the sound with pleasure. It was good to have his brother's companionship once more. Lately, he had been creeping in and out of this room as though entering the presence of the Angel of Death.

"Your Victoria is quite charming. You have had the devil's own luck in capturing her when she is scarcely out, I should say."

"Have I not?" There was pride as well as humor in Charles's voice now. "As soon as I set eyes on the latest Castledon ingenue I knew she was for me and moved in with heavy artillery. She has the most devastating way of making honest observations as if she had never been told young females do not do such things."

"I have noticed" was the reply as Hugo forgot that Charles did not know of yesterday's meetings.

A shout of laughter preceded his brother's next remark. "You should have seen Charity Verewood's face when Victoria referred to local matters as inconsequential nonsense."

"The Verewoods believe the world revolves around Buckinghamshire."

"Mmm. Mama has informed Victoria that she has high hopes of your offering for Charity Verewood."

"Has she, by George! I tell you, Charles . . ." Hugo flung out a hand that knocked a tea cup from the table beside him. "Hell and damnation! There, you see what a prize I would be for any woman?" The sudden return of frustration made him bitter.

"At the moment your activities are somewhat restricted, I agree, but I would swear there is many an Austrian *mädchen* who would vote you a splendid lover. Am I right?"

Hugo relaxed and silenced Waterloo, who was barking at the broken tea cup. "The troops over there are more concerned with the conquest of *mädchen* than martial skills, you know, Charles."

He could imagine his brother's handsome face breaking into a smile as he said, "Gentlemen after my own heart, Hugo. Who wishes to dwell on ways of cutting each other to ribbons when one can make the ladies swoon at the first sight of a handsome uniform?"

Hugo shook his head sadly. "You sound like our senior officers. They think me a madman and not infrequently tell me so."

"And they are right. We are keeping the peace in England and the Empire, adding color and visual attraction to ceremonials and ensuring that the female population is happy and contented. Would you wish us to rush off to have at some fellow's throat just to show how fierce we are? Come, Hugo, it is an obsession with you. The world has never been more settled and at peace."

"But for how long? I tell you, the day will come when we shall all be dying for the want of an army."

"All right, all right." He heard the note of impatience in Charles's voice. "When that day comes, you have my permission to remind me of those words."

"General Kingsworth said the same to me only last month."

"You see? He is a shrewd military leader with fifteen years' experience in the East Indies. He also played no mean part at Waterloo. You, on the other hand, have experienced nothing by way of aggression other than controlling a small mob of factory rioters. Are you qualified to speak on the subject?"

"No, damn you, that is just my point." He brought his hand down on the chair arm and half missed it. "When trouble starts, men like Kingsworth will be too old for the job, and who is to take over from them? No, I am not qualified on the subject, but I should be—we *all* should be!"

"If you continue in that mood I shall call Miss Verewood back. I doubt she has yet left the house."

Hugo had to surrender. "You have found the perfect threat with which to silence me. Her sympathy makes me feel a hundred times worse." He sighed. "Can you guess what it is like, Charles? I cannot wait for the doctor to arrive on the twenty-eighth, yet I fear the moment. The temptation to lift this damned blindfold overcomes me at least six times every day."

The squeak of the chair signified that his brother was about to leave. A hand gripped his shoulder. "Bear it for a few days longer. The worst is over, old fellow." His parting shot was meant to lighten the atmosphere. "If you are Charles's voice. "When that day comes, you have my per- ence will stand you in good stead. Adieu. I'll look in again before retiring."

❋ ❋ ❋

When Charles arrived shortly before the dinner gong that night, Victoria was waiting in triumphant mood, and when he told her he had returned to the sickroom and found the patient not too exhausted, she seemed amused. Looking up at him with dark velvet eyes, she said, "Of course he was not exhausted. It was quite plain to me that he could bear no more of Miss Verewood's platitudes on ill-health—and I cannot say I blame him, for she is most dreadfully prissy and not at all the right company for someone who is so despondent. I am quite put out that she was permitted to visit him immediately upon calling, when I have been denied the pleasure of meeting my own brother for so long." Her lashes lowered provocatively. "Has she ever thought of entering a nunnery? She looks so very like a Sister of Mercy."

Charles regarded her with delighted astonishment for several seconds, then burst into laughter. "That is an outrageous thing to say. Please do not repeat it to Mama."

"Naturally I shall not, for Miss Verewood is such a favorite with her . . . and, I thought, with you all."

He reached for her hand and took it to his lips. "You are my only favorite, Victoria. I am at your feet, as I never was at hers."

"Thank you, Charles," she said, moving quickly because the deep look was suddenly in his eyes. "Come, we shall be late, and your mama will not forgive us."

The next three days passed in a happy state. There were rides with Charles, a morning visit to the rector to make arrangements for the wedding service, excursions into the gardens to gather foliage and flowers to decorate the rooms. The indoor hours were spent writing letters, wrapping gifts and painting cards to go with the presents. And there were twice daily visits to Hugo. She loved the time spent in Hugo's apartment, talking to him as the older brother she had never had and playing with the dogs to whom she was devoted.

One afternoon Victoria tripped through the Mirror Room, humming to herself and bursting with the happiness of youth. At the Verewoods' ball the night before, the gentlemen had flocked around her, leaving Charity filled with chagrin . . . and no wonder, since her own gown of white lace had made the Sister of Mercy look quite dowdy in lavender silk cut in last year's fashion.

Victoria had discovered that her relationships with gentlemen were much more interesting and satisfactory than those with other women, and here was another example. The girl might have the whole of Buckinghamshire commending her goodness and mercy, but Victoria was not taken in. The fact that Charity had been allowed to visit Hugo on her first application, when she had been denied, rankled still, but she hugged to herself the secret meeting about which the girl with the doll-blue eyes knew nothing. Beneath that sweet exterior there was a sharpness Victoria could not like—and if the girl imagined she would capture Hugo with potted meat and remonstrations she was a great deal sillier than she should be at twenty.

With that thought putting a smug smile on her face, she knocked and waited for Stokes to admit her.

"Good afternoon, Miss Castledon. Thank the Lord you've arrived. The captain is in a rare old mood, I can tell you. Threatening to tear off that there bandage and I don't know what, he is. I can't do nothing with him, straight I can't."

"Goodness!" She hurried in, brusquely restraining the dogs, who leaped all over her. Hugo was standing by the window with his back to her, gripping the brocade curtain with his long fingers. She marched right up to him and squeezed between him and the window sill.

"So this is the way you thank me for bringing Aunt Sophy to see you! Have you any idea how difficult it was trying to sort you both out? Do I not deserve a face full of smiles at least?"

"Yes, you do, my dear sister. You deserve a great deal more than that, and I am an ungrateful brute. Does that satisfy you?"

It was said with quiet desperation, and she realized immediately that he was beyond teasing out of his bad temper.

"Nothing will satisfy me until I hear the reason for this, Hugo. I am not Miss Verewood, nor your mama who will not come to visit you because she pretends a dislike of sickrooms—as if you were lying covered in measle spots in an atmosphere of vapors and medicaments. And I am not

Lord Blythe, who has enough on his mind with the estate. Lastly, I am not Charles, whom you would not wish to think you unmanly. I am Victoria, your sister, who will listen to anything you have to say."

He made no response, so she went on. "Aunt Almeira says that ladies cannot have gentlemen friends, only admirers. I cannot agree. I have many friends back in the regiment, and you are my very best friend. Have we not discussed your new cavalry tactics and my wish to become patroness of the Hussars? Did we not discover we are both orphans? Have we not shared a secret about our first meeting? Have I . . . have I *really* not earned the right to be your sincere friend?"

"Please, Victoria," he groaned in protest. "Without your company I should have reached this stage long ago. You know how dependent I have become on your visits—how much of a friend you have been."

"Well, am I not still?"

He pummeled the sill with his clenched fists. "I knocked my luncheon completely into my lap just now. You have no notion how I felt knowing I could not even clean myself up. The dogs rushed at me, and I struck them. That will tell you how angry I am. I cannot reach for a glass of wine or cup of tea when you are here without praying I shall not smash it; I cannot shake a man's hand without wondering if I shall not poke him in the chest instead; cannot see the view from the window, the glow of the dogs' coats, the time of day, the fire that warms me, the pictures on my wall. Dammit, I don't even know what you look like. I have been spending so much time in your company, yet I speak into darkness to a voice that belongs to nothing I recognize." These last words were said in raised tones, and Victoria decided to interrupt before he went on.

"That is a simple problem to solve. I have dark hair in curls below my ears, brown eyes and am dressed in a blue silk gown with slippers to match—quite plain because your mama dislikes over-ornamentation, I have been told." She took his arms and turned him back into the room. "You may know how tall I am by measuring, thus." Carefully raising one of his arms until it was outstretched onto the top of her head, she added, "I wish I were taller, for a patroness should be elegant. I am sure to be dubbed 'Tiny Lady Blythe' by officers and men alike."

Still holding his hand, she pulled him across to the sturdy table beside his desk. "I have seen this chess set every day and wondered how well you play. I do not see why I should not discover the answer. Sit down and take red. I warn you that I am most likely to win, for my uncle taught me several years ago after I had become fascinated by his lovely ivory set."

Reluctantly Hugo allowed her to push him into a chair. "Victoria, if ever you become patroness of my regiment they will rue the day. Your strict discipline will be worse than any they suffer from colonels. I cannot conceive how you propose we shall play chess, but knowing you I am certain you will accomplish it."

"Of course I shall," she told him, thankful his mood was passing. "I tell you which piece I have moved. You tell me your move, and I will guide your hand. Now, face your complete and disgraceful defeat."

Her prowess did not live up to her boast, and the game was quickly won by Hugo, who was an expert on tactics. He went into a long lecture on what she should never have done under such circumstances, and they argued heatedly until Stokes judged it the right time to bring in the tea tray, bestowing a grateful smile on the young lady who could charm his officer out of such a black mood.

Victoria munched muffins and spoke extravagant endearments to the dogs, who sat at her feet, while she gave a disjointed and amusing account of the Verewoods party at Brankham Hall.

"Your friend was very charming, Hugo, and plainly much afflicted by your absence."

"Dear me, was she?"

"How can you pretend such surprise? She has made it plain enough how much you occupy her thoughts." She looked across at him as he sat relaxed with his bandaged head against a cushion. "Are you really going to offer for her, as your mama suggested?"

He was still for a few moments, then he answered, "I know you are an orphan, Victoria, and can sympathize, but someone should have told you that well-brought-up young

ladies do not ask such things of gentlemen—even brothers."

As he was quite obviously amused, she went on. "I see
she sent you hothouse fruit today. I am surprised that she
has not called again. Perhaps you overdid your pretense to
ensure her departure, and she truly believes her visit has
hastened you toward the grave."

He broke into irrepressible laughter. "I trust you did not
speak of Miss Verewood in such manner to Mama, Victoria."

"No," she cried, shocked. "What I say to you remains
between the two of us, I assure you." She hesitated. "Only
because you never appear to disapprove of my opinions."

"Wait until the twenty-eighth. There will be a different
story then, sister dear, for I shall be able to see to box your
ears. That is a severe warning."

"I am quaking in my shoes," she giggled, so glad his
optimism was restored. "We played some capital games last
night. Miss Merrifield shrieked quite terribly when a gentleman told a ghost story and produced a polished skull. It
was so amusing one could not take it seriously. Oh, and
Miss Frere lost her sash when the doctor seized her during
Blind Man's Buff. He was most apologetic."

Hugo smiled. "Had I attended there would have been no
need to produce a scarf. I could have obliged as 'Blind
Man' every time." He set down his cup with great care
and stood up. "It is one thing I could have done better than
any guest. Shall I find you, Victoria?"

"You will stumble. Pray, do not be so foolish." She
laughed. "You would never catch me, for I can flit away so
quickly."

"Oho, if your skill at this is as dismal as at chess, I shall
have you in a matter of minutes."

"We shall see," she cried, jumping up. "I am certain to
win this game."

Quick steps took her into the far corner, but after listening carefully Hugo began to walk unsteadily in her direction. Hemmed in by the desk and a sofa, she remained
where she was, believing he would veer away. He did not.

"You are in the corner by the desk," he said lightly,
"and you are trapped. What you have forgotten, my dear,
is that, unlike guests at a party, I have been in total dark-

ness for ten days and have learned to live by sounds only."

She shrank against the wall as he came nearer, arms outstretched, and held her breath. He was smiling and waving his fingers in a teasing manner, when suddenly, stunningly, she knew she could not let him reach her. Her whole body began to tremble. Breathing became difficult. He was almost upon her when an urgent impulse made her duck beneath his arms and run to the door.

She did not stop running until her own door closed behind her, and then she leaned against it shaking and cold, unable to understand why she had run away from him.

CHAPTER THREE

On Boxing Day everyone gathered at 11:00 A.M. in the Great Hall to open the gifts piled beneath the fir tree. Stokes brought Hugo downstairs and waited some feet away, plainly uneasy in such exalted company. Lord Blythe handed out the packages, his childlike excitement evident as he waited to see what they contained.

With trembling fingers Victoria opened a jeweler's box from Charles to discover a complete set of garnets nestled on white velvet. They took her breath away, but there was more. In a completely unexpected gesture, Lady Blythe had chosen a white Chantilly lace shawl with a silk fringe, and even her comment that it would start the young girl on the road to better taste did not dim Victoria's pleasure in the gift. From Lord Blythe there was a folding fan of white feathers with jeweled sticks and a matching bouquet holder. Aunt Sophy's gift was a tiny gold watch to pin to a dress.

The extravagance of these gifts left Victoria round-eyed with appreciation, but her words of thanks sounded inadequate even to her own ears. Never in her life had she been given such presents, but her natural instinct, to run and kiss the cheek of each giver, was subdued by fears of appearing childish to these grand people. Instead, she exclaimed over them all in turn. It was only then that it occurred to her that there was nothing for her from Hugo. A sharp disappointment had only just pierced her when her better nature said he could not have produced a present, situated as he was.

A quick glance at him banished any selfish thoughts from her mind, for he was sitting awkwardly on the dainty chair, holding parcels in his hands that he could not unwrap. And if he could not do so, how would he know what they contained? Leaving her gifts neglected by her chair, she went across to him.

"My dear brother, if you do not want to see what is inside those boxes, I do, so let us unwrap them before I die of curiosity," she said lightly, sinking to the floor beside him.

He smiled wryly. "Victoria, you fool nobody, least of all me, with your hearty sickroom manner. You know quite well I shall make myself look foolish if I attempt to untie ribbons or open boxes. That is why I am dependent on the first kind soul who takes pity on me."

"Nonsense," she declared. "I should like to know who would take pity on a young gentleman in dashing attire who has an armful of expensive gifts from a loving family. If you were in tatters and begging for food I might then consider it, so kindly cease trying to wring tears and sighs from me. Let us see what this contains. It is a most unusual shape. Can you guess its contents?" She put it into his hands to let him feel it.

Since it was obviously a book, he made a pretense of being greatly puzzled, until she took it from him with a laugh and tore off the wrappings to reveal the title.

"Here is an intriguing box, Hugo. It is from your mama. What could it be?" Feverish fingers tore the paper away. "It is a beautifully tooled leather valise, which will last your lifetime as you go where the regiment demands. I must say that I have not seen a more handsome one before. Oh, and here is something from Charles."

Each parcel was dealt with in turn until there was only the riding crop left, and she was in a dilemma—but only for a moment or two, for she really wanted him to have it.

"There is one other. It is not to be compared with the others because you arrived unexpectedly and there was no time to . . ."

"What is your gift, Victoria?" he asked quietly. "You have already given me so much."

"Here, open this one yourself. It will not break if you drop it, and you will have no doubts as to what it is."

He broke the wrapper with strong fingers and tested the riding crop she had bought in the village.

"You have made an excellent choice. I shall value it, Victoria."

She felt suddenly awkward. "I am glad you are not laughing at the folly of presenting a brilliant horseman with a whip not of his own choosing."

"I would not laugh at anyone who is so confident in my

using one ever again. What would I have done without
your optimism these black days?" He turned his head. "Is
Stokes there?"

"Yes." She was disappointed that he intended returning
to his room immediately.

"Stokes," he called.

The Hussar vanished through the door as Hugo said, "I
have a small gift for you and, in the same manner as you,
had little time to choose, but it comes with my deep affection and thanks."

The soldier reentered, and Victoria could only give a
long sigh as she watched him approach with a wriggling
golden body which he set down on four shaky legs before
her.

"You *dearest* creature! I love you on sight. Oh, how
adorable you are," she cried rapturously, scooping the
puppy up in her arms and crooning endearments into its
satin ears. "You are the most beautiful thing I ever possessed. I shall never let you out of my sight for one moment." Clutching the animal to her breast, she was close to
tears. "Hugo, she is the perfect, the *only* present you could
have given me. I can never thank you enough. You are the
best brother anyone could wish for. I do not deserve to be
so happy."

It was some moments before she turned to the rest of the
family to hold the fat little animal aloft. "Do see her. Is she
not the most noble creature you ever set eyes on? I shall
call her Glencoe, because Hugo's dogs are named after
battlefields and he will only mock her if I name her Nugget
or Guinea. Look, Charles, can you dare resist her exquisite
face?"

"An animal beyond compare, my dear, but I suggest
Stokes remove it before an uncomfortable accident occurs
among all these beautiful gifts."

She was so delighted with the little dog that his strained
manner eluded her. She was unprepared when the group
dispersed to dress for luncheon and Charles walked with
her to her room.

"I am having the happiest of times, Charles," she told
him with enthusiasm. "Your family have all been so very
kind to me. I had wondered, at the beginning, whether they
might not take to me, but any doubts I had have flown.

Such thoughtfulness, such affectionate consideration must have gone into their gifts that I can only believe they will love me as a daughter when the time comes."

"Of course they will, Victoria. There was never any chance that they would not accept the bride of my choice. I trust you will not let them down."

At long last his taut withdrawn manner impressed itself upon her and she looked up in quick concern. "Is something wrong, Charles?"

"Nothing that cannot be corrected, my dear." His voice was cold. "Your youth is one of the things that draws my admiration, but you are out of the schoolroom, and I do not expect you to behave as if you were still in it."

"I do not understand. Have I made you angry?" The light was beginning to fade from her face.

"Not angry—disappointed, perhaps. You were on your knees opening Hugo's packages. *On your knees*, Victoria. I could see that you were not aware of the fact, nor that my parents were embarrassed by your hoydenish behavior. Thank heaven we had no guests with us. As my wife I shall expect you to behave with decorum, certainly not to give a childish display of exaggerated excitement that should be confined to the nursery."

"Please stop," she cried. "I can't bear to hear another word."

"It will have to be said nevertheless." His eyes were hard and devoid of affection: She had never seen him look so much a stranger. "I am prepared to allow you a certain leeway when youthful enthusiasm adds to your charm, but I will not have my future wife capering about the floor like an unruly child. In future, you will sit on a chair as any well-bred woman would do."

They had reached her door, where he turned to face her. "And another thing my dear. While I am happy to allow you to keep a dog, you will please treat it as such. That outburst of ridiculous sentiment did not become you. One might almost have supposed you valued it more highly than my own gift."

December 28 dawned crisp and clear. Fresh snow had fallen during the night, filling in footprints and lying clean and white across the area outside the kitchen door, where much coming and going had yellowed the spread beneath the feet of servants and dogs.

Victoria awoke from a restless sleep to know a fluttering anxiety. This morning the doctor was coming to unbind Hugo's eyes, and the truth would be made plain. No more "supposing" or "of course"; no more "will he?" or "will he not?" It would be impossible to evade the fact that had already been decided at the time of the accident and had been hiding behind the blindfold for two weeks.

She decided to emulate Lady Blythe in succumbing to a headache that prevented her from leaving her room. Charles courteously refrained from disturbing her, merely sending a note containing his wishes for her speedy recovery in time for the dinner party his parents were giving that evening. Had he come to her he would have found no darkened room or atmosphere reeking of vinegar and smelling salts. His beloved was curled up on the window seat, cuddling Glencoe and staring out across the snowbound grounds, in closer communion with the Lord than she had been for some years.

Her confidence in His goodness and mercy had had her believing in Hugo's complete recovery, but all kinds of fears beset her now that the moment of revelation had come. She still had no doubts of the Lord's benevolence, but He *had* taken her parents when she had not wanted to lose them, and He had also taken Hugo's father at a time when the wickedness of the woman who bore him had left him, a babe, alone in the world. Of course, provision had been made in both cases, and she could only wonder now if He might have some reason for depriving this young man of his sight—a reason known only to Himself.

In her prayers she asked that, if this were the case, He might reconsider the matter. Hugo Esterly was a thinking man who could be of great service to mankind in his profession, and if He would spare him this blow she would undertake to mend her own ways and think more kindly of others—even the Charity Verewoods of the world.

This promise suitably impressed upon the One above, she sat reliving her visits to the young man whose nerves would now be strung to a pitch of tension near to breaking point. Her fingers rubbed gently on the fat tummy of the puppy sleeping in her arms and, now and again, she would nuzzle the golden body with her face, murmuring her hopes and fears into floppy ears. Rosie had been dispatched to the lower regions to note when the doctor departed, then to return with all haste with the verdict, so the sleeping Glencoe was treated to her mistress's confessions with no chance of their being overheard.

It was past noon when the servant girl returned and there was no need for her to say a word: the radiance of her expression told it all. Victoria told the girl to go down on her knees with her mistress, but the words of thanks did not come easily through the sudden onslought of pain deep in the pit of Victoria's stomach that so surprisingly resembled the ache Charles put there with his embraces.

Her impulse to run through the Mirror Room to share her relief with Hugo had to be curbed. No doubt he would be surrounded by his family just now, and this was just the kind of childish behavior Charles had condemned in her. In an agony of impatience she waited until just before luncheon before sending Rosie with a note couched in restrained terms, expressing her gladness at his recovery. His reply was immediate.

I read your note with mixed feelings: great thankfulness that I could read it, but puzzlement over the way it was written. It did not seem to reflect the person I know, but when your maid explained that you were indisposed, I understood. Please recover by this evening. I am anxious to see the sister who has been the greatest influence in my recovery.

H.

Victoria clutched the letter against her as her eyes closed. He could see; he had written a letter to prove it. Tonight he would be dining with them all in the confidence that he would knock nothing over nor make any awkward mistake. After a mad twirl around the room, she sent Rosie to say her mistress would take luncheon in her room in order to be completely recovered by evening. Then she danced into the dressing room to select the most suitable dress for the occasion.

Lord Blythe's sister and her husband, with one of their sons and both daughters, arrived during the afternoon for a

stay of two nights, and Victoria was requested to take tea
with Lady Blythe in order to meet the ladies. Aunt Patti
was far too conscious of her blue blood; the daughters appeared rather deficient in it, being pale and frail with
hardly any conversation. Victoria, glowing with new happiness, overwhelmed them into silence, strengthening her belief that women were, on the whole, insipid and uninterest-
ing.

The Massingham girls occupied rooms in the South Gallery near Victoria, so it was the most natural thing for
them to meet upon the sound of the gong and make their
way in a trio of delicate crinolines to the withdrawing
room, where the Verewoods were already assembled with
Lord and Lady Blythe and the gentlemen.

Victoria was certain the corridors were echoing with her
heartbeat as she approached the face-to-face meeting with
Charles's brother. Everyone else present tonight knew
Hugo so well, had seen him walking, eating, laughing,
swinging himself into the saddle, taking a staircase two
steps at a time—all the natural actions of a young man.
Only *she* knew no other than a chairbound figure who
groped and fumbled and who had to be led like a child
who might fall. Only *she* had seen no more than a man
behind a mask. To the others he would be just Hugo again.
What would he be to her?

She was startled by the dimness of the room, for only
half the candle brackets were in use and the lamps were
unlit. The dark-paneled walls loomed in half shadow, with
the oriental jars standing in ghostly isolation on their pedestals and the crimson-covered chairs so far apart from
each other they seemed even more like the thrones of separate kingdoms. Charles appeared at her elbow before she
had had time to register details of figures occupying the
room. He smiled down at her.

"There is no need to inquire whether you have recovered, dearest, for I have never seen such a bloom on your
cheeks." He kissed her fingers with lingering tenderness.
"The low lighting is in deference to Hugo. After two weeks
in total darkness he must be introduced to brightness gradually. What a tremendous day this is for us all. Come and
say your greetings to the Verewoods, then you may offer
your congratulations to my brother."

She walked beside him, as in a trance, toward the bluff, friendly man and his wife, an older, thinner version of Charity. The usual light conversation was automatic, for Victoria was conscious only that somewhere in the room was a young man rising or sitting, talking or laughing, walking or standing at ease, completely confident and assured, needing her no longer.

At last, the Verewoods made a coy reference to how it warmed their hearts to see their daughter happy again, and Victoria followed their glance to the far corner, where Charity was seated amid enormous bell skirts of blue silk net draped over a heavy silk underskirt. The tall, sturdy man in evening clothes standing beside her did not appear to be attending to her earnest conversation. He was looking across at his brother and the girl beside him.

"Please excuse us," said Charles smoothly and tucked Victoria's hand through his arm to lead her over a continent of carpet.

Charity Verewood, conscious now that her companion's interest had strayed, turned to watch them approach, but, for Victoria, she might not have been there. All her concentration was on the man whose face remained in half shadow. Then she was standing before him and Charles was saying, "Here is your patient, my dear, as hale and hearty as I have ever seen him."

She looked up at a face she did not know—a face that was pale, broader than Charles's and forceful by dint of its many shades of perception. She looked into blue-green eyes so vivid that one did not notice Hugo laid no claim to handsomeness. She looked at an expression that was strained and unsmiling. She looked up at a stranger.

The friendly brother-behind-a-mask who had drawn compassionate sympathy from her was gone. In his place was a captain of Hussars, a brilliant horseman with an air of élan even as he stood there, a young officer of the regiment who was being introduced to a girl at a party. With the uncovering of his face he had become a different person from the one with whom she had spent such happy hours of carefree contentment; his blindfold discarded, he had become a whole man who commanded an entirely different set of emotions from the sympathetic girl who had curled up in his chairs and romped on the floor with his dogs.

Now that he could see, Victoria was stripped of her disguise. She could no longer delude him as he sat behind a wall of darkness. In that instant, she felt a searing awareness of her own person, as if his eyes were brilliant lights turned upon her to reveal every detail of her appearance to his concentrated study. She could see the fact in his face, so grave and unfamiliar. She heard it in a voice that had acquired a subtly deeper timbre with his restored vision, and it was apparent in those betrayers of emotion that had kept him in bondage by their blindfolding.

Although it seemed minutes had passed since he had half bowed and said, "Good evening, Victoria," she could not find her voice to answer. What was worse, he appeared unwilling to say anything more.

"Victoria suffered a bad headache this morning which I am persuaded was due to anxiety, my dear fellow," said Charles smoothly to cover the silence. "She is very sensitive to another's plight."

"I confess *I* could not settle to my tasks with any tranquillity until I heard the news," said Charity, smiling up at the man beside her. "You must never again put your family and friends through such trying times, Captain Esterly, or we shall quite wash our hands of you."

"I cannot believe you would be so heartless, Miss Verewood," he replied, his gaze still on the other girl. "I apologize for being the cause of your headache, Victoria."

"No . . . please . . . I gave in to weakness, that is all," she replied, helpless in her inability to accept him as the friend to whom she had confided her foolish thoughts and wishes. How could she have let her tongue run away with her in the presence of this man? What childishness had let her prattle about toy drums she laid in his hands to feel? What had he thought of her temerity in obliging him to play chess with a schoolroom miss who boasted of her prowess in the most immodest manner? Worst of all—and this memory brought a deep blush to her cheeks—how *could* she have demanded to know if he intended to offer for Charity Verewood?

"Poor Miss Castledon," breathed the girl with blonde braids. "Small wonder you succumbed to the headache. You have tried to take upon your shoulders more than anyone could expect you to bear. Happily, you will now be able to concentrate on your wedding arrangements without the burden of the sickroom to spoil them for you."

The chatter was broken by the dinner announcement, and Lady Blythe, true to character, rose immediately. Charles escorted Aunt Sophy and Charity, Hugo took in the Massingham girls and Victoria went in on the arm of their brother. Freddie Massingham chatted gaily to her, but she heard none of it.

They took their seats after Lord Blythe said grace, and Victoria glanced up to find Hugo still watching her. She looked down quickly, heat rushing over her. He had said hardly a word to her, nor smiled once, and she could guess why. He had built up a picture of her and the reality disappointed him. He had thought his brother's chosen wife would be older, more mature. For the past week he had been entertaining her in the belief that she must be a superior well-bred young woman like Charity, and he had now seen she was a little nobody from Brighton.

Unable to stop herself, she raised her glance once more to meet his brilliant gaze across the table. It was as if he could not take his eyes from her. There was no expression of anger there, yet she could not translate the unsmiling concentration into anything she recognized. Shyness led her to turn away, but time and again she looked up to see the same mystery in those startling green-blue eyes.

The gentlemen stayed so long over their port that the ladies began to grow restless. The three mothers clucked and tut-tutted over things dear to the hearts of elderly matrons, and the Massingham girls sat like a pair of wax dolls that had been passed over in a toy shop. That left Victoria a choice between Charity Verewood and Aunt Sophy. It was an easy one to make.

By writing short questions it was possible to have an interesting conversation with the old lady, who had been very dashing in her youth. It needed only a little prompting to set her telling amusing tales of the pranks in which she had involved herself, tales that had Victoria laughing merrily. But even this diversion was cut short when Lady Blythe complained that the girl was exciting her aunt beyond the bounds of acceptability; the over-loud commentary was preventing anyone from being heard.

"I beg your pardon," said Victoria with a sigh.

"I believe Miss Castledon was only employing her praise-worthy talent for kindness, ma'am," put in Charity sweetly. "She has my deepest admiration for her selflessness when there are so many matters of importance to herself and Major Stanford to be decided upon. The manner in which she has devoted herself to Captain Esterly this past week is quite moving. Compassion, however misguided, must be admired."

"Coming from the lips of one whose goodness is known all over the county, that is a very pretty speech, Charity," said her ladyship obligingly.

"Such a blessing to have an admirable son like Major Stanford and then be given another by such a cruel circumstance," sighed Mrs. Verewood, not wanting to leave the subject of Hugo Esterly. "How fortunate for the young man, also, to acquire a family such as he has." She paused delicately. "Of course, now that his brother has elected to do his duty by you there is every reason to suppose Captain Esterly will be freed from any bonds of etiquette that have prevented him from following Major Stanford's example."

"Mama!" breathed Charity in theatrical protest.

"Why is everyone behaving with such simpering intensity?" demanded Aunt Sophy of Victoria in one of her rasping asides.

The girl just shook her head slowly, without looking at the old lady. Something inside her had suddenly stilled, like a stream that has frozen as it bubbles over stones. Charity was quite pink, but not with embarrassment—not *that* girl! Mrs. Verewood looked confidently at Lady Blythe, as the entire room seemed to hold its breath.

Aunt Patti was not well enough acquainted with the situation, or was no more intelligent than her daughters, for she said, "Do not tell me Hugo has been waiting to offer for some young woman. I pray he has not had the madness to form an alliance with a foreign girl from the Continent—although I vow it is just what he would do."

Lady Blythe gave her sister-in-law a withering glance. "Why would he look at foreign girls when there is in this vicinity someone who has all the qualities he could wish for in a wife? I have every confidence he will do what he knows will please me. Now that all is well with him again, I believe I can guess what he will be anxious to settle with all speed."

Victoria saw Charity's glance lower as a smile played over her serene profile, and the bubbling stream could be contained by the ice no longer. She could not believe Hugo would wish to be discussed in this public manner, nor that anyone should take it for granted he would obey anything but his own heartfelt wishes.

"I believe you are right, ma'am," she said clearly. "He has spoken to me quite often on the subject."

Charity's head shot up in shocked disbelief. Victoria gave her a sweet smile and took the greatest pleasure in saying, "He can think of nothing that is more important than his ideas for new cavalry drill. It is his intention to return to Vienna as soon as possible, and he will not rest until he has convinced the stubborn old generals that he is right. He believes there is nothing that would please you more than to hear of his success in this ambition."

Six well-bred faces turned in her direction, each wearing an expression of well-bred shock. Only Aunt Sophy remained as she was until the comedy of the scene impressed itself upon her. She turned to Victoria with a chuckle.

"I cannot imagine what you have said to silence these featherheads, but do write it down so that I may appreciate the richness of the situation, my dear." Her loud voice echoed in the silence, increasing the horror of those demure ladies to whom she referred.

Most opportunely, the gentlemen chose that moment to join their womenfolk, but it was plain to them that they had broken up marked discord. All the dear creatures had unbecomingly pink cheeks and backs that were so straight one might imagine they were starched. For a few dreadful minutes it seemed that the port-induced liveliness of the gentlemen not only failed to cheer the atmosphere but had increased the disapproval hanging so heavily in the air. Then Mr. Massingham of the hearty baritone laugh suggested a game of cards, and corset laces tightened with the sudden relaxing of tense bodies.

The card games varied, the older members preferring serious competition while the younger ones indulged in games of chance that caused merriment and lighthearted squabbling. Charles elected to join the older group, while Hugo was pulled into the antics at the other table, laughingly protesting that his eyes would not be quick enough to allow him to win. Charity immediately seized on that point and announced that she would forego the game in order to sit with him in a quiet corner.

"Come, Captain Esterly, we shall rest over here where the light is not such a trial to you," she said, tucking her hand through his arm and taking him away from the group. "You must tell me your ideas for cavalry drill. If you are to make a brilliant contribution to your regiment it is only right that your friend should be let into the secret."

He went without protest, and Victoria told herself she had caused confusion in the camp of scheming matrons to no avail. He did not need her any longer. Yet a few moments later she had the disturbing knowledge that his vivid blue-green eyes were watching her from the darkened corner. The card game became once more a background to her troubled thoughts. He had spoken no further word to her nor cast a smile in her direction, yet it seemed he could not study her enough but must continue the whole evening.

All through dinner the knowledge that she was under observation had made her own eyes rebels that disobeyed her will not to look up. Each time she did, a strange breathless shyness filled her. He was Hugo, yet he was not. Part of her longed for the friendly comfortable brother, yet she was too fascinated by the strange young officer he had become to wish otherwise. If only he would speak to her, laugh over the things that always amused them, treat her as his friend, she would be rid of the turmoil inside her.

The cards lost their attraction, and Lord Blythe asked Victoria to play to them for a while, smiling at her and patting her hand.

"Something gay for the occasion, eh?"

She went to the piano obediently. Perhaps such an occupation would calm her, after this day of anxieties. Charles came to her side with an offer to turn her music and squeezed her shoulder as she sat on the stool.

"I vow you are delighting the entire company this evening, dearest," he whispered. "No one could fail to notice the radiance of your expression and the elegant gown that sets off my garnets to perfection. Everyone is at your feet, including myself."

"Thank you, Charles. I feel sure you are the only one who thinks so, but I hope my playing will keep them at my feet and not have them walking out through the door."

He paused in the act of setting her music upon the stand and fixed her with a smoldering look. "Do I not wish they would. You are enough to make any man wish to be alone with you tonight."

Quickly she began the little polka she had chosen for her first piece, but her fingers would not do what they should and she had to begin again. The next piece was not a lot better and the third so disappointing she gave her listeners a nervous apology and suggested they might hear better music from another pianist. Charity was called upon, and she agreed at once, begging Hugo very prettily to assist her. He gave a slight bow and excused himself on the grounds that the tiny notes on the sheet would still be a blur to him.

"You would do better with my brother, Miss Verewood. He is renowned for his prowess in the drawing room. I fear I only shine in the field." The deliberate look he threw Charles made it impossible for him to do anything but remain at the piano.

Victoria took Hugo's arm at his invitation and allowed herself to be led to a chair, where he asked if she would care for some refreshment.

"No . . . no, thank you," she told him. He made no move to go, so she added frantically, "Shall you be allowed to ride again shortly?"

"I believe so."

"And . . . and your cavalry drill. Shall you continue with your attempts to persuade the generals you are right?"

"Undoubtedly."

His manner was curt and reserved, as if they had not discussed his plans and ideas at great length. Had she disappointed him so much? Unable to face him any longer, she looked down at the primrose satin of her skirt, wishing he would go away. But after a few painful moments he took the seat beside her and said huskily, "I cannot believe your performance at the pianoforte is usually as bad as it was tonight. Something has upset you, Victoria. I had the distinct impression that there had been a skirmish among the petticoats when we walked in. Dare I inquire the reason?"

"You were the reason," she told him, studying her skirt still.

"I?" He was extremely surprised. "What have I done that would set a group of ladies flying at each other?"

"It is not what you have done but what they wish you to do." She looked up to meet his eyes. "I did not think you would care to be discussed in such a way and turned the conversation in a direction that did not generally please. Aunt Sophy put in the finishing touches."

His glance traveled over her face, taking in every soft line. "You would take on a battery of ladies in my defense? I am honored."

Her confusion deepened. The words were what she might have expected from him but were said with grave sincerity. The laughing banter had gone.

"What is it that everyone wishes me to do?"

She turned her head toward the girl at the piano. "I think you know the answer very well."

"I . . . see."

Silence fell between them, and Victoria grew even more unhappy. Come what may, she must discover the truth from him. If she was to become part of the family, she must recapture the happy relationship between them. Even if he were to address her much as Charles had after her enthusiasm over Glencoe, she must hear it from him so that she could make amends.

"It is not only among the petticoats that there is disharmony tonight," she began. "What have I done to lose your good opinion of me?"

"I beg your pardon? I cannot follow your question."

Her own courage was faltering under the strain of his coldness, but she rephrased the question. "It is all too plain that I have disappointed you somehow."

"No, Victoria," he interspersed quickly. "You could not disappoint me . . . nor anyone else. Never think such a thing again."

The sudden warmth of his words surprised her. What *was* wrong between them that had brought up this barrier? "Then, tell me what I must think. Are you not feeling well?

After the past days the excitement of so many guests might be too much for you. Is that it?"

"In some part, yes. After so long in darkness the sight of movement and color almost makes one giddy."

"And I have been plaguing you over selfish matters. How unkind of me."

"Not unkind—foolish. Foolish to imagine thoughts that are not in my head. There is no disharmony, Victoria. Between the patroness of the regiment and its most valuable officer there could never be." He smiled then, a slow lighting of his face that gave him instant, striking attraction.

"Ah, you *are* still the person I know," she told him in relief. "Without that black band to cover half your face you are a stranger in looks, that is all. It will take some while for me to grow used to the new Hugo. You are quite . . . you are quite different now that you no longer depend on others. You must not forget that I am the only one present who has never before seen you as you really are."

"I had not forgotten."

"Then I am still your friend?"

"I hope you will always be."

Their short period of isolation was broken by Charles and Charity, who appeared before them out of the anonymity of the room. Hugo leaped to his feet.

"You have finished entertaining us so soon, Miss Verewood?"

It was an effort for her to smile, but she managed it. "Shame on you, Captain Esterly. I declare you only notice my performance when it has ceased. But you have never had a musical ear, as I remember."

He bowed his head in acknowledgment. "As I have already said, I am completely undistinguished in a drawing room."

"You are too modest, sir. There are those among us who would have it differently."

Charles intervened with an offer to bring the ladies refreshment, and the brothers went off, leaving the two girls together.

Charity donned her armor quickly. "I am sorry you were obliged to abandon your attempt to shine at the pianoforte. I am not ungenerous enough to imagine you cannot do better, for I am sure it was due to nervousness. I have to say that I feel great sympathy for you. If the company of so few persons of distinction throws you into confusion, the strain of becoming the wife of the next Lord Blythe must *defeat* you. Your apprehension at your forthcoming marriage must be formidable."

"Perhaps," said Victoria hotly, "but I do at least have the satisfaction of knowing my marriage will take place. The strain of uncertainty must try you sorely."

The other girl gasped. This schoolroom miss had the manners of a kitchenmaid. "You might be destined to become a bride, Miss Castledon, but have a care you do not abuse the privilege," she snapped. "To set brother against brother is a dangerous business where men of honor are concerned—or perhaps you would not understand that."

This time it was Victoria's turn to gasp. Whatever could she mean? But there was no time to ask, even if she dared to, for the gentlemen returned with glasses of fruit cup, breaking the tense situation with easy conversation. For the rest of the evening Victoria went over and over in her mind how her own marriage could set brother against brother. The gaining of an heir for Charles would not affect Hugo. There was no question of his ever inheriting the title. Even if Charles had no sons, Freddie Massingham would take the title—and Hugo had a fortune of his own, left by the father who had perished in the Orient. When the departure of the Verewoods brought the evening to a close, she had still not reached an answer to the puzzle.

The ladies retired to their rooms, leaving the gentlemen to cigars and brandy and stories unfit for delicate ears. Charles kissed Victoria's fingers with great tenderness and promised to call upon her in the morning. Hugo gave his good night across the heads of the cousins, but there was no smile to comfort her. Indeed, his whole expression appeared to be one of infinite sadness. She went to her room in very troubled spirits. No matter what he had said, there *was* a strangeness between them tonight.

The ladies took breakfast in their separate bedrooms the following morning, but the gentlemen were up at an early hour. All the gentlemen but one, that is. Hugo's absence from the breakfast table was not remarked upon, since everyone imagined he was tired after the rigors of the previous day. However, shortly before luncheon the entire party was gathered before a log fire to discuss the plans for the day when Dawkins, Hugo's erstwhile steward, entered with a note on a salver and crossed to Lady Blythe.

Lady Blythe took the note, read it through, then gave a strangled cry. "I cannot believe it. He would not do such a thing. Wicked, *wicked* boy to put me through such a torment of anxiety." She rocked back and forth, knowing she held center stage, and determined to make the most of it. "I see now that his brain was affected all along, and we did not realize it."

"My dear," said Lord Blythe. "I do not quite understand you."

"He will kill himself with this recklessness. There is no other explanation but that he is out of his wits." Her bosom heaved beneath the burden of her distress, and the lace handkerchief was waved across her face in an attempt to revive herself as her voice broke on a sob. "To be released from one anxiety only to face a worse! Oh dear, oh dear, could any gentlewoman withstand it with any degree of composure?"

His lordship had had enough. Striding across to his wife, he plucked the note from her fingers.

"Damn the fellow," he exploded.

"Augustus," shrieked his wife. "Such language on top of this will finish me off."

Charles was greatly disturbed by now and joined his father to read the note.

"What has taken possession of him?" demanded father of son. "Is it his wish to defy the mercy of the Lord and break his mother's heart into the bargain? Charles, what devil's work is this? Had you known what he was about?"

"No, sir. I swear he said nothing of his intentions when I left him last night." He was as angry as his parents. "I have known Hugo to be reckless—just how reckless you have no notion—but this is not only completely irresponsible, it is damned bad manners. I am sorry, Mama," he said at the sound of her gasp, "but such ungrateful behavior from my brother forces me to forget myself in my indignation. Here we have all been suffering the severest anxiety on his behalf, doing everything in our power to aid his recovery, and the minute all is well we are treated to a display of manner-

less selfishness that would be insulting even to a mere acquaintance. It is unforgivable."

Victoria could remain silent no longer. She rose and
went to rest her hand on the major's arm. "Charles, what
has occurred to make you so incensed? What has Hugo
done?"

He looked down at her as if returning from a trance.
"My dear, perhaps you will comfort Mama."

"Of course, but over what am I to comfort her?"

He shook his head, still with that dazed quality in his
expression. "This letter from Hugo says that he has this
morning returned to Brighton, on recollecting that he made
a promise to spend the New Year with his friends the
Markhams. He has gone."

"Gone?" She was stunned. "Are you saying he has traveled to Brighton alone?"

"With Stokes to help him, I assume. One day after the
doctor removed the bandages, he is off, without a thought
for anyone. After the care and attention he has received
here, he slinks away without a word, knowing what I
would have had to say to him if he had made known his
intention. By heaven, I shall berate him for this when I
return to Brighton—if he has not succumbed to the infirmity we all prayed he would resist."

Victoria went to Lady Blythe with no hope of soothing a
woman who was bent on extracting the maximum drama
from the situation and found she had even less affection for
her. In no way was Hugo's recovery due to his mama, for
she had merely retired to her room with chocolates the
minute he arrived at Wychbourne—and she would undoubtedly do so again at any minute.

All around her were the sounds of angry voices—
Charles and his father in righteous wrath, Mr. Massingham
and his son indulging in hurt indignation at the insult. The
Massingham girls still sat like wax dolls overlooked on a
toy-shop shelf, except that they both appeared about to
burst into tears at their rejection, and Lady Blythe's sister
reveled in the satisfaction of telling the afflicted woman
how all these years she had nursed a viper in her bosom.

Victoria sank down on the velvet chair, shaken with a
pain so real and fierce it was all she could do not to gasp.
They were all quite, quite wrong. Hugo would not go with

no word of explanation unless there were some urgent reason. The note he left was plainly an excuse to cover the truth he could not at present reveal. Did they know so little of him that they could condemn him so quickly? Had they not noticed the difference in him last night—last night, when he already knew that he was about to leave? Was that what he had been trying to tell her?

The voices around her grew louder and more heated. She looked up. Each of them was so lost in his own feelings he had given no thought to what could have happened to make Hugo leave with such urgency. They did not care about him, only about what his actions had done to their precious dignity. Unnoticed by all those present, she rose and walked out.

The anguish inside her was spreading to her limbs; the stairs seemed like a mountain. There was no question of losing her way this time; her feet took her deliberately to the room where she knew she would find the answer. She did not knock.

Inside, the room was the same, yet devoid of life and reality. No dogs rushed madly to meet her, Stokes's turned-up mustache did not amuse her, not even the ghost of a blindfolded man was there to greet her. The hearth was dead; everything was straightened and unused. Even the clock had stopped at a quarter to eight. She walked slowly through the room, touching his possessions with trailing fingers that longed to find some part of him there but found none.

Those afternoons in this chair were dreams and fancies that had flickered through her mind during a young girl's reveries. The laughter they had shared was the return of some early memory—perhaps of her own mama and papa when they were young and happy together—that she had stored away until now. One day she had wandered lost along this corridor and strayed into the past or future for a while—a sudden moment's departure into another life that had spun golden threads which seemed to her to last a span of ten days.

She halted in the center of the room, lost and frightened. Where was she now? What was real and what was not? Why should all these reflections be covered by a black blindfold? Why should this room she knew so well mean nothing, retain none of the properties she had thought it had? It told her nothing; there was no longer a welcome here. With his departure Hugo had ceased to exist. He had never been.

She passed through the doorway, not bothering to close the door. The memories had escaped already. The carpet along the corridor was the same blue it had always been, the paintings hung there, as before. The heavy bronze statuette still stood on the half-moon table with carved bun feet that reminded her of lions' paws. The door into the Mirror Room opened inward, and she was surrounded by a multitude of dark-haired girls who looked at her from every direction.

Walking toward them as if drawn by their very wariness, she came face to face with her own reflections. Suddenly, she had the answer. It was there in the bruised eyes, the paleness of faces lost in the revelation that had come too late. She saw it in the slender bodies that were melting with longing and in the hands that drifted up so that lips could touch the fingers he had kissed.

Turning away from them with a small cry, she found only another multitude of selves facing her with the same truth. Whichever way she turned, it came back to her twenty fold. Of course his room meant nothing to her. The laughing, friendly brother had never existed; the man she had acknowledged as a beloved stranger last night was Hugo. He had recognized the truth before she had and had run from it, hoping to save her. She pressed her wet cheek against the glass. He was too late. Dear God, he was a lifetime too late!

CHAPTER FOUR

When Hugo arrived in Brighton there was only one place to which he could go. His quarters at barracks would long since have been allocated elsewhere, and all the hotels were filled with New Year's guests. Tired and depressed, he hired a carriage to take him to Bendeaton Street and climbed into its damp interior with the two dogs, leaving Stokes to load his baggage and climb up beside the driver. It was a raw night, without the covering of snow that had made Buckinghamshire so attractive, and the wind off the sea found its way into the cab to freeze the breath of the dogs as they panted with excitement.

There was much traffic abroad, for it was the time when society set out for parties, balls or other pleasant pursuits. Hugo hoped to God Jack Markham was not entertaining or, worse still, out for the evening. Selfishly, he wanted a meal, a bottle of wine and the company of his friends—all in an atmosphere of comfort and peace. The journey had tired him more than he had expected—and his thoughts were not fit to be alone with tonight.

The Markhams' house was in the less fashionable part of Brighton. Three stories high with steps leading to the basement and to the yellow front door, its neat gay appearance reflected the personality of its owners. It was the best Lieutenant Henry John Markham could afford on his pay as a Hussar subaltern.

Hugo's friend laughed in the face of poverty. He had obtained a commission in one of the exclusive cavalry regiments through the influence of a very distant elderly relative on his mother's side who lent his name for the purpose but none of his vast fortune, thereby leaving Jack stranded as a cornet in a regiment that boasted more titles than most of the British Army. Consequently, the young man was hard put to maintain the standard required of the gentlemen with whom he served. Teetering just beyond the reach of the lenders' grasping fingers, he no sooner obtained a lieutenancy through the death in a hunting accident of a foppish young aristocrat than he caught the eye of a doctor's daughter, who persuaded him he could not live without her.

The marriage obliged him to rent a house, for Letty could not live with him in barracks, and they went from week to week, always on the verge of debt, but supremely happy.

Thinking of seeing them again after so long made Hugo impatient to arrive. It would be really too bad if they were not at home. He was not disappointed, however. No sooner had the maid announced him than Jack was striding from the parlor, grinning and clasping his friend's hand heartily in both of his.

"The Devil take you, Hugo! What a friend you are. We heard you were blinded—we even heard you were dead— now you turn up in the middle of a Christmas night like Saint Nicholas himself, as white as a sheet and in company with those two damned beasts. If I weren't so fond of you I should turn you away." He laughed with great gladness as he drew his friend forward. "Letty will be thrown into a great tarrididdle over your arrival."

"Lies . . . all of it lies," said Hugo faintly. "She will be delighted to have some civilized company for a change. I have no doubt she has been pining these last six months."

"That I have," cried Letty, coming to the parlor door on recognizing his voice and seizing his hands. "This has made Christmas perfect. Hugo, I cannot tell you how glad we are to see you. We have been beside ourselves with worry. And to some cause," she added, dismayed by the hollowed eyes in a strained, blanched face.

"Forgive me," he said, kissing her on the cheek. "Word travels too quickly these days."

He was dragged into a cluttered parlor. A bright fire welcomed him and drew the dogs to its side, where they flopped down in complete possession of the hearth rug.

"I have no objection to your making yourself free of my wife's kisses," protested Jack, "but when your dogs claim the fire for their sole benefit, I think you go too far."

Hugo smiled. "Address your complaints to their unfeeling ears, not mine. I have no control over them after six months in Austria."

"Do sit down," urged Letty. "You do not look fit to

make yourself free of any woman's kisses. I will arrange a
meal, then you must tell us the truth to dispel all the rumors. We've been very worried."

She departed to the kitchen to consult her cook, and
Jack pressed Hugo into a chair before the fire, saying with
a grin, "You may avail yourself of what warmth your animals are happy to leave you."

Hugo looked up apologetically. "I have Stokes with me."

"Have no fear, my man will already be fixing him with a
plateful of stew and a corner for the night."

"You are a good friend, Jack."

"Aye, you will be hard put to find another with my outstanding qualities." He stopped smiling. "The latest *on dit*
was that you were in Buckinghamshire in a serious state.
Whatever the truth of the matter, you would hardly turn
up here late in the evening two days before the end of the
year unless there were some urgent reason."

Hugo just nodded, weariness washing over him and an
ache behind his eyes making them smart in the brightness
of the room. After a short pause during which he glanced
around, absorbing the cozy atmosphere of the parlor, he
said, "You are a fortunate man, Jack."

"I know it." He took the seat opposite Hugo and was
about to question him when his wife returned, having arranged for a room to be prepared for their unexpected
guest.

"Cook is cutting some cold meat, and there is a good
soup that will nourish you. At short notice, it is the best I
can do, but if you remain awake long enough to eat even
that I shall be surprised. What a pity Papa is not still
here—he visited for Christmas, you know—for he would
have advised you on your constitution."

Hugo shook his head sadly. "You sound too much like
the young woman Mama would have me wed, Letty. I had
not thought you would fuss over a man so unnecessarily."

"She does not on my account, I assure you," Jack told
him. "I should more likely receive a hearty scold were I to
arrive here looking as you do this moment."

Letty's green eyes sparkled with affection as she glanced
at the husband who loved teasing her. "You will receive
one very shortly if you do not hush and allow me to set my

mind at rest over Hugo's health. Your eyes are undamaged, dear friend?"

"Completely, it would appear. They were uncovered yesterday after two weeks and, apart from a slight reaction to brightness, I see perfectly well. It is good to escape from the sickroom. One's family can be the very devil at a time like this."

Letty and Jack exchanged glances before she said, "You had Christmas with them?"

"Yes. I believe it was beautiful with the snow all around. I did not see it."

The maid came in with a tray so laden she could hardly carry it, and Letty soon had Hugo installed at the circular table with a substantial meal before him. "You will not mind eating here? The dining room is chilled, and you would feel very neglected. Do you not think this is cozier?"

Hugo gave her a tired smile. "It is always cozier in your company. If Jack had not snatched you away from beneath my nose I would not hesitate to offer you my noble name."

Her brown curls danced as she shook her head. "Shameless flatterer! But it *is* good to see you, whatever the reason for your visit."

As Letty predicted, he hardly managed to complete his meal before exhaustion overtook him. After a fortnight of complete inactivity the journey had beaten him badly, and his appetite turned out to be a great deal smaller than the tray anticipated. Overriding it all, however, was the memory of a pair of dark questioning eyes that asked for a reassurance he could not give and a wild young spirit that was about to be incarcerated within the stronghold of aristocratic pride. The thought stuck in his throat; it lay on his chest restricting every movement; it winded him as a fall from a horse; pounded in his head like a hundred hoofbeats.

Already it was clear that he had made a mistake; his friends' company did not comfort him as he had hoped. Here, in this room, he felt even worse. Jack and Letty were ideally happy—hardly the example he should have before him, for it emphasized his own solitariness as never before, and when they packed him off to bed he tossed and turned, plagued by the knowledge that Jack was taking his love in his arms in the neighboring room.

At once, desire for Victoria ran him through like a long cavalry sword. It sickened him to discover that it followed the same pattern as that aroused by the bold-eyed wenches with whom he usually took his pleasure, but with what tender strength would he crush *her* body to him, with what reverent eagerness would his lips light an answering flame in her, with what pride and gratitude would he take the final prize—and afterward, he would not ride away with a careless salute.

Awareness of the direction of his thoughts sent him clambering from the bed to stand at the window in the hope that the sight of passing carriages would take his mind from his disturbing visions. Unhappily he fell to imagining what had occurred when Dawkins delivered his note that morning. His parents would be hurt, unable to understand why someone they had brought up with affection and trust should behave so callously; Charles would feel insulted; his aunt and uncle righteously indignant; Charity Verewood martyred. But what of Victoria? Would she alone guess the reason for his unforgivable behavior? She had known last night that his attitude toward her had changed. Pray God she would believe his disappointment in her was so great he could remain no longer. Better that than she should know his true feelings.

In the morning he descended in a black mood to find Jack eating breakfast alone. Letty's decision to have a tray in her bedroom was born of tact, not indolence. The men would need to talk and could not do so in her company. It would be nice when Hugo married to provide a companion for such times.

Jack bade his friend a warm good morning and offered him some eggs with slices of ham. "Our cook is a treasure. I am astounded that she stays with us when she could better herself by moving on," he said. "Old Cummings went behind my back to her after dining with us one night, but she is still here."

"Happiness is not dependent on money, Jack."

The lieutenant studied the downbent head with a slight frown. "No, it is not. I, of all people, should know that!"

They ate in silence for a short while, then Hugo laid down his knife and fork. "I must arrange for quarters. I shall ride down to the barracks today."

Jack was taken aback. "There is no need."

"Yes. I must get back to routine. I only came here last night because it was too late to arrange accommodation."

"I see. So you will fix up quarters? Your horses are here. They arrived from Chobham in a very good state. I wonder Monty was not injured. I suppose you were riding him when the accident occurred?"

Hugo nodded. "He reared and threw me, but did not bolt. I have trained him to remain steady under fire. One day he will have to face it."

"I dare swear you could train any horse to remain steady—even your brother's Caliban," Jack said. "The major was at Wychbourne, of course?"

"He remains there."

Seeing that Hugo did not intend to elaborate, Jack went on, "He was all set to plague everyone in sight to ensure you were back in this country in time for the wedding. It must be a relief to him to know you will be standing up with him on the occasion." He leaned back in his chair and smiled at Hugo. "Miss Castledon broke more than a dozen hearts when she accepted his offer, I must tell you. I met her on two occasions and was completely charmed. The regiment has taken her to its heart—much too literally, in some instances. Young Harry Edmunds is very seriously cut up about it."

"Poor Harry" was the brusque comment. "This coffee is excellent. I will have another cup, if you please."

"Help yourself, old fellow." Jack was shaken. Despite a night's sleep Hugo still looked drawn. Whatever had sent him posthaste to Brighton had affected him deeply, for he was nothing like his usual self.

"Do you care to come with me, Jack?"

"What? Grace the barracks with my presence when duty does not call? It is enough that I am Officer of the Day for New Year's Eve, confined to quarters there when I could be with Letty."

Hugo looked up at that. "Her loss is my gain. We shall see in eighteen fifty-three in excellent style, old man. The coming year deserves a riotous start. God knows, the rest of it will be black enough."

*　　*　　*

"Help yourself, Hugo," the assistant adjutant said. "Sanderson has transferred into the Tenth, so his rooms are vacant, and there is the corner suite. It doesn't matter to me which one you occupy, and if it should matter to the adjutant when he returns—or to our esteemed colonel— you will already be in residence, and they will hardly put you out."

"Will they not?" Hugo replied unconvinced but made himself comfortable in the corner rooms with every outward sign of permanent occupation, more as a means of keeping himself busy than in the belief he would be allowed to remain in rooms normally given to field officers. He dared not remain idle.

Time, instead of dulling his anger, only served to increase it, Hugo found. As he banged about his new quarters he cursed himself for a weakling. Oaths flew in every direction as he vented resentment over a physical desire he could not conquer; the only way to blot out his overriding sense of guilt was by uncorking a few bottles. Stokes put him to bed that first night with much shaking of his head. He had a shrewd idea of what was behind this mood. He feared there was worse to come.

December 31 was bright and fresh, and the few officers remaining in barracks turned out to a man, with the exception of Jack Markham, who was tied to a small duty room, and made for the Downs on the fastest horses they possessed, galloping with scant care across green undulating country that bewitched horses and riders alike. On one, the devil had a relentless hold.

Hugo gave his horse its head, racing on even when his companions drew rein and called to him. It was good to feel Monty between his knees again and, for a while, the exhilaration of pursuing his favorite pastime dulled the sense of disaster which had hung over the past few days. A great surge of thankfulness drove away guilt and longing. There had been times when he doubted he would ever be able to use muscles, strength, skill and judgment, and his eyes, in perfect combination, ever again. He took the brown stallion straight and true over the spongy turf of the South Downs, racing head down and supremely in control as he cleared low bushes, small streams or sudden marshy basins, then, the confidence, the release, vanished when a farm wall loomed up over a rise and it was too late to veer.

In that split second, years of experience failed him. Monty cleared the barrier with difficulty and landed awkwardly in a barren field whose frozen ruts nearly brought him down. Hugo sat catching his breath, shaken by his own performance, then turned and slowly rode back to the group of officers, who told him he had received his deserts. They did not labor the point when Esterly, usually the easiest of companions, snapped their heads off, wearing a look as black as any they had seen.

After a mainly liquid luncheon, Hugo rode out to a small country dairy owned by a young widow of his acquaintance but, although she rushed into his arms after six months' absence and invited him into the parlor that had witnessed many hours of mutual pleasure, he could not bring himself to accept her comely consolation and left after giving her the present he had brought from Vienna.

Stokes, muttering under his breath about gentlemen who did not know when they had had enough, was pressed into opening another bottle on Hugo's return. If his sense of propriety was offended then, it would have been outraged a few hours later, for the few members of the mess who dined there that night were set on seeing in the New Year flat on their backs.

As Officer of the Day, Jack Markham had to restrict his intake, but he was a reckless young man with great joy in living and could not see that it would matter if he did last rounds of the guard in the happy state of seeing twice as many as usual. He, therefore, had little influence on what happened.

After an excellent dinner the officers got down to the serious business of the evening. With no field officers present and only one captain, barely senior to Hugo, the fun waged fast and furious.

Highly erotic tales concerning the habits of Austrian cavalrymen and even more inflammatory ones about Russian Cossacks had Hugo's audience wild with laughter and bravado. As the level in the bottles lowered, glasses were dashed to pieces in the fireplace after extravagant toasts in the way Hugo had seen it done abroad. A boy cornet swore he could do a Cossack dance and was lifted onto the long polished table for a demonstration. When his inebriated efforts no longer pleased his audience he was dragged off, his spurs leaving long scratches across the wood, and hung by his golden sash from a hat peg, where he dangled and pleaded until they chose to release him.

A mock battle ensued during which half the number quickly lost their senses, the other half their decorum. Jack Markham, who had come out of it more disheveled than most, was dressing himself to the accompaniment of loud complaints that the Officer of the Day should be immune in the expectation of being called out when the twenty-year-old Lord Dovedale proposed that each one still on his feet should take part in a contest to prove his superiority. The winner would be the one who outdid the feats of the rest and would be presented with a bottle of wine from each man.

Clinging to the vestiges of his duties, Jack expressed grave doubts over the idea. He was immediately set upon, stripped of his uniform and his wiry person deposited in the coal bucket, where he decided to stay until the room stopped swaying around him.

The whole thing was quite pleasantly riotous, at first. An aspiring contortionist failed to walk on his hands along the back of a huge leather sofa; another's attempt to balance bottles on his forehead ended in a pile of smashed glass; a third could not lift a bronze bust of the Duke of Wellington with one hand behind his back; and Lord Dovedale himself brought scorn from the others with his rendering of a tenor aria which ended in top D.

Cornet Balesworth, who snuffed out a cigar with a bullet from his pistol, leaving the rest of the cigar intact, appeared likely to win the honor when the game took a serious turn. Hugo was ordered to make his bid, amid friendly mockery.

"He is too large for balancing acts," laughed one. "He could try lifting the 'Duke' instead."

"No, that has already been attempted. It cannot be done again," ruled Lord Dovedale. "Somersaults are hardly for him either."

"He is a fair shot, but Balesworth claims that," put in a fat lieutenant. "The only thing at which he shines is horsemanship."

"I would hardly say he shines any longer," drawled Harry Edmunds from the corner. "That jump this morning would have put even a young girl to shame." He giggled drunkenly.

The atmosphere became suddenly tense. That same remark made of a mediocre rider when all were good-naturedly sober would have brought no more than an oath from its victim, but Hugo was jealous of his prowess in the saddle and still smarting over his performance at the farm wall earlier that day. He was also hot-blooded and very drunk.

Laughter died as he stood up and demanded an apology. All heads turned toward Harry Edmunds, who was taken aback at the way Hugo had taken a foolish taunt, not meant in any way as a slur on his ability. There was nothing for it but to brazen it out. He rose unsteadily and said, "Certainly. I shall go further. On my knees I will claim you are the best rider in England . . . when you have proved my remark does *not* describe the way you jump."

Hugo felt the pulse in his temples pounding. These men would disparage him forever if he did not take up the challenge.

"I will jump anything you name," he said thickly. *"Anything."*

Taken off guard, Harry Edmunds said the first thing that came into his muddled head. "I should like to see the man who can clear the mess table."

There was an outburst of protests, not because the table was too high or wide but because there was not room on each side for such an attempt. Above them all Hugo said, "Done," and called a steward to send word to have Monty saddled and brought around to the mess entrance immediately.

"Hugo, do not be a fool," begged Jack, coming up to him as he pulled on his shirt. "It cannot be done."

"Can it not?" There was bitterness in his voice. "A man can do anything if he puts his mind to it. I shall clear that table or never ride again."

"That is true enough," cried Jack. "You will be dead of a broken back and your horse with you. You cannot bring an animal into the mess."

Hugo turned on him. "Show me where it is written. It will not stop me from doing so, but I shall believe you."

Jack saw something in his friend's eyes that told him

nothing would prevent him using this challenge as a means to rid his soul of whatever gripped it and decided the only answer was to take away the horse. As Officer of the Day he could order the grooms to keep all horses in stables. Unfortunately, he could not go until correctly dressed and by that time Monty was at the door.

Drama had sobered the officers quicker than cold water or black coffee, and more than one was desperately trying to think of a way out of the situation that would satisfy Hugo. Even the lieutenant who had flung the challenge so unthinkingly had sobered enough to know the man was dangerously drunk.

The mess steward entered to say the captain's horse was outside, little dreaming he would see his owner lead the beast inside the building a few seconds later.

With the room cleared of all furniture but the table, Hugo mounted his horse and walked Monty round the obstacle he would have to jump from a near standing position. The silence was complete. Stewards clustered in the doorway, their tough faces registering all levels of apprehension: the gentlemen gathered at the far end of the room, lounging by the wall, watching with shrewd eyes narrowed against the glare of gasoliers as Hugo familiarized his horse with the ground.

It was a sight none of them would forget. A powerful man on a big strong brown charger going slowly around a polished table in a carpeted room. The walls bore regimental standards, battle honors, famous swords, paintings of illustrious former officers of their distinguished regiment and a long shelf containing silver trophies, many of them bearing the name of the man who now defended his right to claim them.

The room was impressively proportioned. Now, with this magnificent animal walking within its walls, it seemed cramped, and the man astride the stallion, tall and broad-shouldered in the blue uniform smothered with gold and scarlet, towered above them as he passed for the third time in a soft jingle of harness.

Jack Markham held his breath and resorted to prayer. He had done his best, but he knew only too well a man must find his own panacea. He looked at the face of his friend. It was a broad face with vivid eyes that normally wore an eager good-natured expression. Now, it was flushed with wine and desperation. What had happened to Hugo in Vienna that had wrought such a change in him? he wondered.

The walking stopped. Monty was backed against one long side wall, and every man present felt his muscles freeze. The soft purr of gas mantles was clearly audible as man and horse steadied themselves for the jump. Then, a quick pressure of the rider's knees, a slight pull on the reins, a cry of "Now, boy," and Monty gathered himself back on his haunches before stretching his great legs out in a magnificent leap that rippled the shining brown coat covering his muscles.

The successful feat had every throat hoarse with cheers, and every man started forward toward the stallion that was rearing up in an attempt to avoid hitting the far wall. The sudden noise after quiet concentration upset the beast, but Hugo had him well under control until the excited soldiers in the kitchen backed into a pile of clean plates and sent them crashing to the ground. Monty had had enough. With a shrill neigh he plunged and reared in fright, his hooves striking part of the oak paneling at the eastern end of the room and splintering it badly before coming down on the window sill to shatter a pair of glass goblets presented by a former colonel. A dozen pairs of hands grabbed at the reins to bring the horse under control, and Hugo slid from the saddle to buckle at the knees and fall against Jack, whose throat was dry as dust.

At 11:00 A.M. the following morning, Stokes decided to brave the captain's wrath and entered with a tray of black coffee. His master was half sitting in the bed, looking greatly dejected.

"Lor', sir, I doubt I've seen you looking more like O'Reilly's ghost than you do right now!" he exclaimed.

Hugo scowled. "If you have nothing civil to offer by way of conversation, Stokes, get out."

"Yessir," he replied calmly. "Them dogs is anxious to come in. I don't rightly know what to do." Stokes cleared his throat. "Taking a look around, it strikes me that they might go to town on your things, Captain. You wouldn't let me do nothing about clearing up when you got back in the early hours, and they're devils with anything lying about."

Hugo cast his glance over the room. His clothes lay scattered all over the floor, boots were flung in different corners and his sword belt dangled from a gas bracket instead of the hook provided. Silver-backed brushes lay in the armchair beside the washstand which was flooded with water, spilled when he doused his head to clear it. Several bottles and glasses stood where he had left them as he dressed for dinner, and the room reeked of spirits.

He sighed and ran both hands through the springy brown hair to clutch his aching head. "What a mess! Stokes, if I ever kick you out again when I am not in command of myself, ignore my orders."

"Yessir," said Stokes in a long-suffering tone, knowing it would be more than his neck was worth to tangle with this officer if he ever took a mood such as he had suffered these past two days. "What shall I do about them dogs?" he repeated.

"Oh, God!" cried Hugo. "Do what you damn well please. Just get out there and quiet them before my skull splits open."

"Very good, sir," he said huffily. "And a Happy New Year to you, Captain Esterly."

The door closed with forceful softness, and the barking of dogs grew fainter. Hugo groaned as he gingerly laid his head against a pile of pillows; they felt like boulders. The coffee grew cold beside him as he contemplated the ceiling. Recollection was returning. There was going to be hell to pay when Colonel Rayne returned at the end of the week. Hugo was no favorite of his commanding officer, who was one of the old school. They had clashed on several occasions over what the older man described as Hugo's unsteadiness and lack of insight. Last night's affair could bring about a request for his resignation from the regiment. For Jack, it could have more serious consequences. He had been on duty at the time.

He groaned and clutched his head again. The devil that had entered him three nights ago fled in the face of truth. With the first day of a new year had come clarity of thought and a return of strength, to show him that his real weakness lay not in his passion for his brother's chosen bride but in his attempt to run away from it.

A love as deep as that he felt for Victoria ruled any man without consideration for time or place, pride or honor. Its grip made even a goliath weak. To be haunted by her eyes, a merry laugh, a youthful voice telling him her dearest wishes, to be filled with pain and desire so physical that it governed him entirely, should not make him a victim of guilt. Only by refusing to acknowledge that he must ride out the storm with no outward sign to betray him was he failing himself and Charles. He, who had sounded forth so often on the subject of battle tactics, was a coward; he, who prided himself on being so much of a man, went to pieces over emotions he could not control.

All the accusations that had ever been leveled at him now gained force. Old Rayne called him unwisely volatile; generals dubbed him hot-tempered and rash; Charles accused him of suffering the mild madness of military rebels who put action before reason. He had vindicated their claims with a vengeance. Only one of his actions would he still defend. The flight from Wychbourne had been essential for Victoria's sake. Cowardice had not been the root cause for *that* decision; the recriminations from his family for his behavior still had to be faced without his being able to give the real reason.

During the next half hour he came to terms with himself and what he faced. Victoria was to become his sister, part of his family. It was impossible to avoid her, so he must learn to govern himself in her presence. The wedding would be the test. He would stand beside Charles as she pledged her life to his brother. After that, he must learn to accept that Charles would take his rights whenever he chose. It was a little while before the heat that flared in him at that thought could be controlled, and some hint of what was to come pressed down upon him.

She would bear Charles's children. His brother had already spoken of the son he must provide. Hugo closed his eyes against the thought of that slender sensitive girl being torn by the birth of child after child until the requisite male lay in her husband's arms. But he forced himself to face it. There was to be no more running away.

The need for more immediate resolution occupied him then. Somehow he must come out of this mess without being asked to leave the regiment. The cavalry was part of his life and, although forced resignation would not bar him from entry into another regiment, he had a fierce loyalty to the Hussars. In any case, he was well known in cavalry circles, and other colonels would hardly welcome a renegade into their hallowed unyielding ranks. Colonel Rayne would be back in three days; in that time he must make every effort to soften the man's anger. There was also something of importance he must tackle immediately.

"Stokes!" he yelled. "My shaving things."

Stokes hovered in the doorway.

"I shall not attack you, man," Hugo said irritably. "A fine slur you put on my character when you hide behind a door rather than face me." Hugo regarded the black-mustachioed face for several seconds before letting out his breath slowly. "And, Stokes . . . in reply to your concerned inquiries after the state of my health today, I am pleased to tell you I feel much more myself."

A grin curled the ends of the thick mustache.

Shortly after luncheon the maid announced him to the Markhams, and he entered their parlor to be greeted by Letty looking very pretty in a silk dress in peppermint-green stripes.

"Hugo, how kind of you to call. A Happy New Year to you."

He kissed her cheek. "And to you, my dear friend. May it continue to bring you your present happiness."

"Sit by the fire," she invited, as her eyes swept over the full-dress uniform, slung jacket and dangling sword he wore. "You look very formal. Is it a duty call on Jack? He is still abed after a heavy night."

"He told you?"

She shook her head, bouncing her ringlets. "It was only too plain his head was ready to crack open when he arrived this morning. I will never cease to be amazed at the behavior of gentlemen. Is the pleasure worth the aftermath?"

He smiled fondly. "It has often occurred to me that ladies have so much more common sense than we, until I see them fit themselves into a gown that restricts their breathing and prevents their passing through a doorway with ease. Is the fashion worth the punishment?"

Letty laughed. "If you were not so charming I vow I

should have given up on you long ago. Have you come for Jack?" she repeated.

"Not in the cause of duty, although I have several calls to make that demand formality of dress. I also wished to see you, Letty, to apologize for my behavior two nights ago."

She was confused. "You were not well. I understood, Hugo."

"There was no excuse for my casual manners in leaving the following morning with no word to you. If one descends to boorishness it should never be displayed to one's dearest friends. Will you forgive me?"

She turned faintly pink. "Hugo, there is really no need for this. I cannot forgive something that needs no forgiveness. Promise me that you will use our friendship whenever you are in need of friends."

He smiled. "I promise. Perhaps you and Jack will have dinner with me tonight."

"I shall look forward to it." She folded her hands on her silk skirts and took the opportunity to say something Jack would scold her for broaching. "You mentioned a young woman your mama fancied as a daughter—someone in Buckinghamshire."

"Yes," he replied warily. "The daughter of our neighbor."

She bit the tip of her tongue delicately. "Shall I have the pleasure of meeting her soon?"

He looked at her quizzically. "I declare you are grown matronly at the tender age of twenty, Letty. If you are to start match-making you'll have to wear a lace cap and adopt a lorgnette. Shall you be joining the mamas at the Pavilion?"

She was vexed with him. His reaction had disproved her theory. Letty had been convinced a mysterious female had been the cause of his abrupt departure from Wychbourne. She dearly wished to know the story behind it, but Jack maintained he knew no more than she. "It is no laughing matter, Hugo. I am waiting for you to provide me with a companion for the times you take my husband off with you."

Hugo was spared answering as Jack entered. He was clad in rather gay, fashionable trousers and plain coat, but he looked strained and worried. Hugo rose as he came in. "Oh, so it *is* you," he greeted. "I wonder you can stand on your feet."

"It is not easy, believe me" was the heavy reply. "I had to see you. My sincere apologies. They won't help the situation, but I offer them just the same." He put out a hand and let it drop. "What can I say? *Nobody* could have persuaded me to listen to reason."

Jack made a face. "Do I not know it? There is going to be the devil of a dust-up when Rayne returns."

"I am on my way to see a carpenter. With luck, and the trappings of the regiment, I'll have the paneling repaired before the end of the week. Replacing the goblets will not be as easy, I think. Copies of the plates that were smashed in the kitchens can be ordered from Glasshorn's Emporium. At this time of year I would not care to wager on their arriving at barracks before Rayne, but I will press Glasshorn to expedite the order."

"Gentlemen," cried Letty, looking from one to the other. "Will you please explain this conversation? What is this talk of carpenters and smashed plates?"

Hugo cast a look at Jack. "It is the aftermath you mentioned that naturally follows upon gentlemen's folly . . . *my* folly, in this case." He moved to the door. "I will be on my way, if you will excuse me."

"Hugo has invited us to dinner tonight, dearest," Letty told her subdued husband. "I have already accepted."

Jack gave his friend a wry look. "You will not be in company with your horse, I trust?"

Hugo gripped Jack's shoulder. "Never again, believe me. That madness has passed."

Colonel Rayne wasted no time. On the morning following his late-night return to duty, Hugo and Jack met in the adjutant's office and exchanged significant looks. The next few minutes were going to prove harrowing.

"How is the old boy?" ventured Hugo of the adjutant.

"Do not ask" was the depressing answer. "He marched through here this morning looking like a blackamoor, and when I handed him your written account of your exploits I thought the Gods of Wrath had invaded the firmament." A broad grin dawned on his face. "Damn sorry I missed it.

Wouldn't care to do it again for my benefit, would you, Hugo?"

"I doubt I shall ever be drunk enough to take such a risk again," Hugo told him gloomily. "Why has he sent for Jack? I mentioned no one in that report."

"The colonel is no fool. He asked for the duty roster right away. He wants two heads for this, believe me."

Jack laughed mirthlessly. "Was it your optimistic outlook that recommended you to this job, Reggie?"

Lieutenant Reginald Wyckham Herrinforth, nephew of the Duke of Meade, gave him a sly look. "No, it was my innate capacity for diplomacy. Not fifteen minutes ago I was agreeing with the colonel that Captain Esterly was a disgrace to his noble family and an embarrassment to his brother."

"There's nothing like having friends in the right places," said Hugo in disgust. "When I am thrown out of this regiment you can handle my application to join another. You will paint such a picture of lies they'll receive me on their knees with reverence."

The adjutant grew serious. "He will not throw you out, Hugo. Surely he will not?" The questioning afterthought sounded less confident.

"Of course he will not," Jack declared firmly. "If anyone is to go, it will be me."

"*Mr. Herrinforth*," shouted Colonel Rayne from his office, and Reggie jumped to his feet.

"I shall announce you. He is in the worst of tempers, so keep the whole thing calm. Confess, then throw yourself on his mercy—silently. He will not stand argument this morning."

Colonel Archibald Rayne was sitting behind his desk when they entered, and the slight movement of his facial muscles was more likely a nervous twitch than an attempt at a smile. A large sandy-haired man with a mustache to match, he had put the fear of God into many young men—and equally as many maidens. The men's apprehension was justified; that of the ladies was not. He was an ineffectual lover, a failing he compensated for by an outward aggression and a tendency to come down hard on particularly virile or well-favored subordinates.

He had had a dreadful Christmas. His daughter had gone into a decline over a nincompoop in an inferior infantry regiment, his son had brought home a bad report from Eton and Mrs. Rayne had pestered him ceaselessly for a new carriage. Hugo Esterly's account of his highly colored exploit had been the last straw. Pale eyes regarded the two specimens of youthful splendor before him and sent an angry message to his brain.

"Good morning, sir," Hugo said.

"The only creditable adjective I can find to use about you is that you are honest—although there is some doubt over that," snapped the colonel, annoyed by Hugo's nerve. "Since I was bound to see the evidence of this disgraceful episode with my own eyes, you had no alternative but to own up." He fixed Hugo with a disparaging glare. "You are nothing but a bloody nuisance to this regiment and everyone with whom you come into contact." His eyes swung to Jack. "And you, sir, are unfit to wear that uniform."

"Colonel Rayne, may I speak?" asked Hugo immediately.

"No, sir, you may not," he roared. "The time for you to speak will be when you make a public apology before the officers of this mess."

Hugo stiffened. Like it or not, he was going to intervene. Jack was not going to be made a whipping boy if he could prevent it.

"Sir, I wish to make an official protest at the presence of Mr. Markham."

"This is not yet an official discussion" was the terse reply.

"Colonel, he did nothing in this affair," he insisted.

"No, sir, that is just the point. *He did nothing.* In the absence of senior officers it was his responsibility as Officer of the Day to put a stop to such conduct. He quite plainly did not."

"*Could* not, sir."

"Could not. *Could* not? What do you mean, *could* not? Is he an officer of this regiment or not? Does he have authority or not? Has he any sense of duty or has he not? Those are the facts in question, Captain Esterly. I do not wish to hear any more of *could not*. And if you cannot remain silent, I shall oblige you to wait outside until I call you."

Hugo was severely shaken. Colonel Rayne was scarlet with exploded anger, and cool reason was only making him worse. Admittedly, he had been drunkenly irresponsible that night, and two valuable presentation goblets had been smashed, but he was going to ruin himself in replacing them, and the oak paneling had already been undetectably repaired at his own expense. It was not as if he had done anything dishonorable or performed his insane jump in a public restaurant. The commanding officer was taking an unreasonable attitude over what was, after all, not the worst breach of mess discipline in the history of the regiment. But knowing further intervention would certainly worsen the case for Jack, he clamped his lips together and raged inwardly.

The senior officer turned his attention to the dark-haired lieutenant. "You have not yet ventured a word, Mr. Markham. I ask you now to give me a complete account of your part in this deplorable affair. I must warn you that your friendship with Captain Esterly should not influence you in any way. You will relate it as through the eyes of the Officer of the Day. Do you understand? Bear in mind that your career is at stake."

"Yes, sir." With a straight face and a steady voice he related the facts. But he was very worried. A court-martial would be hard on Letty. They had no money in reserve. What would they live on if he should fall foul of this man's temper? Then the colonel asked why he had not prevented the groom from bringing the horse to the mess. Jack hesitated for the first time. "I was improperly dressed."

"*What*, sir?" Rayne was scandalized. "What if the guard had been called out?"

There was nothing to be gained by attempting an answer to that, so Jack went on to explain that once Captain Esterly was mounted on his famous charger it would have been more dangerous to try to prevent the jump than allow it.

"Nothing more would have occurred if it had not been for a fall of plates frightening the beast, Colonel. The jump itself was executed superbly, without damage."

"The quality of the horsemanship is irrelevant. Captain Esterly has been at great pains to acquaint the British cavalry with his ideas on equestrian arts," said Colonel Rayne bitterly. "The fact that he did not break his neck, or that of his mount, is sufficient description in this case. You are dismissed."

Hugo remained standing in front of the desk while the older man looked him over with great deliberation. Six feet tall, athletically built, a law unto himself and a great success with fresh young females, this young captain embodied everything he himself could have been—and was not. He had never liked Hugo Esterly. There had been occasions in the past when guilty knowledge of his personal feelings had led the colonel to temper his judgment, but the young man himself had placed the ideal opportunity into his hands, at last.

"You, no doubt, feel secure in the knowledge that I can charge you with no military crime, as I can Mr. Markham. It is nowhere written that you cannot bring a horse into the mess—indeed, in some regiments tradition demands it on certain occasions. I also note your readiness to pay for and make good the damage you caused. As a gentleman you could not do otherwise." He rose and walked around to stand before Hugo. "However, as commanding officer of this regiment I have a right to expect certain standards from my officers. You have never met them."

Hugo blinked. "I beg your pardon, sir?"

"You have never conformed to the requirements of an officer of Hussars—*this* regiment of Hussars. I have bided my time for the sake of your brother, in the hope that you might acquire some of the same steadiness of character that makes him such an excellent officer, but you have made it impossible for me to keep quiet any longer."

"Sir, I . . ."

"Let me finish, if you please," he said in a steely tone. "You left this regiment on six months' detachment to General Redvers and his staff in Vienna, at which time you made it plain that an opportunity to demonstrate your wild schemes was infinitely preferable to the dull routine at barracks. A premature return to assist at military maneuvers at Chobham ended in an unfortunate accident, whereupon you were ordered by the surgeon-major at Chobham to re-

pair to your home for a complete rest. Major Courtland
arranged for an eminent eye specialist to visit you in Buckinghamshire and advised me that you were taking extended
sick leave." He paused to control himself. "Why then, sir,
do you return to this regiment without the courtesy of ac-
quainting me with your intention or asking permission to
do so?"

"It was a sudden decision, taken on impulse," said Hugo
woodenly, dismayed at the way things were going.

"An impulse. Quite so. Like everything else you do,
Captain Esterly—impulsive and attention-seeking. You are
always advocating the possibility of future conflict. I am
only thankful you are wrong and will not be put to the test,
for impulsiveness and vainglory do not make successful
leaders of men."

Hugo's temper flared. This was unfair. "I protest. You
cannot accuse me on a conjecture, Colonel. Until you have
seen my behavior under fire I challenge your right to make
such a statement."

"Your performance at a mere military exercise was not
exactly distinguished, Captain. A good cavalry officer has
command of his mount whatever occurs. He is not thrown
after an unexpected explosion, neither does he return to
duty before being declared fit by the doctor. The safety of
his men might depend on his complete health." Colonel
Rayne smiled thinly. "It is your own insistence on being
prepared for conflict that forces me to use these instances."

Rashly Hugo took the wrong line. "I think there is nothing of which you could complain in my fitness. If there had
been the slightest deficiency in my command of myself I
could hardly have accomplished a jump of such extreme
difficulty three nights ago."

"The ability to clear a mess table while under the influence of too much liquor will be of no help to a troop of
soldiers in the thick of battle" was the furious counter-
remark. "That is the crux of my case, Captain Esterly.
There is much more to being a Hussar officer than circus
tricks and showy displays of swordsmanship at the gallop."

"I know that, Colonel. I am not the complete fool you
imagine," Hugo said hotly. "Unless a man is able to ride
supremely well he would be better off in a damned infantry

regiment, however. What use is a Hussar who cannot manage a horse?"

But the Colonel had got what he wanted. "Before you step into the realms of complete insubordination, Captain, I must warn you that it is a court-martial offense," he said shortly. "I see no point in prolonging this painful interview. For your uncivilized behavior I demand that you make a public apology to all members who have a right to regard the officers' mess as their home." He turned away to circle his desk. "I look forward to receiving either your resignation or a request to transfer into another regiment. You have until the end of the week. That is all, Captain Esterly."

Hugo was stunned. He had joked about being kicked out of the regiment but did not think it would come about. It was unbelievable. He had believed Colonel Rayne to be above vindictiveness of this kind. He turned and went out in a daze. His future was falling down around his ears.

"Hugo," called the adjutant as he passed through. "Sorry, old fellow, but you will have to vacate those rooms you now occupy. They are strictly for field officers, you know."

"Certainly" was the savage reply. "Is it all right with you if I move into the stables until I leave at the end of the week?"

When the gentlemen of the Hussars gathered, as ordered, to hear the apology from Hugo and the severe public reprimand given to Jack Markham as punishment, there were many hostile faces. The request for Hugo's resignation was not popular. Certainly, the man had an obsession with military horsemanship and was prone to rashness over things he felt deeply, but he was an intelligent, capable officer, much admired in the ranks and among the more lively subalterns. Above all, he was a damn good sort—a generous sporting man with none of the superior airs bred in his brother, the Honorable Charles Stanford.

If Colonel Rayne was aware of the atmosphere he gave no sign of it as he left the mess at the end of the painful proceedings. A clamor of commiserations broke out, but Hugo was beyond appreciating their support. Harry Edmunds, in one of the exaggerated gestures he made these days, offered to resign with him as a mark of protest, but Hugo told him brusquely not to be a fool. One ruined career was a high enough price for a few hours of stupidity.

Even Jack, who could not afford promotion so would not suffer from being refused it, failed to break through the barrier his friend had erected to cover his abysmal lack of self-confidence since leaving the colonel. All at once Hugo felt like a man who has had his horse shot from under him in the middle of a charge. His life had stretched ahead in a glowing path of promises. His commission in this celebrated regiment had been a source of pride to him. Even if his acceptance had been partially due to having a brother already serving with it, he had earned his place on his own merit once he joined. His prowess in the field had brought him and the regiment countless honors and trophies, and his own particular troop consisted of soldiers who had never let him down because they believed he would never let *them* down.

With the invitation to join General Redvers' staff in Vienna had come the conviction that his burning ambition for a reappraisal of cavalry tactics would have its head at last. To be brought back to Chobham as an adviser during maneuvers had made those hopes soar. Yet, within a few short weeks, he was brought down with a vengeance. He had seen devotion to his profession as the only means of restoring order in the chaos Victoria had created in his life. Now one weak attempt at another kind of oblivion had completed his downfall.

After three days of self-analysis, recrimination and feverish consideration of his future, he had handed the colonel an application to transfer into any other regiment and removed himself to a cheap lodging in London to await the outcome. The Markhams had begged him to stay with them, but he gently declined. It was difficult enough for them to manage as it was. Gloomily he realized his own finances would be drastically diminished after paying for a replacement pair of Venetian glass goblets, three dozen plates and several oak panels. What colonel would welcome an impoverished junior captain who was a known nonconformer and had been asked to leave his regiment for unmannerly behavior?

Ten days later he returned to his rooms after a light luncheon in a nearby restaurant to be met with the information that a military gentleman was awaiting him in the parlor. His heart leaped. Had they sent word by hand instead of letter? He burst into his rooms, then pulled up a few feet inside the door.

"Charles!"

His brother was in uniform and rose to stand before the fire, facing him. Hugo could not help thinking how impressive he looked. Handsome, autocratic, invincible. There was no smile of greeting.

"As it seemed unlikely you would call on me, I have come to London. It was a damned inconvenience, but my sense of duty dictated it." He tilted back his head. "Have you quite lost yours?"

Hugo drew in a sharp breath and kicked the door closed behind him.

"I would have called on you, except that I had not realized you had left Wychbourne."

"My departure was more civilized than yours."

A faint color flooded his face. "I apologize for that."

Charles loosened his hold on the anger that had been consuming him for days. "Oh no, that really will not do, Hugo. Do you imagine a few casual words to me excuses your conduct? Mama is even yet unable to think of it without resorting to tears. My father is extremely wounded over the incident, especially since the Massinghams were also victims of your ill-manners, thereby causing talk outside the immediate family. As for Victoria, I fear she has taken it very much to heart. After her very real concern and affection during your restriction to the sickroom, it appeared particularly boorish and insulting. She has not expressed her feeling of hurt, but I know it is there by her looks and manner."

Hugo had known it had to come, but preknowledge did nothing to make his brother's words any easier to bear. He threw his hat on a chair and stalked to the fireplace. "You have every right to be angry."

"Of course I have every right," his brother said coldly. The pale blue eyes were full of hauteur. "I will not stand by while my parents and future wife are treated with contempt by someone who has been given their affection and trust."

"No," cried Hugo. "Not contempt. You cannot use that word of me."

"I shall use any word that exactly fits the description. I have had time to consider very carefully, and my opinion has not changed from the time I read your execrable note."

Hugo kicked viciously at a log in the fire. "How like you, Charles. It is always the same. You form an immediate opinion, and the only further consideration you give it is that of congratulating yourself on your astuteness."

Charles countered quickly. "One does not need to be astute to know you possess a wild streak that allows you to be extremely careless of propriety."

Hugo's temper began to flare. "I admit my dislike of blind adherence to existing rules without a thought of whether they still apply, but that is hardly a 'wild streak,' as it pleases you to call it."

Charles walked away from him to stand at the window. He remained cold and calm in anger. "So, it was a wish for reform that led you to disrupt the ceremonial parade last year with your damned new ideas? It was controlled thinking that led to Rayne being forced to apologize on your behalf to Brigadier Foster at a regimental dinner in the mess? And can you dare to suggest it was a genuine wish to improve military efficiency that led you to take a horse over a table during a drunken orgy?"

The two men faced each other, both angry and hurt, before Hugo's mouth twisted bitterly.

"You always keep your trump card until last. You know I have no defense against that."

The clock ticked loudly in the silence that followed. Charles let his glance wander over the cramped parlor, taking in the shabby chairs, the circular table covered with a plush cloth, stuffed birds under glass covers and all kinds of cheap knickknacks. It was the kind of room normally occupied by someone in trade. He looked back at Hugo and saw in the drawn features and angry eyes the man developed from the eager small boy with whom he had grown up. He sighed heavily.

"Hugo, what has happened to you?"

The younger man relaxed and laughed in a short mirthless gust. "Perhaps that 'wild streak' is there, after all."

Charles came over. "No, it is something more this time. I should like you to see a doctor."

Hugo was astonished. "A doctor . . . whatever for?"

"I can only think that fall has done you more harm than we thought. Your eyesight might well have recovered, but a blow on the head can bring strange reactions, I believe." When his brother continued to look at him with amazement, he went on. "I checked with Markham. You had no plans to spend New Year's with him. Why *did* you leave Wychbourne, Hugo?"

Playing for time, Hugo invited Charles to sit down and poured two glasses of wine before taking the other chair beside the fire. Just when he knew he had to say something, a quick memory of Letty Markham gave him an idea.

"I could not give my real reason for leaving, and you would never have believed that I had been recalled to duty. The excuse I gave was a poor one, but the only one I could think of at the time."

Charles held his glass with unrelaxed fingers. "I do not see why you had to leave so abruptly, although I could see you were not yourself at that dinner party. You seemed to be almost a stranger."

"Not a stranger, Charles, just a very wary man."

"Wary?"

"I deserted in the face of the enemy."

"Eh?"

"I admit it was weak and ill-advised, but perhaps two weeks of darkness muddled my head. At the time, it seemed the only way out of a tricky situation."

Charles tugged at his mustache uneasily. Somewhere deep in the recesses of his mind a faint nebulous fear was forming. It did not yet have a name. In fact, he was not aware of its existence—yet he felt irrationally irritated by Hugo's refusal to come to the point and set the fear at rest.

"For God's sake explain yourself, man."

Hugo put as much conviction into his lie as he could muster. It was difficult when the truth made him wish to avoid his brother's eyes, but if any good was to come from the wreck of the past weeks he had to give no sign of it.

"In your own happiness it probably has not occurred to you that your marriage leaves me completely exposed. All the while you remained a bachelor Mama had no case, but she is determined on Charity Verewood joining the family. Her determination has extended to collusion with Mrs. Verewood, with the result that the girl imagines I have been waiting for the bugle to sound the Advance." He took a swallow of wine to sharpen his inventiveness. "That night, Mama made it plain the Verewoods were waiting for my offer, and she could see no reason for delay now that my health was assured." He gave his brother a look that asked for masculine support. "What was I to do? I had only that night recovered from a sobering experience and needed time to think. Charles, you know how Mama is when she is set on something and also how upset she becomes when it does not work out as she wishes. On top of that, Miss Verewood herself adopted such a proprietary attitude toward me during this visit that I took fright." A rueful grin broke on his face. "My inner self shouted 'Threes about!' and I obeyed with alacrity."

From his expression Charles did not appear to be appeased. "You caused such pain and embarrassment because you were not ready to offer for Miss Verewood? Rather cowardly, wouldn't you say?"

Hugo felt his anger beginning to return. "Would you have me ruled by a parcel of females? A fine comment, coming from a man who has neglected his filial duty until it suits him to take a bride of his own choice with no reference to Mama's wishes. I am only twenty-seven."

"That is only too obvious at times."

Hugo rose with a swift impatient movement. "You have already given your opinion of me. I do not think you need to repeat it."

Charles drank his wine calmly. "Very well, you have given me a reason for your behavior. My opinion of it does not really matter, since nothing can alter the fact of your deplorable flight. My real concern is that you have made no amends. Was it your intention to have no further contact with the family who brought you up?"

Hugo turned on Charles, his eyes blazing. "That is a damnable suggestion."

"What *had* you proposed doing?"

"I meant to visit Wychbourne—to explain that I had

been bewildered and not myself. I also intended to put it gently to Mama that I was not ready for matrimony."

"And Victoria? What did you intend doing about your insulting behavior toward her? Yes, you may color, man. She is extremely softhearted and affectionate. I had occasion to warn her not to expend so much of her sympathetic nature that she was obliged to neglect her other, less obvious, duties, but the sight of my brother under such strain brought forth all her tender concern. Are you so unfeeling that it did not occur to you that her very youth must prevent her from accepting such rejection with composure?"

Charles was not only piercing him with the point of a burning sword; Hugo was unable to stop him from twisting it with unaccustomed callousness. "I thought of nothing but the need to get away," he said stiffly. "I meant to explain my reasons and apologize."

Charles rose and put his glass on the mantelpiece. "Your life would appear to consist of nothing but apologies. I hear you had to offer one publicly to the members of the officers' mess. The ones to the family have been delayed while you have been busily ruining your career, I take it. Did you propose explaining *that* to them at the same time? Is that your next move?"

"My next move is to show you the door, Charles." Hugo had taken as much as he intended that day. "If you have come here merely to air your grievances and gloat over my failures without the slightest intention of trying to understand, there seems little point in your staying. I have admitted my fault; I have apologized to you. I have declared my intention of doing so to all those I have offended. I have even allowed you to use words during your chastisement that I would tolerate from no other man. I stand duly humbled. However, my career is my own affair. You were not there, you do not know all the circumstances. All you have heard is the outcome, which, in any other officer's case, would have been more lenient, I swear. Despite the 'wild streak' you insist I have, I believe my acceptance of the harsh verdict was to my credit, and I am determined to continue with something in which I fervently believe if it is the cause of being asked to leave every regiment in the British cavalry." He was really angry now. "I have spent half an hour hearing my character and integrity impugned.

My ideas on cavalry drill are sound, sensible and of great value to the future of armed horsemen. If they make me unpopular I shall still pursue them. Through one foolish lapse I gave Rayne the very excuse he wanted, but he is a biased, nearsighted fool. He has lost the regiment a very valuable officer."

"But he has not" was the unexpected reply. "I am here on official business. You did not think I would gird myself thus otherwise?"

"Official business?" snapped Hugo in thrall to angry pride.

Charles took an envelope from his pocket and held it out. "This contains an official request from General Redvers that you rejoin him in Vienna immediately. He, at least, appears to think your opinion is valuable."

In a daze Hugo took the letter and read its brief contents, registering that it was addressed to Colonel Payne and referred to "your excellent and conscientious young officer, Captain Hugo Esterly."

"That arrived three days ago," said Charles. "It put Rayne in something of a quandary. His 'excellent and conscientious young officer' had just been asked to leave the regiment and had applied to transfer. He was still uncertain what to do when I arrived back in barracks." He pulled at his mustache in an unconsciously pompous gesture. "It did not take a very great effort to persuade him to tear up your application—at least, for the time being. Redvers plans to return to England two days before the wedding, so there is no chance of your missing it."

"I am reinstated?" Hugo was bewildered by this sudden reversal.

"You have never officially left. Rayne could not let the honor of General Redvers' request fall upon some other regiment, could he?"

"And you could not let the dishonor of my forced transfer fall on *your* family."

It was said with such bitterness Charles was shaken. Had they traveled so far in anger? He took a deep breath and let it out slowly. "I also could not let my brother serve in another regiment. There is too much between us for that."

It was the end of a quarrel more deep-seated and emotionally complex than any difference of opinion they had ever had. It left Charles dismayed at the irrational anger that had flooded him today at the sight of the man he loved as a brother. To Hugo, already fighting emotions he did not wish to associate with Charles, the further obligation put upon him by Charles's intercession on his behalf with Colonel Rayne left him unwillingly ungracious—truculent, almost.

"I must thank you for your support," he said tonelessly. "Rayne suggested I should attempt to acquire some of your steadiness of character. He is right. I cannot expect you to protect me from my failings forever."

"Nonsense," said Charles with assumed heartiness. "It was hardly my influence that led to the invitation from Redvers to return to Vienna. He must value your opinion highly." To cover the tension he held up his glass. "I should like some more of that wine. It is of devilish fine quality."

Hugo eased his taut muscles and walked across with the bottle. "It is an extravagance I cannot easily forego. Should you like me to bring you a case from Vienna?"

Half an hour later, Charles left for his return journey to Brighton. They shook hands and smiled, but the first hair crack had appeared in the solid fortifications of brotherhood they had so eagerly and willingly built around themselves.

"You will have no time for visits now," said Charles, "but I am confident that a letter to Mama and another to my father will make the situation a lot easier. Heavy emphasis on the state of your health at the time cannot fail to aid their understanding. You will find time to pen them before you leave?"

"Naturally."

"And one to Victoria? It will make her less unhappy over the affair."

"Yes," said Hugo, wondering what he could put in a letter to Victoria, feeling as he did.

"Hugo . . . one last thing."

"What is that?"

"Promise that you will see a doctor before your departure."

"There is no . . . oh, very well. I owe you that at least."

Charles clapped him on the shoulder, a casual gesture that had suddenly become theatrical. "Goodbye, old fellow. Steer clear of explosives. When I get married I want you standing there beside me to witness it. Do not fail me, will you?"

Hugo's quick reassuring smile was fabricated. "I'll be there, Charles."

He closed the door and walked back into the shabby parlor where the official envelope lay on the plush tablecloth. Picking it up, he reread the general's request and the accompanying orders signed by Colonel Rayne. Flinging the documents down again, he sank into a chair with his head in his hands.

"Damn, damn, *damn!*" he cried in savagely exploding crescendo. "If it had been anyone but Charles!"

CHAPTER FIVE

Hugo's letter caused as much tumult in its recipient as if it had been a declaration of undying love. That he had no talent for words was obvious from the start, but this failing only aroused fierce longing for the man who believed her unaware of the true motive for his leaving Wychbourne. The fumbling misphrased sentences that asked Victoria to forgive his deplorable neglect of her consideration and unselfish efforts to help him through a difficult time only conjured up to the girl a sharp imaginative picture of his desperation as page after page was crumpled by his long fingers in this effort to tell a pack of lies.

The stilted clichés could not have told her more plainly how impossible he found it to write to her. The absence of any real part of himself in the letter brought him startlingly close to her. It made what he did not say stand out with an emphasis it would not have shown in ink on the paper. The lies spilling from his pen showed her the truth in italics.

For several days after his departure from Wychbourne, Victoria had tormented herself with desperate plans. Within eight weeks she was pledged to marry a man who had chosen her from among more noble and wealthy aspirants to his title. Plans for the wedding were made. She had been accepted by his family, given the heirlooms a woman in her position should receive. Charles's regiment had officially received her into its ranks. The officers had given a dinner in their honor, plus a handsome present, and an archway of swords was to be provided by his fellow officers at the ceremony. Apart from that, notices had been sent to the leading newspapers and journals; presents had been arriving at Wychbourne and Aunt Almeira's and invitations sent out.

Did she dare tell Charles it had all been a mistake? The thought set her trembling. Charles would look a fool in the eyes of his family, society and the regiment. She would have to give back everything he had proudly given her; the wedding gifts would all have to be returned. She would be in disgrace—the subject of contemptuous gossip—and her uncle, aunt and cousins would be subjects for ridicule and pity. They would never forgive her. Most of all, her cousins would suffer from her own selfish behavior when the scandal broke.

For a short while she allowed herself to suppose she were strong enough to give Charles back the enormous sapphire. The marriage would not take place and she would be free, but to what avail? Hugo had known there was no answer and, by his going, had told her he could not complete the scandal. The family who had brought him up would cast him off as disloyal and dishonorable; he could not remain in the regiment; he would be shunned by his friends. Most of all, he would lose his self-respect, for the only way they could be together was as social outcasts. Too many other people for whom they had affection would be hurt by such drastic steps.

Robbed of the hope of seeing him shortly and unable to comfort herself by assuring him he was forgiven for leaving without a word, she had only his letter as consolation. Times without number she took it from her small shell-covered box to feel the paper he had held, trace the outline of the words with her finger as if the action put her hand into his as he wrote them and to read the text aloud as he must have done before sealing it.

As week succeeded week she grew quieter and more withdrawn, seeing her wedding day only as the moment when they would come face to face again after their enigmatic parting. There was enough to fill her days, but at night, when she lay in bed with Glencoe at her feet, she asked the Lord in her prayers why he had sent Hugo to Vienna at the beginning of last summer. If he had only been with the garrison during those carefree months, Charles would soon be her brother, not her husband. By the time the wedding was a mere three days away, the Lord still had not given her an answer.

Hugo did not arrive when expected on the day before the marriage. Victoria had spent it in an ache of longing for him to appear. His failure to do so did not bring censure from her, as it did from the others. Her one dread was that he had met with another accident.

It was only when the ladies of the party were preparing

to retire for an early night that Charles came hurrying from the dining room, where the gentlemen were taking part, and took Victoria by the arm.

"All is well, dearest. Hugo has this minute made his appearance."

Relief filled her. "I am glad. What was the cause of his delay?"

He tightened his lips. "Difficulties in crossing the Channel, he says. Nobody but Hugo ever has so many disasters befall him to spoil the plans other people have made . . . but that need not concern you. He sends his apologies—something he seems always to be doing of late," he added dryly. "Unfortunately, he cannot call on you tonight. He is under an obligation to make his peace with Mama and my father. He has not seen them since that affair at Christmas, you know."

"Poor Hugo," she said softly. "Storms in the Channel have hardly improved his case." Her hand went on his arm. "You will stand by him with your parents?"

"When have I not done so?" he asked with a sigh, tucking her hand through his arm. "I will see you to your room, my love, then I must hasten away for the last time. After today we shall have a whole month—no claim of duty or propriety can pull us apart then."

She made no reply. His remark spread a cloud over the joy of knowing Hugo was again under this roof with her. They bade the guests good night and set off along the corridors already lined with potted ferns and green plants as a background to the masses of fresh flowers due on the morrow.

"I wish Hugo would think seriously about marriage," mused Charles as they walked arm in arm. "It would do much to settle his restlessness. Devotion to wife and family would soon banish his obsession to reform something that cannot be bettered."

"Why, Charles," she said swiftly, "if every forward-thinking man did that we should not now have railways, steamships, gas lighting or chloroform. Instead, we should have an island overrun with children."

His astonishment was so great it made him stop in mid-pace. "My dear Victoria, from whom have you heard such ideas?"

She swung around to face him. "Unfortunately, I have heard them from no one. It is merely a matter of common sense. I have thought about Hugo's ideas extensively."

"Then I strongly advise you to cease. Subjects of that nature are not suitable for gentle minds, and society will not expect to hear them voiced by my wife. It is well known in the regiment that I do not support these equestrian reforms. They are unsuited to British cavalry because they stem from the Continent. It really will not do to have you suggesting you do not respect my views."

"I have only tried to illustrate that it might not be for the greatest good if a gentleman were to lose his beliefs beneath the duties of husband and father," she said with unusual persistence. "It is certainly not my intention to discuss such things with society, for the vast majority would not understand me if I did. They are, most of them, complete knobheads."

For several seconds Charles studied her flushed face, then began to laugh with soft sensuality. "By heavens, you drive a man to the limits of his control, Victoria. Such a provocative statement deserves to be met with more than a mere salute on the lips, but tomorrow, my dearest, I shall show you the full measure of ecstasy. You will not care for steamships or gas lighting then, I promise you."

Struggling free from his tight embrace, she reminded him that he had other duties that demanded his attention, and they continued to her room.

Once inside, she did not immediately allow Rosie to undress her. Instead, she sat dreamily before the fire while Glencoe had a blissful hour on her mistress's lap, enjoying the soft rubbing of fingers on her fat furry stomach. The young maid indulged romantic fancies of the bride contemplating the delights of her wedding night. Victoria, however, was dreaming of Hugo, not her bridegroom.

It was the kind of glorious daffodil-and-dewdrop March day with which England woos her countrymen from their winter heavyheartedness. The horses in the paddock threw up their hind legs and whinnied their pleasure; the dappled deer trod delicately into patches of sunshine by the lake; and ducks upon the surface flirted with their reflections in a way that would make any exiled heart fly immediately to England's green land and sparkling waterways.

On that morning, Victoria stood on the threshold of perception. Rosie slipped the skirt of the ivory wedding gown over the hooped petticoats, then assisted the bride into the pointed bodice that covered her throat and clothed her arms with bell-shaped sleeves over lace undersleeves. Very carefully the maid pinned on the great sapphire brooch that was Charles's wedding gift. It was more a donation to the family than a gift of love, but it had been made to match the engagement ring and represented an investment of Stanford money. There was another present awaiting her at the honeymoon lodge, he had told her. Something more personal.

On went the wreath of flowers and the exquisite family veil that turned a beautiful girl into a high-born lady of quality, remote and untouchable. With the donning of that veil Charles has gained his first faint hold on my life, she thought. By the end of the ceremony it will be his entirely.

Dr. Castledon arrived to lead his niece down to her bridegroom. The elderly man was too overcome to speak, so Victoria was left in silence to cover the thick carpet in her bridal slippers, knowing each step was taking her further on a road her heart cried out for her not to take.

Rounding a bend in the first staircase, she had her first sight of the waiting guests. In her absence that morning the Great Hall had been smothered in pink and white carnations, roses and gardenias, cyclamen and great creamy lilies whose scent wafted upward with the heady damp perfume of hothouse plants. Within their encompassing beauty crowded the strangers and friends who had come to see a society wedding. The ladies' dresses were lavish and adorned with an impressive array of diamonds. The gentlemen were dignified in morning suits or dashing in the uniform of Charles's regiment.

She had reached the lower part of the second staircase and the chapel was in view, lit by candles and the sun through stained glass. Her throat tightened. Two men stood side by side with their backs to her, dressed in the impressive uniform of the Hussars—one tall, elegant and golden-haired, the other broader and more muscular, with rich brown hair glowing beneath the dust-flecked rays that struck diagonally through the window. The sunshine caught the gold-fringed epaulettes and elaborate lacing on the blue fur-trimmed pelisses slung over their shoulders; it picked out the twists of gold that denoted rank on their cuffs and the heavy crusting around the high collars; it flashed on sword scabbards that hung with the elaborate sabertaches from wide gold sashes and twinkled fitfully upon the spurs fixed to polished riding boots. They looked proud and impressive, the embodiment of England's aristocratic cavalry officers, but Victoria had never seen Hugo in uniform. It might have been a stranger standing there.

For a moment the flowers, the colorful mosaic of people, the enormous crystal chandelier, the rector in his white surplice and the two blue-uniformed men spun around in a blur of trembling rainbows, but her feet still went on, one before the other, sweeping her inexorably forward. Faces turned as she walked between the ranks. Someone cleared his throat very noisily. A susceptible female sniffed into a handkerchief. Feet shuffled. The rector's overstarched surplice crackled as he assumed a more ecclesiastical stance. The two brothers remained stiffly at attention, staring at the tiny altar.

Foot by foot Victoria approached until she stood beside Charles and the music died away. Everyone in the Great Hall seemed to be holding his breath as silence replaced the boom of the organ. It was nothing compared with the suspension of life Victoria felt as she glanced up through the barrier of lace and met Hugo's eyes.

Hugo felt the world tilt as their glances locked. The message was clear and distressing. Victoria was captive in the same prison; he had run from Wychbourne too late! The blow brought a return of the physical sickness he had suffered on the packet boat from France, and for several appalling minutes he dreaded that he might have to retire and suspend the ceremony.

The exchange of words followed their hallowed pattern while he fought the need to shout *Stop!* and drag her away from this sacrificial altar. His lips remained frozen together while the high collar dug into his throat to choke him, and

sweat trickled down his temples and gathered in his armpits.

. . . forsaking all other . . . Dear God, the words
mocked him. He was breaking one of the commandments
and every principle of honor and loyalty as he stood there
in the holy chapel. Where was his strength? Had he thrown
integrity from the window? Victoria was saying her re-
sponses in a faint but steady voice that shamed him. He must
not only match her courage; he must crown it.

By the end of the service he was as steady as a rock.
When he stood for long minutes with a metal stand supporting his bent arm holding the fur busby, the photogra-
pher saw him as a proud and self-assured young man;
when he gave Victoria the obligatory kiss on the cheek he
was able to say in a confident voice, "Charles is a lucky
man . . . and so am I, to have gained such a delightful
sister."

"Thank you." It had been easy to leave it at that, for a
bride is allowed little time for conversation, but their
glances had hesitantly traveled in converging directions on
too many occasions during the lavish wedding breakfast,
when his should have been on the six attendants and hers
on her husband.

The young bridesmaids gave him a genuine excuse to
neglect further contact with the bride, the Castledon sisters
being extremely coy and flirtatious—a fact that would have
amused him at any other time—and he devoted himself to
their wishes and entertainment. However, the minute he
was left alone while they were presented to Colonel Rayne,
Victoria appeared from the throng and stood before him.
He loved her all the more for the courage he did not possess.

"You are so popular today," she began breathlessly. "I
feared I would never have the opportunity to thank you for
your letter. I valued it."

"I regret I had the occasion to send one." It sounded
insufferably formal even to his own ears.

She was out of her depth but struggled on. "Has your
mama forgiven you?"

"Yes." It slipped out before he could stop it. "Have
you?"

She knew what he meant. He saw it in her eyes. "There

was nothing to forgive. Between the patroness of the regiment and its most brilliant officer there never could be. You told me that yourself."

He swallowed. "Those words were spoken foolishly, Victoria."

"Only if you do not live up to your boast." The sadness in her expression increased as she stepped closer, lost to everything around her. "I heard you had been asked to leave the regiment, until a letter . . ."

"You *heard*?"

"Not from Charles," she said quickly. "The officers talk among themselves. I know no details of the affair, only that the colonel had hardly increased his popularity."

"I see," he said bitterly. "I forget that the regiment had the privilege of knowing you before I did and would naturally entertain you with garrison gossip."

She drew in a little breath and put out a hand. "Hugo, I . . ."

"Captain Esterly, I have been waiting for an opportunity to speak to you," said a clear voice from behind them. "Your duties as best man occupy you so fully, I just had to take this opportunity to approach you."

Charity Verewood glided up, a pale, lovely creature in silver-blue watered silk, wearing a vast representation of her fortune around her neck. She came to rest beside him with a ballooning swirl of her skirts.

"Mrs. Stanford, I have seldom seen a more beautiful wedding. Does she not make the perfect bride, Captain Esterly?"

When he did not answer, she put a hand delicately on the bridal veil. "The number of happy unions this must have witnessed, but none happier than this one, I am sure." Her chaste blue eyes widened at Victoria. "I heard Mrs. Weathercourt-Chyne expressing the hope of a word with you as I passed a moment ago. A bride's obligations are so numerous, are they not? You may safely leave Captain Esterly with me while you fulfill some of them, ma'am." Smooth golden braids shone in the sunlight as she tilted her head to give Hugo a melting look. "You must tell me about your return visit to Vienna. It was unfortunate that duty called you away from Wychbourne at Christmas, but if his presence is so important to a general, an officer must put professional obligations before personal wishes. No one understands that better than I."

The moment was broken, and Victoria moved away, leaving him to follow her with his eyes despite the soft chatter of the girl beside him. She was still beside him when the bride and groom climbed into the carriage for their departure, but his gaze remained on the dark-haired girl in crimson velvet trimmed with ermine until the waving hand and pale face beneath the bonnet were hidden from his view.

"What a happy pair. Plainly so devoted to each other," said Charity softly, noting her companion's silent abstraction with a shrewdness not often apparent in her dealings with others. She slipped a hand through his arm, and he looked down at her from his distant reverie. "A wedding becomes very tedious after the departure of the bridal pair, do you not think?" The smile was cool and sweet. "I know your duties will oblige you to dance attendance on those very youthful bridesmaids—poor man, *six* of them is a daunting prospect—but you must surely be set free tomorrow? I have to drive across to Commerford to see a bay mare Squire Partridge thinks would suit me. Do you care to accompany me? The Commerford hills are looking very attractive at the moment and are perfect for a long gallop." She began walking, making it necessary for him to turn from a view of the now empty driveway. "I should also value your opinion of the mare." Her round eyes grew soft and full of admiration. "There is no one whose word I would trust more than yours."

She had caught him at exactly the right moment. Her soft tones soothed his racked nerves, the blonde perfection of her features was restful after the vividness of a face that haunted him and the prospect of a wild gallop across the countryside of his youth tempted him. He had had a surfeit of emotions today; he longed for something purely physical.

"At what time do you set out?" he asked.

"At any time you wish to name. We need not go directly there. The whole day is at our disposal."

"Nine A.M.," he said in fierce challenge.

"You will not have to wait for me," she replied calmly.

"And if I had said eight?"

"I should have been ready when you arrived."

They were about to enter the house, but Hugo was seized with a sudden reluctance to smell again the carnations that had filled his nostrils with their overpowering perfume. He veered away and led his companion along a side path to the stables.

"You have not seen my latest hunter, I believe, Miss Verewood. You will be vastly impressed."

"But . . . will you not be expected in the house?" she asked in virtuous protest.

"No doubt" was the grim reply, "but I have had rather more than I can stand of gushing matrons and giggling bridesmaids. A short spell of equine company will be far more agreeable to me."

"Captain Esterly!" Charity pulled up, and he turned to face her.

"Do not say you do not agree with me, Miss Verewood." His brilliant eyes flashed in a challenge. "Well? Do you return to the dullness of that garden of assembled flatterers or not?"

Charity hesitated only a few seconds. With him in such a mood she must seize her opportunities. Mama could be conciliated later.

"I am not sure that I dare," she breathed. "You might not offer to show me the hunter again."

Charles jumped to the ground and gave his orders, leaving Victoria to peer through the carriage window at her honeymoon abode. It was a far cry from London or Paris—her idea of the ideal place in which to conclude the ceremonial of marriage. The lamp above the entrance showed a metal-studded door recessed into a red brick archway. It stood open into a hall of wood-paneled walls and floor of polished blocks on which lay a dark-blue and scarlet rug of some age and value. The inevitable trophies adorned the walls: noble animals who had been born for a better purpose than to stare glassy-eyed at others of their species on the opposite side of the room.

Her gaze traveled upward as far as the lamplight permitted. The outer walls of the lodge were dark-red brick with heavy stone lintels and leaded windows—more like a stronghold than a cozy hunting lodge, she thought with a heavy heart.

She sank back against the cushion, closing her eyes against the anguish of her departure from Wychbourne. In all that crowd of well-wishers Hugo had stood taller than most, and she had kept her eyes locked to his until his face had become an indistinguishable blur. As the distance widened, Wychbourne, that vast house that had never seemed to her like a home, had become dear and familiar. Dear and familiar because he was part of it . . . yet it seemed fated to witness only their partings.

The carriage door opened. "Come, my dearest," said Charles gaily. "You will find it very snug inside." He helped her to the ground with great tenderness. "Welcome to Brennen Lodge, my sweet bride."

Victoria found herself swung up in his arms with her cheek pressed against the stiff gold braiding across his chest as he bent over her, laughing softly. "I must hold you closely, my love, or you might float away from me."

Always handsome, there was a triumphant superlative to each of his features at this moment. Beneath the lights his hair had an aura of gilded softness, the blueness of his eyes had deepened with secrets, his smile as he set her on her feet inside and turned away to the servants held a story she could not even guess at. There was a youthful gaiety about her husband that contrasted strongly with his normal dignity; there was a daring about him tonight that should have appealed to her romantic nature. The love locked inside her ensured that it did not.

They passed three-quarters of an hour sitting beside the great log fire while she sipped hot chocolate and Charles fortified himself with mulled wine. Then he crossed to her and raised her to her feet with his hands beneath her elbows.

"It is growing late, my dear. I will conduct you to our room, then return when you have had time to prepare yourself." His arm slid around her waist, and she found herself being taken along a short dark corridor and up a flight of boxed-in stairs lit by flambeaux fixed to the dark paneling. The landing at the top was the approach to only six doors, set close together in a half-moon arrangement, and each lay in relative shade due to the poor lighting of the upper floor. The lodge catered to purely masculine tastes in decor, it seemed. There was even a mute antlered head nailed to the wall up here—a symbol of man's delight in using his superiority to rid the earth of its most gentle creatures. Victoria turned her eyes away, knowing the creature had once stepped delicately in dappled sunshine, like those in the park at Wychbourne.

Charles flung open a door and halted just outside. "Do not keep me waiting long, my beautiful wife," he whispered, kissing her fingers with lingering pleasure.

She could not answer; just backed into the room as he closed the door. The main bed chamber was designed with gentlemen in mind, but Rosie had all the candlebrackets filled and alight, which, with the cheery dancing flames in the hearth, gave reassuring warmth to the shivering girl. Glencoe made her usual fuss of her mistress but received only mechanical pats in return. Rosie removed the attractive going-away dress and the starched petticoats beneath, then unlaced the stays and began to remove the chemise. Victoria's hands went up to clutch the lace-trimmed bodice.

"No. It is rather cold tonight, Rosie."

"But, ma'am, you *cannot*. I mean, will the major not think it odd of you?" stammered Rosie, wise in her knowledge of gentlemen's requirements. "Your nightgown is nice and warm. I have had it before the fire this past half hour."

Victoria acquiesced and thought today had represented a fast-flowing stream into which she had fallen. Now, she was rushing toward the weir at the end of her helpless spinning. The long nightgown was warm, as Rosie said, with sleeves buttoned at the wrist and a frilled collar snugly around her throat, but never before had she been so aware of her own nakedness beneath it.

The double bed she must share with Charles looked large enough, and she was slightly built . . . but suppose, in moving, she should accidentally touch against him? Heat broke out all over her at the thought. How she would ever manage to sleep with that dread in mind she did not know. It would be so very embarrassing. It was difficult to contemplate how she would cope with such a situation. As it

was, her heart was pounding with nervousness. Charles was
a pleasant, amusing companion when they were together,
but to lie in bed with him, was another thing altogether.
Whatever could she converse with him about? It did not
seem polite to go to sleep without a few minutes of conversation. She and her cousin Maude had always chatted until
they felt sleepy, but girlish fancies were not fit subjects for
gentlemen. With Hugo it would be so much easier. They
always had so much to say to each other.

Suddenly, she was pulled into the inexorable glide of water that led straight to the dam, as the contemplation of
being here with Hugo caught at her chest with an unbearable ache that extended down her body into her thighs. It
was so strong she had to bite her lip to prevent a sigh from
escaping. With the age-old wisdom of nature she instantly
knew the things of which they spoke would be sweeter than
any words ever exchanged between them. Her body was
already melting toward his as she imagined him walking
through the door to her. If his lips chased hers as Charles's
had, they would find willing captives tonight.

The throbbing inside her awakening body was so strong
now she pushed aside the hairbrush Rosie was wielding and
went to one of the carved posts of the bed, clinging to it
in a fever of longing. There before her spread the heavy
brocade counterpane and white pillows, telling her something that at once elated and shocked her. If she were to lie
in there with Hugo she would surely nestle within his arms
in only her nightgown, even reach up to touch his beloved
face with her fingertips in the darkness.

She swung around until her back was against the post,
unaware of her surroundings or of Rosie quietly hanging
her clothes away as her head tilted back in despair. That
revelation in the Mirror Room had merely hinted at her
feelings for Hugo. She had known only a fierce desire to be
in his company all the time and to be a happy partner in
everything he did. Now that she had begun to imagine his
taking Charles's place here it opened a floodgate of emotion.

Still uncertain of what her limbs and senses craved, she
recalled Hugo in his room at Wychbourne coming toward
her with blindfolded eyes and outstretched hands, laughing
with the triumph of capture. She had run from an instinct

her body recognized. If she had remained in her corner, what she now felt would have invaded her then. If she had remained in her corner . . . ah, Hugo, she cried silently across the miles that separated them, how foolish we were to run away. We can never escape it now.

A knock fell on the door, and Rosie hastened across to her mistress with a smile on her country-girl face.

"That'll be the major, ma'am," she giggled. "Let me arrange you against the pillows before I let him in."

Victoria climbed into the big bed and sat numbly while the maid twitched the curls into becoming positions and smoothed the counterpane free of wrinkles. The door opened, and she bobbed a curtsy as she went out past Charles, who was clad in a long crimson dressing gown.

Victoria was shaken at the sight of him. Only in this minute did it occur to her that he might behave as Hugo would in this situation. With a dry throat and frozen face she watched him scoop up Glencoe from the foot of the bed and drop her outside the door.

"I do not think we require company tonight," he said with a smile, closing the door and coming toward her. He sat on the edge of the bed and took her hands. "At last, my beloved. I do not know how I have waited for this moment." He bent his fair head over her fingers and kissed them one by one. "How cold you are. I cannot have that." Unknotting the cord of his dressing gown, he took it off and reached forward to place it around her shoulders.

The whole of Victoria's body was shaken by the pumping of her heart, and she could not help feeling the bed was moving with it, too. The sight of Charles in only a nightshirt hardly had time to fill her with acute embarrassment before he was wrapping her in his dressing gown, encompassing her with his arms. She was helpless, for his arms encircled her while his body began to press down on hers as he kissed her.

Charles was a well-built, powerful man, and she found it impossible to move—difficult to breathe, even. Desperately she tried to twist her mouth away from the moist lips beneath the mustache, but success only brought more frenzied searching of her eyes, ears and throat with his mouth. The ache in her thighs returned. Trembling more with nervousness than the cold, she brought up her hands to push him away, but they were caught and held back against the pillow while he continued to caress her smooth throat with a mouth grown eager.

"Victoria, you bring me a sweetness I have never before tasted," he breathed against her shoulder. "You fill me with the desire of a dozen men, and we shall have sons. What sons we shall have!"

She lay still holding herself rigid against the cold that reached into every nerve and fiber. So this was it! Only a few short hours after the ceremony she was expected to fulfill her part of the bargain. So soon after becoming his wife he was demanding the reward for giving her his noble name and its accompanying wealth. She had not expected it so soon, and she could not refuse. He had every right to expect from her something she hardly knew how to do—yet do it she must.

He had lifted his head enough to look into her wide darkened eyes. That intensity she had seen in his was there now, stronger than ever.

"I want you, Victoria. No man ever wanted you as I do. Have you seen it in my eyes? Have you guessed?"

She took a deep breath and summoned up all her courage. "Yes," she said as calmly as she could. "I know what it is you want, Charles."

He caught his breath. "You do?"

She nodded against the pillow. "I . . . I will show you my ankles, if that is what you wish."

For a few seconds he looked at her with hungry, dazed delight, as if he could not believe such erotic innocence could be his fortune, then he stood and flung back the bedclothes with an exultant laugh. It happened so suddenly, Victoria's new-found courage began to evaporate. When Charles began covering her feet and ankles with tiny kisses it fled.

Her nightgown was no longer adequate. A great deal more than her ankles began to feel soft caresses. A hand reached her knee and began seeking higher as his fingers stroked her smooth skin. She gave a small cry and scrambled from the bed in a panic, to stand holding the bedpost tightly. Remembering those stories about theaters where officers went to see the ankles and knees of common actresses, she felt Charles had forgotten where he was.

He was beside her in an instant, prying her fingers from their hold and urging her back to the bed.

"Come, my dearest, there is no need for such teasing."

"No, Charles," she cried shakily. "I do not care for it."

"Then I shall teach you to care for it," he whispered, pulling her to him and sinking his teeth gently into the softness of her neck.

She struggled. "Please. Charles, please do not treat me in this manner. I am not an actress, I am your wife."

Her struggles only deafened him to her pleas. "And you must be my wife. I will show you how to please me." He made her walk across the candelabra, his arms tightly around her. "I know what it is, my sweet love. You wish the room were darker. Some cannot relax if it is too bright." He blew out the candles, leaving only one faint flame, then swung her up in his arms to carry her back to the bed.

There was no more thought in her head now of her duty to the noble house of Stanford. Charles had suddenly become a menacing stranger, and she was terrified of him. Every ounce of her energy was engaged in a battle against him. She cried aloud when he pulled the nightgown from her shoulders and begged him to recover his senses, but he only heightened his assault. He seemed to have lost all control of reason as he whispered of delights that would be hers very soon.

He silenced her cries with his mouth, he suppressed her struggles with his strength, he forced her to accept the passion he could hold back no longer. Victoria was conscious only of blackness, fear and utter humiliation. The nightgown had gone completely, leaving her shamefully uncovered. Her head was spinning from the shock of feeling his hands exploring her body. Her heart was full of the horror of his inexplicable madness.

Just as she felt it was impossible to stand any more, her body was subjected to a tearing pain that surpassed any she had ever known, and Charles gave a sharp cry that matched her own. In the minutes that followed, her feverish brain could think only of getting away from the torment he inflicted on her, wondering wildly where she could hide so that he would not find her again. Where she could hide so that no one would ever find her again. Where she could hide that would cover up her humiliation.

Gradually Charles relaxed his hold on her and rolled away, so that she was free except for an arm covered with thick hair that lay across her breast and made her skin creep. For a short while she lay hardly daring to breathe, then, when he appeared to be sleeping, edged from the bed and seized up the counterpane to cover her burning body. She had reached the center of the room when Charles said thickly, "Where are you going, Victoria?"

Unable to move or speak, she remained where she was, clutching the brocade cover and shivering from head to foot. She heard the rustle of bedclothes as he got up.

"You cannot go anywhere wrapped in a bed cover, my dearest," said the hateful silken voice. "Besides, you look far more beautiful unadorned. Come here to me. Our wedding night is yet only half over."

She was vaguely aware of his unclothed body in the candlelight as he came toward her before she surrendered to the oblivion of darkness and slipped to the floor.

The Stanfords returned to Brighton on a gusty April day that sent the sea crashing over the promenade in white-edged rolls of gray-green water. The house Charles had rented in Brunswick Square was eminently suited to a man of his standing, its elegant interior lending itself to entertainment on a select but generous scale and the stables big enough for the new residents by dint of the fact that three of the major's horses were kept at barracks. Renata, the black mare Victoria had found waiting for her at Brennen Lodge as a wedding present, was stabled at the house with the charger, Caliban.

Delightful though the house was, Victoria was imprisoned in it for a week after their arrival, as the dreadful weather continued to rage. The bride would normally have received callers as soon as she took up residence, but, although Colonel Rayne and Lieutenant-Colonel Hallett, the second-in-command, braved the elements out of courtesy, the fainter-hearted females would not put the toe of a satin slipper outside the front door when the elements were all trying to outdo each other.

Victoria welcomed their absence. She did not wish for
company. An attack of influenza in the Castledon household mercifully relieved her of the obligation to drive out
there, so she spent each day in the blessed interior of her
own house with Glencoe as her one source of comfort. She
felt ill and exhausted, desiring only to curl up with the
puppy on her lap until the click of the door told her
Charles had returned and she must begin the duties of marriage once more. During that time in Brennen Lodge she
had considered each day as it came; now she was in Brighton she forced herself to face the prospect of an entire
week. Later, it might be possible to think about a whole
month.

Her belief that Charles had been attacked by a vicious
form of madness on their wedding night proved wrong.
When she recovered to find herself back in the double bed,
he had explained that a woman's first experience of her
husband was sometimes a little painful, but it was never so
again. He had then repeated the entire terrible ritual. By
morning she had been made to understand that one of the
duties of a wife was to give her husband the pleasure he
demanded; if she was to bear him a son it was necessary to
consummate the marriage.

As time went by, the mirror showed a pale gaunt face
and lifeless eyes. Charles's confident expectation that she
would find ecstasy in the nightly union of their bodies
planted another fear into a mind already fermenting with
confused thought. Could she be suffering from some abnor-
mality that made her different from others? Was she a failure
as a wife? Would Charles be forced to abandon her for another? Would she be branded in the eyes of the world as one
of those unfortunate creatures to be found behind barred
windows in gray fortresses?

Desperate though this idea might be, it was impossible to
banish the fear she now had of her husband. Since they had
been in their new home, however, she had tried to appear
bright in his company and to endure his attentions without
tears or struggles. As she watched the wind swirling the
smoke from chimneys and the rain chasing across her windows, she hugged Glencoe and allowed herself to contemplate the coming seven days as another milestone to be
passed.

On the eighth day the sun came out with springtime surprise, and the wind died away to leave the seaside town sparkling like the blue English Channel. Victoria waited for Charles to leave, then went to her room for a shawl.

"Rosie, we shall take Glencoe for a short walk," she said. "This sunshine is not to be resisted."

"Yes, ma'am," replied the maid, glad of a chance to go out. A month at Brennan Lodge and a week in the continued gloom here at Brighton had lowered her own spirits. Looking after a bride was not the joyful task she had anticipated. Mrs. Stanford was no longer the laughing girl she had been at Wychbourne, and the major appeared remarkably short-tempered these days.

They set out, with Glencoe trotting happily between them, but Victoria insisted on turning away from the popular walking places and following a road that led away from the sea.

"Ma'am, suppose we get lost?" wailed Rosie, disappointed at not seeing the promenade.

"We shall inquire our direction" was the lifeless reply. "I do not wish to meet all the world and his wife. We shall pursue this pathway to its end, then see where we shall go."

They walked for ten minutes, smiling at gentlemen who raised their hats and nodding their bonnets to the ladies who cared to notice them. The area they entered was genteel but not the hub of society smartness that Brunswick Square represented. The houses were very pretty, however, and Victoria occupied herself by noting the gay colors of the front doors. Here was a blue one, there a green. The road bent in a curve and they followed it with interest.

A few yards ahead, Victoria saw a military man descending the steps of a house with a gay yellow door. His uniform proclaimed him as an officer of Charles's regiment, and she slowed her steps. She did not wish to encounter anyone she knew. He reached the pavement and turned to wave gaily to someone at the window before starting to untie his horse. Then something made him look up, and she caught her breath.

"*Victoria!*" He said her name in an incredulous voice, half beneath his breath, and hurried forward, his horse forgotten. "My God, whatever is wrong?"

She was completely overcome. Her legs began to crum-

ple beneath her. Longing to turn and run, she could only
remain where she was as he came up to her and put an
arm around her waist as support.

"You are ill. How fortunate that I am here. Come inside
to my friends where you can rest and recover." Over her
shoulder he told the maid with sharp authority, "Take the
dog back. I will escort Mrs. Stanford to her home when she
has recovered." He bent his head to the wilting girl, finding
it difficult to control the steadiness of his voice. "Can you
manage to climb these few steps?"

She nodded, feeling her eyes fill with tears. Why, oh why
had she not walked in any direction but this one? She had
known it would be painful each time they met, but this was
her final humiliation. What would he think to see her looking so pale and lifeless? Where had all her courage gone
that she should collapse at the sight of him? He was a man
and would guess what ailed her. In that moment she
wished the earth would swallow her up.

Letty opened the door herself and Hugo led Victoria
through to the parlor, knowing if he ceased to support her
she would fall. He settled her in a chair before the fire.
Letty offered a vinaigrette, but Hugo from his squatting position said, "I think a noggin of brandy would be more
useful, Jack. She is about to pass out."

The fiery liquid was poured, and he urged her to drink
it, his hand over hers on the glass. Several sips passed her
lips at his persuasion, but as his eyes dwelt on her face the
fury inside him mounted to explosive proportions.

"Should I fetch a doctor?" asked Jack in some anxiety.

"No, I think not," Hugo replied. He could guess only too
well what had brought about such a drastic change in this
young girl and was filled with throbbing, blood-red impotent pain. Charles had always been inflexible. His understanding of sensitive creatures was limited to the "whip and
spur" method of persuasion. A child of not yet eighteen
would not have the sophistication his brother was used to
expect in his women, but, dear God, whatever had he done
to reduce her to a state of near collapse?

Letty brought a rug to wrap around the shivering girl,
and when Hugo took it with a quick upward glance at her,
she saw in his face the answer to something that had puzzled her for three months. It shocked her—not because a

man should be in love with his brother's wife but because of the magnitude of that love. Jack adored her, but he had never been driven to such desperate emotion, because everything had happily conspired to bring them together.

She put her hand on Hugo's shoulder. "Let me attend her. Another woman is a greater comfort at such a time."

He nodded and stood up. "Victoria, may I introduce Mrs. Letty Markham? I think you have already met her husband. He is with the regiment." He turned to Letty. "Victoria is my brother's wife."

She knelt down beside the chair. "Please drink a little more brandy, Mrs. Stanford. It is doing you so much good."

Jack offered Hugo a draught of spirits. "How fortunate that you were there as she passed, old fellow. Shall I send a servant for the major?"

"No" was the lightning answer. "No . . . need to alarm him. When she has recovered I shall escort her to her house." He tossed back the drink in one movement.

Jack looked past his friend to where his wife was persuading Victoria to sit up to gain full benefit from the fire. "She does look dashed ill, Hugo. Are you certain we should not call a doctor?"

"For God's sake, Jack, leave it alone!" flared Hugo. "I have already stated that I shall cope with it in the best way."

Jack looked considerably surprised. "Sorry. I was only trying to be helpful."

Within a short time Victoria was composed enough to apologize for putting them all to so much trouble.

"Not at all, ma'am," Jack assured her. "We are only thankful you were near friends when faintness overcame you. Hugo could not have paid us a visit at a more opportune time."

"We have met before, Mr. Markham—last summer at the military review on the Downs. You spoke of Hugo with great enthusiasm, I remember. You also had a very beautiful chestnut mare that I much admired."

He smiled. "I still have her. If you intend attending the cavalry races next week you will see her in action . . . and if the results show the usual winner I shall *not* be speaking of Hugo with enthusiasm."

Letty took the empty glass from Victoria and sat on the fender seat beside her. "Gentlemen are so loyal to each other, are they not? Jack and Hugo vie constantly for racing honors and Hugo invariably wins, yet if they were two women one would not now be speaking to the other out of pique."

Victoria looked at the pretty brown-haired girl in surprise. "I never thought I'd hear another woman make such a remark, Mrs. Markham. It is so true, of course."

"And thankfully so," declared Jack with a wicked grin. "If ladies were not forever falling out with each other they would not turn to us for consolation."

"Would they not?" asked Letty with suspicion. "How many ladies have you consoled recently?"

He held up a protesting hand. "None, my dear . . . but did I not discover Hugo patting *your* hand in commiseration last week because you had broken the glass epergne?"

"No. He was patting my hand in commiseration because you had not bought me another," she told him cheekily.

"So much for that loyalty of which you spoke," declared Jack. "He did not offer to make you a gift of one, although I am completely out of funds."

"For the simple reason that I am also out of funds." Hugo realized his friends were allowing Victoria to relax while the attention was taken from her, and he could have kissed Letty for her shrewdness. He went on. "What I win at the races next week will go a long way toward improving the state of my finances."

"Mrs. Stanford," complained Jack, "are you certain I spoke of him with great enthusiasm?"

She managed a faint smile. "Quite sure. Perhaps you were in better funds when he was away in Vienna."

"*I* certainly was," said Hugo. "The Austrians are very hospitable. Their cavalry regiments are full of princes and counts who do nothing by halves."

"I should hope not, old fellow. It is of no use *half* killing an enemy."

"Or *half* winning a race, as you are bound to do next week," countered Hugo.

"Gentlemen, please," implored Letty. "Mrs. Stanford will be reporting to her husband that there is dissension among the junior officers. Neither of you can afford to displease the colonel any further."

Hugo smiled at Victoria, but there was an element of darkness in it.

"It is not the colonel we have to please. Victoria is to become the patroness of the regiment when she is Lady Blythe. It is to her we must cast our eyes for approval."

A tiny hint of color crept into the girl's cheeks at the reference to something so personal between them. "I see now, sir, why you are being so solicitous today," she managed to reply. "It is all for your own advantage."

Jack laughed and clapped his friend on the back. "It is the first train back to Vienna for you, my friend. You are found out!"

Letty had just had another shock. Victoria Stanford was as desperately in love with her brother-in-law as he was with her. What a terrible predicament to be in! Her soft heart ached for them. Was the major aware of the situation? she wondered. No wonder Hugo had left Wychbourne with such haste!

They chatted for ten more minutes before Letty suggested Victoria might like to retire to the bedroom to tidy herself before returning. Victoria liked this girl very much indeed. She made no gushing apologies for the smallness of her house because she was in no way ashamed of it. There was something of Aunt Sophy's honesty about Letty Markham that appealed to Victoria. There was also an enviable relationship between the Markhams and Hugo that reminded her of how she had been all last summer with the love of her family and young men like Harry Edmunds to provide laughter and youthful freedom of spirits. The pomp and dignity of Wychbourne had been unknown then . . . and so had Charles's brand of love.

Jack insisted on Hugo taking Victoria home in their gig, and when they took their leave the grateful girl thanked them and begged Letty to call on her.

"I should be very pleased to do so," replied Letty politely.

"Soon, I hope?"

Letty gave Jack a quick glance. The wife of an impoverished lieutenant did not make casual social calls on the major's lady, especially when the major was next in line for a title. But Jack gave a barely perceptible nod, and Hugo encouraged her by adding, "Since you are both so well attuned over your opinions of ladies who constantly fall out through the pique, I challenge you to prove you are exceptions."

Letty laughed. "The challenge is accepted. May I call on Tuesday, Mrs. Stanford?"

Victoria nodded. "I shall look forward to your company. And if we *should* fall out at any time, I vow I shall not let either of these gentlemen know of it."

The relaxed atmosphere vanished the minute they set off in the gig, each being too aware of the other in the confines of the small carriage. They traveled for some minutes in silence until Hugo said, "I regret not having called on you since your return. Duty has kept me overoccupied this week."

She dared not look at him. "I understand. I . . . I must apologize for . . ."

"No, Victoria," he said swiftly. "Never apologize for anything to me. There is no need."

Concentration was needed to negotiate a bend until the horse was trotting along to Brunswick Square on high-stepping hooves.

"I am glad you asked Letty Markham to call on you. She is a very worthwhile person who has been a good friend to me—they both have." He glanced quickly at the pale profile beneath the bonnet, and his anger flared anew. "I think you need a friend, Victoria, and Letty will answer the need." God knows it cannot be me, he added silently.

CHAPTER SIX

Charles Stanford sat through the court-martial hardly listening to the evidence given in military staccatos. It was only too obvious the trooper was guilty; the trial was a formality. The fellow was a drunken insubordinate bastard at the best of times, and Charles was quite ready to give him the maximum penalty of fifty lashes. Such summary judgment was easy; the case of his wife was less easy to dismiss.

Victoria was tormenting him by day and night. At thirty-eight he had had vast experience with women, yet where his wife was concerned nothing went according to plan. The junior officers had probably raised their eyebrows and muttered about buying a child bride with a title, but Victoria had so captivated him with her fresh beauty and innocent brand of frankness he would have used anything to win her. That very youth still subjugated him, despite everything.

After five and a half weeks she had still not learned to surrender willingly, but the very uniqueness of her reaction only made her even more exciting to him. He was used to courtesans who would oblige a man in any way he wished; Victoria's opposition heightened his pleasure, much as he tried not to admit it. On their wedding night, her absurdly martyred offer to let him see her ankles so affected him it halved his age and doubled his virility, and the impetus had not slackened since. His brief determination to break her vanished beneath the revelation he was still loath to acknowledge—that taking her against her will was the most exciting sexual experience he had ever had.

But lately the blush had gone from her cheeks, and those large candid eyes had grown dark with mistrust, yet, God help him, even her wariness stirred his senses. The oblique edge of sensuality he experienced in performing the daily courtesies, knowing she was nervous of him, was something he shied from facing, yet it was there and too strong for him to resist. He might be ashamed of what he was doing, but he could not bring himself to stop. Small wonder his wife occupied more of his thoughts than a mere shilling-a-day trooper during that tedious court-martial.

The flogging duly awarded, the officers packed away their files and repaired to the mess. The relaxation after a boring duty brought a certain heartiness that helped Charles forget his uneasy problem, and he was laughing carelessly with a senior captain when Hugo burst into the room. His brother came straight across to him, so it was with mild curiosity that he turned to greet him, the smile lingering on his face.

"A word with you, if you please, Charles," said Hugo.

"Is it important, old fellow?"

"Yes." The affirmative was as brisk and cool as the nod Hugo gave by way of greeting to the captain standing there. "Will you excuse us, Fanshawe?"

As Captain Fanshawe strolled away, glass in hand, Charles said, "You look damned hot under the collar, Hugo. What has happened to fire you up this time?"

"Nothing of which you would not approve, Charles, since it concerns you."

Charles narrowed his eyes in sudden speculation through the smoke of the cigar he was smoking. Hugo was alight with real anger, and his manner was aggressive— challenging, almost.

"Whatever can I have done to arouse your formidable temper? I thought you were on late stable duty today?" He leaned an elbow casually on the mantle as he waited for the explanation.

"I have just left Victoria at your home whence I delivered her after she had recovered from a fainting fit outside Markham's house. It was fortunate that I was there to assist her."

Charles straightened. "Fainting fit?"

"I am sure even you have heard of such a thing, Charles." Hugo's hostility was scarcely veiled.

Charles tilted his chin upward in an unconscious gesture. "Are you saying she fell to the ground in the street?"

"Fortunately, I reached her in time to prevent such a thing happening and escorted her inside, where Markham and his wife did all they could for her."

"What was my wife doing outside Markham's house?"

Hugo flung out a hand. "Dammit, Charles, does it matter *why* she was there? Do you not care that she was taken ill?"

The major stiffened and placed his glass carefully on the table beside him. "When you get heated you always jump to hasty conclusions, Hugo. To feel concern does not necessarily oblige one to lose control of rational behavior. I am merely trying to glean all the facts. You have, after all, assured me that Victoria has recovered and returned to our home."

Hugo began shaking with his anger. "My God, you are damned cool! Victoria is your *wife*. Is your first instinct not to go to her as fast as possible?"

"Do not raise your voice, man. My wife's health need not concern every member of the mess," snapped Charles.

"I grant you that, but I would suggest it should concern *you* a great deal more than it appears to."

"And it seems to concern *you* a great deal more than it ought."

Hugo turned a deep red. "What the devil do you mean by that?" he demanded hotly.

Heads were beginning to turn in their direction. Though Charles's reply was hushed it did not lose its effect.

"Victoria is *my* wife. I will be obliged if you will leave me to behave as I think fit." He stubbed out the cigar with unnecessary violence. "I must thank you for doing what any passer-by would have done . . . but Victoria does not need a champion, Hugo."

He made to leave, but Hugo gripped his arm fiercely. "I do not think you know what Victoria needs."

Charles looked pointedly at his own arm where the long fingers held it. "This display highlights your immaturity, Hugo. God knows, we have been treated to far too much of it of late."

His brother's icy calm fell on Hugo's anger like a sudden shower, making him realize how far he had allowed his emotions to carry him along the path to self-betrayal. His hand dropped from Charles's sleeve. He had no right to question a man's treatment of his wife. Worse, he had no right to feel as he did about a woman who belonged to someone else. Vaguely aware of eyes watching them over

the shoulders of others, he said stiffly, "I am sorry,
Charles."

The major gave a thin smile. "Another apology! I suppose you did see a doctor before you went to Vienna?"

"I believe I complied with all your requests in return for
my reinstatement to the regiment" was the formal reply,
before Hugo turned and left the mess, his blue pelisse
swinging from his shoulders.

Charles excused himself from further duty that day and
called for his horse, but his mood was more thoughtful
than anxious as he rode back to his wife. An unpleasant
and chilling suspicion was beginning to bloom from the
seed of a deeply buried whisper he had first heard at
Christmas. Leaping pictures of Victoria bending over Hugo
to show him the boyhood toys she hung on the tree; of her
kneeling in a spread of silk skirts at his feet while her busy
hands tore the wrappings from his presents; of her ridiculous drooling over the puppy he had given her—all these
reminded him of his own pique at the attention she had
given his brother. Surely he had only wanted every ounce
of her sweet vivacity for himself. He had not believed his
anger was for any other reason, had he?

Slowing Caliban to a walk while he questioned himself,
Charles remembered Victoria's enthusiasm over the times
she had spent reading to Hugo and his brother's improved
morale once she began visiting his room. It was only natural that company should cheer him, and who could fail to
enjoy his wife's happy chatter? The thought worming its
way into his mind was ridiculous! Good God, Hugo was
his brother, a man of honor and loyalty, a man he would
trust with his life.

Nevertheless, he rode past his house and around the
square once more, loath to break off his introspection.
Honor and loyalty he would not deny, but Hugo was a
man—a human male—and would have been particularly
susceptible to feminine gentleness during his blindness . . .
and Victoria was too young to realize the potency of her
appeal. His throat began to tighten. Could such a thing
have happened before his eyes without his recognizing it? If
it had, how far had it gone?

Like a sword that comes through the darkness with the
hiss of metal slicing the air, the true reason for Hugo's de-

parture from Wychbourne slashed at him, never to be dismissed. To see Victoria after two weeks of dark enchantment with her would be more than Hugo could bear. He *had* run from the enemy, but Charity Verewood was not the woman from whom he had fled. That scene half an hour ago proved what little use fleeing had been. His brother was firmly caught in the coils of worship like most of the junior officers, but he would have to learn to control the state and Charles was in a position to ensure that he did so.

When Charles summoned a doctor that afternoon, Victoria was thrown into the greatest agitation, and the shrewd little man had no hesitation in ordering two weeks' rest in bed. It was not uncommon for brides to be reduced to such a state by selfish husbands, so he left Charles in no doubt that he meant *complete* rest and emphasized his point by declaring he would call again at the end of that time, when he was persuaded the patient's health would be vastly improved.

Victoria was not aware of her reprieve until three days had passed with Charles behaving in his most solicitous manner. By the end of the week the color was creeping back into her cheeks and some of her spirit was returning. Her time was much occupied by visitors. The Castledons came frequently, her cousins full of youthful gossip and breathless questions about her new life, which obliged the bride continually to ask the Lord's forgiveness after they had left.

Letty Markham was the patient's favorite visitor, for she told Victoria all the regimental gossip, including the outcome of the races, most of which Hugo had won quite easily. Since then, an exciting challenge had been issued by one Count Albrecht, captain of Austrian Hussars, to match himself against any rider the British cavalry cared to name, and Hugo had been selected to meet it. The Count had come to England with General Redvers and his staff, so Hugo already knew the man and was familiar with his riding skill. "Neck or nothing" was the general opinion of the Austrian's methods, Letty told her.

"But Hugo will outdistance him easily," she added with confidence.

"Is he *such* a good rider?" asked Victoria.

"Have you never seen him on a horse?" Letty was surprised.

"No. At Wychbourne he was tied to a chair for two weeks, then duty claimed him."

"Of course," said Letty tactfully. "Then you must accompany your husband to Chobham for the event, where you will see for yourself. The entire regiment will be turning out to support our rider. The race is fixed for the tenth of May."

Victoria's eyes grew wistful. "I shall do all I can to persuade Charles to take me. I should so much like to be there."

The result of the "prestige race" was a close but stylish win for the British cavalry that heaped more laurels on Hugo as an outstanding horseman, but Victoria was not destined to witness his success.

The doctor returned at the end of two weeks and gave a satisfied nod on seeing her. "Splendid, splendid! You have been the perfect patient, Mrs. Stanford. Now, let me have a look at you and ask a few further questions."

Fifteen minutes later he went out to Charles, leaving Victoria stunned and overjoyed. The nightmare of social disgrace and the specter of gray fortresses fled before the gnowledge of her own excitement. The Blythes *must* now consider her of the greatest importance, and Charles would surely view her as the perfect wife.

She could well have been the queen whose name she bore when he came to her after hearing the news. There was that same triumphant superlative of physical attributes that had struck her after their wedding as he approached the bed. Without a word he took her in his arms and held her as if she were the most precious thing in his life. It astounded her to mark the glint of dampness in his eyes when he held her away and said huskily, "I had not dared hope for this so soon. No man could have a more beautiful wife. The child she produces will be perfect." He raised her hands to his lips. "I mean to take the greatest care of you. The very best of everything will hardly be good enough for the mother of my child. You must rest and keep tranquil; visitors will be restricted to those who will not excite you. We cannot afford to run the slightest risk."

"Charles, Dr. Lawton says it is a perfectly natural condition that does not require me to remain in bed any longer," she protested. "Will you not take me for a drive this afternoon? I am so bored with this room."

He shook his head gently. "It will not do for you to expose yourself to the treacherous May winds. Later on, perhaps, when the sun grows a little warmer." He got up, filled with restless excitement. "Lawson estimates that he will be born just after Christmas. We shall go up to Wychbourne at the beginning of December. It is as well I put in hand the redecoration of the nursery wing." He struck the palm of his hand with his fist. "By George, my father will rejoice at this news . . . and Mama also."

In a fit of rebellion she said, "Why can I not have the child here in my own house? Buckinghamshire is so bleak in December."

He gave her a patient look. "The Stanford heir must be born at Wychbourne, my love. They always are."

The relationship between them improved, for Charles was so careful for his child, his love-making became more gentle and less frequent, and it was not long before Victoria learned to escape it by inventing a headache or a bout of sickness. With that powerful weapon in her hands she regained her looks and confidence, although each day brought the hope of seeing Hugo, and each day it was dashed.

Charles cherished her beyond the dreams of any woman. He brought her flowers, chocolates, trinkets—even an ermine cape—but he would not escort her to Chobham for the famous race. Neither did he invite Hugo to the house, and she knew he would not come unasked. They gave a dinner party for the married officers that excluded Hugo because he was single; they entertained Charles's friends and Hugo was not asked because Charles maintained he would feel out of place among so many senior officers. They were all invited to the Castledons', but Captain Esterly was put on unexpected guard duty at the Royal Pavilion on the very night of the dinner party.

Several calls on Letty Markham failed to coincide with one from Hugo, and daily walks brought no glimpse of him. Just when it seemed her only chance would be on her

eighteenth birthday two weeks later, Charles brought home
news that threw her into something near despondency.

"I dislike disappointing you, my dearest, for you have
been looking forward to your birthday party, but I have to
tell you that one of the guests will be unable to be present."

"Oh?" She grew suddenly still.

"There has been further trouble in Ireland—riots and
other kinds of violence—and the regiment was ordered to
send a squadron immediately to reinforce the small garrison we already have there. Hugo departs with them tonight."

"Hugo does not command a squadron. He is only a very
junior captain."

He raised his eyebrows. "How well informed you are on
the details of the regiment, my dear. You will be an asset
to me in the years to come."

"But why has Hugo been sent?" she persisted.

"He is a very promising officer, and this is a wonderful
opportunity for him to take command." He gave a light
laugh. "Hugo has always been such a bloodthirsty fellow.
He will be in his element putting down rioting peasants."

"Is there not some danger in the duty?" she asked, wondering desperately how her husband could have found out
the secret they had tried to hide.

"Certainly there is danger . . . but Hugo will thrive on
it. Colonel Rayne felt it would be his chance to show what
he can do under stress."

As a final test of her suspicions she said, "Could you not
have persuaded the colonel to send someone else, Charles?"

His smile faded. "Why? Hugo is always saber-rattling.
Let him put his theories into practice. They are only Irish
peasants, my dear, and my brother is a soldier by profession. Do you not have confidence in his ability to command?"

Hugo's banishment—for she could think of it in no other
way—heralded the end of Victoria's short period of peace.
Several weeks later the pretended headaches and sickness
became reality and, as her pregnancy progressed, plagued
her more and more. To add to her depression, Letty Markham was called away in the middle of the summer to tend
her papa during a serious illness, and Aunt Almeira was
thrown into feverish entertaining, caused by the double en-

gagement of Lavinia and Charlotte, who were, naturally, her first concern.

Feeling suddenly desperately alone with Charles, who was growing more and more anxious over her as time went on, she read the newspapers every day for any word on the riots in Ireland. The original outbreak had been put down, but the extra troops were to remain to keep the peace. There seemed no likelihood of Hugo returning to Brighton that year.

In September, Victoria had a short spell of improved health. Then she caught a chill that sapped her strength so severely that Charles decided she needed the fresh air of the country and not the damp seaside atmosphere. Nothing could persuade him to change his mind: He would take her to Wychbourne as soon as she was fit to travel.

In the middle of October they went up to Buckinghamshire in the family carriage that had been sent down to Brighton. An outbreak of cholera in London, plus his wife's dislike of trains, had dictated Charles's choice of a means of travel, but Victoria's heart sank as each milestone passed the window. Charles found it necessary to harangue the coachman most of the way in a most irritating fashion. To add to that, the backache that plagued Victoria so often these days made the long drive interminable.

On arrival this time she was only too glad to be allowed to go straight to her room to rest. Since Charles was only staying over the weekend, she asked to occupy her usual apartments rather than Charles's own suite, which was heavily furnished and on the north side of the house overlooking the orchards. He gave his consent, feeling that it was wise to bow to her whims when possible, and she slept in the familiar bed for most of the afternoon before waking at dusk when the haunting half-light beguiled her for a moment into thinking it was another time, another year.

Thinking the reunion with Charles's parents would be most pleasant, under the circumstances, Victoria soon found her mistake when dinner began. It reminded her of the first one she had eaten in this house—for she found herself being discussed once more as if she were not there. Aunt Sophy could not join them due to a chill, but Victoria was the only one who missed her company. Once again, they all sat a dozen yards apart around the long table in a room that grew progressively colder as the long meal went on.

The one topic of conversation was the coming child. Lady Blythe began with the arrangements that had been made for the christening to be conducted in the private chapel, then went into great detail about the repair of the christening robe to be worn by the boy. That subject led to talk of the cradle being made in the village by a craftsman who had supplied cribs for all the notable Buckinghamshire families over the past five decades.

"Do you mean Monk, Mama?" asked Charles.

"Naturally. Who else would do for *our* child but the master craftsman? I have also placed an order for a rocking horse. No, my dear, do not look at me like that," she cooed at her son. "Your old horse will not do for him. It has never been safe since Hugo broke its back legs. We cannot have your son risking a fall like his."

Lord Blyth chuckled. "It is not likely, Agnes. Hugo was eighteen when he broke that horse. He was standing on it while trying to catch a young owl that had flown into the nursery." He turned to Charles. "Do you remember the occasion, my boy? The owl flew out unscathed, but Hugo fell and cracked a rib. Ha, he always was one to get into scrapes. If your little lad turns out like him you are in for some anxious moments."

"I cannot think why he should favor Hugo when he is Charles's son," said Lady Blythe crossly. "You say some singularly foolish things at times, Augustus. Now, where was I? Oh, yes. I have made inquiries about a wet nurse should one be necessary, and I think we shall have a choice of two. Charity Verewood tells me Mrs. Crawley is expecting her fifth child in December, and so is Mrs. Bates. In that dear girl's opinion there is some doubt about the survival of both the babes, and she should know because the rector has been delivering baskets of eggs every week to help nourish the mothers." She gave a theatrical sigh. "The Lord has his reasons for everything he does. We have instructed Sir Christopher Mills to be in attendance during the lying-in, of course. Charity vows there is no better man in the whole of the country. Her cousin would have no other, and one must say her three babes are a credit to her."

Victoria felt her anger bubbling upward like a boiling potion in a cauldron. All three—her husband included—sat discussing the forthcoming heir, the symbol of their continued superiority, the living proof of the virile and noble line of Stanford, as though the woman who had conceived the child and now carried it inside her had had nothing to do with the affair. She knew only too well what she had gone through to provide Charles with his heart's desire, what she must still endure to bring that desire into the world, yet they spoke as if they had created a miracle between them.

She sat watching as they talked and saw them for what they were. A selfish, overindulged, eccentric woman, a man so steeped in wealth he worried himself to distraction over the flooding of a few pounds' worth of meadow, and a younger man so conscious of his heritage it ruled his every thought. She was an outsider and would remain so even while producing others of their kind.

"I must show you the list of names we have drawn up, Charles," continued Lady Blythe. "Your papa and I went through the first one and struck out half as completely unsuitable. The remainder are family names, or those given to royalty over the past five hundred years. You cannot go wrong with any of those, although I must tell you we favor Henry, John, Richard, William and George. Any three of those would be ideal."

"Unless the child is a girl," said Victoria in a tight, angry voice.

Lady Blythe looked up in surprise, as if she had not realized anyone else was in the room. "I did not consider it necessary to make a list against that possibility."

"I suppose not, when the undoubted choice would be *Charity*." She rose to her feet and faced them, trembling with overwrought emotion. "I am surprised Miss Verewood has not been consulted on *every* aspect of my forthcoming child. Her views are plainly considered to be of more value than mine. How unfortunate that it was not *she* that Charles chose as his wife. I am certain it would not occur to *her* to produce a girl to upset your plans."

The major rose quickly to his feet. "Victoria, there is no need for this."

"There is every need. It will explain why I am retiring to my room—not that I will be missed."

She had heard of women "sweeping out" of a room and knew she had done just that. Charles caught up with her and walked by her side in silence until they reached the apartment, where he dismissed Rosie.

"I shall not apologize, Charles," she told him quickly, on a rising note. "I have never seen a more marked display of bad manners."

He nodded curtly. "As you wish. It is perfectly plain that you are overtired and not responsible for your actions. It is bad for you to become so upset, my dear. Please sit in this chair until you are calmer."

He took her hands to lead her to the chair, but she gripped them tightly. "Let me return to Brighton with you, Charles. I have my cousins to visit and the ladies of the regiment. Please, do not leave me here alone. It is so lonely and quiet with no companions to help me pass the days."

"Hush," he said, sitting her firmly in the chair. "Tonight's display emphasizes your need for a place like Wychbourne. Visitors overtire you, walks by the sea expose you to injurious damp breezes and talk of the regiment taxes your brain with things suited only for gentlemen. Your friendship with Mrs. Markham has encouraged your obsession with such things. They are not subjects for gentlewomen . . . or the mother of my son."

"*Our* son," she corrected sharply. "I do not see why you discourage my interest in the regiment. If you become its colonel I shall do a great deal better than that silly, empty-headed Mrs. Rayne, who thinks of nothing but new carriages and her pale-faced daughter. She might have breeding, but she certainly lacks brains. Her knowledge of regimental affairs is abysmal. Besides, I happen to think he is right."

"Who is right, my dear?"

She caught up her words before they fell on his ears and said instead, "General Redvers. He does not believe in letting the Army stagnate."

Charles sighed heavily. "My poor child, no wonder you have reached such a state of exhaustion and bewilderment." He bent and kissed the top of her curls gently. "Stop filling your lovely head with such nonsense and concentrate on your first duty, which is to *our* son." He tipped

up her chin with tender strength. "Do you not understand
how important he is to me?"

She gave in with listless resignation. "It would be an im-
becile who did not, Charles."

The major returned to Brighton, satisfied that his wife
was in good hands. By the end of two weeks Victoria was
at her wits' end to know how she would last until Charles
came again. Lady Blythe had retired into her apartments to
recover from the shock of Victoria's outburst, and Lord
Blythe appeared awkward in the company of a young
woman so visibly swollen and ungainly. After a few days
Victoria decided it would be better for both of them if she
took her meals in her room, and it was as well she did, for
the sickness that had been with her so often returned in
double measure, and the ache in her back was hardly ever
absent.

Miserable and unwell, she was thrown a great deal into
the company of Aunt Sophy, who was the only person with
whom she felt at ease. Many afternoons found her with the
old lady, and they sat before the fire as she spoke about her
youthful adventures that sounded quite scandalous to the
modern girl. But sometimes she would relate tales about
the two boys, Charles and Hugo. Then, Victoria would
treasure every word as she built up a picture of a laughing,
volatile brown-haired boy who had brought as much love
to the family who took him in as they had given in return.

Victoria could not know her face took on a glow, and
her eyes became softly dark whenever they spoke of Hugo,
nor that the old lady had known from the beginning that
Charles had not captured the heart of the young girl he
brought here as his bride. So it was a surprise, when the
cracked old voice shouted at its usual volume, "If this child
is a boy, do not let Charles have sole charge of his upbringing, my dear. He has an excellent character, no one would
deny, but a man with no faults can be extremely dull at
times. I almost pledged myself to a man like Charles, until
I was introduced to a wild young man who never gave me
a minute's peace of mind. Our marriage was short—he was
killed in a duel—and I so regret not having had his son."

Her bright eyes searched Victoria's face and saw the answer she knew would be there. "If your child is a daughter,

let her follow her heart, whatever the outcome. Too many
females allow their lives to be planned by something called
'society.' Those few who do not suffer from it for the rest of
their lives—but they have their moment of freedom that no
one can take from them."

Victoria scribbled furiously on the pad and held it out
with a smile.

Aunt Sophy laughed and patted the girl's hand. "I shall
be honored if you call her Sophy, my dear. She might end
up like me—deaf as a post and a bit eccentric—but she
will have had a full life and some treasured memories." Her
laughter died. "You are not much more than a child yourself, Victoria. Listen to the words of an old woman. You
have the capacity to achieve much in your lifetime. Pray do
not let them prevent you from doing so."

Victoria left Aunt Sophy that afternoon full of thought
and new resolution. When she returned to Brighton she
would redouble her interest in the regiment and try to understand the drill movements better. She would ride more
and perfect her horsemanship. Her present condition had
prevented any riding for several months and she had
missed it. Her declaration to become patroness of the regiment one day might not be so foolish. Why should she not?
If Hugo could pursue his ambition with relentless purpose,
so could she.

Before any of this could come about, however, she must
somehow get through the next two months at Wychbourne
and produce the child she carried, whether it was destined
to wear a coronet or not. At this moment she felt the sickness and aching drag of pregnancy that seemed never to go
these days. Her stomach was so swollen it made movement
labored and difficult, the unaccustomed weight somehow
adding matching weight to her thoughts and spirits. Without Aunt Sophy she did not know how she would reach the
time of fulfillment with any kind of composure.

For a short moment dread rose in her overwhelmingly,
and she stopped to lean against the wall in sudden faintness. If this child were a girl, the whole dreadful procedure
would begin again . . . and go on being repeated until the
required male child arrived. She put her fingers to her temples. The noble Stanfords might be praying for a boy, but
none as ardently as she.

It was growing dim in the house now, and she could hear the servants moving about putting a light to all the lamp brackets in the long corridors. The sound of steps approaching from around the corner made her pull herself together and continue toward her room. It would not do to be seen quaking this way by one of the servants. The future Lady Blythe must keep up appearances at all costs.

The man came around the corner quickly and had covered several yards before he knew she was there. When he did the shock acted quicker on his brain than on his feet, which carried him several paces nearer, even after a great sigh had escaped him. Victoria was not aware of the moment her feet stopped—of the moment when everything stopped. Every breath, every heartbeat, every drop of blood in her veins, every muscle, every blink of her eyelids froze as though she had been petrified in a spell cast by the vivid blue-green eyes that met hers.

The seconds ticked past as they stood six feet away from each other, unable to speak. She saw the pain in his face as his glance flew straight to the skirt that spread out over the swell of his brother's child. Outwardly, he was a paladin in a proud uniform; inwardly, he became unmanned and defenseless. Those eyes came up to search her face with hungry anguish, and still they said nothing to each other. An eternity stretched between them as battles were fought and lost, knights jousted and fell, kingdoms crumbled beneath the invader. She answered his pain with her own as her cheeks grew wet, but no words seemed adequate to repulse the force that stormed their defenses.

She had faced him on that evening here at Wychbourne with innocent wonderment; she had stood helpless beside him as she pledged her life to Charles; she had almost collapsed at his feet after her honeymoon—but this was worse, far worse. Her swollen body must mock at him, must seem like her final sword thrust. Charles's seal of ownership was there for all the world to see.

"Why . . . *why* did no one tell me?" he said painfully, still rooted to the spot.

There was no answer she could give. It had not occurred to her that Charles and the Markhams had had their own reasons for keeping him in ignorance.

He took a step backward. "Have no fear. I shall leave at once."

"No!" The cry echoed all she had ever felt in her life. "If you go this time I shall feel completely deserted." Her hands flew up to cover her treacherous lips.

He was beside her immediately. "I thought it was what you would wish me to do. Forgive me." He put an arm around her shoulders and led her to an alcove seat nearby. "Forgive me," he said again. "The shock of coming upon you when I thought you were so far away has affected my wits."

She said through fingers that covered her face, "I thought you were in Ireland. It was as if your spirit walked along this corridor in some ghostly prank."

He could see she was trembling. Taking her fingers in his, he gently drew her hands away from her face. "I am no ghost, Victoria, merely a captain of Hussars on leave from a lonely and isolated garrison."

She gazed up at him, knowing she should tell him to go. "You have no idea how lonely I have been since Charles brought me here. Aunt Sophy has been my salvation."

"As she has been mine, at times. What are you doing here alone?"

Her eyes evaded his. "I have been unwell. Charles felt the sea air did me no good. I am to remain here until . . ."

His thoughts were more collected now. "I have this minute arrived and was on my way to pay my respects to Mama." He dropped the fingers he still held. "When I have done that duty I should be pleased to entertain you and my great-aunt to tea." He paused. "But only if you would like it, Victoria."

"I think you need not ask me that," she said in an attempt at casualness. That was all that could be between them. "Will there be muffins?"

His eyes still held remnants of shock. "I would not dare to ask you if there were not muffins." He helped her to her feet and walked back along the corridor beside her until they reached her apartments.

Still seeking reassurance, she said, "Hugo, you will stay?"

He nodded slowly. "Until the end of my leave . . . or until you tell me I must go."

Wychbourne was a different place with Hugo within its walls. Lady Blythe emerged from her room, Lord Blythe managed to forget his flooded meadow for a while and Victoria saw something of the affection between the Stanfords and the man they had chosen to be their son. It was a different bond from the one they had with Charles, but it was none the less stout for being self-made.

Victoria felt relaxed and happy. The only tense moment came when she bade her parents-in-law good night, and Hugo was obliged to escort her to her room. They set off along the familiar corridors, striving to think of light conversation until Victoria said, "Have you brought Stokes with you this time?"

It was the perfect subject, for Hugo was able to speak on it for most of the way. "You have touched upon the reason for my taking leave at this particular time. Stokes has just taken a wife." His slow smile broke out. "Yes, poor Stokes met his match in the village in which we are garrisoned. She is not Irish, however, but an English girl employed by a traveling circus. I defy you to guess her duties." His sideways glance brought a happy shake of her head. "She rode the elephants. There . . . I knew you would find it amusing, and so did I, much to Stokes's annoyance. I have seen the fellow take a huff before, but never the great gathering-up of his dignity that greeted my mirth at his request to marry an elephant girl." He slipped his hand beneath her elbow to assist her up the stairs. "But marry her he did, and her name is on the roll-call."

"But not her elephants, I trust?"

He laughed. "God forbid! Five horses and two dogs are enough to take around with one. Here is another amusing thing. Stokes would get no dinner if he did not cook it himself, for Mrs. Stokes knows nothing of housewifery."

She smiled. "Poor Stokes. What possessed him to take such a wife?"

He looked down at her with a wicked expression on his laughing face. "Wait until you see Mrs. Stokes. You will get the answer to that question and understand why Stokes sleeps with his rifle handy."

They arrived at her door and all humor fled. Suddenly, good night was the most difficult thing to say. Hugo avoided it altogether.

"Do you still play chess, Victoria?"

"Yes, although I have not done so for some time."

"I challenge you to a game tomorrow."

"Perhaps I shall play better with only my own pieces on which to concentrate."

"Ah, but I shall also play better with my eyes uncovered." He gave a mock bow. "Until tomorrow, when may the best one win, ma'am." He turned and walked away, but she watched until he turned the corner.

They played chess on the neutral ground of the conservatory, where Hugo won all the contests and replied, to her protest that he might have allowed her victory just once, that overwhelming defeat was the best spur for renewed effort.

"Once a man begins to feel sympathy for his enemy he will soon find himself the loser, my dear Victoria. It is one of the first rules of battle."

She put her head on one side and studied him. "You are still studying the tactics of warfare in this time of peace?"

He frowned. "Victoria, have you not heard of the declaration of war between Russia and Turkey only this week?"

"I must own to have taken no account of the outside world since leaving Brighton. It is all too easy in a place such as Wychbourne to forget that the world moves on outside its walls."

He looked very serious. "Victoria, the Russians have been gathering for an invasion of Turkey for more than two years, but the heads of our fighting forces have seen no reason for alarm. This is what I have been predicting."

"How does it affect us or our fighting forces? Russia is such a long way from England."

He shook his head sadly. "Oh, Victoria, Victoria, you echo the rest of the complacent ones! Let me explain. Russia has her eye on the Mediterranean route, but, in order to get her ships through from the brand-new naval fortress at Sebastapol, it is necessary to capture Constantinople. With that port taken from the Turks, the way would be open to the Balkans and Egypt. Now do you see how this outbreak of war up in the Balkans affects us? We *cannot* stand by while a poor nation like Turkey is swallowed up by the greed of a greater power. But how can we rush to Turkey's aid with an army that is half disbanded, completely out of date and lacking youthful vigorous leaders?"

"Are you saying we shall soon be at war?" she asked, appalled.

"We shall be obliged to make a show of strength—and that is just what we do not have. The signs have been there for anyone with sight to see, but of what use is a tiny army trained on the methods we used at Waterloo—nearly forty years ago? Why do you think I have been advocating reforms in cavalry tactics for so long? Come with me and I will demonstrate what I mean."

In the nursery, with toy soldiers spread upon the table, Hugo explained his theories to her and illustrated them with the tiny horsed men.

"I have employed these methods in Ireland with great success," he said. "General Redvers approves them, yet the majority of our military leaders believe that what was good enough to win the battle at Waterloo is good enough to win anything. They are wrong, Victoria." He straightened up. "Once, I believed that if a majority is in agreement, their opinion must be the right one . . . but I know I am right this time."

Loving him, longing to take his hands and tell him she believed in him, afraid of what he was telling her, she could only stand across the table gazing at the soldiers formed up on its surface. "If there is a war, will the regiment be called upon?"

"I should hope so." The quick reply was spoken before he thought, and the next minute he apologized. "Forgive me. War is not a subject I should bother you with at such a time." His embarrassment over her condition was plain. "Coming direct from the unrest in Ireland, I suppose such things fill my mind too much." He smiled gently. "You are a very sympathetic listener to a man who is known as a saber-rattler."

"Was it dangerous?" she asked in sudden anxiety.

"For the poor devils in the mob, it was. We were able to charge into them with swords drawn; they were on foot with cruder weapons. Even so, they dragged two of my men from their horses and kicked them unconscious. Mob violence is not pleasant to witness, Victoria."

She picked up a toy soldier and studied it. "Thank you for assuming I shall not faint away upon hearing such things."

"It did not occur to me. You will not, I trust?"

She smiled and shook her head. "I have never seen you ride, Hugo. I feel my education is not complete. Will you not give me a demonstration of your equestrian skill? Think of the honor to have the best cavalryman in England giving one a personal display."

"Are you laughing at me, Victoria?"

"I could never do that."

For a long moment the tension was there again.

"Tomorrow, if it is fine, I intend to ride across the park. If you care to watch from your window I shall do my best not to disappoint you," he said with a bow.

The day was so warm Victoria insisted on accompanying Hugo to the stables, then walked beside him as he led his latest hunter around to the paddock that led to the deer park. She wore a warm shawl over her woolen dress, but Hugo, striding along beside her in breeches and brown plaid coat, was very concerned with finding her a seat sheltered from any sudden breezes.

"I declare, I had not thought you would ever behave in so foolishly cossetting a manner, Hugo," she laughed. "You will soon be as angelic as Miss Verewood."

To her surprise he did not join in her laughter.

"I am not certain you should be outside at all on a day like this," he muttered. "Mama will probably berate me if she hears of it. I know so little about . . ." he broke off, leaving the subject in the air.

It was the first time her condition had been mentioned between them, for although he had been solicitous and gentle, that was his natural manner. Now, Victoria grew shy and tongue-tied, and the silence was beginning to grow unnatural when the sound of a horse approaching made them both look up across the park. A female rider was approaching at the gallop, exhibiting her skill. She slowed to a trot at the paddock and came up to them knowing all attention was focused on her. The smart black habit and veiled hat suited the classic coldness of the girl's beauty.

"Captain Esterly, good morning. I see you were just setting out for Brankham Hall. How fortunate that we did not miss each other on the way. It was so lovely a morning I could not resist coming to meet you. I did not expect you yesterday, although in your letter you said you would call as soon as you arrived at Wychbourne."

Hugo took off his hat. "Good morning, Miss Verewood. It was good of you to ride over so soon. I had not meant my words to be taken as a summons, I assure you. It was simply that I felt eminently responsible, having advised you on the mare in the first place."

The doll-blue eyes grew even rounder. "You must not feel any sense of guilt. Please, do not. I would not have bought any horse without first asking your opinion, you know that, and I would not have mentioned it at all except that you asked in each of your letters and it did not seem possible to conceal the truth from you."

She sat stiffly erect, black skirts arranged over her legs so that only the foot of her tiny boot was visible. Looking up at her, Victoria saw her as the Virgin Huntress who hounded unsuspecting males to their deaths.

"Good morning, Miss Verewood," she said clearly.

Charity shifted her glance to the figure she could not have escaped seeing and affected surprise. "Good morning . . . oh, *good morning*, Mrs. Stanford. Please, please forgive me. I did not immediately recognize you." Her glance flickered over the pregnant girl. "You look so . . . my dear ma'am, no wonder you are so pale." She held out her arms for Hugo to lift her down and, when he had done so, stood very close to him, gazing up full of shocked concern. "Captain Esterly, how could you have acted in such an ill-advised manner?" She swung around to look at Victoria. "Believe me, I would have come to Wychbourne sooner had I known you were here and in need of feminine care. Please come inside at once. The time of year is treacherous for even those of us who . . ." she broke off delicately. "I dare not think what damage has already been done."

Victoria felt an arm go around her and begin to press her back the way she had come. Charity smelt of sweet lavender, pure and fresh, before it has been cut, beheaded and stuffed into little bags. The soft virtuous voice was insistent in her ear.

"I cannot believe Lady Blythe knew of this, for she would never have allowed it. It is the greatest pity Major Stanford cannot be here at this delicate time, but Captain Esterly cannot be blamed for ignorance in a matter that should not, after all, be his responsibility. I do feel you should not place such a burden upon him when you have Lady Blythe so anxious for your welfare." She urged Victoria along the path with great firmness and determination. "Captain Esterly has been in Ireland, where you cannot imagine the danger he has faced. No doubt he wishes to relax and follow his own desires for once. You cannot know what he has been through, or you would not load him with further responsibilities."

"It was a great deal worse for the rioters," said Victoria, bringing them both to a halt. "Hugo had a horse and a sword; they had only their fists and their feet. You see, I *do* know what he has been through, Miss Verewood." She skillfully twisted free from the encircling arm. "Strange as it might seem to you, I am not ill. This is a perfectly natural condition that allows one to walk abroad in the warm sunshine without loading anyone with responsibility or casting Lady Blythe into a fit of palpitations. A stroll in the garden will not hasten my union with the Lord, you know."

Charity cluck-clucked with her tongue. "It is one of the worst symptoms when a female grows fractious, ma'am. I insist . . ."

"You will insist on nothing," cried Victoria hotly, knowing the morning had been completely spoiled. "When you are in a position to speak from experience, your arguments might hold more authority. I suggest you wait until you are in that happy position."

Charity blanched with anger but knew she could win this battle with one swift blow. Turning on her heel, she hurried back to Hugo, where a tirade of fierce words sent him in Victoria's direction.

"I think perhaps you should go in," he said earnestly. "Miss Verewood does know a lot about such things, and I was unhappy about your welfare all along."

Her flashing eyes scalded him with dark fire. "I think you might have championed me after I saved you from

broth and potions last year. I will go, Hugo, only because
you will be made to look foolish if I defy you. As for Miss
Verewood, it is my earnest hope that her horse tosses her
into the village pond so that she emerges dripping and covered with weed right beneath your eyes. My only regret
will be that she is probably stuffed so full of her own reme-
dies she will not catch so much as a sniffle."

Her quick retreat into the house prevented her from
seeing the surprise on Hugo's face turn into delighted
laughter that still filled him as he galloped off with his
neighbor.

As soon as they were distant figures Victoria reemerged
and sat on the seat Hugo had chosen for an hour, determined to have the last word. At the end of it she was cold
and unhappy, but Charity Verewood had been defied.

She remained in her room for the rest of the day, working on a water color of Glencoe, and decided to eat dinner
alone. Her low spirits would not lift, and the ache in her
back suggested it had been foolish to remain so long in the
garden that morning after all.

Soon after breakfast the following day, Rosie came into
the bedroom bearing a note, and Victoria opened it swiftly.

*I trust your absence is to punish me for my deplorable
lack of support yesterday, not because you are feeling
unwell. I have to drive into Mexford today. Mama is
agreeable to your accompanying me as the weather is
so warm, and the journey is through quiet lanes.
Please come. If I am still in disgrace you have my
permission not to speak to me the whole journey long.
I leave at eleven A.M.*

H.

She crumpled the note with a swift surge of happiness.
"Rosie, I shall wear my lavender velvet with ribbon ruch-
ing and the cashmere shawl. Be quick. I leave at eleven."

Hugo was waiting for her with his hand outstretched,
and she took the note with great curiosity.

*In case we are not speaking, this is just to say good
morning. I am glad you decided to come.*

She looked up at him and gave a shaky laugh. "You are absurd."

His smile cut at her, as usual. "I am also relieved. Come, let us start right away." He took her arm. "Have you visited Mexford before?"

"No, but I would visit anywhere on a day like today. Is it the start of an Indian summer, do you suppose?"

"I hope so," he replied as he handed her into the rig and jumped up beside her to take the reins. "There is really nothing as beautiful as Buckinghamshire in early autumn. You should see the golden beeches along Mexford Heights. They have been the subject for many artists." A quick flick of the wrist set the horse off at a comfortable trot, and he glanced down at her. "If you are not too tired we could return that way. It adds a few miles to the journey but is worth the effort."

"Let us do it, by all means. I know so little of the area. Last December was hardly fit for outings."

"So you told me at the time."

"Yes, yes . . . of course." Her bonnet hid her profile from him as she watched the cylindrical privets lining the drive as they passed them one by one. "Why are you going to Mexford?"

"My father wishes me to collect an inlaid ivory box from the estate of Sir Gervaise Garland. His possessions were sold last month. My father's manager bid on his behalf, but heavy rains have prevented the collection of the box. It is intended for a Christmas present for Mama."

"How pleased Lady Blythe will be."

"Yes." He negotiated a bend. "Why do you not call her Mama?"

"She has never yet invited me to do so. However, I imagine Miss Verewood will call her so with no difficulty when the time comes."

He looked away and said nothing.

"Thank you for asking me to accompany you," she said several minutes later. "We should accept the beauty the Lord gives us while it is there. Suppose it should never come again?"

"That is a strange remark for one so young. It would come better from Aunt Sophy."

A faint smile touched her lips. "Letty Markham will not

draw her curtains against the sunlight lest the Almighty take it away altogether. Do you not believe in the wrath of God, Hugo?"

He avoided an answer. "You have found a friend in Letty?"

"She is the only female who earns my respect. Her honesty and humor are such as one normally finds only in gentlemen. I am sorry to say it, but ladies more often than not arouse in me the desire to shake them until their empty heads rattle."

He whistled through his teeth. "You do not mince words, Victoria. Do you make no allowance for the poor creatures?"

"Not when I see them become wax dolls like the Massingham sisters, or fall into the vapors because someone at a ball is wearing ribbons in exactly the same shade. And—you must forgive my saying it, Hugo—I cannot admire the woman who invents a delicate constitution when things do not go her way." She glanced up quickly at him. "How will your mama cope with her sons going to war when the time comes?"

He let out his breath in a long sigh. "I . . . it appears I should not have spoken on such a subject to you the other day, for Miss Verewood gave me a severe lecture on agitating you unnecessarily. Please forget all that nonsense of which I spoke. I am inclined to get carried away. It is quite likely I exaggerated the situation." He gave her a rueful smile. "You must be more severe with me and not encourage unseemly conversation between a gentleman and a lady who is far too kind-hearted."

She grew pink. "What nonsense! I declare you are growing more like Charles every day. I had always thought you had more . . ." She broke off painfully, knowing they were treading on dangerous ground. They drove in strained silence until they reached their destination.

They collected the ivory box from the late Sir Gervaise's estate manager, drank a glass of wine with him while he showed them some of the other treasures waiting for collection, then set off on the return journey along the top of Mexford Heights, after Hugo had checked that Victoria was not feeling too tired. In fact, the deep ache in her back had returned, but it was such a beautiful day she did not wish to miss the sight of the trees in all their autumnal splendor. They branched off up the side of the hill soon after they left the village and were soon several hundred feet up with a view across Mexford toward Brankham Hall on a faraway hill and Wychbourne lying serene in the midst of extensive parklands.

For a while both looked down on their corner of a green and pleasant island, lost in their own thoughts, until Hugo broke the silence by saying, "In March, I advised Miss Verewood on the purchase of a mare. In my opinion it was an excellent animal, but it became sick soon afterward and went lame. She wrote to tell me of it. I was obliged to answer."

She grew still. "You are not obliged to tell me this."

"I was angry to think I had been duped into believing the animal sound," he went on, as if she had not spoken, "and felt an obligation to recompense Miss Verewood, who had acted on my word. When I was granted leave, I wrote to tell her that I would look into the matter as soon as I arrived. That is why she rode across yesterday."

"I see." The pain in her back was growing worse— beyond easing by shifting in her seat. She did not wish to hear about Charity Verewood. That she would capture Hugo in the end was beyond doubt, and the whole family would rejoice.

"The outcome of my investigation satisfied my conscience and resulted in the dismissal of a stable boy at Brankham Hall. Unfortunately, the poor beast is ruined forever by his bad treatment, and the Verewoods have lost money on the deal. I am sorry for it, but it was not my fault, as it turns out."

They were well up on Mexford Heights now and veering away from Wychbourne onto the straight Roman road that stretched for a mile and a half until the long slow drop down to the east of their destination. For a short while Victoria forgot her discomfort in the beauty of the long lines of flaming autumn beeches that stretched along each side of the road in seas of gold, crimson, brown and russet touched by the sun and set afire with color that must fill the artist with a longing to achieve such aesthetic perfection.

"I did not exaggerate, Victoria. Do you agree that it is a

splendid and moving sight?" he asked, turning to her with pleasure on his face.

She nodded, robbed of speech by a violent gripping of her stomach that stood perspiration on her forehead and set wings of fear beating in her temples.

"Is anything wrong?" he asked quickly.

"No, I think the wine did not agree with me, that is all," she managed to say. "It does not spoil my enjoyment of the ride. I think I shall never forget this morning up here. How I should love to do a water color of those trees."

"Perhaps you will, later on," he said with a slight frown. "Does wine usually disagree with you, Victoria?"

"Many things do, at present. It is quite usual, I assure you."

Ten minutes later, another spasm as violent as the first told her the pain was not the mild indigestion she felt from time to time. The pain in her back had grown infinitely worse and she longed to ease it by lying flat. Wychbourne suddenly seemed a long way away. A third onslaught on her body forced her teeth into her bottom lip to silence a cry that would have betrayed her.

Hugo had urged the horses on. The trees were flashing past like gilded ribbons and all she could do was to hold the sides of the gig and pray for a sight of Wychbourne's ancient walls. All too soon her courage failed, when a sharp thrust more frightening than any other made her grip Hugo's arm.

"You must get me home as quickly as you can," she gasped. "I feel most dreadfully ill."

The only time Hugo had experienced real fear was during those two weeks of blindness; even then, it had been tempered by hope. The fear that caught at his throat at the sight of Victoria's face was total.

"Is there anything I can do?" he asked desperately, easing the reins. "Tell me what I must do."

"Take me home. Just take me home as fast as you can. I feel sure it is the child. Hurry, Hugo."

Dear God, he thought. It will be almost three-quarters of an hour before we reach Wychbourne, whether I go on or turn back. Why did I bring her up here? God Almighty, *why?*

"Hugo!" Her hand gripped his arm as another spasm shook her. "Help me. Please get me home."

The cry brought him an instant idea hatched from desperation and confronted him with a decision he had not time to consider. He stopped the gig, took off his coat to spread on the floor of the small carriage and made Victoria lie on it while he padded her around with two rugs. Then, the decision taken, rightly or wrongly, he told her gently what he intended doing.

"It will take almost an hour if I use the road we're on— and then only if we go at the gallop. I mean to cut across country. It will be difficult and I shall have to take it slowly, but it can be done and will get us to Wychbourne in twenty minutes. You will feel that I am not going with all speed, but this way you will reach help as swiftly as it is possible to do so. Trust me, Victoria."

"Do you think I would not?" she said faintly.

He reflected wildly that his own trust must be put in the horse, for if the beast shied from the task, not all the skill in the world would be of any use. Standing on the seat and pulling gently on the reins, he coaxed the animal to leave the road and set off down the grassy slope. The horse did not take kindly to the idea of a wide-open hillside after the clear-cut road he had been following. Hugo longed for one of his own horses instead of a plodding old gelding who was past adapting to new ways but did not allow his anxiety to pass to the horse. Talking in quiet encouragement, he eased the animal downward in a steady pace, knowing the first onset of panic could cause it to bolt and throw them all down the hill.

Now he had taken the decision, Hugo wasted no time wondering whether he had been right, but it occurred to him they might be facing the wrath of God Victoria had mentioned a short while ago. Deep inside him, was the conviction that something terrible was about to happen. He felt it in the accelerating wheels of the gig; in the white stones that jolted them whenever he could not avoid passing over them; in the tenseness of his legs as they braced against the wooden seat and in the rhythmic pumping of blood through his brain. He heard it in the panting of the horse as his nostrils flared nervously; he heard it in every gasp from the girl on the floor; in his own tightly con-

trolled instructions to the horse; and in the stillness of the
deserted hillside.

Ahead was a wide swath of trees which must be crossed
before they reached the lower slopes. He knew of a path
that skirted a quarry but had ridden on it only once before.
Would it be wide enough for the gig? Dandy, the horse,
took exception to the solid block of tree trunks ahead and
tried to veer away from them. The carriage began to slip
sideways, and it took a strong arm to pull the horse around
to face what he dreaded with rolling eyes and high-stepping
hooves.

Hugo glanced quickly at Victoria and met large eyes that
asked questions he could not answer. He smiled a reassurance he did not feel. There was no time to soothe her fears;
at this moment it was more important to soothe Dandy.

"Come on, boy. It is only a few trees. You've seen trees
before," he said softly and drove him into the dark shadow
of the copse where the sun created pools of gilded haze as
it broke through the thinning autumn foliage. It was
hushed and still in there, so still that their quiet progress
through the deep spread of crackling leaves sounded like a
brace of Roman chariots.

He spotted the path almost immediately. It was the only
way they could traverse the copse, but it was damnably
narrow and a bare three feet from the edge of the quarry.
For a split second he hesitated, then guided his horse onto
it as Victoria moved convulsively at his feet. He had been
blessed with the eye and judgment of a natural horseman;
he must put them to the test now.

During the next six minutes he coaxed Dandy along that
path, inching past sections where the edge had been
washed into the quarry by earlier heavy rains. Sweat
damped his armpits and shoulders, and stood out on his
brow. At every shuddering breath from Victoria he redoub-
led his efforts. Faster. They must go faster. The beauties of
the copse went unseen. Variegated leaves against blue heavens; hoary crab apples, sweet chestnuts scattered on the
ground and bursting from their green cases; rambling black-
berries, blood-red in the sunshine; leaping squirrels; birds
scavenging in the damp bracken; and the sweet smell of
moist, rich earth were lost on Hugo as he made his painstak-

ing race against time, fighting the urge for speed with the iron hand of caution.

Then they were out onto the green slopes that led down into the farmlands. But the lower they traveled the damper it became and the more difficult it was to keep going. The wheels sank into the mud, dragging back on the shafts as Dandy tried to plod his way through the sticky patches. Another glance at Victoria showed Hugo the time for caution had passed. Her face was pinched with fear and as pale as a cameo. The time he had saved by coming down the hill was not nearly enough.

Driving Dandy was no use now. Leaping from the gig, Hugo squelched through the lush grass to take the horse's head. Foot by foot, he urged the beast forward, never once losing his temper with an animal that was doing his best and scrambling to the back whenever the wheels stuck to put his shoulder to the carriage. There was a driving urgency on him. He knew nothing of childbirth, but Victoria looked extremely ill and something told him it would be too late if he did not hurry.

At last they were beside the river where a narrow tow path provided firm footing again. The horse had caught some of the excitement and sensed that a great effort was demanded of him, for he responded to the light touch of the whip and his master's hoarse command, "Go like hell, boy!" The gig fairly raced over the path toward a farmyard through which it had to pass before reaching the road.

The farmer looked up in amazement to see the Blythes' gig hurtling along beside the stream. Where in perdition had it come from? The tow path went up only to the mill and ended in its yard. Captain Esterly looked like a wild banshee standing on the seat in his shirt sleeves yelling at him to open the gates. The gig was almost upon him before it dawned on him that if he didn't open the gates, the captain would drive right through them.

Hugo was about to pull Dandy to a halt when he saw the gates being unfastened. Thank God, he breathed, and flashed past the farmer calling, "Get Dr. Anson up to Wychbourne immediately. Hurry, man, hurry." He repeated the message to the farmhand, who held open the other gate and swung out of the farm approach onto the road. Here he gave Dandy his head until they curved into the drive of Wychbourne House and thundered up the graceful approach.

The horse was flecked with lather when they pulled up in a spray of gravel. Hugo leaped down and began lifting Victoria gently into his arms, wrapping the rugs around her as he did so. Her paleness terrified him, and so did her burning body. They exchanged looks that said everything they need not put into words. It was all there—the regrets, the apologies, the fears—and as he strode into the house shouting for a servant to gallop for the doctor, Hugo knew his intuition had been right. Something terrible *was* about to happen.

Servants were told to go and prepare Mrs. Stanford's maid and inform Lord and Lady Blythe that she had been taken ill. In a voice cracked with tension and shouting, he put the fear of God into everyone within range. They could only imagine there had been an accident, since Captain Esterly was coatless, sweating and covered in mud.

Hugo carried Victoria into her room and laid her on the bed, instructing Rosie to keep her mistress warm and to give her only water until the doctor arrived. He could do no more than squeeze Victoria's hand and assure her everything would be all right before tearing himself away, haunted by her pallor.

Desperation sent him running down the stairs, yelling for his horse to be saddled. Charles must be informed at once. Snatching up his coat from where it lay in the gig, he leaped into the saddle and set off like the wind for the telegraph office in Aylesbury. A servant could have gone, but he himself would get there quicker by galloping over the property of neighboring families who knew him. There was an anger inside him that had to find expression in violent physical action. When he got back, the doctor's gig was outside the front entrance. It was there all night.

It was impossible to go to bed. Lady Blythe retired in real distress, for once, but Hugo and Lord Blythe remained in the study before a log fire with a bottle of brandy to fortify them. All the afternoon and evening had been spent in the greatest anxiety. There was no doubt about a premature birth; it was simply a case of keeping mother and child alive. The doctor had confirmed to Hugo that time had been all-important in getting the patient to Wychbourne and clapped the young man on the back as he assured him he had done everything possible, under the circumstances, although he could not imagine how anyone could drive a gig down from Mexford Heights without overturning and crashing to the bottom.

Even so, Hugo tormented himself with blame. He should never have taken Victoria out in a gig in her condition. He should have listened to Charity Verewood the day before when she insisted that females in that condition should remain quietly in a room to retain a serene attitude of mind. Time after time he referred to the railway timetable that told him Charles could not possibly arrive until midmorning, and he strode up and down the study carpet until Lord Blythe said wearily, "When you have seen a little more of life you will learn to sit still when nothing can be gained by exhausting one's nervous energy, Hugo."

The young man turned a strained face toward his father. "No, sir. I think I shall never be like you and Charles. My temperament is too restless for that. How could I sit still when there is so much weighing on my conscience?"

"Nonsense, boy. You cannot be held responsible for the ways of nature—that is the job of the Almighty."

"But Victoria has done nothing to . . . why her?"

Lord Blythe stood up and went to warm his back at the fire. "That is a question you should never ask, for you will never stop. Why my brother? Why my infant daughter? Why your father? Why Victoria's young parents? The list is endless. The Lord has an overall plan and we cannot expect it to fit our especial requirements." He studied the young man he had chosen to rear. "He has been very good to you, Hugo. You have a fine manly body, a good deal of intelligence and considerable skill in your chosen field. You have wealth and breeding, and when I die my estate in Bedfordshire will be yours. There has to be a discount side."

"I will allow that," Hugo cried, "but why should Victoria pay it on my account?"

"I have a feeling it will be Charles who pays," said Lord Blythe quietly.

Hugo put his head in his hands, then looked up over the top of his fingers with bloodshot eyes. "Of all the people to cause it, it should be me!"

Lord Blythe walked across to the small table and picked up a decanter. "Have another glass of brandy, my boy, and try to relax."

The grandfather clock ticked loudly all through that long night, and Hugo found himself regulating his paces to the slow tick as he counted the minutes away. He had never before noticed how many inexplicable noises filled Wychbourne at the dead of night, nor how the wind whistled as it became trapped in a corner of the projecting wings.

Lord Blythe's eyelids drooped, and he slept while the oil lamps burned low, but Hugo relived the previous day in a hundred ways, each different from the actuality. He tried making bargains with God, then abandoned that for straight prayer. He vowed to put Victoria out of his mind; he swore to transfer to a regiment in India; he even wildly contemplated marriage with Charity Verewood as the only solution to his unhappy life. The night wore on minute by minute with no word from upstairs, and his torment continued.

At 4:30 A.M. a servant entered and said in a low voice that the doctor wished someone to go up. It did not occur to Hugo to wake his father. Taking the stairs three at a time, he arrived in Victoria's sitting room before the doctor was ready for him, and a tearful Rosie went into the bedroom to fetch him.

Dr. Anson was stout and bucolic, but one thing he did know about was midwifery. He had plenty of practice in his village, and there were few who could handle the situation better than he. His manners were rough, but a newborn child was safer in his hands than those of some specialists. Even so, he had a grave expression on his face as he came out to Hugo.

"I did my best, Captain Esterly. The child was a boy."

"*Was?*"

The doctor wagged his head. "Never had a chance. Much too soon, you know."

Hugo reeled. "And Mrs. Stanford?"

He shook his head again. "It's touch and go."

"Dear God!"

"Major Stanford has not yet arrived, I suppose?"

"No."

"Then I should like you to remain here in case you are

needed. She is very weak. It is not likely she would know you were not her husband in her last moments. I will call if she asks for someone."

"Is there no chance, man?" asked Hugo desperately.

Bushy eyebrows went up. "Dear me, yes. There is always a chance until the last one has gone."

Half an hour passed in dazed shock until Hugo was jolted out of it by the opening of the outer door to admit his brother. Charles was in uniform, his cloak thrown over his shoulders. He carried a riding whip, and his face was red from the night chill. He pulled up at the sight of the younger man.

"What in blazes are you doing here?"

"Anson asked me to wait nearby. No, Charles, I should not go in."

"Why?" The question was terse and hostile.

"He said he would call if someone was needed. Thank God you are here. I thought you could not arrive before eleven."

"I took the train to London the minute your message arrived, then hired a phaeton and drove through the night. Damn Anson! I have not galloped up here to be told he will call if I am needed. My wife and child are in there." He pushed past his brother and went into the bedroom.

Hugo felt suddenly beaten. He did not belong here. That bedroom door closed in his face told him the truth more cruelly than before. The corridors could easily be sinister at this hour, dimly lit and stretching forever, full of the ghosts of those who had walked along them. The Mirror Room was a small version of purgatory, with his own face accusing him from every direction like the demons of hell rising up in the faint light of one guttering lamp. He reached his sitting room and dismissed Dawkins, who had been waiting up for him.

"But, Captain Esterly, you have had no sleep," he protested.

"Get out, man," he said savagely. *"Get out!"*

"Yes, sir." The valet feared the worst had happened and, at once, relayed the news of Mrs. Stanford's death to those below stairs, whereupon the women burst into tears, and a faint glisten was to be seen on many a male cheek.

Dawn came up without shame. It proclaimed the joys of

living as if nothing had happened. The brown-haired man standing so silently watching it from his window found it incredible that a morning of such pure gilded beauty could follow last night. The growing light revealed the deer that had been there all the time—shy, gentle and innocent. The birds of the air burst into simultaneous song that told all those who heard it to rejoice in the sound. The gray walls of Wychbourne emerged out of the darkness for one more day; solid and impregnable, indifferent to the dramas played out within them. Life went on.

The door of his room opened and he turned quickly. Charles was standing there with a wild look in his blood-shot eyes. His face was white, jaw working with an enormous emotion as he faced his brother across the width of the room.

"I want you out of here by midday. If you were any other man I would kill you."

Hugo felt the world close in on him. *Dear God, forgive me.* He gripped the back of a chair as Charles went on. "You destroyed my son. From the moment you took Victoria off on one of your wild jaunts they stood no chance."

"I did all I could, I swear," said Hugo brokenly.

"All you could to ensure he would not survive."

"No . . . believe me. Charles, you are overwrought. You do not know what you are saying."

"I know the facts. My dead son lies out there to condemn you." He was fighting to control himself. "We are no longer brothers. You have betrayed every principle of brotherhood. I forbid you to have any further contact with my wife. There are to be no more dishonorable assignations behind my back."

Something inside Hugo flamed up like a rocket to burst inside his head. He had thought Victoria dead. Charles had flayed him with a tirade about the infant without giving him the news that delivered him from hell. Snatching up his riding crop, he took three strides across the room.

"I take that from no one, you damned . . ." He broke off abruptly as the bursting rocket fizzled out, realizing how far they had come in anger. He had been about to strike this man who had grown up with him in a bond closer than blood. He drew in his breath in a painful gasp as he lowered his arm.

"My God, Charles, where are we traveling?" he asked at last.

"You may travel where you please so long as you are out of this house by midday and never return to it."

Charles left his brother standing in the middle of the room as he strode out.

Victoria had slept for most of the day and would have gone on doing so if Dr. Anson had not arrived shortly before eight, still a very worried man. When his rumbling voice penetrated her slumbers it took an effort to open her eyes. The beautiful cessation of all feeling that had overtaken her was a state she was loath to give up, but he wished to probe her yet again and there was nothing to do but submit.

She knew the child was lost, but the knowledge left her indifferent. He had been created violently and had died the same way. Charles had done his duty by planting the seed; she had been expected to do hers by producing the finished product. The boy would then have become a symbol of a name and birthright, taken out of her hands so that he could, in his turn, fulfill his duty. How could there have been any love within her? How would there be for the next one, who would be created under similar violent conditions and even more anxiously snatched from her arms?

She gave a small cry, and Dr. Anson apologized. "Forgive me, Mrs. Stanford. You have been through quite enough of an ordeal. I shall leave you in peace now. Here is a sleeping powder. Your maid will give it to you after I have left." He tried to smile, but there was something in his face that prevented any comfort from reaching her. "You are a great deal more resilient than you look, ma'am. With rest and care we shall have you back to perfect health before Christmas." He snapped his bag shut and gathered up his jacket. "I will call again in the morning. Your husband is waiting in the sitting room. I wish to have a quick word with him before he comes in to bid you good night. Try to rest. Your recovery is in your own hands."

He went out and pulled the door to behind him. Rosie began straightening the bedclothes and tidying away the bowl of water and swabs the doctor had used. Victoria could hear male voices in low conversation outside and waited for Charles to come in to her. There was a vague memory floating in her head of her husband standing beside her at some time during the night, so they must have sent for him, but her most vivid recollection was of Hugo's anguished expression as he left her here. She longed to see him again, if only to blot out that memory. He must surely be smiling at the thought of her recovery.

The sound of voices outside ceased. The sitting-room door opened and closed, but Charles did not come in. She did not care. The numbness was wearing off. The probing had awakened throbbing pain which she was anxious to put to sleep again. There was nothing in the world she wanted more than to return to oblivion. All the ugly problems would start to crowd in on her soon enough. For now, they must allow her to hide from them beneath a layer of laudanum.

She asked Rosie to prepare the sleeping draught, and the girl had just gone through into her small closet when the door was pushed open to admit Charles. He came to stand at the foot of her bed, holding on to one of the posts. The arrogance in his stance had gone. The proud set of his shoulders had tilted downward as if under a heavy weight. Burning blue eyes appeared almost sunken into his gray face. He was a stranger.

"Have you any idea of what you have done?" he asked with difficulty, clutching the post for support. "You have not only killed my son, you have denied me the right to have one at all."

He did not shout or gesticulate; he did not lose control and curse her with a string of oaths. His very quietness was frightening.

"You would not give me love. You cannot give me a child. You are of no further use to me."

PART TWO

CHAPTER SEVEN

During the winter of 1853–54 the British government grew increasingly uneasy over the sudden conflict between Russia and Turkey. It had begun when Czar Nicholas demanded that the responsibility for the Church of the Holy Sepulchre in Jerusalem should be that of the monks of the Greek Orthodox Church rather than the Roman Catholic monks of French origin. Violent clashes between rival monks led to an ultimatum from Russia: Unless Nicholas. was obeyed, and further, unless he was proclaimed legitimate protector of the Orthodox Church throughout Turkey, Russia would use force.

In an ill-advised effort by France and Britain to calm the situation, the British fleet was sent to show the flag in the Dardanelles, a strategic passage. Nicholas countered by marching troops into the Turkish-held territories of Moldavia and Wallachia. The Anglo-French committee wavered and waited. At first, the Turks appeared well able to hold their own, until their entire fleet was destroyed in one attack—an act of war that aroused extraordinary fury among the allies.

In March 1854, Britain and France declared war on Russia in support of Turkey, and the British generals began looking for their army. It barely existed. What there was of it was completely inexperienced in battle and led by officers accustomed only to parading before the public in handsome uniforms that made them the darlings of the ladies.

Chosen to lead this army were elderly men in doubtful health, whose experience of warfare dated from the Napoleonic wars, when campaigns were fought in traditional style with gentlemanly courtesies on both sides. Even worse, the Commander of the Cavalry, Lord Lucan, had a long-standing feud with his brother-in-law, Lord Cardigan, who was chosen to lead the Light Cavalry. The latter, an infamous commanding officer generally hated by captains and subalterns on whom he waged perpetual war, was an eccentric and unreasonable man who pursued quarrels to ridiculous lengths and allowed them to govern all his actions. Any man who had once fallen foul of his lordship's temper was never likely to be forgotten, and the old quarrels were quickly revived. The Light Cavalry could not believe their ill-fortune in being given the Earl of Cardigan as commander but were ready to suffer such a burden for the chance of crossing swords with the enemy.

Rumors spread daily. Regiments waited jealously for sailing orders, but when the coveted sealed papers arrived, they were hard put to bring their numbers up to strength. A mad bout of recruiting and transferring began in order to muster a respectable force. The cavalry regiments had the additional problem of providing suitable mounts for their troopers and, since no one had heeded the warnings of officers like Hugo Esterly, had to accept the best animals from the considerably disgruntled regiments forced to remain in Britain, who considered it further insult to have to hand over their prime horses in exchange for a lot of broken-down hacks from those who were going off to fame and glory. They little realized the coming conflict was not going to be a mere show of strength.

All of a sudden, the subject of war and the inadequacy of the army had become a universal topic of conversation even among the gentle young creatures who were normally kept from anything unpleasant by their protective menfolk, and, on a day at the start of April, Victoria Stanford sat talking to her friend Letty Markham in the parlor of the little house with the yellow door.

"Two regiments of Dragoons have already begun preparations for sailing. We *must* soon receive orders, Letty, or I vow I shall start writing letters to some of those influential gentlemen who have been pleased to grace my dinner table these past few months. They were happy enough to pat my hand whenever the opportunity occurred, so I do not see why they should not pay for the privilege now."

Letty laughed. "Do not tell me you are prepared for intrigue, Victoria. Shall you be making secret visits to ministers, in carriages with drawn blinds, and become known as 'The lady in the black cloak'?"

"If the situation becomes desperate," Victoria replied, "although I would hesitate in some instances. Several el-

derly war horses of Charles's acquaintance believe they are
still in the first flush of youth, you know." She gripped her
hands tightly together. "They *must* send the Hussars. It is
such a fine regiment. Think of the honors to be added to an
already impressive record."

Letty smiled with real affection. "You truly count yourself as part of the regiment in a way I never shall. If they
are ordered to war I shall accompany Jack because I could
not bear to be parted from him, that is all." She looked up
as her maid entered with hot chocolate and little cakes.
"Put the tray there, Maisie."

When the girl had gone she poured chocolate for her
guest and offered the cakes. "Have you told the major of
your wish to travel with the regiment?"

Victoria nibbled her cake and shook her head. "I do not
anticipate things where my husband is concerned. If and
when the orders arrive will be the time to broach the subject. I am determined on going, Letty."

The other girl nodded. "I know and am thankful. It will
be good to know you are there, even if we are restricted to
nodding our bonnets at one another."

Victoria paused in the act of drinking and set her cup
onto its saucer again. "What a remarkable person you are,
my friend."

Letty shrugged her shoulders as she selected a cake.
"Then it is a great pity there are not a few more like me,
for it seems no more than common sense. Military protocol
has to be observed, and I would be a complete goose if I
did not realize that our friendship cannot be taken into
consideration on such occasions. There are those officers'
wives who firmly believe I am no more than a social
attention-seeker, but I do not give a fig for them. I value
our friendship, Victoria."

"Do I not know it." She looked at Letty thoughtfully.
"We have not fallen out these past nine months as the gentlemen predicted, have we?"

Letty shook her head, and Victoria went on, after a
slight hesitation. "Have you had any word from Ireland
recently?"

"Only that Hugo is beside himself with anger that we
find ourselves so unprepared at such a time."

"So I should imagine. He always maintained that we

should be ready for war, even in the midst of peace. It must be frustrating to be stranded in such an isolated spot when so much is happening."

Letty wiped her fingers on her napkin. "Jack says they will be brought back very soon. If the regiment is to go they will need every man and horse."

The faint color that touched Victoria's cheeks did not go unnoticed by her friend. Letty sighed inwardly. It was six months since Victoria had lost her child and nearly her own life, but, instead of the experience shattering her, it appeared to have given her strength and calmness of spirit that she had not had before. Letty was continually surprised at the change. The young girl had become a woman in so short a time. Letty could not help feeling there was something deeper behind it all.

Looking at her now as she sipped her chocolate, she saw a young woman dressed in expensive fashion who was, perhaps, even more beautiful for the sadness in her large eyes. She had found the answer to that sadness in social success. In those few months she had flung herself into the military life with great dedication, playing the part of Major's lady with such flair that she was already regarded as the toast of the regiment. The troops revered her, the subalterns adored her and the senior officers had become putty in her hands. Her popularity with the ladies of the regiment was not as unanimous, naturally, but some of the troopers' wives had reason to be thankful for her intervention on their behalf.

Mrs. Stanford was to be seen at parades and reviews mounted on her magnificent mare Renata and could always be found taking a morning ride on the Downs with an entourage of Hussar officers, if the major could not accompany her. As if this were not enough, the house in Brunswick Square had become the scene of dinner parties that had Brighton society by the ears. Other hostesses might have prouder ancestry, greater wealth or a more elite circle of friends, but Victoria Stanford could be relied upon to entertain her guests with refreshing novelty. In vain, her rivals tried to outdo her, little realizing it was her personality, not her hospitality, that was the core of her success.

Still, Letty sighed. Beneath her friend's new veneer of maturity lay an emotion that revealed itself now and again in unguarded moments. That she was still deeply in love with Hugo Esterly was plain, although he had been in Ireland for nine months where Victoria could not possibly have seen him. She saw through her friend's casual inquiries about him. What she did not know was the relationship between the major and his wife. Victoria would not talk about the two months she had spent at Wychbourne last autumn and spoke only of her husband in terms relative to the regiment or social activities.

Jack had told his wife Charles Stanford had become a more unapproachable man and was often to be seen with a glass in his hand, but added that forty was no age and everyone confidently expected Mrs. Stanford to be in a delicate condition again shortly. Letty was not convinced. Her own wish for a child had not yet been granted, and she could not believe it was simply a matter of forty being considered no age. Jack was only twenty-five.

Victoria broke Letty's train of thought by saying, "I met Mrs. Rayne yesterday while purchasing some muslin. What an exceedingly tiresome woman she is! In less than ten minutes I was given a catalogue of her domestic woes that began with the loss of a wheel on her outmoded carriage while she was returning from Sir Hubert Franklin's dreadfully overcrowded soiree and ended with the 'disgrace' of her daughter's attachment to an officer in the 44th—or is it the 54th?—Foot. My cousin, Charlotte's husband, is in that regiment and knows the young man well. An excellent officer with good prospects, he says. It is merely the fact of his family's being in commerce that turns the Raynes against him, you know." She put down her cup. "I feel very sorry for the girl. If her heart is set on him, of what use is it to tell her he will not do?" She looked away out of the window. "They already have orders to embark, you know. What if he should fall in battle?"

Letty gave the sensible answer. "Mrs. Rayne will say it was all for the best."

Victoria swung burning eyes back to meet her friend's cool green gaze. "Her daughter will never agree, nor forgive her." She sighed. "What creatures of manipulation we are, Letty. If you ever have a daughter, do not rely on me to help persuade her what is 'all for the best,' for I have never yet discovered for whom it turns out the best."

Letty laughed. "I shall remind you of that speech when

you forbid your own daughter to . . ." she broke off and
rose to her feet as the door opened to admit her husband.
"Jack, you are early!"

Jack Markham pulled his wife to him in a bear hug.
"The orders have come. We sail from Portsmouth in ten
days," he said in a voice vibrant with excitement. Then he
gave an exultant laugh. "Ha! They could not fight a war
without us. When the Russians hear *we* are on the way
they will relinquish all claims to Turkish territory. Letty,
think what a trip it will be for you. Can you be ready in
ten days, my love?"

Letty struggled free from his arms and said, "We have
Mrs. Stanford with us, Jack. What are you about?"

He immediately turned and bowed to Victoria with a
grin on his face. "Ma'am, forgive me. This news has robbed
me of my manners, but I promise you the entire regiment
is going wild with excitement. The colonel is counting
horses with breakneck speed, the regimental tailor has
locked himself in his workshop with bales of cloth, a cutler
has been engaged to sharpen all the swords we can muster,
saddles are being refurbished . . . and half the officers are
applying to get married." His ebullience made his voice
husky. "I have seen nothing like it before. Even old
Paddington-Smyth was heard to murmur that he was
dashed if he would not purchase a new pair of riding boots
for the occasion. *That* will tell you the extent of the jubila-
tion." He dropped into a chair and wiped his brow with the
back of his hand. "Gad, the next week or so is going to be
hectic. We are nowhere near full strength, even with Hugo's squadron ordered back to Brighton. The recruiting sergeants will be out in force from today."

"But Hugo once told me it takes a long time to train a
soldier," protested Victoria.

"And so it does," Jack agreed with a nod. "These new
fellows will have to be trained as we go along—especially if
they have never sat upon a horse in their miserable lives.
With luck, it will all be over before we need them, but
fighting for one's life is the most effective form of training
ever devised, you know." He gave a rich laugh.

It was a sign of the close friendship between Victoria and
the Markhams that he should discuss such things in her
presence, although the formal form of address was main-

tained between the youthful lieutenant and the wife of his major for reasons of protocol.

"Did you learn our destination, Mr. Markham?"

"No, ma'am. We are to march to Portsmouth on the twelfth to await transports . . . but it will be for the Balkans, there is no doubt. They say it is beautiful there in the summer." He got to his feet as Victoria made to leave. "Please, do not go on my account."

A smile crossed her face, suddenly grown pale. "If we are to sail in ten days there is much preparation to be done—the first part of which is to persuade my husband that I am indispensable to the regiment."

Brighton seemed a district of Paradise to Victoria as her carriage made its way through the streets to Brunswick Square. Hugo would be here in a few days. All she had to do now was fight for her place with the regiment when it left England—and fight she would with every weapon at her disposal. If she were left behind the only purpose left in her life would be gone.

In her agitation of spirits her mind flew back to the night Charles had learned she would never bear another child. It had been a turning point, Charles's words had burned through her as the minutes ticked away. She had pushed aside the sleeping draught with a cold hand so that she could think the better, and pain had washed over her body, heightening her complete humiliation. She had allowed herself to be used by them all.

It had started with Aunt Almeira persuading her that a girl could have no greater honor and happiness than an offer of marriage from a man like Charles Stanford. Lady Blythe had been insufferably rude under the guise of aristocratic eccentricity, yet she had made only a token stand against her. Why had she not asserted her right as the woman's successor? Oh, and why had she not laid the ghost of Charity Verewood once and for all?

Her fevered mind had dwelt on memories of her honeymoon that filled her with shame. Why had no one told her she must expect her husband to ask sacrifices of her—not that Charles had asked! Had she so little pride that he could reduce her to the role of chattel; had she so little character that his usage of her set her trembling with fear of him? Surely it was not the natural role of a woman to submit herself to such treatment at her husband's whim?

Then, when the desired result had been produced, she had been treated only as the impersonal machine designed to bring forth the long-awaited son. Charles had laden her with gifts, flowers and extravagant care, but not for love. With the child within her she had become an echo of his self-gratification. When his dream of an heir was smashed, he had cast her aside.

All through that terrible night she had faced those truths and had examined her own weakness. At eighteen, she had her life still to live; until Charles decided to be rid of her she was tied to him. Those were the facts: She must build a new life around them—but never, never, *never* would she humble herself before anyone again. His contemptuous dismissal of her had been her birth. She was now a person in her own right, the slave or machine of no one.

As the carriage neared her house, Victoria reflected that she had been true to her vow that night, but her greatest test was upon her. If Charles refused to take her to the Balkans with him she would be powerless. Not all her resolution would get her on the boat if her husband said no. Without the regiment and Letty she would have nothing. In this moment Charles had her in the palm of his hand once more, and she already knew she would sink to begging for his permission, if it became necessary. If he refused she might never see Hugo again.

When Charles arrived late for luncheon he found a composed young woman in yellow silk awaiting him, and Victoria was careful to give no hint of the turmoil inside her as she listened to his concise report of the situation.

"I fear the time I can spend with you during the coming days will be curtailed," he said. "We could not have foreseen this situation, or Rayne would never have allowed the remounts to fall so far behind in standard. Who would have believed we would be plunged into war so suddenly?"

"Who indeed?" she said softly, thinking of one who had.

"We have only enough fit animals to mount half the regiment. Our equipment is not all that could be desired either." He leaned back and dabbed at his mustache with his napkin. "Apart from those problems I have to provide myself with campaign equipment, tent and two more horses. Ten days until we sail—it will not be half long enough for all that has to be done."

"I am sorry, Charles, and quite understand that you will be busy." She tried to keep her voice steady and push down the sudden lightning resurgence of the fear she once had of him, now she was in his hands once again. "Ten days will not be long enough for anyone, but I pity most those troopers who have wives and children they must leave behind with little or no support while they are away." She allowed a short pause before saying, "I understand that officers may take their wives. I was this morning with Mrs. Markham when her husband arrived with the news. She is this moment preparing for her journey."

"No doubt," said Charles airily. "Markham might find it deuced expensive to take her, but even more so to leave her behind. She is rather fond of bonnets, I hear. There will be none where we are going—that is one economy of which he can be certain."

Victoria saw the subject slipping away and said quickly, "I do not think a shortage of bonnets would weigh with her . . . with *any* woman who accompanied her husband. Her only wish would be to see to his comfort and ease his hardship."

"Oh?" Up went his eyebrows, and she saw the coldness of his eyes. "In what way would she comfort and console him, Victoria?"

She knew he was well aware of her hopes and was baiting her, as he did so often these days. "By ensuring that he had regular meals when his duties were over, by keeping his clothes in good repair and by listening to the confessions and fears he could not impart to another man for fear of being thought a weakling," she said with as much steadiness as she could muster.

"And?" he prompted.

She began to tremble inwardly. "And by performing the normal duties of a wife."

"Hmm," he mused, "I wonder if all those ladies who accompany their husbands regard it as merely 'the duty of a wife' as you seem to do. Do you think they do, Victoria?"

She clenched her hands until her wrists ached. He was plainly going to refuse her, so she would put up with no more of his sadistic playing. He had torn off her wings six months ago. If he was about to transfix her with a pin onto green baize, she would make it swift.

"Charles, I feel I could be of great service to you and the regiment at such a time. If you would but consider . . ."

"Naturally you will be of great service to everyone, Victoria. Rayne gave his consent to my request this morning and expressed his pleasure at the prospect of your continued company."

She was stunned. "You . . . you *agree* to my going?"

A smile twisted his mouth. "When a man has a wife he avails himself of the blessing—however limited it might be." He rose and made for the door. "I must be on my way."

Victoria followed him in a daze, unable to believe victory had been handed her on a plate and wondering why Charles should be so determined to take her along. She stood beside him as he fastened the sword belt around his waist and took up the fur busby.

"You will not find campaigning pleasant, Victoria, but your great interest in military affairs should be satisfied by the end of it."

"My great interest in military affairs has caused your name to be constantly on the lips of men of influence, Charles," she told him breathlessly, still lost in the wonder of getting her wish.

"Perhaps we should invite the Russian Ambassador to dinner. A word from you might do more than a show of armed strength."

His caustic comment left her untouched. The joy of knowing that before long she would be with Hugo day after day was enough to cancel out any other feeling she might have.

"With only ten days in which to prepare I doubt I would have time to entertain the Russian Ambassador."

"Your baggage allowance will be limited to just two trunks, by the way. What you decide to do with your other clothes and personal belongings is your own affair, but your jewels and furs will be deposited in the bank vaults with the silver, the china and paintings. You cannot, of course, take that bitch with you."

Victoria looked down at Glencoe and felt a spasm of

sadness. Parting would be a wrench for them both, but if Hugo meant to send his dogs to Wychbourne she would be in good company. The golden animal had been the recipient of her mistress's innermost thoughts and resolutions— no one knew Victoria Stanford as that dog did—and part of the girl would be left behind at Wychbourne when she sailed.

"Shall I be allowed to take Renata?"

He turned at the door. "If you do not you will grow extremely footsore. It is a great shame to take a thorough-bred beast to war, but there is no time to find you another. I doubt there will be a horse of any quality left in the area by morning. If things get.bad, I might be glad of the mare myself. Men have been known to have as many as four horses shot under them. War is a dangerous affair, Victoria."

"I know," she replied, suddenly remembering Hugo's description of an occasion when men galloped into a jungle where hidden cannon blew them to pieces. She shivered, Jack Markham's description of the Balkans in summer might be greatly off target.

Three days before they marched off to war, the officers of the garrison at Brighton held a grand farewell ball. It was a brilliant affair that was discussed for years afterward by local residents who remembered the air of reckless excitement, the laughing young men in colorful uniforms, the romantic music and the tears of the young women, many of whom were seeing their loved one for the last time on this earth.

The ballroom had been decorated with banks of spring flowers that filled the hall with the sweet scent of England and softened the stateliness of walls hung with heavily embossed wallpaper. At vast expense, a huge circular aviary had been placed in the center of the ballroom to house exotic birds from tropical climes which filled the evening with color and liquid warbling. Two bands played the music of Paris and Vienna for the waltzes, polkas and quadrilles, while crystal chandeliers threw brilliant light over the distinguished company below. Aside from local dignitaries, the guest list read like that of a royal garden party. Friends and relations of the military men flooded into Brighton for the occasion, until there was not a hotel room to be had, nor a guest room empty in the elegant houses so soon to be vacated.

The more impecunious subalterns were hard put to meet the costs incurred by this splendid hospitality, but, already caught in the reckless mood of young men riding out to meet their destiny, they sold some of their possessions to defray the cost and basked in the aura of adulation.

They were the golden boys, England's heroes, off to defend the oppressed in the name of their own splendid country. They were the sons of those who had shown Napoleon the folly of tangling with the might of Britain, young men who bore the names of some of the noblest families in the land. For a short while creditors gladly tore up outstanding bills; inflexible fathers smiled benevolently upon their wild sons; disapproving mamas were won over; and elusive maidens were willingly captured. The wine was heady; they drank deeply of it. Several months later they were to lie stiff and glassy-eyed in great piles of scarlet and blue, the wine of youth spilled onto foreign soil.

Victoria entered the ballroom with many emotions fighting for predominance within her. Lady Blythe's histrionics had already put her out of patience with her mother-in-law, and Charity Verewood, whom she had been obliged to entertain as the Blythes' guest, had aroused the usual antagonism from the moment she arrived. Pride was there in no small measure when she saw the officers of her own regiment in their excessively flattering uniform, gallant and courteous as they danced attention on their partners and showed them the tropical birds between dances. There was sadness, too, at the sight of her cousin Charlotte, whose husband, Captain Jenson, was preparing to march away with his infantry regiment and leave her behind. Poor Charlotte put on an air of sophistication, yet she cared very deeply for the young man she had married only two months before.

It was useless to deny that the overriding emotion that would govern the evening was the sweet pain of knowing that shortly she would see Hugo again. That Lord and Lady Blythe had brought Miss Verewood with them purely because of Hugo was very plain, but Victoria found it a tormenting situation. She did not know the full extent of the

quarrel between Charles and his brother, only that Hugo
had left Wychbourne on the morning after his desperate
drive down Mexford Heights and Charles had not spoken
his name since then. That the parents were hoping to bring
about a reconciliation between their two sons was fairly
evident, but Hugo had sent word excusing himself from
dining with them before the ball, as he had only arrived
from Ireland late the previous night.

Victoria knew that he could arrive at the ball at any
time. It was difficult to calm her heartbeat. She would twirl
in the waltz to meet his eyes over her partner's shoulder;
would look up and see him standing in the doorway as he
had stood in the dimly lit corridor at Wychbourne; would
be returned to her seat by a laughing partner to find him
kissing the fingers of Charity Verewood. Victoria's mind
flew back to that ball at Aunt Almeira's. Charles had said
then that the evening only began for him at the supper
dance. So it would for her when Hugo came tonight.

He was very late and his arrival was lost in the general
mêlée of taking supper. At first Victoria caught only a
glimpse of the back of his head through the crush of people. Then the gap closed as guests shifted and cut off her
line of vision. She felt a crushing sense of anticlimax. The
moment had never come. Why had she not instinctively
known he was near? What had happened to that heart-
stopping exchange of truth between them as their eyes met?
How long had he been there?

Charles's conversation flew past her, as did that of everyone around. In that instant it came home to her how far
apart she and Hugo now were—separated by a multitude
of barriers. For the past six months he had been in Ireland.
She did not know the country, the village, the quarters he
had occupied during that time; could not picture any details of his life there. He had slept, awakened, eaten,
laughed, danced, hunted . . . loved? All these things he
had done, and she had had no part of them, had no right to
any part of them. She should not expect his arrival tonight
to be any concern of hers, should not expect that he would
report to her the minute he entered the room. *He was not
committed to her*. The truth did not prevent the pain
of knowing her whole world was over there across a sea

of faces, while she must eat wafers of ham and larks in aspic and he behaved like a stranger.

Her dance program had been filled soon after her arrival, and her partner for the first dance after the supper interval somehow managed to find her in the crowd and bowed before her. She took his arm and walked beside him onto the floor, exchanging the same kind of remarks she had made to most of her partners. Couples broke away from the solid mass to walk into the ballroom, and, in the shifting pattern, her partner led her right into the path of a tall captain of Hussars who was talking to a girl of classic beauty with fair braids around her head.

There was no time for Victoria to prepare herself. Her eyes flew to his, but he gave a barely perceptible nod of polite acknowledgment before turning back to his partner. She felt her cheeks flame with color as she took her place in the dance. Her humiliation had been beneath the eyes of Charity Verewood.

Hugo had dragged himself to the ball out of a sense of duty to his parents. After delaying his arrival as long as possible, all his arguments with his conscience had been of no avail, and he had surrendered to the better side of his nature. As he walked the short distance to the ballroom he told himself this evening was sure to rate on his list of disasters. His father had indicated that he and Lady Blythe were anxious to repair the division between their two sons before they went off to war, and he could not deny the request. He did not feel that a ball was the right occasion for such a vain hope, however.

The words he and Charles had exchanged could never be withdrawn or completely forgotten. Even allowing for the emotional heat of the moment, their brotherhood was shattered forever.

After six months, what could a man say to another who held him responsible for the loss of his son and the near death of his wife? What could a man say when he was guilty, not only of that but of coveting the woman he had very nearly killed? What could a man say when he still could not forgive the slur of his honor in the suggestion that he had made assignations behind his brother's back?

The memory of that dawn at Wychbourne lived with

Hugo wherever he went and whatever he did. Guilt had layered upon him as the weeks passed until he was bowed down with it. During those months he had received news of Victoria through the Markhams. Outwardly she appeared to have recovered complete health and vitality and was the toast of Brighton once more. He loved her, so was glad; he loved her, so was consumed with jealousy of all those who could receive her smiles and share her company. The tiny hamlet where he was garrisoned had never seemed so lonely and bleak as it had all through that dreadful winter. His quarters were crowded and damp, the road became a sea of mud after November, there was no hunting, and the only other officer was an effeminate cornet called McKay, who was hardly congenial company for a man of his own type.

The outbreak of war had been his release, although his prophesies had proved sadly true with regard to the lack of readiness throughout the army. He was glad to rejoin the regiment for some real campaigning—riding against his own countrymen with a drawn sword was not to his taste. Not the least consideration was that sailing orders would relieve him of the obligation to his family that was proving so difficult. Unable to go to Wychbourne any more, he could do nothing but write regular letters, to which he received dramatic outbursts from Lady Blythe in reply and saner missives from his father that were underlined with regret. He supposed rejoining the regiment must go some way toward healing the breach between himself and Charles. Comrades-in-arms must surely put aside past quarrels.

Yet, as he walked beneath the covered entrance to the ballroom, Hugo was a man at his most vulnerable. Ahead of him lay a battery of hidden guns, and the ground he must cross to reach them was hostile and covered with obstacles. He was entering unarmed to face this and must somehow acquit himself with distinction. He knew himself for a coward. The prospect of behaving as he must to Victoria alone almost brought about a retreat.

He saw her almost immediately as his brother led her into the supper room at the far end, and he halted just inside the door when Lord Dovedale greeted him with pleasure.

"Greetings, Hugo. So the little men in green have not made away with you after all."

Hugo smiled, abstracted. The sudden heat and vivid color after the night chill brought about the giddiness he had sometimes experienced since that business with his eyes.

"Good to see you, Anthony. Splendid, is it not?"

Lord Dovedale knew he did not mean the ball. "Cannot wait to have a crack at them, old fellow. Saw your people a moment ago, by the way." He grinned knowingly. "You have kept remarkably close about a golden-haired beauty who is awaiting your arrival with such impatience. Damn nearly consoled her myself."

"Eh?" Hugo was startled.

"Miss Verewood, old boy. I was presented, but it was all too clear no one would do but the gallant Captain Esterly."

Damn, thought Hugo in despair, at this unforeseen obstacle. *How can they expect me to make a decision now?*

There was no time to brood on this, for the thinning crowds showed him his parents and Charity, who spotted him immediately. He made his bows to the ladies and received a warm handshake from his father.

"Forgive my lateness, Mama. Bad weather delayed the crossing so that we did not reach barracks until late last night."

Lady Blythe, in black watered silk with the Stanford emeralds cushioned upon her plump breast, sighed delicately.

"I must be grateful for any time with my sons that the Lord grants me before they are torn from my bosom. The trials of a mother are not generally appreciated. I shall need all my courage in the coming days."

"I think you need not worry on my account, Mama," he said dutifully.

"Not worry!" she cried. "Even now you look dreadfully pale. I suppose that the sea voyage made you ill, as usual. What will you do on this wretched journey?"

"I shall survive," he said shortly, but before he could turn the conversation, Charity said in her clear tones, "I know of an excellent remedy for the miseries of sea travel, Captain Esterly. I will tell you of it before you leave."

"Thank you. It is most kind." To break away from such

talk he added, "Do you not wish for supper, Miss Verewood?"

She smiled. "Yes, indeed. We were about to go in when
we happily spotted you."

He offered his arm, and they joined Lord and Lady
Blythe to stroll across the polished floor, halting for a few
minutes to admire the birds, then moving on. Hugo did not
eat much. He was still queasy after the sickness that had
incapacitated him on the packet from Ireland, and his
brain was trying to come up with a solution to this latest
problem.

Charity Verewood had been out some three or four
years. In a military garrison town, or in London, she would
have had offers galore, but the Verewoods, like his own
parents, preferred a rural life, and their daughter was a
diamond amid gravel. Hugo had been her companion
whenever he had visited Wychbourne and found her very
agreeable. But her beauty was of the remote kind. Whenever he had allowed himself to study her well-proportioned
body, his feelings had seemed more sacrilegious than pleasurable.

Tonight, she was flawless in silver gauze over white, with
a magnificent set of diamonds that cascaded to the valley
between the swell of her milky breasts. But even this hint of
her female charms suggested that they would feel cold beneath his hand if he attempted to cup them. Extremely eli-
gible, of excellent birth and an heiress into the bargain, she
was seen by his parents as the perfect partner for him. That
Charity wished for the union was quite plain. Charles had
never glanced her way, but the connection by marriage to
the noble Stanford family would be a step in the right social direction.

Loving Victoria so totally, he could do no better than
marry a girl who would never demand a great passion from
him. But he hesitated. If she had no desire for his heart and
body, might she not lay claim to his soul? Something told
him he might find himself in a stranglehold of vines that
would cling until he was crushed. He shook himself free of
the image to answer a question she put to him and knew he
must either make her an offer tonight or make it plain she
must look elsewhere.

"I cannot believe that there are not those who wish they had heeded your words, Captain Esterly," she told him earnestly. "You spoke to me of the need to be ready for war only last October, did you not?"

"And you persuaded me that I was being unnecessarily foolish, did you not?" he replied in a half-teasing manner.

She did not color or laugh his remark away, as most young women would have done. "I had not appreciated the situation, that is very plain. I should have known you would base such an opinion on wise observations." Her eyelashes lowered. "I shall pray for our victory . . . and your safety, my dear friend. May I hope for the continued solace of regular correspondence while you are away? I found your letters from Ireland of such great interest."

"Then the power of my pen must be greater than I thought, for my days there seemed fearfully dull to me." He was playing for time. Her request for letters gave him the ideal opening for the question of their future together, but here, surrounded by those taking supper, was not the place. He looked around for a quiet corner and, in that moment, saw Victoria walking toward him on the arm of a balding major. Caught off guard, he saw her lovely eyes widen in shock. He gave a stiff nod in her direction, conscious that Charles was probably somewhere near, watching him. Shaken, he took Charity's arm and led her to a seat in a corner of the rapidly emptying supper room.

For the length of the waltz Victoria suffered from the deepest hurt and disillusionment. A polka followed the waltz and between the dances she was caught up in a group of officers and their wives that prevented her from returning to her place with the family. She saw Hugo and Charles standing together in formal attitude and knew by her husband's face that he was being coldly polite for the benefit of society. Hugo looked strained and determined, but not once did he make any further acknowledgment of her presence. Even when Jack Markham eventually returned her to her seat at the end of the polka, Hugo remained engrossed in his conversation with his father and another elderly gentleman until her next partner claimed her for the quadrille.

At the conclusion of that merry dance Victoria felt she must retire somewhere to think and departed to the quiet

seclusion of a room set aside for the ladies, where she sat
for some moments trying to use her newfound determination to overcome her distress. Whatever had occurred six
months ago, there was no reason for this. He was deliberately avoiding her, was treating her as if she were the merest
acquaintance.

It was certain to be noticed by everyone in the regiment.
Speculation would be rife. Why was he doing it . . . why,
why? Was it his wish to punish *her* for the rift between
himself and Charles, the nature of which she had never
been fully aware? Did he blame her for keeping him at
Wychbourne when he would have left again immediately?
Had the sight of her, caught in the toils of premature birth,
destroyed his love? No, when she had last seen him bending over her before the doctor had arrived that love had
been in his eyes in overflowing measure. What had happened since then that induced him to hurt her—no, humili-
ate her—in front of a girl he knew she so heartily disliked?

Her hands twisted together as she reminded herself of
the vow she had made, but it was easier not to be crushed
by Charles, for whom she had no feeling, than by this man,
who was her soul's salvation. At this moment she had no
resolution; she *was* crushed. She rose to her feet as another
lady entered and forced herself to return to the ballroom
where a cotillion was in progress. Her partner would have
looked for her in vain.

With the hurt still beating in waves against her composure, she walked toward the crowd lining the floor and
rounded a pillar to confront a small group of officers, the
nearest of whom was Hugo. Their glances locked in confusion. There was no chance of avoiding him. The young
men greeted her warmly.

"Ah, ma'am, I regret to tell you Mr. Curtis is off to cut
his throat," said one with a chuckle. "Finding no trace of
his partner, he felt his life and career no longer of importance."

She smiled automatically. "When I see him to apologize
for my absence I shall advise him to wait awhile. If he
wishes to be heroic it would be better to offer a Russian his
throat. Think of the greater honor to the regiment."

They all laughed, except Hugo, who gave a slight bow
and murmured an excuse for departing. Without time for

consideration she said, "One moment, Captain Esterly.
There is something of particular importance on which I
need your advice." Having gone that far, she added, "If
you would be kind enough to fetch me a glass of lemonade
I would be glad of a word with you."

To her horror he hesitated until, caught in the impossible position in which she had put him, he reluctantly offered his arm.

With the color mounting in her cheeks and her inner self
telling her she had laid herself open to even more harrowing treatment, Victoria walked with her silent escort to the
room where drinks could be obtained. Miserably she
waited until he brought her the lemonade, when he said,
"If you will excuse me I will endeavor to find Charles. He
will give you any advice you need."

At the realization that he was about to walk away again,
quick unexpected anger saved her. "Hugo, have you left
your manners in Ireland? I receive more courtesy from my
fishmonger."

He drew in his breath as if she had slapped him. "Perhaps your fishmonger is credited with more honor than I.
Excuse me, if you please."

He made to turn away, but she said hotly, "No, I will
not excuse you." She took a step nearer him. "No one shall
treat me in this offhand manner, least of all you. If there is
some reason for it you will tell me. What is all this about
honor?"

He was trapped, her anger had made his position impossible. "Victoria, this will do no good. Will you allow me to
fetch Charles . . . or my father?"

"Not until you tell me what I have done to merit your
public contempt—a contempt you saw fit to display before
Miss Verewood."

His eyes flashed. "A fine opinion you hold of me. First, I
am less courteous than a fishmonger; now I am a bound-
er."

"Then tell me what opinion I must have of you," she
cried in desperation.

He glanced around as if expecting there might be eyes
fastened upon him, watching his every movement. Then he
said stiffly, "Charles directed me to have no further contact

with you. He doubts my honor where his wife is concerned."

It was the last thing she had expected and left her conscious only that she had forced such a statement from him
in this public place.

"Hugo, that is quite unforgivable! How dare he say . . .
I am so sorry. If he had told me, I . . . how *could* I understand your behavior?"

His eyes darkened with anger . . . passion? She could
not tell which. "He did not expect that we should be in
each other's company again so soon. I deeply regret this,
Victoria. If it had not been for my parents, I should not be
here tonight, but duty obliges me to make some effort at
their especial request. However, the regiment is off in two
days and we shall not meet again."

She shook her head in a daze. "No, Hugo. I travel with
you to the Balkans. You cannot possibly avoid the wife of
your major when she is with you day after day."

He stared at her in horrified disbelief. "Has Charles gone
mad? Victoria, you cannot! We are off to *war*. Have you
any notion what it will be like?"

Seeing the concern that sprang from his love only as rejection, she flung back at him, "Have *you* any notion what
it will be like if I am incarcerated at Wychbourne?"

Inquisitive faces were turning in their direction. He drew
her to an alcove that offered more privacy. "At Wychbourne you would be safe," he urged in a low insistent
voice. "At Wychbourne you would not be exposed to hardship and the rigors of a campaign."

"At Wychbourne I would be *stifled*," she said through
frozen lips. "It would be a prison sentence. The Stanfords
have no real fondness for me, and I would be fed an undiluted diet of the sanctimonious Miss Verewood. Would you
condemn me to that?"

"Instead of an undiluted diet of battlefields? Yes!" was the
heated answer. "You cannot go, Victoria."

"Letty is going. Have you treated her and Jack to your
dictatorial attitude on the subject?" Seeing she had silenced
him for a moment, she went on. "Or have you another
reason in my case?"

He stood for a moment with his jaw working. "You

know full well it would be intolerable. A tented camp offers
no privacy; its occupants are thrown together in an inti-
macy one does not find in barracks."

"And?"

Her obstinate attitude incensed him further. "By heaven,
is that what you truly wish, Victoria?"

She had grown as pale as he was flushed. "I think you
know what I truly wish." It was soft and sad—a plea for
his understanding of her need to walk in his shadow, if all
else were denied her, but he was wiser in all things than
she and forced himself to say, "There is a vacant captaincy
in the Lancers. I will apply to transfer, for I cannot live
side by side with you under such circumstances."

"Hugo . . . no! There is no reason for you to . . ."

"Forgive me, Mrs. Stanford," said a voice beside her. "I
come to claim my polka. If this unmannerly fellow detains
you much longer there will be none of it left to dance."
Harry Edmunds gave her a wicked smile and bowed to
Hugo with slight mockery. "Arriving too late to find any
partners does not entitle you to dally with those promised
to your friends, Hugo." He offered his arm, which Victoria
was obliged to take, and led her away, saying, "Captain
Esterly might have a great deal of dash, but his performance in the ballroom is deplorable."

"So I have heard," she struggled to say, conscious that
Hugo was watching them as the young lieutenant slipped
his arm around her waist. The ball was turning into a
disaster.

The Stanford party left the ball in two carriages. When
they arrived at Brunswick Square the ladies said their good
nights and went immediately to their rooms, leaving the
gentlemen together.

Lady Blythe kissed the two young women on the cheek
and went into the room Victoria had prepared for her, wiping the corners of her eyes to hint at tears that were about
to flow in the privacy of the boudoir. Victoria was not
taken in, but the girl walking beside her along the landing
appeared greatly affected by the performance.

"She is taking it so bravely, under the circumstances, do
you not think?"

"Oh, there is no doubt her stoicism is an example to us all."

"Indeed, yes," agreed Charity, missing Victoria's sarcasm. "To give up two sons in the defense of their country is a great sacrifice."

Victoria continued to look straight ahead as she walked. "They are not yet slain and in their graves, Miss Verewood. I think we need not take out our black dresses and mourning jewelery just yet."

Charity drew in her breath sharply. "I cannot blame you for forcing yourself to be less than sensitive to another's suffering, Mrs. Stanford, since your husband insists on your accompanying him to the Balkans. It will not do to be easily overcome by hardship and anguish, but it seems a great pity that you are so unused to tending the sick. You have my sincere wish that you will survive the ordeal, ma'am." She stopped at her door and turned a bright smile upon her hostess. "I must express my gratitude to you for allowing me to be a guest in your house. We have not always perfectly understood each other in the past, have we?"

"That fact does not prohibit my accommodating you when my parents-in-law bring you as their guest, Miss Verewood." She turned to go, but Charity put a hand lightly on her arm.

"You are soon off to an uncertain future. Can we not part as friends? If we are to be sisters . . ." Her voice trailed off delicately.

Victoria felt a sudden lack of air in her lungs. "Sisters? How is this?"

Lowering her eyes modestly, Charity said, "Captain Esterly tonight expressed his earnest desire that I should be waiting for him when he returned, and I gave my promise. He is too gallant to ask me to share the life to which he goes, but it is only a matter of time before we are united in marriage." The doll eyes gazed at her in triumph. "Can we not say goodbye in sisterly affection?"

Victoria's bosom heaved as pain knotted there and thrust up against her throat. The vision of sweet acid before her began to blur as she faced the implications of the girl's words. How could he take such a marble creature as his own? She felt herself swaying as thoughts of Charity in Hu-

go's bed set blood and pulse pounding into an aching anguish that spread over her entire body. Stepping back as if
to escape from the mental ravishment, she found herself
saying, "So, you have had your way after all! You and
Lady Blythe make excellent conspirators in the trapping of
a man when he is under stress and cannot escape." She
took another two steps back in agitation. "If I cannot escape becoming your sister, I fear we shall never be friends.
Unfortunately, you possess all the characteristics I most
dislike, and I cannot see any hope of improvement. Our
goodbye will, I hope, be final."

She turned in a swirl of chartreuse silk skirts and hurried
along the corridor to her own room. Once inside, she
leaned against the bedpost and let the tears slide unchecked
down her cheeks, as her own body cried out for the rapture
that would never fill the cold limbs of the girl Hugo had
chosen to take for a partner.

When Hugo would have left immediately, Lord Blythe
caught his arm and cast a stern eye at Charles. "This is
your home. Have I your permission to ask your brother to
remain for a short while?"

Charles gave a stiff nod. "If you really wish it, sir."

"Of course I wish it, sir. You are well aware of our
hopes—your mama's and mine. She has been extremely
under par over this affair, and I must speak to you on the
subject. Will you invite us to take a glass in your study?"

Charles led the way into a book-lined room of little character since no resident remained long enough in the house
to make it peculiarly his own, and they all took a seat in
silence. A footman brought a brandy decanter and glasses,
then departed, closing the double doors softly.

Lord Blythe took a pull at the brandy after warming the
balloon glass with his hands. "Excellent quality, my boy."
He cleared his throat. "You two are off to war, and we
are proud of you. We have always been proud of you—the
son of our union and the son of our choosing. You are
brothers." He looked into the glass and cleared his throat
again. "After your mama had meningitis I was grateful for
your understanding of the way her illness changed the
sunny personality she had. You have both been discreet
and showed no signs of the embarrassment she must have

caused you, at times. I believed the bond we all had was behind your continued devotion to her in these trying years, but you have now allowed your personal differences to cause her infinite distress. Perhaps I have kept from you just how fragile her disposition is these days, but you are both intelligent men and must know that your present behavior plays on a mind that has become a little childish." He looked most uncomfortable and Hugo's easy guilt returned.

"There is no knowing how long this war may last, and she might succumb to her weakness at any time," he went on. "I ask you both, as gentlemen, to take this into consideration." He took aonther draught of brandy. "In the conflict we might lose one, or both, of you in the cause of our country. Our grief would be extreme, that goes without saying, but it would be unacceptable if we thought you had parted as . . . if there had been no . . ." He stood up, leaving the brandy unfinished on the table. "Dammit, gentlemen, let us have an end to this for all our sakes." He left the room, blowing his nose on a silk handkerchief.

The brothers remained standing where they were at their father's departure, each balancing a brandy snifter in his hand. The heavy tick of the clock echoed the mood Lord Blythe had left behind him. Hugo felt no inclination to speak.

Charles swirled the brandy in his glass and watched it as he said, "My God, he asks a lot of my sense of duty. You are only in my house because he requested it." He tossed back the last of the drink and placed the glass gently on a bookcase. "I suggest you leave now."

"Just like that?"

"Yes. You can find your own way out."

Hugo banged his glass down angrily. "Do you intend making no attempt at reconciliation?"

"I see no reason why I should."

"Dammit, man, we shall be riding together into battle. It is an impossible situation, not only from a personal viewpoint but a regimental one. You are my senior officer."

"As to that, I shall perform my duties meticulously—as I shall with every officer beneath my command. I do not need a personal relationship with them in order to do it. In the future, you will receive nothing from me that any other man cannot expect."

Hugo's temper flared. "I want nothing from you. I shall fight this war on my own merit, and you can go to hell."

Charles gave a grim smile. "I shall find you already there. You will never last out a campaign for all your mock heroics. Look at you now—wild, irrational speech, a complete lack of self-control. I pity the men under your leadership. Their self-proclaimed hero will turn out to be nothing more than a fancy jockey when put to the test."

"You will live to take that back," said Hugo through his teeth. "You like your pound of flesh, Charles."

"When it is my lawful due."

Hugo had no answer to that and lost some of his anger in a return of remorse. He pushed his fingers through the unruly hair in a gesture of helplessness. "Is there nothing to be saved between us? We had a bond that I believed immortal—a bond that has lasted twenty-eight years. Father is right. Who knows what lies ahead? Do we not owe it to them to make some attempt at understanding? Are you prepared to face the enemy swords with this between us?"

"You ask me that after robbing me of everything I held dear for my future?" challenged Charles coldly. "A bond, you say. Where was that bond when you set your covetous eyes upon my wife? Where was it when you took her and my unborn son careering across the countryside in a gig, performing a downhill race only an insane man or a puffed-up fool would contemplate? There never was such a bond on your part or you would have regarded it as sacred."

Hugo rubbed his eyes wearily. "Do you think I am not aware of the consequences of my actions that day? Everything I did was for the best, I swear. Do you think I have not also suffered these past six months? There were days when the utter isolation nearly defeated me—you were responsible for sending me there—and my conscience plagued me the whole time. Do you think I have not said *if only* so many times that it has made my head spin? Charles, do you think I have not wished over and over again it had been *anyone* but my own brother? In twenty-eight years you must know me well enough for that."

"I was your brother when you began to covet my wife."

"And I left immediately. Dear God, you know only too well I did."

"It was the coward's way out—I told you so at the time. I believed you were man enough to master it, but events proved you had no intention of mastering it. You *happened* to meet Victoria in the street and took her to your friend's house to recover from a fainting attack, instead of escorting her home and informing me immediately. Then you came across from Ireland when I left her at Wychbourne for rest and quiet and proceeded to amuse yourself at my expense."

"Damn you! That is unforgivable."

"What you did is unforgivable. Do not speak to me of reconciliation. You cannot be true to anything." He looked supremely arrogant as he accused his brother. "Despite my directive, I saw you just tonight taking my wife into a quiet corner again."

Hugo was losing any hold over his temper. "I had no choice. Since you had not told Victoria of your words to me, she was in great distress over my behavior. It was a choice between a few minutes of quiet explanation or a public snub before officers of the regiment. I cannot believe you would have wished me to submit her to that."

"I did not wish you to submit her to many things, but you did."

"But it was all done with honorable intentions," cried Hugo hotly. "I have nothing on my conscience on that score."

"God, but you have a strange conception of honor. Can you deny you still have a passion for her? Ha, I see you cannot answer."

"I have enough regard for her to beg you to reconsider taking her with you. War is bloody and terrible. There will be things that will make a man sick to his stomach. You cannot put her through that. Charles, you cannot put Victoria through such an ordeal."

"I am merely acceding to her own earnest desire. Since she cannot be a mother to my son, she wishes to concern herself with the ruffians of the regiment . . . but I have my own reasons for agreeing." He was gripping the edge of the bookcase in his anger but, unlike Hugo, he was quite controlled. "She will see you day after day, month after month as you ride about the camp; she will watch you ride off on patrol and never know if you will return; she will see you crack and fall apart before her; she will see her brave hero disintegrate as his boasts crumble before the reality. And you—you will know she is within arm's reach and will be tormented by the knowledge. I wonder how long it will be before you can both stand no more?"

"You will never know the answer to that brutish question," flamed Hugo. "When she told me the news tonight I resolved to transfer to another regiment."

"Then I charge you with cowardice," snapped Charles.

"Charge me with what you wish. I will not aid you in something designed to hurt her." Hugo felt the blood pounding in his temples.

"Then I challenge you to prove you have some vestige of manhood. I challenge you to see this campaign through to its end as an officer of our regiment, constantly in her company. I challenge you to show her you can live up to the brave picture you paint of yourself."

"*No!*"

"Are you an adolescent boy that you cannot master yourself sufficiently to overcome the desires of the flesh?" Charles was white around the lips, and all the overweening arrogance of his forebears was in his face. "Transfer then, for I will not have my troopers led into needless slaughter by a conceited sentimental weakling."

Hugo took two steps forward and struck his brother across the face.

There was a petrified silence. Hugo stood, chest heaving and eyes blazing with horrified anger, hardly able to believe he had been so violent. Charles was swaying slightly, a red mark flaming against the whiteness of his face. At last he tilted up his chin and said in painful, labored tones, "Your lack of self-control might yet solve your problem. There will come a time in the heat of battle when my back is turned to you. In the mêlée who is to know who delivered the fatal sword thrust?"

Hugo closed his eyes for a moment against the shock, then began to move away backward across the room. "May God forgive you for that, Charles," he breathed. Then he turned and went out.

* * *

The night before the regiment was due to leave, Rosie was
on her way to her mistress's room with a strange message.
It was one of the last duties she was to perform for Mrs.
Stanford, for she had asked to go back to Wychbourne.
Being a lady's maid in an elegant house was one thing; the
prospect of tents, hardship and soldiers cutting each other's
throats was another. On the morrow she would go up to
Wychbourne in the big carriage with Glencoe and some
small items of furniture that were to be kept at the big
house. Her tread was light tonight. This household was too
fraught with undercurrents to be a happy one, and she was
going home to her own village.

After curtsying to her mistress, who was writing farewell
letters, she said, "Alice says there's someone waiting to see
you, ma'am."

"Alice?"

"Yes, ma'am. He's in the kitchen. Seems desperate to see
you, she said. He's been waiting since four o'clock."

"Why haven't I been told?" asked Victoria, dragging her
attention away from her letters. "I have been in all day."

"Seems she didn't think you would wish to be disturbed
and hoped he'd go away. Only he didn't. She can't leave
him in the kitchen, and she's waiting to go off for the
night."

Victoria was getting quite cross. Had her servants abandoned their duties a day in advance? "Go and find out who
this man is and what he wants, Rosie."

"Oh, ma'am, I know who he is."

"You know? Then why have you not told me? Really,
girl, one might almost believe you had never been trained
in domestic service. Who has been waiting several hours to
see me?"

"It's Trooper Stokes . . . and he won't say what he's
come for," Rosie blurted out with a touch of defiance.

"*Stokes!* Oh, why was I not told instantly?" cried Victoria, full of apprehension as to why Hugo's servant should
be so persistent. Surely it was not bad news? Hurrying
down the stairs, she directed Rosie to show him into the
music room at once.

"But, ma'am, he's a *trooper*," wailed Rosie, hurrying behind her.

"He is an acquaintance of mine, nevertheless. I take it he is not in company with his horse," she said tartly.

Stokes looked quite ill as he walked across the rose-patterned carpet toward her, and Victoria felt her stomach muscles tighten.

"Good evening, Stokes. It is a pleasure to see you again after all this time," she began with a semblance of calm. "I apologize for the long wait you have had. My maid has only this minute informed me of your visit."

"Thank you for seeing me, Miss Cast . . . I mean, ma'am." He was plainly in great distress. His proud military bearing had gone and there was no trace of the ruddy joviality she was used to seeing on his face. "Believe me, I would not have come to you, only I'm real desperate, ma'am," he continued miserably. "The captain'll likely skin me alive when he finds out, but there's things that have to be done at times."

Victoria was too relieved at hearing Hugo was apparently not the subject of the visit to take in all he said, but his whole demeanor aroused her quick sympathy.

"Stokes, just tell me why you have come. We shall worry about Captain Esterly later."

"Yes, ma'am." He looked at his boots. "It's Mrs. Stokes, you see. She drew 'not to go.' "

Victoria began to understand. When a regiment was sent overseas the number of soldiers' wives allowed to accompany their husbands was six per troop. To decide who the lucky ones should be, a ballot was held. The women drew papers on which were written "to go" or "not to go." Those who lost were given a ticket to their family home—if they had one and had not been turned out for marrying a despised soldier—and left to fend for themselves until their men returned, sometimes as much as twenty years later—if they returned at all.

Stokes went on. "I don't know which way to turn, ma'am. Captain Esterly has done what he can, but we only got back three days ago and there's been no time. As it is, he's going around in circles trying to get himself equipped and the horses reshod, so I can't expect him to do more than he has—which not every officer would do, I can tell you."

"I am sure he has been as helpful as time permits," she agreed. "Has your wife no family?"

"No, ma'am. She was brought up in a traveling circus."

"Ah, yes. I remember Captain Esterly telling me. Could she not return to her friends there while you are away?"

"They've gone to Germany touring the towns on the Rhine. There's no one else. The captain generously offered to send her to Wychbourne at his own expense, but she'd never make a kitchen maid, ma'am, and I know what them servants is like there. Dawkins would never rest until she was dismissed. If there was time the captain could've found her employment in the village nearby, but we're off tomorrow. Besides which, she's not too good at anything but elephants. That's all she's ever done, you see."

Victoria could imagine the extent of Hugo's success if he tried to find employment for an elephant girl in his home village.

"I can see your dilemma, Stokes, but what are you going to do?"

He turned his busby around and around in his large hands as he watched the twirling plume. "I'm not going to accept charity, ma'am. Me and the captain had words this morning after he said there was nothing else but to take his offer to supplement the cost of simple lodgings until we get back. He went off in a right black temper, and I've been walking up and down, up and down, trying to pluck up the courage to come here."

"I am sorry you felt you had to build up your courage to see me. I thought we were on better terms than that," she said gently.

He looked up with a flush on his doleful face. "It's very kind of you to say that, Miss . . . Mrs. Stanford, but I wouldn't have come on this errand unless I had to. When a man takes a wife he must look out for her, mustn't he?"

"If he is an honorable man, certainly," agreed Victoria, beginning to feel some of his desperation.

"Yesterday, I bumped into Miss Caddywould—your maid—in the street, and she told me she wouldn't go to the war if all the horses in the regiment pulled her there. It occurs to me that if you are going without a maid, my wife might be of some help to you." He grew slightly redder. "She's had no training, but she is a good laundress . . .

and I'm teaching her to cook. If you could say she is your
personal servant, she gets to go on the ship with us. I don't
want charity—I can afford to keep us both—but if she goes
as your maid she can travel with the regiment all the time."

Victoria looked at him in dismay. "I have engaged a
maid. I am so sorry." At his reaction she added quickly,
"Would you like me to ask on your behalf of the other
ladies who are going? There is time even now."

He shook his head numbly. "They're all fixed up. We got
back from Ireland too late. I beg your pardon for troubling
you. Miss Caddywould didn't say anything about a replacement or I'd not have taken up your time when you
have so much to do."

"Nonsense," she said, knowing she could not let him go
like this. "It has just occurred to me, Stokes, that I have a
duty to the regiment. If you sail without your wife you will
be bad-tempered and inefficient. That will put Captain Esterly in one of his black moods, and *he* will be bad-
tempered and inefficient." She smiled. "In no time the entire regiment will be the same . . . and the war will be lost,
all for the want of Mrs. Stokes."

The poor worried trooper was looking at her as if she
had gone mad. "What does all that mean, ma'am?"

"That you may return to barracks before your absence is
noted, and prepare your wife to travel with me tomorrow. I
did not really take to the girl I engaged last Monday." She
pulled the bell rope for a footman to show her visitor out.
"I have a feeling I shall get on far better with Mrs. Stokes."
A little gurgle of laughter broke through. "I have always
wanted to know about elephants."

Stokes could hardly take it in. "I don't know what to
say, ma'am, except the regiment got a real lady the day
you joined it. I shall be able to rest easy tonight, and Zarina will perk up right away."

"Who?" choked Victoria.

"Zarina, ma'am. My wife was known as the Great Zarina—Ranee of the elephants."

Victoria fought to keep a straight face. "I see. Please
bring . . . your wife at nine tomorrow morning. I suppose
you travel to Portsmouth by train with Captain Esterly?"

"No, ma'am. The captain has been detailed to bring a

squadron in. It seems a bit hard when he had less time to prepare than the other officers, but he's unmarried and considered to have less to attend to. We're riding to the docks through the city." He hesitated, grateful beyond his ability to express it. "Good night, Mrs. Stanford. If I can ever be of real service to you, you will not find me wanting." He gave a grin that turned up the ends of his mustache. "I've got to think of a way to break the news to the captain now."

And I have got to think of a way to break the news to Charles, she thought as he went out.

There were hitches.

The transports did not arrive in Portsmouth dockyard on the expected date. The infantry and cavalry officers who had traveled there by train were obliged to put up in hotels in the city, where a great burst of social activity began as sight-seers and relatives or friends of the departing men poured into Portsmouth and Southsea, complete with retinues of servants. Balls and dinner parties were speedily organized, theaters were packed with elite audiences, trips around the harbor attracted wide-eyed giggling young ladies more lost in admiration of the young naval officer than the wonders of shipbuilding he showed them, and everyone forgot about the war for two or three days. Even those women who had desperately marched behind their husbands, holding onto life as long as they were in sight, had a short reprieve before abandonment.

Among those who did *not* forget what lay ahead was Hugo. He was stranded in a hotel in Havant, a small village outside the naval port, and fumed over the delay. These few days could have been used to great advantage at Brighton, where he had been forced to accept inferior equipment because he did not have the time for selection. He had set off with the squadron he had commanded in Ireland, plus the effeminate Cornet McKay, feeling half prepared for a campaign. Now he was stranded with his men on the outskirts of the city, waiting for orders to march through to the transports.

Despite his urge for action, he felt a new happiness these days. For the first time in eighteen months he walked like a

proud man. The guilt and doubts had flown; he was free,
confident and decisive. Hearing Charles accuse him of all
the things he had called himself had somehow laid all the
ghosts, sorted out the truth from imagination. His brother's
contempt had banished self-condemnation, enabling him to
see clearly—more clearly than he had since taking that
black band from his eyes so long ago at Wychbourne.

His single crime had been taking Victoria out in a gig
when she was plainly too ill to stand such a trip. The journey had been suggested with the best of intentions, and his
subsequent actions had been right. That had been no insane
careering downhill; every foot had been taken with skill
and calculation. He had atoned twofold for the tragedy that
followed. Charles had verbally flogged him twice. The slate
was wiped clean.

Victoria was traveling with her husband, so there would
be other sons, without doubt. As to the rest, he would stay
in his regiment and lead the men who respected and
trusted him—and he would still be there at the head of
them when they returned to England victorious. That he
surely knew. Life as he had lived it for the past twenty-
eight years was over. He had written to his "parents,"
thanking them for all they had done and explaining why he
must say goodbye. From now on he was a man on his own,
a man dedicated to his profession. The future was his to
decide, and his blood ran young and eager at the prospect.

Five days later he received word that the regiment would
embark at eleven the following morning and promptly set
his men on a frenzy of cleaning and polishing. He had
heard that the people of the city had turned out every day
in the hope of seeing these renowned horsemen pass
through, so they must look their grandest. To a naval port,
the sight of cavalry in full uniform was virtually unknown
and bound to cause a great deal of excitement.

Even knowing this, Hugo was unprepared for the hysterical outburst of patriotic pride that greeted them as soon as
they passed the city boundary. The road from Cosham to
the dockyard—a matter of some five or six miles—was
lined on both sides with citizens, from babes in arms to
nonogenarians, who would go to their Maker knowing they
had witnessed one of the finest sights an Englishman could
see.

It was a balmy spring day, with the blue clarity of sky over sea, as Hugo rode at the head of his men, aware only of worn, wrinkled faces; hard features full of the forced cunning brought about by poverty; sweet young girls with a beauty that struggled against a consumptive pallor; grubby children with noses that needed wiping and half their breakfast clinging to their mouths; old men with the glaze of reminiscence bringing youth back for a while—all united in this carnival moment that brought color, spectacle, release from grinding tedium and pride in a country that had done nothing much for them except keep them free.

Halfway to their destination, the cavalry squadron was met by the full band of the 44th—or was it the 54th?—Foot, and the crowd was treated to the sight of meticulous regimental maneuvering while the Hussars halted to allow the band to reform in the opposite direction in order to lead the cavalrymen in style.

They set off again, with the delirium rising to fever pitch. The sun shone down, striking off the gleaming instruments in dazzling flashes; highlighting the gold braiding, badges and buttons on the soldiers' uniforms; catching the subtler glints of harness, spurs, accouterments and chain straps beneath sturdy chins; and glossing the horses' coats as they rippled over the animals' muscles. It shone on the scarlet infantry jackets crossed with white pipe-clayed straps; on the white gloves, blue overalls and shining black boots; on the leopard skins worn by the drummers; and on the scarlet tassels attached to the trumpets. It enhanced the blue Hussar jackets and slung pelisses smothered in gold lacing; the leopard skin saddle cloths and scarlet-and-gold embroidered shabraques; it showed to advantage the polished horse leathers, black riding boots, decorated sabretaches, engraved scabbards, white gauntlets and black fur busbies with scarlet bag and tall plume.

As if that feast of color were not enough there was the sound of martial trumpets, the thud of drums, the tramp of boots, the jingle of harness and the squeak of leather saddles as the horses clopped along the city streets, immune to the racket and din around them, carrying mustachioed warriors who looked proud, invincible and completely fearless.

The crowds thickened. The flags, emblems and even

shawls and aprons waving in the air appeared to Hugo a sea
of rippling cloth that blotted out the faces. The volume of
cheering increased as the band broke into "The Girl I Left
Behind Me," and women began leaving the crowd to run
beside the troopers, holding out flowers, mascots, bottled
beer—even pies. They were laughing, crying, pulling at the
men's legs, catching at the reins.

Some boasted their trade with laughing invitations to
provide a last hour of comfort before they sailed; there
were tearful mothers who saw their own sons in these sons
of England; and there were young girls wanting to touch
these dream men in glittering uniforms who suggested
strength, courage and an indefinable quality they would
never find in the drunken louts who inhabited their lives.
Some knelt in prayer as they passed, others threw blossoms
at their feet, a few looked with a hunger that stilled their
bodies and chilled their hearts. These husbands, sweet-
hearts, sons were going to war and might never return.

Hugo had begun by being cynical. It was well known
that the British soldier was despised by everyone, regarded
as the lowest of the low; yet now he was being feted as the
hero of the hour, the savior of the country—which he had
always been. But as they progressed, even he felt a lump in
his throat and the thump of pride in his heartbeat. His
squadron looked immaculate, they rode like ramrods in
their saddles, and when he gave the order to present swords
in salute to the city dignitaries outside the dockyard gates
they performed the drill as one man.

Police were out in force to hold back the crowd surrounding the gates, but just as they were passing through, a
slender girl in brown dress and shawl broke through the
cordon and threw herself beneath the hooves of the front
rank of the squadron. Hugo registered a vague impression
of a white face beneath dark hair as he passed, then a cry
went up and the column behind him wavered.

Turning in his saddle, he saw one of his men jumping
from his horse and running to the two policemen lifting the
girl clear of the road.

"Sergeant, get that man back on his horse this minute,"
he said furiously and halted the squadron.

Sergeant Cairns wheeled and rode back to the group of
which the trooper had formed one but appeared to have no

success in retrieving him. Hugo cursed roundly. Was their
grand march to be ruined right at the last? He would have
the culprit flogged for insubordination, he resolved, turning
Monty and trotting up to the scene of the trouble. At close
quarters he saw that it was Trooper Pitchley, a young hard-
working soldier, who looked as white and ill as the girl.

"For God's sake, has Pitchley taken leave of his senses?"
he asked in a low voice.

The sergeant looked up at his officer with a wooden expression. "It's 'is wife, sir."

"The devil take her," breathed Hugo and edged his
horse toward one of the policemen. "Constable, would you
kindly escort the young woman to the jetty? I will take up
the matter there." He swung his eyes round to the trooper.
"Remount at once, Pitchley!"

During the short ride to the jetty Hugo had time to guess
the situation, but it did not alter his angry expression nor
sweeten his tongue when Pitchley was brought before him.

"I'm sorry, sir, and that's the truth, but it was more than
flesh and blood could stand. She's my wife, sir."

"So I believe. What is she doing here?"

"I give my oath, I don't know, Captain Esterly." It burst
from him with uncontrolled heat as his face flared with
color. "She walked from Brighton behind us, but I said
goodbye to her last night. She must've come in behind the
column today." Suddenly he seemed to crumble and his
face worked convulsively. "As God's my witness, I never
thought she'd try to do away with herself. What am I going
to do?"

Hugo took a deep breath. "Has she absolutely nowhere
to go?"

Pitchley shook his head, tears sliding down his cheeks.
Next minute he was sobbing like a girl. Hugo sighed and
cursed young fellows of eighteen who saddled themselves
with a wife. This boy had probably seduced some scullery
maid, then felt honor-bound to do the right thing by her.
The girl's parents had most likely thrown her out for dis-
gracing the family by marrying a shilling-a-day man, and
here they were in this fix.

Instructing the man to stay where he was, Hugo walked
across to where the constable had deposited the girl on a
seat.

"She looks werry ill, sir," said the policeman, who had daughters of his own. "That man of yours ought not to go orf and leave 'er like this."

"He has no choice. He is a soldier," Hugo snapped. "In the service of his country he is expected to do many inhumane things. It is a pity the public is not more aware of the fact."

"Yes, sir." The policeman's voice was small. This gent looked ready to make mincemeat of anyone who ventured to criticize his fancy soldiers, and he was twice his own size in heavy riding boots and tall plumed hat. "Well, I'll be getting about me duty. You did say as 'ow you'd deal with this, me Lord," he added for safety's sake. "Good day to you, I'm sure." He rolled away with his official gait, hoping he gave an impression of competent nonchalance.

Hugo looked at the girl. She could not be more than sixteen, and something about her large eyes and smooth dark hair stirred him. He had intended giving her a piece of his mind but said merely, "Are you feeling better now?"

She nodded sullenly.

"You have rendered your husband liable for punishment, you know." She made no comment, and he added angrily, "If you had wanted to kill yourself before his eyes you should have waited until we were at the gallop."

Her head came up. "You never went at the gallop."

He stood there, considering. They were already loading the men and horses. There was no time for arrangements of any kind.

"Mrs. Pitchley, are you expecting a child?"

"No, sir."

"Are you quite certain?"

"On my word of honor, sir."

He made up his mind. "Come with me, then."

Ten minutes later the last file of Captain Esterly's squadron went up the gangplank with one extra in their midst, while their commander engaged the quartermaster in deep conversation at the top.

When the coast was clear Hugo strolled along the deck to watch the loading of his own horses and felt immensely sorry for the beasts as they were swung up from the jetty by a sling under their bellies. They dangled helplessly as they were brought up and over, to be lowered into the hold where well-padded temporary stalls had been fitted for the journey. From the language floating up from the hold he deduced that the animals were reluctant to settle in their new quarters. He felt sympathy with them. Every time he stepped onto the deck of a ship his stomach protested, and it was a shrewd guess that it was Charles's knowledge of his debilitating aversion to the motion of a ship—worse now than ever, since the accident at Chokham—that had governed the allocation of his own cabin in this transport. As he went below he felt the same dread and reluctance as the horses and prayed for a calm and speedy voyage.

Three hours later the ship was ready to move out of Portsmouth harbor, but just before the gangplank was pulled up, a dark-haired young woman in brown was carried screaming and kicking down onto the jetty. She had been found on board without a pass and ordered off. Her distracted husband insisted Captain Esterly had given his permission, but a token search of the ship had not located that officer, and the quartermaster was not taking instructions from any horse soldier on his own ship. Trooper Pitchley had to be put under restraint as the wooden ship drew away from shore with an ever-increasing gap and set course for Spithead, where she was to anchor until morning.

Those watching in great crowds from privileged positions in the dockyard, and the citizens who had fought and scrambled for a place on the pier to watch the vessels pass through the mouth of the harbor, thought it a magnificent spectacle. The strains of a military band floated back to them across the water, and many a tear-filled eye saw a glimpse of Hussar blue that could have been a loved one waving a last farewell.

Maria Pitchley saw her husband's ship depart with a great cry inside her. She had nowhere to go, and the prospect of getting work with the baby inside her was very faint. The little bit of money Ted had pressed on her last night would not last more than a week or two. The long walk from Brighton and the events of the day had left her very tired, and it was blowing up cold. It would get colder as night wore on.

As the great wooden ship glided past looking so near, she knew she should have been on it, and the memory of

Ted's face as she had been carried from the ship started the tears sliding down her cheeks. Then, like a match being set to gunpowder, a fierce and terrible determination exploded inside her. England had taken away her man; she would see the old country gave her a living in return. She was strong and knew how to wheedle when she had to. That officer nob had been taken in completely. What she could do once she would do again.

After five minutes the ship was showing her stern; after ten she looked a lot smaller. When she was no more than a tiny model in the distance the girl stopped watching and turned away to face the world with a firm set to her mouth.

CHAPTER EIGHT

As the only lady aboard the *Sirocco,* apart from the women of the regiment who were somewhere in the bowels of the ship safely out of the way, Victoria was smothered with flattery and warm attention from the moment they slipped from Portsmouth harbor. The troopers, who already loved her, spread the word to the seamen, who were superstitious over women on board, and they declared their willingness to adopt her also. The ship's officers had no need of persuasion; they knew a raving beauty when they saw one. In consequence, wherever she moved about the decks Victoria met with smiles and offers of assistance and was amused at finding it necessary to fend off the approaches of the free-and-easy seafaring officers, who were experts at instant and short-lived flirtations.

Not the least of these was the captain of the *Sirocco,* Byron Porchester, who fell an immediate victim to expressive brown eyes and mobile features, finding as Charles had that Victoria's youthful charm was a challenge to his approaching middle age. So it was that at dinner that first night while anchored at Spithead, she found herself being entertained by bright-eyed young men contesting for the attention of their female companion.

There was one exception. Hugo, pale and unusually reserved, said no more than good evening to her and retired early. Though Victoria knew that their relations had to be formal, she felt the evening ended with his departure. She was unprepared for what followed.

Captain Porchester nodded at the closing door. "That is a very serious young man, Major. He is going to need a sense of humor in the days to come."

Charles smiled. "A sense of humor will not help him, sir, and I doubt you will see him on his feet again until we reach port. I understand his baggage contains arrowroot, a vinaigrette and a basin. From the look of him tonight I would say his knees are already growing weak—and we are still at anchor."

A hoot of laughter greeted this and increased when Charles added, "Believe it or not, his father was a naval commander."

Victoria left the gentlemen to their cigars and retired to the cabin she must share with Charles. It was minute, walled with miniature compartments and so low Charles had to bend his head to avoid the beamed ceiling. It smelled of tar, tobacco and stale air—hardly an attractive place in the pale light from a swinging lantern. Although they were at anchor, the strong currents around the Isle of Wight were heaving the ship in slow but steady undulations.

Sitting outside the door was Zarina Stokes, waiting to render assistance to the mistress who had enabled her to travel with the regiment. Victoria felt fresh amazement as the girl followed her into the cabin, for Zarina was quite unlike any soldier's wife she had ever met. How well she now understood Hugo's laughing comment that she would understand Stokes's marriage when she set eyes on the elephant girl.

The glamour of the big top walked with the girl; it was there in the beautifully dressed chestnut hair, the slanted green eyes and the gilt of pendulum earrings that were put through her lobes in the way of gypsies. She walked spread-footed, with her body curved forward and head held high. The brightly colored clothes she favored fit her opulent shape with not an inch to spare. At first sight Victoria could hardly believe Stokes could have persuaded such a creature to show the slightest interest in him, but once the interview had begun it was plain that a circus upbringing had stamped the sophisticated veneer upon a gentle, orphaned girl who had longed for someone of her own on whom to lean.

Strangely enough, Charles had been amused by her, and any anger Victoria thought he might have felt at her employment of the wife of Hugo's servant was banished by his definitely rakish manner toward the girl. In any event, Zarina was the ideal girl for a campaign. A compulsion to address Victoria as "missus" instead of "ma'am" and a complete lack of a lady's maid's finesse were outweighed by her ability to dress and arrange hair in a matter of minutes—a relic of performers' quick changes. Add to that the girl's shining gratitude to her employers, and the Stanfords had hired the perfect servant.

In no time, Victoria was in her nightgown, the russet silk gown and hooped petticoats hung above the inadequate locker and everything tidied away.

"Good night, missus," Zarina said, stepping out of the cabin in her vivid emerald-green dress as if the gangway outside contained an audience waiting for her entrance.

Victoria was left alone in the tiny cabin. How alien the sight, sound and smell of everything around her. How far away were all the shadows of the past. The lantern swinging above her head filled her with excitement. Aunt Sophy had told her to fulfill her need to make something of her life, and this was the first step upon the path. The cabin was cramped and the bed unsprung and uncomfortable, but she must be prepared for some discomforts. An army on the move had no luxuries.

Constantinople! The very sound of their destination thrilled her—minarets, exotic trees and oriental spices. She could not wait to arrive. The Russians were confronting the Turks of Silestria, and the British were hastening to the Black Sea to provide the show of strength that would make the Russians back off. Everyone predicted a return to England by Christmas, but Victoria was determined to gain the greatest value from this expedition. It would be over in a few months, and she might never have the chance of such an adventure again.

Charles entered on a waft of cigar fumes that clung to his tight-fitting jacket. He made no attempt to be quiet in his movements, and Victoria knew why. Despite his words, he did still have some use for her and indulged it with silent dedication. Invariably, after an evening when other men had showered her with attentions, his masculine desire was at its greatest, and since the night of the ball he had been at his most demanding. After the loss of her child he had taken her with an impersonality that merely satisfied a need, and she had lain still and cold. Like counting the linen and checking the daily menus, it was one of her duties.

He banged about the tiny cubicle used for ablutions and dropped his spurred boots carelessly upon the planks. She kept her eyes on the lantern when he came to stand beside her, the reek of spirits strong on his breath. Inside her, the hurt that had sprung up at the dinner table grew like a flame beneath the bellows of his presence.

"How soon I have been proved right in my decision to allow you to accompany me," he said smugly. "You have made the finest of impressions upon the captain and crew."

She turned to look at him with stony eyes. "What a great pity you did not."

His head tilted up at the complete unexpectedness of her words. "I beg your pardon?"

"Are you sure there was not some mistake made over you and Hugo when you were children? He does not have the stomach of a sea captain's son, as you so cuttingly pointed out to the assembled company, but then they could hardly have thought you had the good breeding of a true aristocrat. Are you quite certain it is *you* who is the future Lord Blythe? Nobility is more than a name, Charles."

He stared at her for several seconds, then walked away. She was not troubled that night.

A fresh breeze blew up in the Bay of Biscay, taking the ship badly off course and delaying their arrival at Gibraltar so that the hoped-for two or three days ashore were reduced to five hours in which to take on supplies. No one was permitted to leave the ship.

Victoria stood on deck, looking longingly at the great gray rock. With the certainty of invitations from the British garrison there, she had looked forward to a change of company. Being the only lady among so many attentive males was an enviable position, except that she had no one in whom to confide. How she wished Jack Markham had been with the *Sirocco* instead of with another ship. Letty would have been the perfect companion.

"Have we been such dull company that the sight of land brings a sigh of longing from you, Mrs. Stanford?" The forthright voice of Captain Porchester teased beside her.

She turned with a smile. "Is it not true that that which is out of reach acquires an attraction in excess of its worth?"

"It is also true that familiarity brings a lack of enchantment—the exception to that being yourself, ma'am," he said with an audacious flourish. "I fear there will be a mutiny among the officers when you leave the ship."

"Your authority will surely bring them to heel."

He grinned. "I shall be leading it, ma'am."

It was difficult to guess his age. Silvered hair and weathered face contrasted with keen youthful eyes and the vigor found in men who lead an active life. There was a vagabond attraction in his rangy figure and manners that had a jauntiness not to be found in military men, but the intensity in his eyes when he spoke brought up a barrier in an instant. She knew to her cost what that look meant.

"I know very little about ships, Captain Porchester, so you must not think me foolish if I ask why you do not prefer to command a steamship."

He laughed. "Ah, you have touched upon a very sensitive subject, ma'am. It is something over which seafaring gentlemen argue incessantly. You would not understand the finer points."

"How can you be sure I would not?"

He was taken aback. "It is not a subject of interest to ladies."

"Well, of course it is not, until gentlemen feel moved to explain it to them," she said crisply. "It amazes me that the simplest facts never occur to men of intellect. Women are obliged to travel in ships; do you think it never puzzles them why sails should be rigged when there is no wind and furled when it is blowing from all directions? And if the breeze is coming *from* the direction in which it is desired to travel, how is it that the ship ever arrives at its destination?" She paused to give him a stern look from beneath her lashes. "Would you eat a strange-looking dish put before you by your housekeeper without inquiring of the ingredients? Of course you would not! And what if the woman replied that a gentleman would not understand culinary intricacies? Am I wrong in supposing you would demand to know with what the devil she was trying to fill your stomach?"

Byron Porchester began to rumble with laughter that turned into a hearty shout. "I concede defeat, ma'am. I hereby issue you an invitation to visit the wheelhouse when we get under way, when I will explain anything you wish to know."

The captain mentioned the incident to Charles over cigars that night and admitted he had been outmaneuvered.

"It gave me food for thought, and damn if she is not right. I *would* demand to know what the devil I was being given—have done, on more than one occasion in the Orient. Those little yellow men are experts on poisons, you know." He laughed. "You've got yourself a wife in a million, Major. There cannot be many like her."

"Yes," agreed Charles tautly. "So I have been told."

The idyll of blue Mediterranean and sun-washed coastline vanished forever for Victoria. It was bitterly cold and rained incessantly between Gibraltar and Malta, where the officers went ashore to a dinner arranged by the Governor. Victoria found it brilliantly dull. It left her with the impression of having spent an evening in the company of a score of Charity Verewoods—a person she had found difficult to banish from her thoughts since the night of the farewell ball.

It made her wish for Letty even more fervently. The only relief from the insular stuffiness was an interlude on the balcony with a French attaché, who parodied the principal guests so wickedly she could not stop laughing. Unfortunately, his Gallic nature obliged him to press kisses upon her fingers which, he seemed to think, reached to her shoulders, and she had reluctantly assumed an outraged dignity before sweeping off in a rustle of skirts. It was a pity, for he had been the most amusing guest present.

Only later did she realize he had subtly reminded her of Hugo, who was reported as too ill to attend the dinner. Cornet McKay told her his commander was growing feverish through constant sickness and lack of food.

"I must say it is a frightfully good thing we are not bound for Australia, ma'am," he drawled with affected weariness. "I doubt Captain Esterly would survive the ordeal."

"How I agree with the first part of that statement," she replied, "for I doubt *you* would survive the responsibility put upon you by his demise."

He watched her walk away and said to himself, "By Jove, that was extremely uncalled for!"

Two days out from Malta they were hit by a cyclone. For a day and a night they were at the mercy of the elements that seemed bent on destroying them. The first hint Victoria had of it was shortly after breakfast, when the deep rhythmic motion to which she had grown used broke up into a pattern of heaves and jerks, long anguished shudders, plunges, tilts and breathtaking upward swoops. The ship echoed with running feet, nautical shouts and the sounds of canvas being lowered and sheets secured.

Within minutes it was impossible to stand still. In the cabin, Zarina was attempting to shake out the folds from the dress her mistress had selected for the evening, when she was hurled to the opposite side, the trunk sliding after her and bruising her leg. Victoria sent her back to her own quarters, saying she could manage on her own until the storm abated. Lunch was brought to their cabin, but she and Charles found it a skilled art to eat with any kind of success and abandoned the meal.

By five, they had entered the eye of the storm and sat as tranquilly on the sea as if they were in dock. Dinner was a gay affair prompted by the ship's officers, who knew the worst was to come, and Victoria settled to sleep with no more thought of perilous seas. But all hell was let loose by midnight, and she awoke in a panic to find Charles pulling on a pair of trousers over his nightshirt as he tried to keep his balance.

"Charles, what is it?" she asked quickly.

"More bad weather," he said with a grunt as he was thrown against the bulkhead. "I must take a look at those horses. Don't light the lantern; it is far too dangerous. Remain where you are and hold the bars at your head for support. I shall not be long."

He went out, leaving her alone in the dark cabin. Now he had gone she was conscious of the eerie scream of wind as it battered taut ropes and rushed through narrow places; of the thud of water bombarding the wooden hull as it lifted in the air; of the crash of china and furniture as it shifted from side to side with every change of level; and, worst of all, the shrill scream of horses locked below-decks, in darkness and suffocating heat where they had been confined for nearly two weeks in narrow stalls.

Although it had not seemed possible for conditions to be worse, within another hour the *Sirocco* was twisting around like a spinning top, apparently rudderless and listing to port. A tremendous lurch sent Victoria headlong from her bed to the floor, where she bumped her head and grazed her knee, but before she could recover her sense of direction there came an awesome groaning followed by a crash from above that suggested the entire ship had been split asunder. Icy cold and trembling, she clawed her way to the bed and pulled bedding from it to wedge herself between a locker and the bunk. Piled around with pillows and blankets, she huddled on the floor, too frightened to think what might be happening.

In the darkness, and all alone with that infernal noise on every side, it occurred to her that Orpheus must have experienced something similar on his journey to the underworld, and her fancy put her on that same road. The note of a trumpet resounding along the gangways added to the theme, the Last Trump sounding, and the insistent call, repeated countless times, dinned into her head the message that all men must stand to their horses.

The trumpet call became mixed with the increasing screams of the beasts and the wind outside into a whirling medley of high-pitched notes that set her teeth on edge and her courage rocking. Unable to seek out human contact, the minutes dragged through her brain that attempted to count each sixty seconds. Before long, the flat crack of pistols somewhere below told her they were shooting the horses. With a mind too vivid for composure, Victoria began to see each animal falling, its great noble head hitting the floor, never to be lifted again. Her hands went up over her ears, then the blankets, until she was curled into a tight ball with her head completely smothered.

She was still there at dawn when Charles returned, exhausted and angry at the night's work. Whether she was asleep or so numbed that it resembled sleep, she was not sure, but when his hands pulled the blankets from her she could not believe it was light. His face was drawn and dirty, his eyes bloodshot, and there was an air of resignation about him.

"Victoria, how long have you been here like this?" he asked wearily.

She shook her head, then gave a gasp as the stiffness in her neck caught her. "It was impossible to remain in one place without wedging oneself in."

"You are all right?" he asked, helping her to her feet. "I could not leave the horses to come to you."

"I knew that. How many are lost?"

"Too many." He led her to the bed, fetching the pillows and rugs to put around her, then gave her a glass of brandy. "This will steady you."

"I shall never forget this night," she said through her shivers. "The scream of the horses and the sound of shots is still in my head."

He swallowed his brandy in one draught. "If you insist on becoming part of the regiment, you must accept its misfortunes. There is worse ahead."

"Has it occurred to you that I might have been hysterical after a night such as this, as most women would?" she asked, dark eyes snapping.

"Not you. You have never been sensitive to deep emotion, Victoria."

In the morning they counted the toll. Nearly half their horses had been lost when the terrified. creatures had smashed the stalls in their frenzy. Some had kicked each other to death, others had been thrown off balance and broken legs, several went mad with fear and had to be shot there and then. One of the masts had snapped and fallen overboard. Some cables had shredded and whipped back to sever the hand of a seaman. Other human casualties were a trooper with a seriously gashed head and a broken ankle, seventeen suffering from chronic seasickness, including Hugo, who had risen from his bed in a delirium to obey the trumpet call and been thrown down a companion way. He was suffering serious contusions and had been ordered to remain permanently in the sickbay under observation and restraint until they reached Constantinople.

All they saw of Constantinople was a distant impression of minarets piercing a purple haze. Orders had been received to proceed direct to Varna, a town on the shores of the Black Sea not far from where Silestria lay besieged by the Russians. A steamship was sent to take them in tow. They were fortunate. The enormous force that had been disembarked at Constantinople, to occupy the huge barracks at Scutari loaned by the Turks, was in a state of chaos.

The barrack building proved to be without either furniture or amenities and spread with rotting garbage and sew-

age from a broken pipe that disgorged into the building.
The whole place was overrun with rats, lice and wild dogs.
The soldiers forced to camp outside the walls found the
stench indescribable, and the vermin inside immediately
spread to the tents and their environs to make their life a
misery. There were reports of men seeing their ration of
salt pork and biscuit—the only one they had in a day—
literally walking away from them and of sleepers having
their fingers gnawed by rats, while lice reduced the victims'
bodies to areas of swollen red lumps.

As if that were not enough, orders arrived in steady suc-
cession, each countermanding the previous ones, until the
embarkation officers and the commissariat staff gave up in
despair. Regiments were impossibly split up, with two
companies at Scutari, three at Varna and the rest with
headquarters, at God knew where. Cavalry squadrons disembarked with all their horses and marched two miles inland to bivouac, only to be chased by a galloper with orders to get aboard again immediately and proceed to
Varna. Horses that had smelled fresh air and freedom
fought against returning to the purgatory of stalls between
decks.

The harbor was chaotic. Quays were covered with equipment, ammunition, harassed officers and blaspheming seamen. Horses and guns blocked every avenue, and Turkish
peddlers found their fresh vegetables being inadvertently
tipped into the sea to join the floating filth and swollen
carcasses that already made it a cesspool.

Those aboard the *Sirocco* had been spared the miasma of
that place, so Victoria did not appreciate that Varna was
pleasant in comparison. It was a clean enough town, but
not ideal for disembarkation, as the ship had to stand offshore while small boats plied to and from the quay. The
soldiers and their equipment were taken off with efficiency,
but it was a different matter when it came to lowering
horses into cockleshell craft; the beasts were terrified and
dangerous.

Victoria stood on deck to watch the activity in a cool
dress of flowered cotton and a straw bonnet. It was a hot
June morning that threw a haze over the shore, making
their destination indistinct, and she strained her eyes to get

a good impression of this strange land upon which she was to make a temporary home.

Shouts and splashes drew her gaze down to the filthy water where kicking horses had upset a boat, throwing all the occupants into the sea. The animals were swimming for the shore in great glee at their freedom, while the sailors and Hussars cursed as they scrambled through the odorous flotsam surrounding them.

To one who had no responsibilities it was a fascinating and exciting morning. The ship was alive with scurrying men and the sounds of winches squeaking, chains rattling, rough commands, shrill neighing and sea chanteys. Everything was bustle, from the deck to the shore. Strange odors reached her from landward and mingled with those of tarred ropes, boiling stock from the galley, human sweat and horse manure—the latter being almost overpowering, now the hatches were open.

All this sent a thrill of adventure through Victoria. The sun blazing down upon brown water that was moving with boatloads of black, bay and white horses, blue-and-gold-coated Hussars, piled equipment and one containing squabbling, drably dressed soldiers' wives, released spirits that had first been imprisoned within her on that morning in the Mirror Room at Wychbourne. Here was life and excitement; here was something she could share with Hugo, could understand as part of his life, could see with her own eyes instead of dutifully waiting at home. Oh, she would not have missed one moment of it!

For this she could almost feel gratitude toward Charles—if he had refused her request she might just as well have entered a nunnery. For this she was prepared to endure his hostility, his insufferable patronage, his sexual advances. He would not find her wanting in courage, strength or willingness to see to his needs, for at any time he could send her back to England. How much worse it would be then, having tasted this existence.

Byron Porchester appeared from the wheelhouse and strolled across to stand beside her. "Ah, ma'am, 'tis a sad day indeed," he said with real regret as he looked out at the shore. "So many brave men. How many will return?"

"You must not be so melancholy, sir," she said. "They go with eagerness to do their duty."

"Aye, mebbe," he said heavily. "And what of you, my dear Mrs. Stanford? You surely do not intend to stay with them? It is no life for you."

She smiled. "Captain, I thought you knew me well enough now to realize I am no stay-at-home. Women have a particular role to play in life. We are the gentle peacemakers, the soft voice of comfort after the roar of the aggressors. In the same way that you cannot sail a ship without first learning how it is done, we cannot create peace if we have not seen war, neither can we provide comfort from something of which we have no understanding."

He took one of her hands and raised it to his lips. "I salute you, ma'am. You are a remarkable woman." He paused, turning to see the reason for her rising color and intense interest in something behind him, and saw a young military captain he did not recognize at first glance. Peering with narrowed eyes across the brilliant sunshine, he took in the hollowed yellow face, burning eyes and sagging shoulders.

"My dear sir, are you quite mad?" he exclaimed. "You are in no fit state to walk off this ship, Captain . . . "

"Esterly," said Hugo, pulling up short at the sight of Victoria. "Good day, ma'am."

"Good day," replied Victoria, shocked at his appearance and in complete agreement with Captain Porchester. But as she was about to repeat his advice she caught back the words, remembering Hugo's dislike of being treated as an invalid. It must be bad enough knowing he was regarded, with unsympathetic masculine justice, as a target for ribaldry, without having the misfortune to encounter her the minute he appeared on deck. Unlike the men, however, her own gratifying lack of aversion to the sea did not prevent her from feeling extremely sorry for those unfortunate enough to suffer in that way. Constant sickness during her pregnancy had seen to that.

The sea captain was not as sensitive. "You can barely stand, man. I insist on sending for a stretcher. There have been enough mishaps already."

"No, sir, I am completely capable," Hugo insisted.

"I am captain of this ship, sir. You will do as I say."

Victoria put her hand on the older man's arm. "I think

Captain Esterly would not put anything at risk. He is a very sensible man, I assure—"

"What is amiss?" Charles came from behind the wheelhouse and summed up the little scene immediately.

"We are discussing the possibility of this gentleman being taken ashore on a stretcher," said Captain Porchester.

Charles ignored Hugo and spoke directly to the man standing beside his wife. "None of my officers goes ashore unless he can take himself," he said tartly, as if Hugo were trying to malinger. "We are going to a war, not a convalescent home. You have my permission to proceed, Captain Esterly," he added over his shoulder. "Come, my dear. Captain Porchester has kindly invited us to lunch aboard. We shall find the harbor less congested this afternoon."

He held out his arm, and she went across to him, conscious of Hugo's careful progress down the Jacob's ladder. *Please do not let him slip,* she prayed.

It was mid-afternoon when they were rowed ashore, and the heat was intense as they stepped onto the quay. It seemed as congested as it had looked all day. As far as the eye could see there were milling soldiers in scarlet, blue or rifle-green jackets, mixed with Greeks and Turks in rags or exotic boleros and baggy trousers. Cavalrymen were accoutering horses, who were being driven mad by swarms of flies that settled on their heads like moving masks; infantrymen were unpiling arms with more haste than care; red-faced artillerymen manhandled guns into positions where they could be harnessed to the horses; others piled cannon balls and shells in great mounds as they were unloaded from small boats.

Victoria was glad of Charles to guide her through the bedlam to where a trooper waited with Renata and Caliban already saddled, but it proved impossible to move off for another hour, until the entire detachment was mounted and formed up. The sight of two squadrons of Hussars on the march was familiar to Victoria, but never had she ridden at the head of them as she did now. Charles helped her mount, then led her across to the long column headed by Hugo on his famous horse, Monty. Their eyes met as she passed him. This moment would have been supreme if it

had been at his side that she rode, and her look told him
so.

Charles gave the order to move off, and they began their
ride to camp through the narrow uneven streets thronged
with inquisitive peasants who gaped at the sight of these
splendid men, half of whom were riding horses just now
provided by the remount officer to replace those who were
lost at sea. Against the English horses they looked short,
rough-coated and poor, but the loss in animals had been so
severe throughout the entire force, the remount department
had been forced to buy them where they could from deal-
ers who knew they could charge twice their worth.

The early twilight had begun when they reached the
campsite, a huge open plain beside a lake where thousands
of English and Turkish soldiers were already under canvas
and going about the usual chores of setting guards, throwing out cavalry piquets and eating a meal of unappetizing
quality. To Victoria it represented real campaigning for the
first time.

The ground was covered in bell tents in neat rows, with
ropes spread out all around them. Rifles were piled in pyramids every twenty yards or so, and fires burned outside
the mess tents, casting picturesque shadows over the canvas
and the industrious soldiers as they went about their duty.
It seemed to go on for a mile or more, and the thought of
becoming a part of it made Victoria throb with excitement.

The excitement began to dim when it was discovered
that all their own tents and equipment, which were following in bullock carts, had gone astray somewhere along the
route, including their rations for the night. They could do
nothing but remain in their saddles until the carts showed
up, an extremely heavy dew making it impossible to sit on
the ground. The officers—Hugo and a more senior captain
called Foster, Cornets McKay and Lancing and Charles—
organized the watering of the horses at the lake, leaving
Victoria alone on the open area designated for their tents.

She was not alone for long. Her cousin Charlotte's husband, Captain Jenson, appeared out of the near darkness
and grinned at her surprise.

"We have been here two days. The news of your arrival
reached us this morning. I have been waiting for you to
ride in."

"How lovely it is to meet you here," she cried in delight at encountering someone she knew in this foreign spot. "We are in a fix. Our tents are lost—gone who knows where—and dinner is far away. I am only thankful Charles and I had luncheon on board; the others had none."

He laughed in his usual happy manner. "If that is all your trouble, ma'am, you are fortunate. My tent and dinner are yours to share. By George, this will be in my letter to Charlotte tonight."

"And I shall also write," she declared. "News from me that you are hale and hearty will be more reassuring than your letters, which she will believe are couched in terms more pleasing than truthful. As to your invitation, I accept, I accept! You are quite the most welcome gentleman I have encountered today."

Without Captain Jenson she would have spent a miserable evening, for the wagons were not located until ten, and the soldiers set up the tents in darkness, aided in their work by pretending the tent pegs were the heads of the Turks who had gone astray with the baggage. In consequence, the detachment of Hussars turned in with empty stomachs, although its officers were all entertained by infantry officers, who hospitably shared dinner with them, including bottles of tolerable wine they had been swift to buy in Varna during the two days they had spent in the area, knowing there would soon be none to be had.

Victoria passed her first night under canvas full of a strange kind of restlessness. The air of unreality that had hung over the meal in Captain Jenson's tent in company with Charles and two infantry officers persisted now that she was lying on a folding bed in the large tent Charles had provided for their use. He had said hardly a word to her since their arrival, too angry over the loss of the equipment to be even impersonally polite, and now he was asleep in the companion bed, leaving her awake with her thoughts.

How far removed she was from her previous life. Lying here surrounded by several thousand soldiers, she was only one hundred miles from the enemy. The voyage had been a suspended existence between one life and the other; tonight, she was part of a war. From now on she would spend each day with the sounds of trumpets, rifles and thundering hooves. She would grow used to eating off a wooden chest within the sloping canvas walls of the tent and drinking wine beneath the swinging lantern on the tent pole, while the sounds of a military encampment went on around her. She would push open her tent flap with an experienced hand and learn to hold her skirts free of the dew-laden floor. In time, the sounds of the night would not keep her awake. Dogs howled in the distance—or were they wolves?—and insects set up an orchestra of uneasy notes. The horses moved restlessly, blowing through their nostrils and stamping to shake off the dew that fell like heavy rain. Soldiers coughed with consumptive distress, and the guards moved along their patrol routes with low-voiced conversation.

Midnight, and she was still not asleep. The dew that had settled on the tent created a chill inside that made her curl tighter beneath her blankets and slip down until the tip of her nose was covered. Finally, she accepted that sleep would not come until she allowed herself to think about Hugo lying in the next tent.

He was her reason for being here. To be near him day after day was all her life. To share each alien experience, to exclaim over, question and enthuse about each aspect of the campaign with him was an aching desire within her. There was so much she wished to know, so much she longed to discuss, so much she yearned to tell him, yet she must lie here in dutiful neglect beside his brother. But it was not that that kept her awake. On the ship he might as well have been still in Ireland for all she had seen of him, yet today he had been there all the time, looking so ill, yet going about his duty with dogged determination and refusing to acknowledge her presence by the slightest sign. Apart from his greeting on the deck of *Sirocco*, when he could not avoid speaking to her, Hugo had behaved as though they had never met—as though she did not exist. Tonight, she had never been so near him, yet so far away.

All the next day troops marched in, as transports brought them from Scutari, and the camp swelled. Rations were somehow found for the men, who had gone a whole day with only a mug of tea to warm their stomachs, and the officers descended on Varna for chickens, vegetables and wine to grace their makeshift tables. There were plenty of eggs and fresh fruit for those able to pay the price, and the officers could. But the soldiers were adept at beating down the prices and stuffed their pockets full of apricots, greengages and plums, or returned to camp with a watermelon or a great scarlet pumpkin, tied in a handkerchief.

Victoria could not tear herself away from watching the road, which grew dustier and more indistinct as the day wore on. Long snakes of scarlet-coated soldiers wound their way up from the harbor in a never-ending tail, until it seemed to her there could be no more—and still they came. The tents now stretched as far as the eye could see in every direction, and the air was filled with a steady hum that never abated. At last, toward evening, her tired eyes saw the glitter of sun on harness and the blue jackets of Hussars. The second detachment of the regiment was now marching in with a small figure in cream and brown alongside them.

Letty was as delighted to see her friend as Victoria was to see her, and they fell upon each other with embraces and eager questions. The new arrivals had been caught up in the confusion at Scutari, disembarking and embarking again the same day. Letty described the scene with lively humor, but it had not really been amusing. Several horses had been lost when they jumped into the sea with fright and swam in the wrong direction until they drowned; Lieutenant Lord Dovedale was suffering from a concussion, after being thrown from his horse that was too much of a thoroughbred to take kindly to Turkish bullock carts; and three soldiers' wives had vanished into Constantinople, vowing they had had enough of campaigning. The ship had sailed without them.

"If you only knew how I have longed for your company," declared Letty.

"As I have for yours," Victoria replied happily. "Now you are here we shall be constant companions."

But it was in Hugo's tent that the Markhams ate dinner that evening. Charles would not have them as guests in his home in England and saw no reason for changing his ruling.

Early the following morning, orders came in for the cavalry to strike camp and march to Devna, a village some twenty miles upcountry, at first light the next day, and Victoria was awakened by Zarina shortly after 3:00 A.M. in preparation for the march. As they left soon after five, Victoria could not help reflecting that it was just as well they were moving, since six regiments of French infantry had arrived in Varna, besides three detachments of English Rifles and the major part of the 17th Lancers, who had also sailed from Portsmouth.

The day was one she would remember as her first real march, for they did not arrive at the new camp until well after noon—the longest time she had ever spent in the saddle. For the greater part of the journey she was too fascinated by the countryside to feel tired. Their winding dust track led them over gentle hills colored by wild flowers, through woodlands that gave relief from the beating heat of the sun and across plains of such rural tranquillity it seemed wicked to fill them with war-like horsemen.

Victoria rode at the head of the column with Charles but sought Letty's company at each halt, when the nature of the march made it natural for all the officers to drop to the ground in a common group to eat breakfast or slake their thirsts. The two ladies were very popular and had a gay time with young blades like Hector Balesworth and Harry Edmunds, who threw Victoria tragic glances every so often from beneath his lashes. Hugo was with the advance party—probably with the deliberate intent of Charles, thought Victoria—and she had no sight of him until they reached their destination.

Another wide plain of lush meadows and a plentiful supply of water looked very attractive to the soldiers and the two officers' wives who arrived exhausted by the excessive heat and fatigue of the march, but it was paradise to those women of the regiment who were forced to follow their trooper husbands on foot, with an occasional lift on one of the baggage wagons. Trooper Pitchley saw the state they were in and knew his Maria could never have stood such conditions with the baby inside her. Perhaps it was all to the good that she had not been allowed to come. He could not write to her, for he had no address. All he could do was trust the Almighty to see her right.

Life settled into a routine, and the troopers made themselves as comfortable as possible. Day by day detachments marched in from Varna, until the Light Cavalry Brigade was complete.

One day there was a great stir as the notorious Earl of

Cardigan, commander of the Light Brigade, rode into camp and, with the overbearing military eccentricity for which he was renowned, decided to change the position of all the tents—not once but twice—until everyone was hot and resentful and at least a mile further from the water than they had been before. From that day he made a nuisance of himself wherever he went by insisting on parades and reviews, immaculate uniforms and the severest punishment for the slightest offense. He also indulged his favorite sport, officer-baiting.

Victoria became something of a mother-confessor to the cavalry officers. Not a day passed that some subaltern or junior captain did not come to her tent or accompany her on a ride over the hills and spoke bitterly of the unfairness of their commander. One had been publicly reprimanded before the entire regiment for being seen in camp in a forage cap instead of a shako. Another had been ordered on a dangerous patrol with the remains of fever still on him and told to be a man. Yet another had been refused permission to leave camp until further notice because he had had the temerity to point out that the temperature was one hundred degrees and he felt his men could be excused wearing fur-lined pelisses on pardae. Lord Cardigan stormed, penalized the captain, and the men sweltered in their full-dress uniforms to satisfy their commander's whims.

Victoria met this handsome, egocentric major general at dinner one night with Colonel Rayne and thoroughly disliked him. Charming and persuasive with ladies, Lord Cardigan did not know he was talking to someone who distrusted older men who flattered her with a silken tongue. He was often to be found riding past her tent to inquire how she was, and she was thankful when he was sent with a large detachment to ascertain the position of the enemy. News had been received that the Turks had raised the seige of Silestria without help, and the Russians had retreated to a position unknown. The Anglo-British force surrounding Varna sat and waited to hear what they must do next, while the politicians and generals tried to conceal their embarrassment. The armies could not be sent home again, yet they could not sit at Varna indefinitely.

June passed into July, and the temperature soared to one hundred and ten. Victoria and Letty began taking a daily ride in the coolness of early morning before breakfast, accompanied by any officers who felt so inclined. It was on one such ride that they came across Hugo exercising Monty in the hills above the camp. Harry Edmunds hailed him, and he trotted across with reluctance when he saw the ladies.

He looked better than when he had left the ship, but Victoria remembered him at Wychbourne and knew the voyage had taken its toll of his vitality. In all the time they had been at Devna he had been merely polite. She had received stiff salutes in passing, brief greetings at dinners to which they were both invited and adamant refusals to enter into conversation with her at any time. For six weeks she had watched him go about his duties meticulously, knowing Charles was watching every movement for the slightest fault. He had taken patrols during the day and at night, mounted piquets, drilled his troop strictly by the book, inspected horses, written reports, administered discipline . . . and scrupulously kept his distance from his major's wife. He was often in the company of the Markhams, yet moved away when Victoria approached; he rode with his brother officers, yet never joined the young men accompanying the two ladies on their morning exercise. This time he was trapped, and the fact was in the depths of his eyes as he bade Letty and Victoria an unsmiling good morning.

"We're glad to come across you, for we are unusually short of escorts this morning," Letty cried saucily. "We are used to six, at least and are wondering what we can have done to make everyone desert us."

He gave a faint smile. "And I was wondering why I should be in such great demand that I was hailed from such a distance. I see now that I am expected to stand substitute for four men."

"Something you are well able to do, sir, when you set your mind to it," said Letty with a laugh. "Take off that downcast look and entertain us. We have seen little enough of you on our morning rides. Can it be that you feel we are not in your class as riders?"

"So you are not, madam," he replied in quick teasing. "Why else do you think I have encouraged all my friends to flock around you? They have let me down this morning."

"Shame on you! For that confession you shall suffer our company all the way back. What say you, gentlemen?"

Harry Edmunds and Lord Dovedale—now recovered from his fall—agreed, and further suggested he should provide the eggs for their breakfast. They rode in a group for a while, chatting lightheartedly as they were prone to do these days to cover the growing sense of frustration and worry over the condition of the horses, which were becoming pathetically thin and ill in such an unsuitable climate.

With careful nonchalance Victoria edged Renata nearer Hugo until they were riding side by side and slightly behind the others. He sensed what she was doing and made to quicken his pace.

"Hugo, just one moment, if you please," she said quickly.

He remained coldly remote, not looking at her. "I am sorry. It is not possible."

"*Not possible!* Is it not?" she cried in sudden hurt anger. "I shall make it possible." Raising her voice so that it was clearly heard above the chatter of the others, she said, "I challenge you to outdistance me, Captain Esterly. We shall see if we are not in your class, as you so ungallantly suggested just now."

Carried away by the passionate need to hurt him, move him in some way, see that he suffered as much as she, Victoria urged Renata forward on a mad gallop downhill before she fully considered her action. The hot morning air brushed her cheeks, making them burn, and the jacket of her blue habit felt too tight to contain the bursting within her breast as she heard hooves thundering behind her. In that short moment she had everything.

Monty flew past with long deep strides, and Hugo brought him around in superb style on that slope, so that she was forced to veer and rein in a hundred yards further on. Hugo was beside her as she halted and he was extremely angry—a mood that transferred itself to Monty, who fidgeted and danced sideways, snorting through his nostrils as his rider breathed heavily with more than exertion.

"That trick was not worthy of you, Victoria," he snapped.

She was also breathless with more than exertion. "You

have not been behaving in a very worthy manner yourself," she flung back at him. "How do you think it looks when you so pointedly ignore me? Every other officer at Devna offers me warm friendship."

His eyes flashed. "Then you do not need mine."

"I do not need such a complete reversal of manner that not only the officers but the men are beginning to look strangely at me when you pass by like a stiff-faced statue."

"You should never have come on this campaign."

"But I am here and intend to remain. Do you mean to continue this ridiculous pretense that we are even less than acquaintances?"

"Yes."

"Why?"

"It is a matter of honor. Charles doubts mine where you are concerned."

"So you told me at the ball, but you are being quite nonsensical about it. How can there be anything dishonorable about you having a conversation with me in the presence of others? Does he question the honor of every gentleman who speaks to me?" She was angry and flung out a hand to point at the distant figures they had left. "Does he doubt Lord Dovedale and Mr. Edmunds because they ride with me?"

"I suggest you ask him."

She looked at him in despair. He was not only acting like a stranger—he was one. To what distant place had he retreated since the night of the ball? Had Charity Verewood beseiged him so that he had abandoned all he had previously held dear? No, it was impossible to believe that . . . yet she had lost him as surely as his manner suggested. He was not acting a charade these days; there was more than honor behind his hostility.

Through stiff lips she asked, "Are you afraid of Charles? Is it really necessary for you to walk away whenever I approach, or dig in your spurs if I trot past?"

"I would not do it if it were not." He pulled at the reins to steady his horse. "I suggest we rejoin the others."

"And I suggest you are a coward," she cried through her hurt. She was unprepared for his reaction.

"By God, not you also? Has your husband been instructing you on my character?" He was blazingly angry, and

she thought he had never stirred her more than at this moment on a foreign hillside with the sun glinting through his
windblown hair as he sat the tall restless stallion.

"We do not discuss you—we do not discuss *anything*.
Charles seems always too busy these days."

"Then perhaps you should concentrate more on your
husband and less on trying to captivate every officer in
sight," he suggested tightly as he swung his horse around.
"At the risk of appearing even more ungallant I am about
to return to our friends—whether you accompany me or
not."

Six days later, all other problems were set aside when a
vicious form of cholera quickly ran through the French
camp and struck the British cavalry overnight. By morning, twenty-five men were dead, including Major Packer,
second-in-command of the Hussars. Victoria was shocked
and frightened by her first encounter with sudden death—
Major Packer had dined with them the previous evening,
laughing and entertaining them with stories of his one attempt at training a string of race horses. She could not believe he would not laugh again.

Too upset to eat breakfast or go riding, she remained in
her tent all day, sweltering in a temperature of 109°,
haunted by Major Packer's face and staring at the spot in
which he had sat less than twelve hours ago. The air was
oppressive, Charles, as his new second-in-command, was in
conference with Colonel Rayne, and Letty had gone with
Jack and several Lancer officers to the village of Schumla
on a day's excursion to see if there were better goods there
than in Devna.

A headache had developed by the time Charles returned,
but he had even more shocking news for her. In Varna the
epidemic was out of control, and those encamped there had
lost as many as four hundred in one night. In their own
camp there had been more deaths during the day, the
most tragic being one of the troopers' wives, who had been
much loved by the men for her kind and cheerful nature.

Charles brooded over dinner, and Victoria retired early,
trying to cool her forehead with cologne that was warm in
the bottle and virtually useless. Her dreams were night-
mares in which she saw herself running from a great green

monster with outstretched hands that kept laughing with increasing hollowness in Major Packer's voice.

Zarina awoke her in the morning with the usual cup of tea, but Victoria quickly noticed an air of nervousness about the elephant girl as she glanced around for any sign of the major arriving.

"Missus," she whispered conspiratorially, "Stokes said I was to tell you this private. The captain got took with the cholera two hours ago and won't go to his bed. Stokes says you're the only one can talk some sense into him before it's too late. Please come, Missus, they're gone in a matter of four hours, with no one to mourn them."

CHAPTER NINE

"You're doing yourself no good, sir," Stokes insisted. "Walking up and down like that only aggeravates the pains—take my word for it. Captain, it's a fact," he pleaded. "I shan't tell you again."

"Good. Your silence will bring one less thing to plague me," grunted Hugo. He continued to drag himself along the few feet of space within his tent, holding onto the center pole as he passed, while a cramping pain doubled him up once more.

He had thought the sea journey produced the most misery he had ever felt, but this was far worse. Apart from the vomiting that left him shaking and cold, there were tearing claws at his stomach that could not be borne silently, however hard he tried. At the onset of the attack in the early hours, life had not run out of him in the most appalling way, but now that had ceased the cramps seemed worse.

He took out his pocket watch. Two hours and a quarter since that first fearful knowledge. Some men died in that time. Determinedly he put one foot in front of the other and made for the tent flap, before turning to pace back the other way. To lie down would be fatal; while he was on his feet he could not succumb. A man could not die of cholera if he was standing up. If he kept moving for a quarter of an hour, he could do so for the next. On no account would he take to his bed.

He reached the bed as another cramp brought cold sweat and an onrush of fear in its wake. As he was hanging over it, fighting to keep his breath even, there was a rustle behind him.

"Thank the Lord you've come, ma'am," said Stokes's voice. "Please get him to go to bed. All that walking up and down is weakening him."

"I shall do what I can, Stokes," said Victoria's hushed voice. "Thank you for letting me know."

"Well, ma'am, I thought as how your being . . . friends . . . with the captain . . . I mean . . ."

"It is good of you to show such concern over Captain Esterly. He has a loyal man in you."

The spasm over, Hugo turned in exhausted anger. She was standing just inside his tent, dressed in a gown of some yellow material that hung in full folds. Her long dark curls were caught back with a ribbon, and her face was pale. He had never seen her with her hair down, and the sight made him angrier.

"I shall have your hide for this, Stokes. Escort Mrs. Stanford back to her tent at once."

"No, Stokes," she said quietly. "Just wait outside for a few minutes."

Stokes gave Hugo a tragic look. "I'm sorry, sir. I've always done what you said before, but there's times I don't hear you too well, and this is one of them." He nodded his head at Victoria. "Call if you want anything, ma'am."

"Stokes!" Hugo roared through a throat made dry and husky through constant retching. Turning to Victoria, he said, "I shall be obliged if you will leave immediately."

"No, Hugo."

"I cannot believe Charles sent you."

"He does not know I have come."

"Then I insist you leave."

She came forward several paces, paler than ever. "You are extremely ill. All other considerations must be forgotten at such a time."

He was at the end of his tether. "Keeping alive is my only consideration. That is the only thing in which I have any interest. I do not want advice, assistance . . . or anything else from you. I thought I made my views clear enough last week."

She stood her ground, the light of determination still in her eyes despite a growing hurt. "Very clear—but I am more concerned with compassion than honor. I have no intention of leaving until I have persuaded you to see sense. Since you *cannot* leave, and I *will* not, I think you must give in to the inevitable."

"Are you not content with what you have already done? Is it your wish to destroy everything around me?" An attack of pain in his lower abdomen grew so severe he was forced to bend forward in an attempt to relieve it, and he felt her arm around him for support.

"I would not be here if I wished to hurt you," she said on a breath. "Please listen to advice and lie on your bed."

The familiar lemon-and-sweet-hay perfume swept over him, with luring promises of past pleasures reborn. In the midst of the uncontrollable shaking which followed each spasm he found time to wonder rather wildly why he should have to face this extra torment when he already had enough to combat. Though he was drained, exhausted and near capitulation, her next words brought back his fighting spirit.

"Hugo, stop this nonsense and let Stokes make you comfortable or I shall have risked Charles's anger for nothing."

He pulled away and went across to the tent flap, which provided a convenient hold to steady himself. "You *have* risked it for nothing. I did not ask you to come. I do not want you here. It is abundantly clear that you know nothing about cholera. Its deadlines depend as much on fear as virulence. A strong man can *believe* himself into his grave from the moment he first knows he is a victim." The tent began to blur and he blinked to clear the sweat that was running down his face.

Behind Victoria his bed beckoned. A great longing to double up on the blankets and shut out the world began to insinuate itself into his brain in a louder voice than his own, which suddenly sounded far away in his ears. "The only way to fight this is to stay on one's feet and *know* that recovery is certain. That is the only way, Victoria," he finished painfully.

The yellow dress had grown smudgy now, and the grass inside the canvas pyramid was undulating in a way that revived the nausea inside him. Dear God, surely he was not about to start retching again? In a great burst of desperation, he set himself walking, brushing past Victoria as he went. She had broken his regular pacing and the symptoms were returning. A hand caught his arm and she was beside him, looking up with eyes that appeared wet, but it might have been his own blurred vision giving that illusion.

"Recovery *will* be certain if you let me help you." She walked beside him, smelling sweet and clean after the wretchedness of the past two hours. "Please give yourself some ease by lying down."

"I must keep walking." He was not sure if he had spoken aloud or not.

"If I only knew the right thing to do." Her voice held a note of despair. "If I could only be sure this was the best way to fight it." Suddenly, she was before him, taking his face between her hands. The wetness in her eyes was now overflowing. "Tell me the truth, Hugo. Tell me what I must do. I am so frightened—more frightened than I have ever been in my life." All that short life was there in her eyes. "If I lose you, I shall have nothing—you know that."

He caught at the center pole as he felt the tent start to spin. He tried hard to focus on the face that haunted his life; all he could see was his brother standing in the book-lined library in Brunswick Square. *Are you an adolescent boy that you cannot master the desires of the flesh? She will see you crack and fall apart before her. I challenge you to see this campaign through to its end.*

He dragged up words from deep within himself. "I have only one aim in life—to survive this campaign to its end. I shall not do it unless you leave me to recover and go back where you belong." With some pale savagery he added, "You cannot lose what you have never had."

The vision of Charles vanished in time for him to see the effect of his words, but she went in a swirl of skirts while he stood holding the pole. He was viciously angry now. The feeling of sickness vanished and the returning vision of Charles put new strength in his feet. Several minutes later, Stokes entered with a brawny trooper and the men took Hugo's arms to keep him walking up and down. A look at his pocket watch showed that twenty minutes had passed since he last looked. Twenty minutes more of his life. It was not finished yet!

After luncheon, Victoria put on a straw bonnet and walked the short distance to Letty's tent, knowing she would find her friend alone while Jack was out on patrol. The unbearable heat had taken toll of the brown-haired girl, who was resting on her bed with a damp cloth over her eyes. She uncovered them and managed a smile when her visitor entered.

"Hello, Victoria. Mrs. Stokes has told you the news, of

course? Jack went to Hugo's tent as soon as we received your message this morning, and I called again less than half an hour ago. You would not believe the improvement in him!" She paused fractionally. "I believe he is over the crisis, truly I do. There is every chance that he will survive, Victoria."

"Thank you, Letty." It was the first time since sailing that the two women had alluded to any interest Victoria might have in the young captain. Even now, it was quickly pushed away.

"The heat, plus anxiety for Hugo, has given me a headache. Jack is gone on patrol, so I hope to sleep for a while." Letty raised herself on the pillow. "Are you quite well yourself? Should you be about in this terrible heat?"

"I have been thinking and am come to enlist your help," said Victoria, sinking onto the only chair. "I have been told that many men *believe* themselves into their graves because cholera frightens them into succumbing from the moment they know it is on them. They see their fellows dying all around them—sometimes within a matter of an hour or so—and give up all hope immediately."

"Are you surprised, Victoria? Jack said six hundred died in one night at Varna. It has spread to the fleet and the Turkish troops that have marched in to join the Anglo-French force. It is said that our poor Guards are reduced to half their number. *Half their number,* mark you, and they have not yet been in battle."

Victoria was appalled. "It cannot be true, Letty."

The girl nodded. "Jack had it on good authority from a captain who rode up from Varna yesterday. It seems our Guards were encamped in one of the unhealthiest spots in the Balkans. The Turkish troops will not go near it but, since we did not ask its fitness, they did not think to tell us what they knew. Our men are being moved as soon as possible."

"Charles tells me there is a rumor afoot that we are to move also," Victoria confided, "but we hear so many conflicting stories I do not believe any of them until they happen. It will not affect my plan."

Letty looked at her curiously. "Are you certain you are well enough to discuss plans, Victoria? You look as if there is a fever upon you."

"If there is, it is a fever of impatience," she said shortly.
"I wish you will listen to what I have to propose."

Letty considered her for a few seconds, then said quietly,
"Go on."

"We are the only two ladies here at Devna, and I have
come to believe that we should earn our places with the
regiment."

Letty became suspicious. "How?"

Victoria forced herself to speak plainly. "Hugo is recov-
ering from something that is killing most of its victims. He
is a very determined and intelligent man, and he has
friends like you and Jack who care about him—besides
Stokes, who, I truly believe, would die for him if necessary." She took a deep breath. "All through the morning I
have been thinking about those who have none of those
advantages. Letty, out there are men lying among their
comrades with no one to give them any attention, hope or
reason to believe they are not already dead men. All they
see are their fellows being covered with blankets and taken
out one by one. They hear the trumpet being sounded over
the graves, knowing that the next one will be over their
own. Would you not give up under such circumstances?"

Letty shivered. "Whatever has brought such melancholy
and morbid thoughts to your head? No wonder you look so
white and exhausted. It does not do to dwell on such
things, Victoria."

She grew angry in an instant, surprising even herself. "I
had not thought to hear such words from you, Letty. Do
you tell me you can glibly speak of six hundred dying in
one night and our poor Guards leaving the earth in such
great numbers and not give a thought to the fact that those
numbers are human souls? Each one is a man with a family, loved ones, friends. He is a father, husband, son. In
England, there are women destined to hear that he is no
more. A piece of paper will arrive, and that is all they will
ever know of him again."

The girl on the bed pulled her wrapper closer around her
and swung her legs to the ground. "If one thought of all the
tragedies in life it would be impossible to find any composure, Victoria," she said quietly. "The ways of the Lord are
mysterious—*you* should know that, dear friend—and we
must accept His decisions."

"Pray do not speak to me of accepting His decisions," Victoria flared. "Forgive me, Letty, but life has been very good to you, and I do not believe you have any idea of what it is like to be forced to do so. I will agree that the Lord has His reasons, but I happen to think He expects us to help ourselves from time to time."

Letty was looking angry now, but Victoria was not going to be stopped, even if it meant a quarrel. Since she'd left Hugo's tent that morning, a great deal had been going through her head and heart. The Almighty had come in for a great deal of criticism until Zarina Stokes had come in with the laundry, acting as His messenger, Victoria thought. She had swung in in her usual graceful manner, with the basket on her hip and her red hair piled high.

"Missus, isn't it grand? The captain is on the mend. Stokes said I was to tell you if you hadn't sent him to get another man and walk the invalid up and down until he could stand no more, there's no doubt Captain Esterly would be in a bad plight by now." The girl had neither guile nor sauciness on her face. "You can rely on us not to say anything, missus, but Stokes and me reckon you saved him . . . and that must be about as much comfort as anyone would wish for. Don't go upsetting yourself any more about him."

The girl's words had returned again and again, until Victoria suddenly saw what she must do. Her natural instinct had been to come straight to Letty, but she would do it alone if necessary.

"Victoria," Letty was saying, "if you are not suffering from a fever brought on by melancholia, will you quickly come to the reason for your visit? I have a headache, the heat is trying me very severely . . . and so, at the moment, are you."

Victoria rose and went to sit beside the girl on the bed. "It has occurred to me that we are here for a purpose," she said urgently. "I will admit it was a purely selfish motive that led us to travel with the regiment, but we need not remain selfish." She took her friend's hands. "It is the duty of our husbands to look after the men under their command, is it not? I see it as *our* duty to perform those services that can only be considered as nonregimental. A woman's soft voice inquiring after them, reading letters from

their loved ones at home, hearing the last thoughts that
could not be told to their fellows lest they be thought unmanly, knowing someone cares about them as a person, not
as a fighting machine—all that could make this terrible
time bearable for them. It might even raise the spirits of
some enough to make them fight it, as. . ." She broke off
quickly. "It might even save one or two. Letty, will you
come with me to the hospital now?"

The frown on the pretty face deepened. "I cannot believe
the major approves this plan, Victoria."

"He does not know of it."

"As I thought. He will soon put an end to it."

"He will not. I am determined upon it. Do I go alone?
Are we to fall out over something that should unite us?"

Letty was unhappy and showed it. "Have you thought
what this really means, Victoria? It sounds very high-
minded and commendable, but the hospital is a terrible
place just now. It is surrounded by the most unimaginable
smells, and there are groans and moans coming from beneath the canvas day and night. I dare say one could not
move among the sick, for I believe they are scrambling all
over each other. The language to be heard would dismay
anyone. They are common soldiers, Victoria . . . and you
are the wife of a major."

Victoria could hardly believe her dearest friend could
think in such terms. She rose at once, disillusioned and upset.

"Well, Letty, you have taught me a lesson in mistaking
the character of a person. Yes, I am the wife of a major
and could choose whether or not I traveled with my husband on this campaign. The wives of these soldiers could
not." She went over to the tent flap. "If Jack were halfway
across the world without you and he were dying, would
you not be grateful to the woman who put a last glass of
water to his lips or wrote to tell you his last words?"

Letty rose. "This is different. These men are . . ."

"Are what?" challenged Victoria. "Would Jack leave
them on a field of battle because he is a gentleman and
they are not?"

Letty stared at her friend, then looked down. "You have
brought reality too near, Victoria. I am sorry you have
found me wanting."

Immediately, Victoria was across to her and taking her
hands again. "Come with me, dear Letty, for I doubt I shall
have the courage to do it alone."

Victoria returned to her tent at 5:00 P.M. Her dress
was wet and sticking to her back, and the dark curls hung
limply against her neck. The ache that had begun in her
throat as she ran from Hugo's tent that morning was still
there, making her voice hoarse, and unshed tears widened
her eyes.

Pushing up the flap, she walked in to find Charles, already washed and out of uniform, sitting in the chair reading a copy of *The Times* that had arrived that day. His
eyes looked at her over the top of the newspaper, then he
slowly stood up.

"I would doubt the advisibility of walking during the afternoons while this weather is upon us," he said. "Since you
are not wearing a habit, that is what you must have been
doing."

"I have spent the afternoon in the hospital, Charles," she
told him as she unfastened her bonnet strings.

"In the . . . *hospital?*"

Swinging around to face him, she tilted up her chin as he
often did when prepared to argue. "I shall go there every
day until the cholera has ended."

"Might I inquire for what purpose?"

"For the purpose of humanity." She put a hand up to lift
the hair away from her neck. "Charles, have you seen
them? There are so many they cannot be fitted beneath the
canvas, and some are lying outside in the shadow cast by
the tent. Surgeon-Captain Morrison tells me he will have to
leave men in their own tents if the epidemic increases. I
was horrified. Imagine the feelings of those having to lie
beside the sufferers, wondering if they might not be next.
Something will have to be done."

"My dear Victoria, are you telling me you have been in
company with Captain Morrison within that vile hospital
throughout an afternoon that, I am told, reached a temperature of one hundred and twelve degrees?"

She could not decide if he was angry or amused. "I was
lucky—I came away at the end of it. Those men have to
remain there. I saw poor Trooper Miles—his wife is with

us—whom Captain Morrison told me quietly would not last out the day. What is to become of Mrs. Miles, stranded out here in the Balkans?"

Charles folded his newspaper and threw it onto the table. "She will be married again by tomorrow night. Soldiers' wives can do nothing else but go from the graveside to the marriage service. With luck, she will have four or five offers from which to choose."

Victoria looked at her husband and marveled at his calm attitude toward something she found so tragic. "You make it sound so . . . so . . . *inevitable.*"

"On a campaign there is no help for it. What will you do, Victoria, if you are left a widow?" That intensity was in his eyes once more.

Recognizing the baiting mood he had often adopted since the loss of her child, she refused to be drawn. She said instead, "Is there not another large tent that could be used as an extension to the hospital? We cannot allow sick men to lower the spirits of the others."

"We?" he asked with raised eyebrows.

"The regiment . . . its officers," she explained, "and also Mrs. Markham and me."

"Ah, I thought Mrs. Markham might be involved in this."

"You have it wrong, Charles. It was I who persuaded her. She believed it was below our dignity to visit and comfort mere troopers, until I pointed out that she would be grateful to anyone who would do as much for her husband." He stood looking at her, still with that intensity in his eyes, every inch the handsome aristocrat, and she knew he was waiting for his opportunity. Suddenly, she could hold back no longer. "Did you know that Hugo was taken with cholera last night?"

He gave no sign of his feelings, apart from allowing a shadow to fall across his natural expression. "I heard a report that one of my captains had succumbed. I was not surprised."

"What if he should die?" she whispered painfully, watching his face.

"It would be unfortunate. I do not see where we are to get replacements for all these casualties."

Her hands clutched the sides of her skirt, and the heat suddenly oppressed her more than it had all afternoon. What had happened to love, friendship and loyalty? Her husband's love was no more than selfish desire; Hugo's love had died. Letty had disappointed her today—her one true friend. Hugo was simply "one of my captains" to his brother; loyalty had fled.

Then she remembered the events of the afternoon. Love she had written in letters to England; friendship had been rife among fellow sufferers; loyalty had abounded in the promises made by comrades to carry out the last wishes of those who would be buried by sunset. It was crystal clear what her own salvation was to be. She had sailed with Charles for purely selfish reasons—to be with her one love. This morning Hugo had rejected her, thrown her love in her face, shattered her soul. He did not want her! First Charles, then Hugo had shown her she was of no use to them. But in that stinking overcrowded hospital tent she had been wanted. Her smiles had brought an answering spark of warmth to dulled eyes, her words of comfort had fallen on grateful ears, her offers of help had been accepted with unbelieving thankfulness.

Her foolish dream of becoming the patroness of the regiment had been that of a child. She no longer wished to be the revered and respected great lady—when Charity Verewood married its most brilliant officer she would step into that role quite fittingly. Now, her heart and soul cried out to belong, to be needed, to be of some use . . . to be *loved*. There among the sick troopers she had found what she sought . . . and not one of them had told her to go back where she belonged!

Aware that Charles was watching her closely, she dragged her mind back to their conversation. "If these men are left lying in their tents you will have cause to find many replacements, Charles. Surely some arrangement can be made to extend the hospital."

"At some later date, Victoria. We received orders today to move camp to Yeni-Bazaar, some miles upcountry, to try to halt the epidemic. We march at five A.M. on the day after tomorrow."

"March? But what about the sick?" she cried.

"They will be left here with most of the medical staff and a party of gravediggers. It is pointless moving if we intend taking them with us."

"I . . . see." She turned away, sick with disappointment. Her salvation was crushed before it was born. "I must send for Mrs. Stokes," she said to cover her feelings. "We are dining with the Lancers tonight, I believe."

She heard him come toward her, and his hands fell on her shoulders.

"There is no need to send for Mrs. Stokes," said a silken voice in her ear. "I am well able to unhook your dress for you."

Growing still, she said, "But I should very much like to take a bath."

"So you shall, my dear. The presence of your husband will not prevent it." Her dress slipped to the ground, and Charles turned her to face him as his hands began to caress her shoulders. "I had no way of knowing how very well you would adapt to campaigning when I decided to bring you, my dear. I am constantly being told of your excellent qualities as I move about the camp. During the months we have been here your capacity for friendship and your insatiable interest in the affairs of the regiment have made you universally admired." He smiled. "Even Lord Cardigan was heard to express a fondness for you." His finger began to follow the strap of her chemise down to her bodice. "In short, you are the perfect officer's lady—a fact that could not suit the situation better."

Victoria was dropping with fatigue and longed for rest and solitude, but she read something new in Charles today. "I am glad you feel justified in your decision," she said woodenly.

"More than justified, my dear. Rayne has approved my appointment to lieutenant colonel. You are now only one step from becoming colonel's lady—something for which you have ambitions, I believe."

She recognized his buoyancy of manner for what it was, and his pride served to increase her dispiritedness. The news gave her no pleasure.

"I have every confidence in your filling the part to perfection, Victoria," continued Charles, slipping the straps of her chemise from her shoulders and bending his head to brush her skin with his lips. "So you see, I really cannot have you wandering about the camp like some trooper's woman, can I?"

Rising up in her with extreme violence was the knowledge that she could not bear to submit to him at that moment. The touch of his hands was making her skin crawl; the silken tone as he spoke the overtures to his cold passion brought a return of her bridal fear of him; the intense light in his eyes burned like a sword thrust through her body as past-remembered anguished nights told her it would be the same again if she could not escape.

Taking several steps backward, she said, "I think you cannot compare me with a trooper's wife, Charles. There has been ample evidence from all quarters that I have made many friends among the officers, who are all pleased to seek my company." She took another step back. "You said yourself that General Estcourt and even Lord Raglan spoke highly of my evident knowledge of military matters."

He began following, forcing her back toward the bed. "Quite so, my dear, but much as it pleases me to know the officers seek your company and are graciously received, I cannot have you neglecting your husband in the process . . . can I?" he breathed against her mouth as his arms compelled her to arch over, close to his body.

In anger and panic she began to struggle, fighting with something near delirium in her desire to escape, to salvage something from a day of events that had brought her to her knees. Her naked fear sent Charles's desire rocketing. Her next words brought a violent response from him.

"No, Charles, no! I am exhausted. I have been trying to give comfort to the men all afternoon," she pleaded desperately.

"Now you must comfort your husband," he said with savage finality. "If you have forgotten how to do that, I will soon remind you."

Victoria had not forgotten—could never do so—and her tears flowed for Hugo, for the pitiful creatures in the hospital and for her own lost hopes and dignity that day. For the first time since leaving England she felt utterly defeated.

The Light Cavalry Brigade had been in its new camp at Yeni-Bazaar for two weeks when those who had been thrown into a dilemma by the relief of Silestria decided what to do with the enormous force that was dying off in hundreds around Varna. Cardigan had discovered the position of the enemy.

The Russians had retreated across the Danube, but the situation could hardly be left as it was. Though Britain and France had made their show of strength, it was unthinkable to send their forces back without having fired a shot. Vivid reports on the cholera epidemic had caused raised voices at home—not about the deaths but the manner of them. If men were dying, let it be in some glorious battle that established superiority over the upstart Russians. At length, in mid August, orders were issued to invade the Crimea and capture the strategic port of Sebastopol. The war was on again!

Every day conflicting instructions were received, but there was no doubt that a vast fleet of transports was being assembled in Varna harbor, and the soldiers began to believe they would be going into action at last. Spirits rose, and men were heard singing about their work once more. Cholera was still raging, but any man would sooner face the Russian bayonets than remain in that accursed place to join his comrades beneath the sod.

The infantry began embarking almost immediately, and the cavalry received orders to prepare to follow. In overpowering heat and reduced to three-quarters strength, the Hussars struck camp and set off on their tiring journey to Varna, where they had landed so eagerly almost three months earlier.

Two members of the long column covering the dusty ground that threw up a cloud to stick in the throats of travelers had no eager anticipation in their breasts. Victoria and Letty were bound for a hotel in Varna where they must remain while their husbands sailed for the Crimea. The commander-in-chief of the British force had forbidden any officers' ladies to travel on the official transports—and that was that! Victoria had pleaded with Charles, who had appealed to Colonel Rayne, but when that gentleman prevailed upon higher authority the answer was still no. The reason for the ban was soon obvious. Due to lack of space on the crowded transports, each officer was allowed only one horse, what he could reasonably carry by way of baggage and would be obliged to share a cabin with two or three fellow officers.

If Victoria had thought the scene at Varna chaotic when they had landed, what she saw there during the last week in August exceeded it a hundredfold. The harbor was only deep enough for trading vessels; standing offshore was a vast fleet of six hundred steamships and old sailing vessels that were to be taken in tow. Into these hulls had to be packed more than fifty thousand men, half as many animals, batteries of guns, an arsenal of ammunition, tents, cooking equipment, medicines and stretchers, spare boots, greatcoats, blankets and saddles and enough rations to feed this force for an indefinite period.

The Hussars camped in a field just outside the small town, finding many regiments spread around in similar manner awaiting embarkation orders. Some had been there for almost a week and described the chaos caused by this monumental expedition. Victoria and Charles had dinner with Captain Jenson, whom she was pleased to see again, but he was gone the following morning. She stepped out of her tent to find the side of the hill that had been covered by infantry tents the night before bare and green. A small regret lingered inside her that she had not waved her cousin's husband off, nor wished him God's blessing. By midday the hill was occupied by French Lancers—and so it went on, no regiment knowing when it would be called to the ships.

During their two days in camp, inquiries revealed that a hotel room was out of the question for Victoria and Letty, for Varna had been swept by a severe fire on August 10, which had destroyed a quarter of the town. The ladies had no alternative but to return to Constantinople while their husbands were fighting. Until arrangements could be made for passage, they were invited to stay with a kindly staff officer, who had commandeered a house near the harbor.

Past caring where she went from now on, Victoria agreed to these arrangements and waited for the departure of the regiment in a mood of quiet tension, while one by one the ships filled up and stood out to sea. The orders arrived late on the night of September 1; embarkation began just after dawn the following morning. After three months in a tent, Victoria could not believe it would be the last time she would wake to look up at the sloping canvas over her head.

Charles was as silent as she as they watched the regiment march off along the sloping road to the harbor, before mounting and following in their wake. She watched her baggage and that left behind by Charles being installed in her room in the town, then turned to her husband as the soldier went out.

"You must go. They are embarking fast."

"Yes." He seemed lost for words for once. "I have no idea how long it will be before I can join you in Constantinople. Once we take Sebastopol the whole issue should be settled swiftly."

"Will it be difficult?"

He shook his head confidently. "I think not. If we can beat Napoleon we can take a small Russian fortress easily enough."

"I pray you are right," she said, thinking of the men now, compared with when they had left England.

He hesitated, then took her hands to his lips. To her surprise there was sadness in his eyes. "It is a great pity you cannot see out the campaign. You have worked so hard at it . . . and I have been most excellently cared for. No man could have wanted more."

"Thank you, Charles." There seemed no other way of answering.

His fingers played with hers. "Victoria . . . if I should . . ." It was never completed and he slowly released her hands, turning away as he did so. "I shall endeavor to bring you a souvenir from the Crimea so that you can show your friends when you return." He turned at the door, still reluctant to leave, yet saying nothing.

Victoria wished he would go; she wished the entire day were over; she wished . . . oh, she wished she were seventeen again and dancing at Aunt Almeira's ball with laughing young men who were not riding off to be cut to pieces. She remembered the swirling couples in her aunt's hall and how her own heart had reveled at its awakening. Why had it not remained dormant?

"Goodbye, Victoria."

The picture faded, and she stared at the tall fair-haired

man who stood in the doorway. He could have been a stranger.

"Goodbye, Charles."

His boots clattered on the stairs. It occurred to her that she ought to say more . . . but he was gone. Hollow hoofbeats rang on the narrow street until there was no more sound.

CHAPTER TEN

Although it was now October, the heat was as oppressive as it had been when the armada left for the Crimea nearly a month before. Victoria sat at her window writing a sad letter of condolence to Charlotte, but her hand would not let her form the words she wished to say. It stilled each time her mind filled with pictures of the happy-go-lucky Captain Jenson.

The news had come through only last week of a great battle at the River Alma on September 20, at which the Russian forces had been driven back from their strategic position on the heights by courageous redcoats fighting uphill at a complete disadvantage. There were conflicting stories of the number of casualties, but there was no doubt they ran into thousands. There was also no doubt that the Light Cavalry had not been engaged in the battle—a fact that had incensed infantry and cavalry commanders alike. The Russians had retreated but could have been routed completely by a cavalry pursuit. For some reason best known to himself the commander-in-chief had kept his glittering regiments of cavalry sitting handsomely in their saddles to watch the chance of a lifetime slip away before their eyes.

Victoria and Letty could not help but feel thankful at the news, although they were well aware that their husbands were smarting with injustice at the slurs that were being cast upon their ability by the regiments of Foot. One, in particular, would be beside himself with frustration in the regiment of Hussars, but Victoria would not let herself think of him.

Other disturbing factors tormented Victoria to distraction. Inexplicably, tents, blankets, stretchers, medical supplies, chloroform and ambulance wagons had been left on the landing beaches two days' march back, so the treatment of the wounded had been makeshift. Dying men had been left with no shelter from the cold night, the injured had been carried from the battlefield in ways that could only increase their suffering, limbs had been amputated with nothing to deaden the pain but a sleeve to bite on and blood poured from wounds because there were no bandages. Those who had been considered to have a chance of recovery had been loaded onto the transports standing offshore and were now on their way to the hospital at Scutari—that same building that had been untenable three months before!

Listening to such words made Victoria ache deep within herself. A mixture of anger, impotence and protective pity made her restless with inaction. Captain Jenson, she had been told, had lost both legs in a shell burst and had died two days later. Whenever she thought of his good-natured face smiling at her across a wooden box dinner table inside his tent at Varna it was impossible to be still. *If I had only been there!* Whenever she thought of his forty-eight hours of agony, of his fevered cries for Charlotte, of his loneliness as he lay dying among rows of broken men, she pressed her hands to her temples. *If I had only been there!* Whenever she thought of the comfort she could have brought him and hundreds like him, she lifted her head and cried silently, *If I had only been there!*

The paper before her lay open and innocent of ink. What could she write to Charlotte? The pen began to move. It drew patterns that told lies. It spoke of how William Jenson had felt no pain before he died; it told of loving messages he had breathed at his last; it balanced the recipient's grief against her husband's gallantry in the field. It wrote "The Crimea" at the head of the paper and made no mention of a month in Varna. It wrote with mercy in its tip.

Victoria sealed the envelope and went in search of Letty, who was sketching in the garden. Her friend glanced up and smiled. They had grown close during their enforced residence in Varna. Victoria knew how much Letty longed to be beside her husband and admired the strength that allowed her to sit patiently drawing when her mind was so full of fears. On September 20, it had been clear and beautiful in this Balkan port while the two armies had been slaughtering each other at the Alma. There had been nothing to tell the two ladies of the fact—no shot, no cry, no clash of steel. Could it not be like that again? At this very

moment could not their loved ones be . . . No, it did not
do to allow such thoughts.

"I propose walking to the post office with letters. Shall I
take yours, or is your inspiration at a low ebb this morning?" asked Victoria, studying the small drawing on Letty's
lap.

"Everything is at a low ebb this morning," Letty confessed, getting to her feet. "I cannot help thinking of Jack.
It would be better in England than this place. We are so
near, yet so cut off."

"I have never felt so rootless as I do sitting here waiting
for a ship to put in on its way to Constantinople," Victoria
admitted. "I shall call again at the harbor master's office to
discover if we cannot get some kind of passage soon. I
swear I shall go into a decline if I am obliged to remain
here much longer."

The two young women set off to post their letters in a
mood of mutual disconsolation. There was a hint of thunder in the air. There had been several severe storms in the
past week, and they did not look forward to another. Letty
did not like lightning, and thunder now reminded Victoria
of the shooting of horses at sea. They were discussing these
dreads when a voice hailed them.

"Mrs. Stanford! I could not believe my eyes, but it is
indeed you."

Victoria half turned. "Captain Porchester! How very delightful. I cannot tell you how relieved I am to see you. I
had begun to think British ships did not put into Varna."

Where a military man would have raised her outstretched hand to his lips with an elegant bow, Byron Porchester patted it affectionately while his twinkling eyes
smiled into hers.

"Nor they do, ma'am, unless they have need of repairs. I
had not guessed my misfortune would have this happy outcome." He laughed in a rumbling crescendo. "Will you
present me to your companion, my dear lady, before my
officers catch up with me and steal my thunder?"

Introductions were made and an explanation of their
presence in Varna. The captain was returning from Scutari,
where he had taken some of the wounded and victims of
the cholera that was still raging.

"Our forces have taken possession of the village of Balaclava that lies before Sebastopol, and they are encamped there with some permanence, I hear. I am under orders to return to Balaclava harbor but have had to put in for repairs," he told them. "If I had been traveling in the opposite direction I would willingly have taken you both aboard, ladies. Any of my officers would be glad to give up his cabin for your sakes."

"I believe you, sir," said Victoria with sudden sweetness. "I have not met a finer group of gentlemen. However, none could outshine his captain in charm and courtesy."

"Ha, ha ha!" boomed Captain Porchester. "You have a pretty way, ma'am."

She looked up from beneath her lashes. "Not at all, sir. It is simply that I remember your kindness to me during the voyage."

"It was a pleasure to have the company of such a gracious lady aboard my ship," he replied gallantly.

Victoria was looking at Letty, who appeared surprised at this exchange. "Mrs. Markham, I cannot describe to you the skill with which Captain Porchester guided our vessel through the most terrible storm. I was crouching in my cabin quite *terrified*, thinking we should surely founder, but we came through in the manner for which our great seafaring nation is famed."

Letty's eyes widened fractionally and her lips moved rather stiffly. "Indeed, Mrs. Stanford? A miraculous escape, to be sure."

Victoria turned her full battery of charm onto the middle-aged man. "All due to Captain Porchester—quite my favorite seafaring officer. I still remember the great privilege you bestowed on me by conducting me over your vessel and answering all my questions so kindly."

He beamed. "I recognize genuine interest when I see it." He turned to Letty. "Are you a lady of inquiring nature also, Mrs. Markham?"

"Most definitely," Victoria said quickly. "Unfortunately, Mrs. Markham traveled with a captain who believed ladies should not concern themselves with matters of great interest to gentlemen. Unlike you, sir, he did not appreciate that females wish very much to understand the skills that are beyond their own reach. She has envied me my good fortune in traveling in *Sirôcco*. Is that not right, Letty?"

Byron Porchester rose to the occasion immediately. "My dear lady, may I attempt to repair the omissions of your ungracious host by offering to conduct you over my vessel while we are in Varna?"

"How very magnanimous!" Victoria cried. "Think, Letty, how fortuitous it was that we should meet Captain Porchester this morning! To think your ambition is to be fulfilled so immediately. I declare, it is the first happy day we have had since being left so alone in Varna." She let her shoulders droop, and her eyes began to fill with tears.

"Dear, dear . . . yes, that is a great pity," murmured the captain. "We cannot have that . . . dear me, no. Mrs. Stanford, can I not cheer you both a little by asking for your company at dinner on *Sirocco* this evening? My officers and I would be honored if you would accept." He rumbled with embarrassed laughter. "We get lonely at times, too."

Victoria raised her eyes to his as her hand went to her bosom. "I have seldom heard a more beautifully phrased invitation, sir. It would give me the greatest of pleasure to renew my acquaintance with your officers, and I know Mrs. Markham would benefit from the company of cultured gentlemen after a month in this place. Her spirits have been very low after hearing of that dreadful battle."

"Of course they have been," he agreed sympathetically. "We shall do our utmost to put such things to the back of your minds for one evening." He sketched a salute. "Two of my officers will wait on you at seven this evening. Until then, I bid you good day, ladies, and look forward to your company."

He went about his business, having noted their address, and the ladies continued on their way from the post office. Letty was very quiet, and Victoria let her remain so for a little while. Then she said, "I vow I shall be hard put to know which of my gowns will look well enough for tonight. After so long folded in a trunk I fear none of them will flatter me."

Letty could remain silent no longer. "I must tell you that *I* have now had a lesson in judging character, Victoria, and am greatly disappointed, I did not think to see the day you would put yourself so forward with a mere acquaintance. My cheeks burned at what impression Captain Porchester must have of us—accepting a dinner invitation with a half-dozen gentlemen while our husbands are fighting."

Victoria burst into merry laughter and took her friend's hands. "Letty . . . oh, if you could but see your disapproving face! I know Captain Porchester. He is a very charming but susceptible man. He is already feeling sympathetic toward us, and by the time we return tonight he will have promised to take us with him when he sails."

Letty still did not understand. "But he is not going to Constantinople, he is going to . . ."

"Balaclava," finished Victoria triumphantly. "And where is your beloved Jack?"

The other girl gripped Victoria's fingers until they hurt. "Dare we?"

"It is not a question of daring," Victoria replied, her eyes gazing at some faraway place all of a sudden. "I have to go to the regiment. I have known it since they sailed."

Hugo crushed the letter between his fingers and sat for a long time trying to come to terms with what it contained and all it implied. The mail had been delivered that morning, but he had been away from camp all day on outpost duty, returning hot and weary and dispirited. The letter seemed unnecessarily to complete his feeling of disenchantment with life.

Closing his eyes and taking a deep breath, he silently repeated the shocking phrases. *My sincerest sympathy in your loss . . . a great blow to us all . . . always so very generous and kind to me . . . your papa feels her absence most deeply . . . to come at a time when you are under great stress and danger.* Charity Verewood knew how to comfort the bereaved with well-thought-out words, but they did not comfort Hugo. Lady Blythe, the woman who had replaced his mother, had died very suddenly from a heart attack, more than five weeks ago, and Charles had said nothing to him, although the intelligence must have been his for some time.

Lying back on his bed, Hugo grasped the crumpled letter while youthful memories paraded before his eyes. The laughing pretty woman he had called *Mama* was prone to spoil him, for he was never told to go away when he approached, and she had loved to take him on her knee. Later, her interest in his exploits became indulgent but less absorbed, until it struck him one day that he actually knew more than she did.

From that moment of revelation he had found the situation reversed. She sought comfort from his affection, and he became indulgent. That indulgent fondness continued long after he needed anything in return, long after her tragic encounter with meningitis, long after he had been forced to watch her grow into a self-centered, eccentric woman. No matter what happened afterward, he could never forget the life and future that woman and her husband had given him.

He screwed up his eyes in pain. The letter of farewell and gratitude to his family when he left England had come easily out of his need to sever himself from anything in his past. Now, he knew the numbness was wearing off. He had thought himself strong and invulnerable—prepared to live as a man alone—but this had hurt him. Out of the past had come a lance to reach him in his armored fortress and pierce the crumbling walls. By his own hand he had renounced any claim to their future bond, but those past years counted still and it took some time to ride out the knowledge that Charles could remain silent on something that was so close to them both. Where did the realms of hatred end?

As it only takes a short while for complete feeling to return once numbness breaks, so Hugo admitted to things he had banned from recognition since that night after the ball. He had read the letters he had received from Charity avidly for their references to Wychbourne, his parents, Aunt Sophy and the life he had known since babyhood. They had told him of the horses, the summer countryside through which he had ridden countless times and of his dogs whom he had sent to Wychbourne for good when he left England.

Weakened by the wound brought about by his latest letter, he faced up to the bigger pain of loss. When he had left Brunswick Square on the night of the ball, he had rebuilt his life by cold rejection of all those who had brought about his destruction. Charles went by his own choice, his family had been abandoned of necessity, and he had seen Victoria as the siren who had bemused him.

His passion for her had shaded into anger—the anger

that cries out against the hopelessness of love—and she had become the target for his rejection. From that night he had seen Victoria as the cause of everything that had happened to him. She had caught him off guard when he had been blinded to reality; had tugged at him with her frailty after her honeymoon; had made it impossible for him to leave again when he arrived at Wychbourne unaware of her presence there.

Charles had challenged him to live beside her day by day, and he had created an illusion of possibility by rejecting her. He had told himself she would see his strength, his completeness, his lack of need of her, and it had been easy until she deliberately confronted him. His careful plans had not allowed for that and, finding it impossible to be indifferent, he had resorted to hurting her as the only outlet for the emotion locked within him.

He sat now in the anguish of numbness long past, knowing the truth. He watched her constantly as she moved about the camp, separated from him by his own determination; listened for every sound of her merry voice on the still air at Devna. He admitted to jealousy of those who could receive her smiles and confidences, to burning sleeplessness when he thought of her in the tent with his brother. He grew hot at the memory of her face when she told her love in words for the very first time such a short while ago. His head went down into his hands. How could he have left her without some sign that would soften his departure?

The tent flap was pushed up and Jack Markham walked in, his sword clanking against the pole.

"He has done it again! That old gentleman is a bigger enemy than the damned Russians," Jack declared in disgusted tones. "Our fellows are just about done in—half of them still with fever upon them—and he has called them out on inspection because he found one of my troop with a button missing from his tunic and must needs look closely at all the others." He unbuckled his sword belt and threw the weapon down angrily. "We are being mocked, Hugo. As if it were not enough to be forbidden to charge at the Alma and have to see the infantry drag past us covered with honorable wounds, asking us where we had been all day, our noble Lord Cardigan now asks us to have a care to our appearance lest we become too untidy. Are we soldiers or dolls, man?"

Hugo rose and poured them both a drink. "Our esteemed colonel told me our chance will come, Jack, so we can do nothing but rest in impatience. Please do not set me off on the subject of Cardigan. I shall be hauled in front of the regiment for yet another reprimand, for he will hear my rage from where he sits." He gave Jack a tin cup of wine and sat on the corner of a wooden ammunition case while his friend eased himself from the tight-fitting stable jacket and loosened the collar of his shirt.

"Aye, you had best hold your tongue for a while," advised Jack darkly. "One more outburst will get you placed under close arrest—and I have no fancy for another officer of equal rank moving into this cramped space to chaperone you."

"If we are forced to watch the enemy ride away from us once more while we sit in neat rows doing nothing, I shall be unable to hold my tongue, Jack, close arrest or not."

"All right, my fierce friend." Jack held up a conciliatory hand as he sank onto his bed. "Protest, rant and rage, vent your frustrated cavalry spirit—but do it out of earshot of the noble earl in future. That you are still in this regiment is miracle enough. It will not do to chance your arm too far."

Hugo gave him a frowning look. "You begin to sound too much like Rayne for my liking."

A short silence fell, then Jack said, "Have you noticed how our colonel plays safe these days? He's a sound enough man for regimental duties, but I cannot think he is going to distinguish himself in battle. Oh, I do not question his courage—that goes without saying—but if we are ever faced with the unexpected, I doubt he will take a gamble."

"He is too old—like all our commanders," said Hugo angrily. "The Alma was won through sheer grim determination of the regiments. If there was ever a plan of battle, I never saw evidence of it—and we were in the perfect position to watch the whole thing, were we not?" he added bitterly. "I tell you, Jack, this war is going to be long and bloody. Why did we not march straight into Sebastapol and take it while they were still retreating to within its walls? You know we should have done so, I know it, and all those

damned wretches in the trenches know it. Our chance is
lost. They have regrouped *outside* the fortress, and any
siege must now be incomplete. As long as there is a route
inland they can bring in supplies and reinforcements. Crimean winters are extreme and we are now in October. Our
men are still dying of fever and cholera, and the horses are
in a piteous state." He rose and paced the tent, head in the
bent position he was forced to adopt within the sloping
canvas walls. "Only today Tilden's horse dropped dead beneath him. The man was obliged to walk back from patrol
because I could not put the burden of two men on one of
the other beasts."

He gripped the center pole and waved his tin cup almost
in Jack's face. "It is criminal to let the poor creatures grow
so thin and weak. Where are the supplies? If we are not to
take Sebastapol immediately, why are we not shipping in
stores as fast as we can? Where are the stables for our
animals? They stand tormented by flies and the burning
sun by day, and shiver in the open at night. I have peti-
tioned Rayne on three separate occasions for permission to
erect huts against the bitterly chill nights, but he says there
is no wood available." Well and truly roused by now, he
snapped, "It seems there is *nothing* available. I cannot even
buy oats for my horse."

Jack looked up from beneath bushy black eyebrows.
"The word is that we are going into winter camp at Scutari. I heard it today."

For several seconds Hugo gripped the center pole, then
sagged wearily and walked to the tent entrance to gaze out
over the camp. "May this army forgive them," he said, "for
they died at the Alma for nothing."

By morning the news was around the entire cavalry
camp, fostering a mood of resentful resignation. Those who
had seen Scutari on the way out dreaded the move, those
who had been suffering from recurring cholera since being
at Devna felt a journey would finish them, and those who
were still relatively fit put a further strain on their reserves
by indulging in invective concerning the bastards who
thought up the idea of fighting right up to the gates of the
citadel, then sailing away again.

Hugo had spent a bad night. The intermittent shelling
between Sebastapol and the besiegers in the advance

trenches was too familiar a sound to disturb him, but there was enough on his mind to keep it too active for sleep. Cornet MacKay was detailed for morning stables, so Hugo used the short time before breakfast to write a letter to Lord Blythe. It did not mention that he had only heard the news from Charity. He penned a brief note to her also, thanking her for her condolences and giving her the latest situation—not forgetting to say how much he appreciated the tins of pâté and the cigars she had sent for his birthday that had finally reached him.

Stokes entered with breakfast—black coffee in a tin container, gray bread and some fruit—and shook Jack awake.

"Mr. Markham, sir, it's seven o'clock."

"What is so remarkable about that?" Jack demanded, rolling over.

"You're taking a foraging patrol at eight. You told me to remind you."

"What is this, Stokes?" asked Hugo, looking at the tray.

Stokes smiled. "Breakfast, Captain Esterly."

"Where are the eggs?"

"There won't be no more, sir. You ate Betty last night, if you remember."

"So we did. The ham, then?"

"All gone, sir."

Hugo's face was a picture. "Gone? It cannot be."

"Ah, well, sir . . . Mr. Markham asked Lord Dovedale and Mr. Edmunds to lunch yesterday when you was on patrol, and there was nothing else for it but to use the ham. I didn't have prior knowledge of the fact or I could've tried to borrow a bit of extra salt pork."

"Jack!" cried Hugo through clamped teeth. "I would be obliged if you entertained your guests out of your own pocket in future."

"Sorry, old fellow," Jack grunted, swinging his legs to the ground. "It was a long-standing invitation to return their hospitality."

"Why did you not ask them on a day when I was in camp?"

"There wouldn't have been enough ham for *four*, sir," put in Stokes hastily.

Hugo turned on him. "Dammit, Stokes, it was *my* ham."

"Yessir," said the trooper unabashed. "I could make

some of that porridge if you feel really hungry, Captain."

"No, Stokes. It will be a long time before I bring myself to eat any more of that mess you call porridge," Hugo vowed in disgruntlement.

"Yessir. Well . . . there's breakfast, then. I'll be seeing to your boots, if you'll excuse me." He turned to Jack Markham, pretending not to notice the expression on his own officer's face. "Any news, Mr. Markham?"

"There has been no mail since Monday, and I told you then that my wife and Mrs. Stanford were still in Varna," said Jack patiently. "Of course, that was written two weeks ago, so they could be in Constantinople by now. I have assured you that I will inform you when I get word, so that you will know where Mrs. Stokes is. Now, I suggest you clean Captain Esterly's boots before he inquires what became of the rest of his cigars."

"Oh Gawd, yes, sir," said Stokes, his mustache quivering, and ducked beneath the tent flap with alacrity.

Around midday Hugo called for his horse to be saddled. There was word of supply ships newly arrived in the harbor, and he was determined to ride down there in the hope of beating the other officers to it. Difficulty in obtaining any kind of equipment made a man seek every opportunity, and he wanted a blanket for Monty and another horse he had bought when they auctioned off the belongings of the officers killed at the Alma. How he kicked against the order that had compelled them to bring only one horse from Varna; he doubted he would ever see his fine trio of chestnuts again.

Trotting through the camp, he was hailed by Colonel Rayne, who was in the company of Charles outside the colonel's tent.

"One moment, Captain Esterly, if you please."

"Good morning, sir . . . Colonel Stanford," said Hugo tonelessly from his saddle. "May I be of service?"

"Yes, you can oblige me by dismounting," snapped Colonel Rayne. When this was done, he continued. "I have just received a message from the Earl of Cardigan asking why a trooper of your patrol returned on foot without his horse when you came in yesterday. Why did I hear nothing of this?"

"I cannot say, sir. My report was handed to the adjutant, as usual."

"I see." He was thrown off his stride. "Well, I was dining in the French lines last night and had no time to read routine reports. However, you still have not explained the incident."

Hugo was aware of his brother's presence but could hardly protest at being questioned in front of the second-in-command. "The horse died from starvation, exposure and mishandling, Colonel. Since the rest of my troop horses are on the verge of doing the same, I did not feel justified in allowing two men in one saddle."

The older man grew red in the face. "I did not ask for one of your heated tirades on how this regiment should be run, sir. If the beasts are mishandled, it is your fault. As troop leader they are your responsibility."

Hugo felt his anger growing. "I cannot keep healthy animals if I have no food for them, nor wood to build some kind of shelter against the weather."

"And neither can anyone else, Captain Esterly. Find me a grain store and a timber yard within a hundred miles of here, but please do not treat me to an impertinent lecture on what should be done."

"I am sorry, sir." He meant it. He knew it was no fault of his colonel that supplies were not reaching them but felt the man could do a little more to badger those responsible, even if he made himself unpopular for once. "I have arranged for a remount for Trooper Tilden, sir, so we are up to strength again."

The sandy-haired man sucked his mustache as he drew in his breath.

"Why is it always your troop on whom misfortune seems to fall?"

Hugo kept silent. He did not know a suitable answer. "You are summoned to his lordship to explain the incident, Captain, so I caution you to watch your tongue. You have earned his displeasure on two previous occasions."

"Is the summons immediate, sir? I was on my way to the harbor."

"I should imagine when a brigade-commander issues a summons he expects it to be obeyed immediately," Charles put in smoothly. "All the more so if the offender is a junior captain. Lord Cardigan is known to have no fondness for them."

Colonel Rayne smiled thinly. "I think Colonel Stanford has a point. I just wish it were not a junior *Hussar* captain on whom he picked. Captain Esterly, do you think you could make an effort to avoid further clashes with his lordship?"

"I do not clash with his lordship, sir," said Hugo quickly. "It is he who clashes with me."

The colonel was not amused. "I think you have said enough on the subject, sir. A little less levity and a little more attention to regimental duties would stand you in better stead for the days to come. You had best go for your interview immediately."

They moved off, and Hugo watched the straight back of his brother for a few minutes before mounting Monty and returning to his tent in a black mood. The interview with Lord Cardigan meant changing into full-dress uniform to ride into Balaclava, where the Brigade-commander had taken up quarters on one of the ships because the state of his present health made it inadvisable to live under canvas. All the junior captains prayed he would remain there.

His mood slid deeper into depression when overtones of a storm at the outset of his journey grew into a full-scale thundery downpour that soaked him to the skin before he reached the harbor. Half an hour of kicking his heels on deck and fifteen minutes listening to a lecture on his shabby appearance and the fact that his lordship would not countenance a cavalryman *walking* on a patrol, under any circumstances, raised Hugo's temper, as he left the ship with angry strides, to the same heat as the sun that had come out to set the steam rising over the tiny town.

His mind fixed on seeking out the newly arrived vessels, he approached the jetty and was pulled up short at the sight of eight or nine horses being held by local navvies.

"By God, I cannot believe what I see," he breathed viciously. "Those are two of my chestnuts, *they* are Jack's Merlin and Mayhem, and beside them are several from my brother's stable." Immediately his blood was up. Those animals had cost several hundred pounds, and no one was going to pirate them after they had been left in Varna in good faith.

He ran up the gangplank and pushed past a seaman at the top, vaguely registering the fact that the vessel appeared very much like the one in which he had left England. They all suggested torture chambers, as far as he was concerned, and he saw too little of the men who sailed them to make any friends. The captain of this one would be far from a friend when he had finished with him. Swinging around the wheelhouse with great energy, he came upon a figure standing at the ship's side, studying the hills that rose up all around, enclosing the tiny harbor. She turned at the sound of someone approaching, and all thought of horses went from him.

After a month without her he could see how she had changed since leaving England. The green cotton gown was well washed and crumpled, but she was so unconscious of the fact, one did not count its importance. Her face was finer and an unfashionable golden-brown that highlighted her dark eyes to an extreme of beauty he could hardly believe. The limpid innocence they had once held had been replaced by a luminosity that was at once anger, yet joy, at his present helpless self-betrayal. In seconds he drank in greedily every detail of the girl he had thought lost forever, while his spirits soared.

"I knew nothing of your arrival," he breathed, "so how did my feet carry me here?"

"Does it matter?" The words were as soft as his.

"Not a bit."

Her eyes searched him as if she would catch up on all the days she had missed. "You are wet through." The sentence was as caressing as an expression of love.

He felt his youth flood through him with vigorous warmth. "You say that more prettily than Lord Cardigan." Foolish words. He longed to shout to the four winds that he loved her.

She drew nearer, and the lemon-and-hay perfume was all around him, drugging his senses to everything but her. "You left Varna without a word—not even a glance in my direction," she whispered. "I might never have seen you again."

Walking to meet her, lost to the barriers and constraints that had been between them, in the unexpectedness of coming upon her when his defenses were shattered, he took her cold hands fiercely in his.

"Forgive me. Forgive me. Do you think I have not regretted it every moment since then? I have missed you beyond belief . . . beyond endurance. Only a fool could believe it possible to shut you out of his life."

For a moment she closed her eyes against the ravishment of his words, and he was shaken by the desire to make them fly open again lest he lose forever the amber surrender in them. Her lashes came up and it was there in double measure.

"Never go away again without the comfort of a goodbye. I could think of nothing but your lips cold and silent forever . . . your ears no longer able to hear my words. I could think of nothing but men galloping. Hugo, I . . ." Her voice broke on the welter of emotion brought about by the impact of his ardent return into the man who loved her.

"No, you must not think such things . . . say such things." He laid his fingers gently across her lips, then moved them up to chase a tear that hung on her lashes. In that moment her frailty left him breathless with pain. Drawing her against him as if to offer protection, he stroked her hair tenderly. "You should never have come. This is no place for you."

Her face tilted upward. "It is the only place for me when you are here."

The protective feeling vanished immediately. Her mouth was only inches from his, and he was no longer master of himself. Tightening his hold around her, he breathed, "My love . . ." but his head shot up when a voice nearby said, "You are in full view of the harbor, Victoria."

Letty stood a few feet away, an expression of understanding on her pretty face. "The situation, at present, makes reunions rather emotional, but they are better conducted in less public places." She smiled at Hugo. "Having said that, I shall be happy to receive a warm welcome from my dear friend." She stood on tiptoe to offer her cheek for his automatic kiss. "You have always been a great deal too dashing with the ladies, Hugo. To be seen embracing *one* on board ship would cause gossip. To bestow your kisses on every woman in sight will bring no more than amused head-shaking from your fellows." She tucked her hand through his arm. "How did you know we had arrived? Is Jack here?"

In something of a daze he murmured, "No . . . no. He is gone on a foraging patrol. I cannot think what he will say when he sees you here. How long do you remain?"

Victoria slipped her hand through his other arm, seeming to recover more quickly than he. "This is not a visit. We have come to rejoin the regiment," she said quietly.

He swung around to face her, recollection of his brother, his vow, returning in full force. "You cannot! We are under constant fire. There is no provision for ladies in the encampment. The whole idea is impossible."

"How very unwelcome you make us, Hugo," pouted Letty. "It might be that you will change your mind when you see we have brought two of your horses with us, besides Jack's and Colonel Stanford's."

Filled with the realization that he had so nearly weakened where Victoria was concerned, Hugo sounded even more discouraging when he said, "Believe me, for the horses I shall be everlastingly grateful—you have no notion of the situation here—but you will not be allowed to stay in the cavalry camp, I guarantee."

"Then we shall live elsewhere," declared Victoria. "We are determined to stay, are we not, Letty?"

"Yes, we have brought all the baggage that was left behind, extra food supplies and the horses. Hugo," Letty said hotly, "you must give us your complete support. Say that you will."

Hugo looked at Victoria and heard himself say helplessly, "Of course I will give my best support."

The cavalry was encamped on a hill two miles above Balaclava, near the village of Kadikoi, where they were in an excellent position to counter any attempt by the Russians to retake the tiny harbor. As the small party rode up the rough road that bright, chilly day, Hugo pointed out the encampments of various regiments of an entire force occupying the vast hills around Sebastopol.

Victoria saw it all with amazed eyes. The hinterland of the Russian naval base stretched in a series of undulating hills and long valleys for as far as they could see, and tents dotted every visible part. It would appear the little sea fortress further along the coast was practically under siege by land, and she could understand Hugo's bitterness at the failure of the commanders-in-chief of the Anglo-French forces to march straight into the town after driving back the enormous Russian force at the Alma. Instead, they had been sitting here for three weeks while the enemy regrouped before the walls of Sebastopol and put up great earthworks to defend their port. Assault on the objective now would mean a bitter battle, he said, and there was even talk of retiring to Scutari for winter quarters.

She watched him as he rode beside them, talking of his views and feelings, and knew it was as it had previously been between them. She felt no desire to analyze why he had hated her, then loved her again. Content with the present, her only wish was to remain where she could see him and know he was safe. That month in Varna had been a lifetime. When she had thought of Captain Jenson with his legs blown off, she had thought of Hugo. While she had longed to be of some comfort to the injured and dying, it had been Hugo lying in pain that she had pictured. Here, in the Crimea, she could rest content, knowing she was at hand whatever happened.

They entered the camp and saw immediately that things had changed drastically since the regiment left Varna. There was a lack of permanence about the site, as though there was no point in making the place comfortable or convenient. There were fewer tents, and the much-trodden ground between them was thick mud that sucked at the horses' hooves as they threaded their way to headquarters. Passing some of the horse lines, Victoria was appalled to see beautiful creatures that had been the pride of the cavalry reduced to mangy-coated nags with ribs showing too clearly through emaciated bodies and tails that had been eaten to stumps.

The troopers and officers past whom they rode warmed Victoria's heart with their delighted greetings, but the change was there in their faces, as it was in Hugo's. They had seen death by violence now and were experiencing hardship, danger and uncertainty. There was a hardness, an undertone of seriousness in the way they moved about, and the glamour of their appearance had begun to fade. They were here for a deadly purpose.

Hugo hailed a passing trooper to ask where he would find Colonel Stanford and was told he had gone to his tent for dinner. Taking that to mean Charles had decided on an early luncheon, Victoria asked the man to conduct her to her husband and turned to Hugo and Letty.

"I will see what Charles can arrange for us, Letty. Have no fear, We shall not go from here on any account. I trust your husband will return by the time we have settled the matter." She turned to the man beside her friend. "Thank you for escorting us here, Hugo. I am most grateful." It was all she was allowed to say, but words did not matter any longer.

It was a short distance to Charles's tent. Giving her horse to the trooper, she lifted the flap and entered without announcement. The interior was spartan—a bed, a table of wooden boxes, a tin jug and a bowl for washing. Charles was sitting on the bed to eat a plateful of gravy—soaked meat, washed down by a tin cupful of wine, and he looked up with an alertness born of wartime conditions. For a few seconds he sat looking at her, then slowly lowered his knife and fork.

"Victoria!" He came toward her with half-frowning delight, and took her hands. "Give me time to believe it is really you I see. I had thought you in Constantinople by now." He let out a long breath. "How am I to explain this to the commander-in-chief?"

"We shall think of a way," she said calmly.

Next minute she was pulled into his arms and his lips were on hers, hard and demanding, as always. She felt the desire mounting within his body and knew it was her turn to use him at last. Dragging her lips away, she murmured against his neck, "Now I have gone to all this trouble to join you, you cannot let them send me away."

He found her mouth again and spoke against it. "I cannot and shall not!"

CHAPTER ELEVEN

Two days after Victoria and Letty moved into a small half-cottage in Balaclava, not far from the harbor, the great bombardment of Sebastopol began with a tremendous roar. Victoria awoke to the sound, believing it to be a storm, but over the doomed siege town lay a pall of black smoke that increased after each shattering salvo. She called Letty to come to her room, and the two young women watched in silent awe their first evidence that war was an earnest game.

Victoria felt her stomach churning. At this distance it was a tremendous spectacle, but over there, a few miles distant, a town was being destroyed. Proud houses were falling apart, crushing their owners beneath the walls; women were going about their tasks in terror; animals were rushing headlong; mutilation and death were stalking the streets of a pretty port. It was such a painful thought she turned her eyes away, only to see something worse. There was a similar pall over the hills above Kadikoi. Why had she imagined the battle to be one-sided?

They rode up to the cavalry camp after breakfast, as usual. Outside in the streets, the noise was deafening, and it was plain that not only were the batteries on the hills pouring shot and shell into Sebastopol, but the British men-o'-war anchored outside the harbor had moved in closer to bombard the target from the seaward side. Heavy smoke layers hung over the whole area, bringing a morning twilight to a dull day and filling Victoria with a premonition of Stygian darkness to come.

Their progress into the valley revealed the drama even more vividly, for they could then see the red flash of fire from the mouths of cannon in the hills above as the shells flew whistling downward to find their mark with a roar that joined the universal thundering. They were close enough to see the gunners moving around their weapons when the smoke cleared, but all that was visible of the Rus-

sian batteries was a row of smoke puffs that blossomed and
faded like momentary flowers in the distance.

The Light and Heavy Cavalry were in their saddles and
formed up just north of their encampment, waiting for the
assault that should follow the bombardment. They had
been waiting since an hour before dawn, when the piquets
had come galloping in with reports of large groups of Russian cavalry on the move beyond the heights, but, although
they remained in their saddles while the morning wore
away, no orders came to advance. At last, around midday,
they heard there was to be no assault of Sebastopol's advance defenses that day.

The Hussars rode back to their lines with jingling harness, the men in faded uniforms, their faces etched in lines
of strain, angry that they had yet again been prevented
from taking an active part. Victoria received only a swift
salute from Hugo as he cantered past, his vivid eyes stormy
and his uniform splattered with mud.

"There goes one gentleman who will either explode or
get himself put under arrest if we do not soon match our
steel with the enemy," observed Lord Dovedale dryly to his
lovely companion. "Poor Esterly came in from outlying piquet this morning with his blood up, confident that his report would have us on the move within minutes. Much
more of this and he will be unable to hold back. He is an
impetuous fellow at the best of times."

Victoria watched Hugo's back. "Why did they not make
the assault?"

He gave a weary smile. "Dear ma'am, I am not yet in
the full confidence of our worthy commanders. They probably felt it was not *quite* the day for it."

She asked the same question of Charles when they went
to his tent. He was angry, she could tell, but he merely said,
"They have their reasons, my dear. We do not see the overall plan as they do."

She sat on his bed and pulled off her hat. "What plan
can they have if we are to move out to Scutari shortly?"

He turned and smiled. "That rumor is scotched. We are
to remain here until Sebastopol falls. At the rate we are
pounding them, it will hold out for three days at the most."

A week later it showed no sign of crumbling. Victoria
and Letty had grown used to the continual rumble of big

guns, although they were firing less frequently now. Not only was the fortress withstanding the bombardment, but large numbers of Russian infantry and cavalry were massing some five or six miles away from Balaclava. In the expectation of imminent attack the Allied cavalrymen were forced to sleep beside horses ready-saddled and were turned out every morning just before dawn where they would sit shivering for hours without breakfast or a drink to warm them.

The young women visited the camp every day and found everyone growing dispirited and exhausted. There was no sign of an assault on the fortifications—in fact, no sign of an attack on any kind, except the shells, which were fast running out after a week-long bombardment. The troops were despondent at having to sit every day waiting, achieving nothing; there was another outbreak of cholera to weaken their numbers; and they were beginning to feel the icy fingers of a Crimean winter reaching out to them. The high level of sickness was making it necessary for men to be on piquet duty for twenty-two out of twenty-four hours, and the horses were in such a state regiments could only mount three-quarters of their men.

The general atmosphere affected the two young women, and persistent rain prevented their usual visit to camp for two days running. This did not improve their spirits and both ended up suffering from headaches that made them cross and impatient with each other. They retired early, and Victoria was consequently quite snappy with Zarina when she entered the tiny whitewashed bedroom with great energy and no lack of noise early the following morning.

"Can you not learn to move more quietly?" she complained. "I am not yet ready to awaken."

"Oh missus, get up quickly," Zarina said breathily. "I just heard there's a big battle started. The Russians have attacked and captured our guns on the hill, and there's thousands of cavalry riding down on Balaclava."

Victoria shot up, filled with icy terror. "Where did you hear this?"

"It's all over the town. This time it's true, missus. The Turks are rushing into town like terrified sheep. Seems they ran away and let the Russians walk in where they liked. I stopped a soldier in the street and asked the truth of it, and he said the infantry boys are hard at it and our cavalry are all turned out in the North Valley waiting for the enemy to come." The girl was as taut as if she were about to go before an audience in the big top. "I got that idiot lad to saddle the horses. Everyone is going up to the Heights to watch."

Hardly knowing what she was doing, Victoria flung on her riding habit and rushed in to find Letty doing the same. They said nothing, their apprehension too evident for words. Victoria's throat was dry and fear hammered at her heart.

An air of tension hung over the little town. Mounting their horses, they set off quickly, following the many riders who were leaving the harbor area for a ringside seat. This was the moment, an end to the waiting. Here was, at last, the hour of glory.

Turks were flying down the road, loaded with pots and pans, kettles and whatever possessions they had managed to snatch up, shouting in alarm and signaling riders to turn back. Staff officers galloped back and forth in desperate haste, dodging the overladen ammunition wagons that were stuck in the mud. The Turkish drivers whipped and kicked the poor bullocks in a frenzy of panic, but the beasts were broken by semistarvation and incapable of pulling such loads any more. Several times the women had to draw in to the side as ambulance wagons rushed past in urgent bumping progression.

Up on the hills, large dark masses of troops could be seen, but Victoria could not tell if they were British, French or Russian. Trumpets were sounding in the clear air, the bombardment being in a hiatus, and soon she heard the light chatter of musketry all around her, carrying on the lovely, hazy autumn stillness. Why today? she wondered. Why, on a day such as this, when the world is so beautiful, should men be destined to see their last of it?

In the valley Monty shook his head restlessly, setting the harness jingling and the flies rising from his eyes only to settle again seconds later. Hugo sat motionless in his saddle, gazing through narrowed eyes down the sun-washed valley nearly three-quarters of a mile wide and flanked by

heights on both sides. It was empty and still, sweet grassland lying dozing beneath the growing heat of morning.

Less than an hour before, the southern slope of the
South Valley had been covered with battling cavalry, after
the scarlet-jacketed Heavy Brigade had charged coura-
geously uphill at a force several times their superior. Admiration and pride burst from Hugo's breast. It had been
highly unorthodox but instigated by the desperation of the
situation; it had been a maneuver after his own heart—
cavalry used creatively under extraordinary circumstances.
The Light Brigade, formed up in readiness, had cheered
their comrades on as they waited for the order to chase
after the retreating Cossacks and complete the rout, but the
cheering had died an incredulous death. Lord Cardigan
had continued to sit his charger while the Russians retreated, amazed but thankful, to the safety of their lines.
They were now reformed at the far end of the North Valley
behind their battery of twelve heavy guns and together
made a dark block of men in the far distance.

Hugo's head was thundering with rage at his own impotence. Was there to be no end to the appalling mishandling
of this campaign? Did the commanders of this force have
any idea of trying to win it, or was it their intention to kill
off their own army with disease and ineptitude? He was
surrounded, at this moment, by six hundred or more of the
finest cavalrymen in the world—yes, even though they
were exhausted and fever-ridden—yet they had been sitting
here in neat rows since 4:00 A.M., like glittering toys on
parade. It was infamous!

A somnolent hush had fallen over the valley. After the
earlier gunfire, the shouts and screams of infantry on the
hills and the *huzzahs* of the cavalry as steel clashed against
steel and horses neighed in fright, the peace was intense
against his eardrums. Once the stillness of inactivity had
been broken by an aide-de-camp galloping up with a message, and muscles tensed. But that had been thirty minutes
ago, and still they sat.

Looking along the ranks of his troop, Hugo saw his own
mood echoed in the men's faces—those who were not dozing in their saddles. They had been out on night piquet and
had had no sleep. This sun warmth after the frost of dark-

ness was taking its toll. Up ahead, his brother was sitting
straight in the saddle, gazing down the valley also. What
were his thoughts? he wondered.

Movement caught his eye on the slope to the rear, a staff
officer slithering and sliding with the utmost speed down
the very steep incline who could only be Captain Nolan,
for no one but an exceptional horseman would be daring
enough to attempt the descent. Hugo knew him as a passionate advocate of cavalry reform but thought his ideas
just a little too advanced to be sound. Always an excitable
and impetuous fellow, he now rode like one demented. A
staff officer risking a crashing fall down a hillside could
only be carrying an urgent order. Did it connect with the
last one, and would it bring some action from their divi-
sional commander?

From where he sat in the middle of the Light Brigade
Hugo could not see what was happening to his right, but
the cavalrymen who had been despondent and weary were
drawing themselves up in the saddle and a buzz of conjecture was running through the ranks.

"What is it, Clive?" Hugo called across to Captain Foster, who was on the right of the regiment and in a better
position to see.

"No idea" was the laconic reply. "There is a lot of
damned arm waving from Nolan which seems to impress
no one very much. Oh, a moment," he corrected himself.
"They are coming across to our noble Lord Cardigan.
What do you say, Hugo? Are we off at last?" There was a
tinge of excitement in his voice that Hugo quickly suppressed.

"Off back to camp. He brings the order to retire, no
doubt."

Hugo watched the staff officers in white-plumed cocked
hats move along past the busbies, shakos and lance caps of
the Light Cavalry regiments until they halted before Lord
Cardigan. For an order to stand down there was a great
deal of discussion going on, and a sudden feeling of expectation began to grow inside him as he saw nods in the direction of the enemy. Was a body of cavalry approaching
over the hills? Had they received intelligence of an advance
about to take place? Were they, at last, to prove their
worth and live up to their badly shaken reputation?

There was an air of tense expectancy now where there had been despair. Something was afoot. Every bone felt it, and men had sloughed off their weariness, hunger and sickness. The mood transferred itself to the horses, who threw their heads about to set their bits clanking and stamped with hooves fidgeting to be on the move. Their riders spoke to them in soft-voiced reassurance.

Lord Cardigan left the group and faced his brigade, passing on the orders he had been given with no sign of emotion on his face.

"The Brigade will advance. First squadron of the 17th Lancers to direct."

He turned his horse in perfect style and walked out to take up his position some way out in front of the men, who could never be too glitteringly regimental for his taste.

Hugo was thunderstruck. He did not believe what he had heard. There was only one direction in which they could advance, and that was down the valley to the great row of gaping cannon mouths backed by a solid wall of three thousand Cossacks. They were being ordered to charge huge tubes of metal on wheels that belched shot and shell sufficient to blow up everything within range. They were being ordered to fight twelve-pounder guns with swords and human flesh. They were being ordered to make the supreme but senseless sacrifice for their country. He and six hundred and seventy-two other men were being ordered to commit suicide.

Nevertheless, one by one the officers gave their separate commands, voices betraying no trace of reaction in having to tell their men that life was over for them from this moment on. Hugo turned to address his troop and spotted Stokes, mounted on a broken-down pony, at the end of the rear rank. The man sent a visual appeal to his officer to allow him to remain with his comrades, and Hugo passed him over.

" 'A' Troop of the Hussars will advance on command," he said calmly, seeing in that moment the faces of men he had known for years and who had served him well. They looked dazed and uncomprehending—but there was not one who let fear distort his features.

Turning back, Hugo swept the valley with his glance once more. On the heights on both sides were the guns of

Russian artillery regiments, angled downward to rake the grass of that sleepy vale with every kind of deadly shot. Before they had covered a quarter of the distance they would be brought down by this crossfire, but any who survived would then be within point-blank range of the block of guns at the end. Even if, by some chance, a few managed to ride beyond the cannon and kill the gunners, they could not carry away the guns. There were Cossacks and Lancers waiting with pointed steel. His reason and professional pride cried out within him at what they were about to do. England would surely be sorrowing over this October morning for years to come.

The officers had finished shouting their commands, and to Hugo, sitting in his saddle was like being poised on a compressed spring that was about to be released. The mid-morning peace was suddenly cut by the sharp metallic scrape of steel as swords were drawn from scabbards, each one held securely by a sword knot around the wrist. Then borne on the quietness came Lord Cardigan's command.

"Sound the advance!"

Instinctively Hugo looked ahead and to his right, and Charles turned his head fractionally to lock his eyes to those of the man he had denied as his brother. There was no flash of understanding in that last moment; just an unmistakable challenge that said, *This is your moment for a sword thrust in my back.*

The shock had hardly registered when the ranks began to move forward in perfect alignment, as at a military review. Hugo's ears were full of jangling harness, the squeak of leather and the snort of horses moving after such a long spell of inactivity. He heard the grunting of men as they shifted in their saddles and the nervous cough of a sick trooper in the rear rank. Cutting across these regimental noises, the bees rose humming in great clouds from beneath their feet, and somewhere high above a bird was singing its heart out.

He felt peculiarly alone as he rode two lengths ahead of his men and some distance behind the regiment in front—surrounded, yet isolated. A quick glance along to the left showed him Jack Markham riding steadily, looking neither right nor left, lost in his own thoughts. He had been a good friend.

They broke into a trot, keeping perfect formation, as they had been trained to do. Up on the hills to his left the sun caught some bright object and flashed a blinding light in his eyes for a moment. The sound of hooves had increased to an awesome rumble. They were well out into the valley—a colorful moving mass in the cup of Nature's hand. Hugo's breath quickened, and sweat began to dampen his armpits and groin. They were level with the batteries on the heights. Why did they not fire?

He turned his glance up to where the dark shadow of troops broke the azure skyline on each side and wondered on their inactivity. Then he looked again between the bobbing ranks ahead at the mass of guns they were approaching and knew the answer. This charge was so supreme in its daring, so inexplicable in its madness the Russians could not believe what they saw. The gunners were stunned into immobility.

They were almost half way to their objective when suddenly Captain Nolan, who had brought the order, galloped out from the ranks, waving his sword and shouting like a maniac at Lord Cardigan trotting so superbly at the head of his brigade. Hugo was disgusted with the man. They all felt as he did, but it did not do to put on a show of adolescent hysteria in an anxiety to increase the pace. They had a long way to go, and the horses must not be winded too soon.

At that minute the sky seemed to split open as the guns on the hills opened fire, and Captain Nolan let out a scream that sounded like something beyond the grave. His horse swayed and crashed back through the front ranks in a frenzy. Nolan's body remained in the saddle after death, and Hugo winced as the corpse galloped past him, burst open to the heart and crimson with blood. Hardly had he registered that sight than he realized the row of backs before him had gaps in it, and Monty's feet had begun to dance away from motionless bundles on the ground. *Dear God, they are going down in threes and fours!*

The air that had seemed so full of autumn was now a purgatory of whistling shells that shattered men in seconds; a hell where screams and cries beat on his ears with hollow echoes that increased in volume; a charnel house where death and torment attacked from both sides with red-hot metal.

His nostrils were full of the reek of acrid smoke, singeing flesh, blood and sweat. He was riding over burst horses and broken men. Monty was urging forward, not liking the loneliness of command, seeking to join the comfort of a crowd, and Hugo held him back with a steel hand. The clear blue day was lost in a haze of smoke; the guns could no longer be seen. A voice somewhere, probably that of fear, had given the order to gallop, and he was now racing along enclosed by lathered horses with fear-rolled eyes and foaming mouths.

The thunder of hooves was a roaring background to the fusillade of round shot and explosive shells that rained down on them from both sides, flying out of the gray pall to take off a man's head as if it were butter or rip open a horse to release a mess of blood and entrails. Hugo saw it with abstracted eyes. Horror supreme leaves one immune.

The madness of battle had taken over. The ranks behind him were pressing on, urging those ahead to go faster. Men with tears of rage running down their cheeks pulled alongside, and he had to order them back. As gaps appeared in the neat rows he roared at his men to close in—they must charge as a solid body to have any effect—but the tumult was so great his voice could hardly be heard above it. Riderless horses were trying to force their way between the mounted men in their frenzy to stay in a situation they knew.

"Close up, close up," he yelled. "Keep in formation."

A low whistle sped at him, and his busby was wrenched from his head, the chain strap tearing at his chin. A swift glance to his left revealed the round ball bouncing over the grass to take off the leg of a black horse who collapsed and sent Jack Markham headlong.

God have mercy on him. The thought vanished in a sharp gasp as a burning pain in his shoulder made his left hand tighten on the reins and sent splatters of blood across his body. There was no time to see the wound, for a brilliant light flooded over him as he shot out into the sunlight once more.

Dazzled by the sudden brightness, he didn't realize for several seconds that they were close on top of the guns, and the full enormity of this charge was apparent. Wicked elongated barrels yawned in between a mass of mounted soldiers who watched them rush to certain slaughter. He could see the pale blurs of gunners' faces and behind them the solid block of horses and uniforms brightened by the glitter of steel and fluttering lance pennants. Sick at heart, he saw their own ranks had been ravaged to half their original number and shouted hoarsely to his own troop behind him.

"Keep steady, men, and strike at their throats."

He was no longer aware of noise. When the battery opened fire it was a silent affair; blossoming barrels, tongues of orange flame and thick black smoke that swirled around him. The row of broad blue backs ahead of him disintegrated into flying fragments of unrecognizable form, and Monty rushed on through a shower of blood-rain. A Lancer officer loomed up before him, his mouth open in a shriek of agony, but Hugo heard nothing from that blood-covered skull. He swerved to avoid a runaway horse dragging a dead Hussar whose foot was caught in the stirrup. The man had only one arm.

The silence in Hugo's head was complete; his ears refused to take any more sound. Thirty feet away from the guns, the smoke and flames belched again. Monty threw up his head, checked his stride, stumbled, staggered and crashed into the wheel of one of the guns, twisting high in the air and throwing his rider head over heels past the gunners.

The pain in Hugo's left arm as he hit the ground made him cry out, but he was scrambling to his feet and setting about him with his sword before the artillerymen had made a move. They went down still showing their astonishment at what the Light Brigade had just done.

"Hugo, over here," cried an anguished voice, and he turned to see Cornet McKay holding a riderless horse. As he ran for it he realized his left arm was growing numb and the pain in his shoulder was biting deeper into his chest. Mounting was not easy, as the horse kept turning away, but he dragged himself into the saddle and pulled the horse around just in time to see the boy's chest laid open to the bone by a Cossack sword. The young officer's face crumpled with disbelief before he tumbled from the saddle, and Hugo slashed at the Russian with personal hatred until he was a mass of blood.

Looking away, he saw that he and the other survivors had passed the guns and now confronted the huge body of cavalry. Formation had broken, and steel was clashing against steel in a mêlée of mounted men. To his left, two of his regiment were being surrounded by Russian Lancers intent on spearing them to death. He set his horse at the group at full gallop, crashing through the enemy and scattering them with his sword and the impetus of his charge.

Three seconds later, the beast beneath him gave a shriek and fell sideways, pinning Hugo's leg beneath its brown flanks and giving him no escape from the Lancer who trotted up and thrust his long weapon deep into his victim's chest. Hugo was overwhelmed with pain. Everything began to blur into unconsciousness even while he fought it with all his will.

When he came to, the scene had altered. It was all over. Englishmen were staggering past him through the pale smoke, uniforms torn and bloody, eyes searching painfully for a horse or sturdy comrade for support. Others were lying forward over the necks of their mounts, covered in wounds and staying in the saddle by sheer force of habit. The ground was covered with moaning bundles of tattered uniforms who were trying to crawl to safety with legs open to the shin bone or a mere stump of a limb. Horses limped forward, valiantly supporting the weight of soldiers who clutched the stirrup iron with desperate hands. They were all retreating.

Raising his head, Hugo saw parties of Russian Lancers trotting among the wounded who begged for water, replying by spearing them to death. Gathering his strength, he clawed at the grass, clutching great tufts of it to aid his effort to pull himself free of the dead horse. The numbness had gone from his arm and was instantly replaced by screaming pain when he put pressure on it. Gasping and struggling, he watched the Lancers drawing closer. *I must return.*

Groping his way to his feet, he heard his breath rattling in his throat and saw blood from the lance wound in his chest. Walking was impossible pain, but every step took him further from the guns and nearer his own lines. He refused to think of the mile and a half he must cover. He was not alone. Through the obscurity he saw the remnants of the proud Light Brigade drag-footing their way back, each man an island of agony and endeavor.

He came upon a horse standing quietly beside its dead master, halted by the rigid death grip on the reins. *I must return.* Unable to bend, he cut the reins with his sword and leaned thankfully against the sweat-glistened flanks, gathering his strength to mount. There was a mile and a half to go, and the guns from all three sides were still firing upon those who were dragging, clawing and crawling back along the valley, showing no mercy for the wounded and dying.

The struggle into the saddle brought a fresh burst of blood to soak the front of his gold-laced jacket. Overwhelmed by weakness, he lay across the horse's neck watching the grass sliding past his feet. It was covered with spent balls and shell fragments; pieces of torn cloth with the badges of fine regiments attached; broken swords; photographs and treasured letters; hard biscuit carried in a pocket against hunger; lance caps with their unique square tops; Light Dragoon shakos; Hussar busbies; and severed men who had worn them with honor.

The visions blurred as something exploded just ahead of him, and a man who had been stumbling along fell on his face with a scream. Choked with smoke, Hugo slid to the ground to look down at one of his own troop. It was Pitchley, whose wife had thrown herself beneath their horses at Portsmouth, and Hugo knew he must help the man for the sake of that desperate girl.

"Take the horse, Pitchley," he croaked. "I have both my feet."

The boy could not speak but took the hand he was offered and somehow hooked himself securely over the saddle as the horse trotted off into the drifting grayness. Hugo watched his support go, knowing he must walk back, then turned, in hope, at the sound of hooves. The Cossack was racing at him with sword arm raised, like the Devil venturing forth from the fires of hell, and he could only thrust feebly at the rider's leg as the blade slashed down upon his head turning him upside down in a blood-red darkness.

I must return. I must return. The words were on his lips

when his senses brought him back to a world of red mists. *Return where?* It did not seem possible for anyone to feel such agony and remain alive. His face was masked with blood—the Russian sword had smashed into his skull with great force—and his left eye was closed or blinded. The left cheek was a raging fire. *I must return.* Fevered though his thoughts were, that fact stood out clearly. The reason eluded him, but his body obeyed the impulse.

He began crawling on his knees and one hand. If he concentrated on a foot at a time he could make it. *Never think of a mile and a half. Just a foot at a time.* Through his blurred right eye he could see shadows moving slowly in the same direction—shadows that sobbed and gasped—and he knew he was among friends.

Three feet. That is one whole yard. Just one thousand seven hundred and fifty-nine more. No, never think of a mile and a half—just a foot at a time. Eight feet. That is as high as a doorway at Wychbourne. Twelve feet. If Charles stood on my shoulders we would reach that far. Twenty-two feet. He could think of nothing to compare with that and thought of the agony of his body instead. Taking in great sobbing breaths, he lay on his face, feeling the warmth of the grass on his right cheek. He wanted to feel it for all time, but there was an urgency in him now. *Six more feet. I must be nearly there. No, there is a mile and a half. God give me strength. A mile and a half.*

The smoke was thinning. Up ahead was the sunlight. Every movement burst his chest further open, and his head seemed split in half. Blood was clotting in his mouth and running down his throat in a thick slimy stream. *Get into the sunlight. I must reach the sunlight.* Flat on his side now, he stretched out the fingers of his one useful arm in an effort to reach the brightness on the grass and brought up his knees to push himself forward. The smoke began to wisp away, leaving the valley stretching ahead beneath the October warmth.

This was as far as he could go. He had done his best. No man could be expected to do more, surely. Unashamed, he lay on the grass and cried out from the torment of his wounds. High above him a bird was still singing its heart out at the beauty of the morning.

And so ended twenty minutes in Hugo Esterly's short life.

The crowd on the hillside watched in stricken silence as the entire Light Brigade vanished into the smoke at the end of the valley. It had been exciting to see them set off like mechanical toys down below, but the thrill of pride had changed to horror when a supply officer cried out, "My God, they are going the wrong way. Those men are going to charge a full battery of cannon!"

Indeed, the disastrous truth was soon all too obvious. Someone had made a tragic blunder and sent them galloping at the wrong guns. From their advantage of height the spectators could see the tiny gun emplacements that had been captured from the Turks that morning and were now only lightly guarded by Russian infantry, but as the bright ranks had advanced down the valley, the expected sweep to the right did not come. The Light Brigade had been sent to attack the wrong target!

The chatter, the excited murmuring died away, leaving only the faint echo of drumming hoofbeats to float upward before smoke hid the regiments from view. The Heavy Brigade, which was some distance behind in support of their comrades, dropped from a trot to a walk, then halted. The order to retire was given, and they returned, knowing no one—nothing—could prevent what was about to happen.

For ten minutes or so it almost seemed that five regiments had vanished from the face of the earth, until sharp eyes made out tiny stumbling figures emerging from the point whence they had disappeared and realized that the scattering of dismounted men was all that remained of the Light Brigade.

The women, wives of the Lancers, Light Dragoons and Hussars who had been longing to go into action, took it very quietly. Those who gave way to tears did so in silence. The others clutched their shawls around them, shivering in the warm sunshine, stared down into the valley with set faces. They had never before seen an entire brigade go down within ten minutes and could not accept the fact.

Victoria knew her life would never be the same again.

What she had just witnessed was beyond credibility, beyond humanity. As she watched, more figures were emerging into the sunshine with the disorientation of pain, some leaning on each other, some crawling like the beasts of the fields. It was terrible, it was depraved, it was obscene. She had lived this nightmare once at Wychbourne, after Hugo had spoken of such things, and woken to find the deer park tranquil and unspoiled. From this one she would never escape.

Time passed.

"I have to go down there, Letty," she said tonelessly. "We both have to."

The girl beside her had grown old within twenty minutes. Did she look the same way? A glance was all that passed between them before they mounted and turned the heads of their horses down toward Kadikoli. They set out at a walk, hesitant, reluctant, frightened, yet their pace quickened as they covered the several miles, as if their reserve of subconscious courage overrode their frailty.

Victoria had only one thought in her mind. It had been there since the first hoof moved in that charge and was pushing at her heart, her head and her stomach. *God give me the strength to face what I have to face,* she prayed as they reached the approaches of the valley and rode into the aftermath of battle.

Confusion was total. Regiments were mixed together, distinguishable only by their headgear, and she looked desperately for the fur busbies of the Hussars. Down here it was hot, the high hills throwing back the sun into the hollow below, and the air was filled with the stench of war.

Abandoning Renata, Victoria began picking her way through stretchers, medical boxes, kneeling attendants, survivors, her eyes seeing nothing but faces—only faces. Horses were being led away through the confusion by men she did not bother to scrutinize. He would not be among them. Limping, hopping troopers were assisted with difficulty through chaos, but they did not have a captain's knots on their sleeves, and she walked past. Her feet took her over the soldiers who lay masked by blood, for none had the right build, the rich brown hair or enough gold lace on his jacket to be the one she sought.

She walked alone, not knowing or caring that Letty had gone her own way. Her riding skirt clung to her hot damp legs, forcing her to hold it up higher as she continued her search. There, *there* was a Hussar busby lying on the grass beside an officer! She pushed past a torn gray horse and through several Lancers sitting together slaking their thirsts, seeing none of them. *It was not him!*

"*Clear a way there! Stand back . . . Stretcher bearer, over here . . . water, someone give me water . . . leave him, Corporal, there is nothing more we can do . . . where are the bandages? They cannot have run out . . . this man will have to have his leg off . . . get this man off me, for Christ's sake. He has just died . . . make way. Make way there!*"

Victoria was oblivious of the words around her. Surely she had not looked at every man. There were others coming in all the time. Was that a captain's sleeve behind the cart? Yes, but the officer lying so still and white was a Light Dragoon. She must turn and search again. Had she really looked at every face?

"Mrs. Stanford, ma'am, we've been looking for you. Mrs. Stanford? *Mrs. Stanford!* Are you all right, ma'am?"

Victoria turned blank eyes to the trooper.

"The colonel is in the hospital tent. His foot is crushed and he has a sword cut on his arm, but he's all right. I'll take you to him. This is no place for a lady, ma'am."

Awkwardly, the lad put his arm behind her to coax her away from the frightful scene. She went because he might be there with Charles. It was a long walk—the length of a nightmare. Her husband was lying on the grass outside the tent. Inside, the doctors were performing the indescribable rituals of their trade with a glass of brandy as their only anaesthetic.

Charles presented a neat appearance after some she had seen. Blood had dried rust-red on his sleeve, and his left foot stuck out at a stomach-crawling angle. His face was pale and patchily blackened by smoke, which emphasized the colorless quality of shocked eyes. Apart from that, the gold-encrusted jacket was neatly buttoned to the neck and his busby still sat at the correct angle on his head.

His right hand went out to her, and she took it, hardly

noticing its warmth against her ice-cold fingers. Automatically she knelt beside him, and he spoke with unusual emotion.

"They are saying it was a mistake, Victoria. I can tell you it was the most tragic mistake known to warfare."

His words relit the picture in her mind as those small galloping figures were led past the right sweep straight into the guns.

"It is rumored the Lancers are finished, and the Dragoons have no more than a dozen left. *A regiment of twelve men!* As for mine, I dare not inquire." He remained quiet for a minute or two, staring at the late-afternoon sky. "I think I have never been so tired. You cannot know what a comfort it is to have you here. I had not thought you could be so courageous . . . so loyal."

His voice died away as his eyes closed again, but the hand remained clasping hers until they came to tend his wounds. The doctor's swift comforting smile went through her, and she walked on cramped painful legs among those lying around the makeshift hospital, lifting the blankets even from still, shrouded forms so that no face was overlooked. *He was not there.*

When she arrived back in the valley the scene had hardly changed; men were still willing their shattered bodies to cover a few more yards to safety. Each one of the faces that stared back at her was the wrong one. The Lancer just coming in could not be him; the corpse across an officer's charger that was being led by a trooper of Hussars was that of Cornet Balesworth, the champion shot of the regiment. The man without a jacket and covered with blood from a shoulder wound was too lightly built. They were shooting horses all around her.

Breaking into a stumbling run, her feet took her over the ground their hooves had covered that day. The first part was rough and uneven, forcing her to lift her skirts high and stride out over the humps, then the valley smoothed into regular grassland.

"God bless you, ma'am," cried the stumbling, bleeding man holding up his arms as she approached. She paused, but he was a trooper of Dragoons, and she walked past.

The valley was vast; it had not looked so big from above. She turned left toward a blue-uniformed figure and walked

with increased pace. It was impossible to see his sleeves, for
he was lying face downward and doubled up in agony.
Shaking hands turned his head. He had only one eye, and
the other that stared sightlessly up at her was brown. The
body just beyond was already being tenderly straightened
by a woman who rocked back and forth singing a keening
song. There was no need to approach.

"Jeannie? Is that you, Jeannie?" asked a Dragoon in his
delirium as she drew near but received no answer.

Her steps quickened. There was a long way to go to the
next one. She reached the bundle that had been a Hussar.
It had no face, but a sergeant's braid on the sleeve told her
what she wanted to know. She was running now, past
women who were sitting like statues beside their dead husbands and past soldiers crying unashamedly as they took
personal effects from beloved brothers and lifetime comrades. Her feet flew over the grass that was littered with the
debris of battle, going faster and faster as shots rang in her
ears to signify that yet another beast would feel no more
pain.

Up ahead was a Hussar officer lying against a brown
horse that was rigid in death. She could see the brave gold
lace of his jacket, the sword still in his hand, the brown
hair tumbled over his face. She was running, running to
him, over patches of thick clover, over autumn flowers
vivid with color. A hare shot away in fright at her noisy
passage, but her eyes were fixed only on that figure far out
in the valley.

Breathless, sick with fear, she reached him, then gazed
helplessly at the lieutenant's insignia that decorated the
blue cloth. Distraught, she turned away, but a hand
clutched her skirt with such desperate urgency she was
held there. Fighting to free herself, she heard a voice she
knew.

"Stay for just a minute. It is so very lonely out here."
Young Harry Edmunds looked up at her with eyes that
were fast closing, and something inside her broke. Sinking
to the ground, she took his head in her lap, stroking his
face with fingers that grew wet.

"It was a beautiful summer that year, Victoria," he murmured.

She nodded. "Yes . . . it was . . . a beautiful summer."

Letty came to her when it was dusk and no longer possible to see far into the valley. The few survivors had ceased
coming in hours before, but Victoria had watched and
waited even after they brought her back with Harry Edmunds. The young lieutenant had died soon after she
reached him. The last small light of her youth had seemed
to die with him.

Letty's arm went around her shoulders and drew her
away. They walked close together through the straggle of
men who had nowhere to go because their regiments had
vanished at twenty past eleven that day. The advancing
night brought bitter chill, but fires were forbidden lest they
betray their positions to the Russians, who had successfully
carried away the captured guns and now had possession of
the Woronzoff Road that led from Balaclava inland, giving
them access to the siege town. No hot meals could be prepared, nor hot drinks to warm the stomachs of those who
had fought to save the loss of Balaclava itself. Since the
camps had been struck at dawn in case of a retreat, the
survivors just rolled themselves in their cloaks and slept on
the frost-hardened ground.

The ladies were lucky. Colonel Rayne had allowed the
officers' tents to be erected, and it was to the one shared by
Jack and Hugo that Letty took her shivering friend, wrapping her in a blanket and fixing a cup containing brandy in
the shaking hands.

"He did not return, Letty."

"No," said the girl gently, "but there is still hope. Mrs.
Stokes is searching for her husband, who is missing."

Victoria felt inordinately distressed. "Oh no! Stokes was
such a *good* man." Her eyes began to register again and
saw the dim, shaded lamp on the table and the paleness of
her friend's face. "How selfish disaster makes us, Letty, for
I have not even inquired about your beloved Jack."

"He lives" was the simple reply. "By God's mercy he
was hit before reaching the big guns. They are at this moment digging out a ball from his thigh and another from his
neck." She tightened her hands into fists. "I am not as
staunch as you, my dear friend. I could not bear to stay

within the realm of his pain. You are my comfort. I only wish I could be yours."

There was a rustle outside, and a voice said, "Mrs. Stanford, ma'am?"

"Yes. Who is there?" asked Letty.

"Trooper Connaught, ma'am."

Victoria's head shot up. "Come in, please."

The flap was raised, and the soldier entered with a salute. She knew him as a cook in the regiment. He held some things in his hand.

"I was asked to give these to Colonel Stanford, but he's got a bit of fever and don't seem to know who I am. Would you take them, ma'am?"

"What are they?"

"Effects found on the body of his brother." He put the items one by one on the table. "Watch, a miniature, some money, and two letters—one addressed to your husband, ma'am." He straightened up.

She struggled to swallow the block in her throat. "I should like to see Captain Esterly's body."

The man winced. "Much better not, ma'am."

Her throat was still thick as she stood up. "After all I have seen today I can face anything."

"But, ma'am, he . . . some Frenchies brought him in not long ago and . . . well . . ." He turned to appeal to Letty. "It's better to leave things as they are, ma'am . . . really."

Letty took Victoria's arm and held her tightly. "I think Connaught would not recommend staying away without good reason, Victoria."

The man saluted and left, and Letty coaxed Victoria to sit once more. She sat like a marble statue, fixing her eyes on the watch and seeing only his face.

"He was my whole life, Letty."

"I know."

The watch ticked quite loudly, macabre in its continuing life in the face of death. "What shall I do now?" It burst from her like a moan.

Letty took her hand. "What he would want you to do."

She put her head back and closed her eyes against the tears. "He would want me to be strong, and I am not. He would want me to use life to the full, but how can I do it without him? He would want me not to grieve, but oh, Letty, I do . . . *I do.*"

Her body rocked back and forth in torment, until Letty took her rigid hands against her own breast and cried with her, tears shed for all those women whose world had been darkened that day.

PART THREE

CHAPTER TWELVE

When they brought Charles to his tent at ten o'clock Victoria was sitting there alone, having left Letty when her husband was carried in, exhausted after his ordeal at the hands of the surgeons. The orderlies placed their second-in-command none too gently upon the makeshift bed and departed. He looked pale but composed, he smiled at her once the men had gone.

"I am luckier than most. I return whole and find a devoted wife awaiting me. I know there is no chance of anything hot to drink, but you should find a little brandy in the flask inside my valise."

She remained where she was, looking at his blanched handsome features, knowing she would never hate anyone as she now hated this man.

"Victoria, are you all right?" It was said with surprising concern.

Painfully, wrenchingly, she brought it out. "Hugo is dead. You have not once inquired after him."

His whole demeanor changed. She saw the upward tilt of his chin as the noble House of Stanford settled on his shoulders. "So that is the way of it!"

"You have not once inquired after him," she repeated, "and yet he thought sufficiently of you to carry a letter to be delivered to you in the event of his death." The consuming anguish was making her voice shake. "I have read the letter and destroyed it. It did not belong to you. He owed you no words—he owed you *nothing*."

Charles raised himself on his uninjured arm. "How dared you read a letter addressed to me!"

"How dared you speak to Hugo of honor, when you have none yourself!"

"You go too far, Victoria—even allowing for the trials of the day."

So deep was her grief, so empty her future, so bitter her hatred, nothing would have stopped her saying what she must say.

"What kind of man could do what you have done? What manner of arrogance can make a man believe himself fitted to take responsibility for another man's soul?" It came out of her with a passion she had never before displayed, that her upbringing condemned. "You allowed Hugo to believe he caused the death of our child and endangered my life that day. The doctor told us both, in each other's presence, that a malformation brought about a premature birth and would preclude any further children. It would have happened if I had been sitting quietly before the fire with your mama. I heard the doctor tell you that Hugo's brilliant descent from Mexford Heights saved valuable time and probably my life." She fought against a tidal wave of tears. "How could you have put him through such torment of mind? How could you have questioned his honor, when everything he did was above reproach? How could you—" she caught her breath—"how *could* you have let him die still believing it? His letter asked for your forgiveness." The memory of Hugo's words, badly expressed but sincere, completed her breakdown and she put her face in her lap in a frenzy of sobbing. "Dear God, it is he who must try to forgive *you*. I never shall."

Those wounded at the battle of Balaclava were being shipped to Scutari in transports that were not fit to answer their description of "hospital ships." The same vessels that had conveyed men, horses and equipment from Varna were hastily transformed by the addition of a sprinkling of medical staff and a small chest of medicines to each. They were overcrowded. 'A ship fitted to accommodate two hundred would set sail with well over a thousand men suffering from cholera, recurrent diarrhea, fever, supporting wounds or amputated limbs.

The battle casualties were heaped in with the cholera sufferers, who scrambled over the raw stumps of men's arms and legs as they tried to reach the primitive sanitary arrangements, setting them screaming with pain. In many cases, the sufferers were too weak to move, and with no one to assist them, the lower decks were soon overflowing with blood and filth where sick men soon died and wounded men quickly fell sick. Germs bred in the ill-ventilated bowels of the ships, so men who had embarked suffering in one way arrived at Scutari with additional ills.

Surgeons operating during the voyage found the heavy rolling of the ships brought ghastly errors of judgment when cutting off a limb or probing a deep wound and were forced to leave gangrenous wounds to grow worse. The men who endured the voyage knew only one way to keep sane: They fixed their minds on their arrival at Scutari when they could say goodbye to their ordeal. They could not know their last hope would go when they were carried over the threshold of the Barrack Hospital.

One of the transports being used in this way was *Sirocco*, and Letty persuaded the embarkation officer to allocate Charles and Jack to that ship, where Byron Porchester had promised the ladies cabins for themselves and their husbands. The sea captain was very distressed by Victoria's appearance. He had seen her vivid and provocative on the voyage from Portsmouth, melting in her defenselessness at Varna, but now, empty, stony-eyed and lifeless. Remarking on the fact to Letty, who appeared to be taking control of the situation, Captain Porchester repeated his assertion that a battlefield was no place for a lady.

Letty had a suspicion that the breezy man was a little too fond of Victoria but silently vowed to take advantage of his penchant for her friend if his help would make things easier for them. She was herself extremely worried over Victoria's condition. The girl went about her duties, looking after her husband with silent efficiency, but something had died inside her. When word had come of the move to Scutari she heard it with dazed indifference and began packing the few things they were allowed to take with them. Details of the voyage did not appear to interest her; Letty had arranged everything.

Jack Markham was weak and feverish, but Charles Stanford, although strong enough, was in great pain. His foot had been crushed when others had ridden over him to reach the guns. Victoria was meticulous in her nursing of him, but Letty believed she spoke no word to the man who had survived while his brother had been lost. Hugo's death had cast a dark shadow over Jack and herself, but she was selfish enough to concentrate on happiness at Jack's safety and her efforts to bring him back to complete recovery. To this end she used all her energies to make the four of them as comfortable as possible.

Letty's maid had remained in Balaclava with her husband, who was one of the few survivors of the charge, and Zarina Stokes agreed to serve both ladies, going about her duties faithfully but sadly. Stokes had disappeared with no grave or epitaph, like many others, and Zarina was a widow. She had lost her proud walk and air of flamboyance, but she was lucky to have food, somewhere to live and a small wage. The other soldiers' widows were stranded and destitute, unless they remarried, or ensured their survival some other way. With the present state of supplies and conditions before Sebastopol, life would be punishing enough for the men; there would be nothing to share with those creatures who had followed the army from England.

It was Letty who took command at Scutari when they arrived to find that the horror on board was nothing to that at the great Barrack Hospital. The approach was appalling enough. Only a short ferry ride across the Bosphorus, Scutari had no jetty—just a rickety landing stage that would accommodate no more than caiques or rowboats. The sick and wounded had to be lowered from the transports into these smelly vessels and rowed over choppy seas to shore, where a gang of sulky, unwilling Turks carried them the short distance to the hospital. Frequently, notification of their arrival had gone astray, and men suffering unto death were left outside in rows, with nothing but a torn, gaping uniform to keep away the November cold. Even so, many would sooner have stayed there than enter the building itself, which effused a stench that nauseated those outside its walls and enclosed those whose moans could be heard night and day.

The day before *Sirocco* put in at Scutari, an English gentlewoman called Miss Nightingale had arrived with a party of nuns and trained nurses to give urgently needed help in the hospital and was given bare rooms running with lice and rats by way of accommodation and advice to remain there. The administrators of the hospital refused to let her or the women anywhere near the sick men. They received no food or water, and there was no furniture in their tiny cells.

Charles and Jack were obliged to walk to the hospital, since only those with no legs at all or those in the last throes of death fevers were allowed to use the limited number of stretchers. Victoria and Letty supported their husbands to the doors of the building and were then turned away, Letty with a sinking heart at having to say goodbye to Jack and to leave him in such conditions. Scutari was a dolorous place with nothing but cemeteries, brothels and other places of vice that naturally sprang up around a military settlement, along with mean, vicious traveling peddlers, starving dogs and vermin bloated on a superfluity of rubbish.

Byron Porchester was pressed into immediate service by Letty, who decided she and Victoria must go into a hotel in Constantinople, and, true to his word, the sea captain took them to that city and found them rooms in a quiet comfortable hotel well frequented by English people of quality. He left, promising to call on them each time he came down to Scutari and pledging to do what he could about transporting the rest of their baggage from Balaclava when an opportunity arose.

Letty thanked him very warmly. Victoria spoke as though her thoughts were elsewhere. She did what Letty suggested, ate sparingly and automatically and allowed Zarina to make her look neat and presentable but cared nothing for what went on around her. If Letty said they must travel to England, she would go—or back to Balaclava or to Varna . . . or to the ends of earth. It did not matter.

Charles, being a senior officer, was housed in the more reasonable General Hospital a quarter of a mile away from the converted barracks, and Jack was lucky enough to be sent there also. Every day it could be managed, the ladies went across on the ferry with delicacies they could purchase in Constantinople, but, although Letty took her gifts to Jack and stayed to cheer him, Victoria handed hers over at the door. There was nothing she and Charles could say to each other.

The news from the Crimea was frightening. Cholera had broken out again with great virulence, the advancing winter was sweeping the British Army on the heights with sleet showers that froze on men and beasts alike, deluges of rain had made the only track from Balaclava to the hills—the

only route, since the capture by the Russians of the Woronzoff Road, by which supplies could be taken up to the
troops—into an impassable sea of mud in which the pack
animals struggled until they sank lifeless to their knees.

Then, on November 14, came the final blow to the army
that had marched so bravely through the streets of English
ports. The Crimea was hit by a hurricane that blew away
tents, supplies, furniture, equipment—everything needed
for survival by those encamped around Sebastopol. Horses
were snatched up and carried for miles in the teeth of the
gale; an entire flock of sheep disappeared. The hospital
marquees went in a trice, leaving the patients lying in a sea
of mud, exposed to the fury of the storm. The last remaining trees needed so urgently for fuel were uprooted and
tossed away like matchsticks, and the wagons were
smashed to pieces. In the morning, as men crept from beneath saturated greatcoats, they heard that every ship in
Balaclava harbor had been smashed and sunk that night,
taking down with them all the supplies for the winter.
There was now no warm clothing, no huts, no extra food,
no blankets for men and horses, no fuel—no hope!

Hospital ships became more crowded than before, the
men piled into them like livestock. As well as those suffering from cholera, dysentery and rheumatic fever, the ships
carried appalling casualties from another battle at Inkerman, when the Russians had attacked in thick fog and pre-
cipitated a gruesome and bloody bayonet-against-bayonet
struggle. They had been driven back but had left dead and
wounded in great mounds.

For several days high seas in the Bosphorous had prevented Letty and Victoria from crossing to Scutari, but
when they were, at last, able to do so, the sight that met
them was so shocking, Victoria was brutally shaken from
her apathy. Boats stood offshore unloading men for the
hospital. Littering the ground between the landing stage
and the entrance to that grim building were hundreds of
creatures in rags, bearded and filthy, half starved, shivering, covered in clotted blood and pus and demented with
pain. They were once the pride of the British Army; now
they were scarlet shadows.

The two women stood speechless, until Victoria whispered, "Letty, we have to do something to help."

Letty shook her head hopelessly. "We cannot help. If Miss Nightingale and her trained nurses are not allowed even to wipe a man's brow, they would not hear any words of ours on the subject."

Indeed, they did not get even any word on the progress of their own husbands on arrival at the hospital doors. An angry, distracted doctor in crimson-soaked clothes ordered them away.

"Can you not see the state of our emergency?" he roared. "This is no time for genteel visiting by ladies of quality with arrowroot and eggs in their baskets."

"Do you not need arrowroot and eggs?" Victoria demanded heatedly.

"No, ma'am. We need a hospital—a real hospital. In fact, we need three of them. If one more shipload arrives the men will either remain out there on the ground or be forced to lie on top of others in this God-forsaken place. They will receive no attention for two weeks either way."

"Then why will you not allow Miss Nightingale's nurses to use their skills and humanity, sir?" cried Victoria. "Will you let our soldiers die rather than swallow your masculine pride?"

He became viciously quiet. "I, ma'am, would have taken Miss Nightingale's help with thankfulness when she first set foot in here. I am a doctor and I will save life by any means at my disposal. If I thought that filthy water out there in the harbor would save just one man, I would bring it drop by drop in my cupped hands. But I am also a soldier and must bow to the commands of those of higher rank who are afraid that a few Sisters of Mercy will make them appear foolish back in England. Stand back, please," he said swiftly and moved toward a stretcher being brought in. Over his shoulder he added, "Miss Nightingale is now fully employed from sheer necessity . . . but even that courageous lady will not prevent complete disaster." He pushed past them. "And neither will baskets of arrowroot and eggs."

Realizing that chaos did indeed reign within the hospital, they moved away, feeling distressed and helpless. Men begged for water in faint voices, but they had none to give. On an impulse, Victoria took an egg from her basket and offered it to a glaze-eyed Guardsman, suggesting he ask to have it coddled for him when he arrived in the ward, but the man snatched it and ate it whole in its shell before her astonished eyes.

"They are *starving*," breathed Letty. "Let us go. It is too terrible."

As if she had not heard, Victoria walked away from her friend to where she had spotted a Guards officer sitting against a wall and sank down before him. He raised blood-shot eyes to hers and said painfully, "Forgive my manners, ma'am. I cannot stand."

Her eyes avoided the stump of his right leg. "My hus-band is Lieutenant-Colonel Stanford of the Hussars, sir. He is in the hospital, already on the mend. I know he will not mind my offering another the things I brought for him to-day." She put the handle of the basket in his hand. "There are eggs, arrowroot, fish and some wine. May I hope you will share them with these poor men?"

He looked blankly at the contents of the basket. "Alas, I am not Jesus Christ, ma'am, who fed the multitude with five loaves and two fishes."

Ridiculously she felt tears start in her eyes at the sound of so beautifully cultured a voice coming from a dirty rag-ged outcast. Beneath his degradation he was a gentleman.

"You have already done so much that is beyond belief, sir," she said gently.

He put his hand inside the tattered scarlet jacket and brought out a creased envelope. "Would you think me im-pertinent, ma'am, to ask you to post this to my mother? It is a very personal matter that needs an urgent reply, and I am not certain when it will get off once I get in there." His eyes turned toward the hospital.

"Of course." Overcome by the moment, she took the let-ter and returned to Letty, trembling with some indefinable anger. The envelope was addressed to the Countess of Kingsmere.

Several attempts by the two young women to speak to Miss Nightingale were unsuccessful, since it was impossible to gain entry to the building. They returned to Constanti-nople upset and depressed. Victoria had reawakened and could not rest in comfort knowing what was happening across the narrow stretch of water in Scutari. Until well into the night she sat gazing from her window, lost in thought, her eyes on the distant hospital, dark in the winter moonlight.

Gradually emerging from her state of shock, she began to feel again. Again, she felt as she had at Varna when men were going down with cholera and had no one to console them or give them hope. That time Charles had told her the second-in-command's wife could not go around the hospital tents, but he was not here now to prevent her. The more she considered it, the greater grew her conviction that here lay her salvation. She had turned to it before when Hugo rejected her; now that he was gone, it was the one thing that could make her life worthwhile.

The minutes passed as she came to terms with herself. Hugo had loved her as she had loved him. She knew that for all time. It would be a betrayal of that love if she let her own life be wasted as his had been. Ahead of him had lain a brilliant career in the army; could she not make it possible for some other young man to conclude what he had begun? Her thoughts went to the youthful Guards officer of that morning. Would an answer to his letter ever reach him?

In her mind she traveled painfully back to Wychbourne and an innocent child telling a blindfolded figure that she would be patroness of the Hussars. In her personal grief she had abandoned the regiment—forsaken those who still remained. She had foolishly dreamed of leading a host of glittering horsemen; could she refuse to help the ragged broken survivors? If only one man could be saved by her efforts, she would have repaid to Hugo the debt he was owed.

Burning now with impatience, she knew herself hopelessly ill-equipped for what she proposed. But as she gazed at the outline of Scutari where the casualties had been exposed to the elements that morning, she knew there were many things that needed only the natural qualities of a woman to perform. It was to that end that she would direct her energies.

The following morning saw the two ladies, together with Zarina Stokes, take the ferry to Scutari. With them were three small boys laden with boxes, and no sooner had the party arrived than the three began walking among the men who were being landed from the ships, offering cups of milk, slices of bread spread with butter, pieces of goat cheese, raw eggs and jellies. The men took what they were offered, as many seeming unable to bring themselves to eat as those who wolfed the items whole, but each one was grateful for the milk held to his lips by gentle hands.

Victoria went about her task with an aching heart, seeing in each pair of eyes the pain Hugo must have suffered and in each broken body the one she had never found out in the valley. Within a quarter of an hour it was clear that her store of courage was lower than she had thought, and it was an effort to continue.

Her problem was solved in an unpleasant way by a loud voice saying behind her, "Stop this at once!" and she looked up to see the same doctor they had encountered yesterday, just as angry as he had been then.

"What do you mean by this damned dangerous practice?" He peered closely at Victoria. "You were here yesterday with eggs and arrowroot. I thought I told you then that Lady Bountifuls had no place at this hospital."

Victoria rose to her feet, shaking. He was a youngish man, aged by despair, with a shock of red hair and fierce eyes. He had on a filthy white coat and trousers, and his hands were stained reddish-brown.

"It seems that manners have no place in this hospital either, sir," she said.

"No, madam, not when men are dying in thousands," he snapped. "I am not an aristocrat in a scarlet uniform—just a doctor who is too far beneath their uptilted noses until he is expected to perform miracles. I cannot afford the time for fancy manners when limbs are waiting to be amputated."

"Then why are you out here, sir?" she pointed out acidly.

"To prevent the harm you are doing with your high-minded helpers. Most of these men are starving, besides suffering from dysentery or cholera. Eating food such as you are giving them will shortly cause them great agony, even death in some cases. They require special diets."

She was still trembling. "Will they receive special diets in there?"

Suddenly, he sagged and put his hand through his hair. "No . . . no, they will not. I still cannot allow you to increase their suffering by this ridiculous indiscriminate feeding."

"Tell me what we must give them, in that case," she cried. "If you have none in the hospital I will purchase it myself."

"We could not allow that," he said firmly. "These men are our responsibility."

She looked back at him with intense eyes. "They are the responsibility of us all, sir."

He grew angry again. "I don't know who you are, madam, but you are making extreme nuisances of yourselves. Do you realize that the British Army is dying here at the rate of three hundred souls per week? What we need cannot be supplied by society ladies living in luxury in Constantinople who trip across the Bosphorus with baskets of eggs because they have nothing better to do."

Victoria grew quiet. "We have come down from the Crimea where we watched our husbands fight in the battle of Balaclava. We have been with the army since it left England, sir, and no one has ever doubted our genuine wish to help. We know men are dying; we have seen them."

He did not grow embarrassed or awkward, just apologized rather wearily. "I have seen so many ladies of the kind I mentioned, madam, that I cannot grow used to true strength and courage. I repeat, there is nothing you can do in the hospital—even Miss Nightingale will have no ladies who are not trained in nursing—but if you really want to be of some use, come with me. I know where your presence will be really welcome."

So forceful was he that Victoria, Letty and Zarina fell in behind him without another word and picked their way over the stony slope toward the great grim Barrack Hospital. He veered away from the entrance. One side of the building had been leveled by a wall that contained a row of gratings high up in it, and the doctor walked purposefully to an archway at the end of it. His strides were so long, the young women had a job to keep up with him.

Getting closer, the ladies were forced to put their handkerchiefs to their noses, but the red-haired man seemed unaffected and strode beneath the arch into the relative darkness of a series of connecting cellars. There, he waited for his female companions to catch up, making no attempt to assist them down the slimy steps.

After the daylight, Victoria found it difficult to see anything, but the smell of urine combined with shuffling noises and whimpers told her there was something alive down in the cellars. She strained her eyes against the darkness and gradually made out human shapes. She heard Letty gasp behind her as she realized what they were seeing. The cellars were crammed full of women and children.

As her horrified gaze penetrated the murk she saw filthy faces, distinguishable only by the eyes that glowed like those of animals cornered in a dark lair. It was difficult to decide how many were there, for some were sitting, and the rags they wore merged with the rags that served as beds on floors covered with refuse of every description floating in an inch or so of water.

Silence had fallen at their arrival. It was so nightmarish a sight Victoria could not accept that the *things* crawling in the filth littering the floor could be infants, nor that the bundle of cloth rolled into a ball in one woman's arms could cry like a newborn child. Every nerve jumped when a cackling voice from the darkness suddenly cried, "It's a penny to come and gawk, lidy. For tupence, me pretty sir, you'd get a lot more." Her shriek of laughter was immediately augmented by bawdy invitations to the doctor.

The ladies could stand no more and fled up the steps, followed phlegmatically by the doctor. Victoria stood in the air fighting down waves of nausea. Judging by Letty's face, her friend was doing the same. Zarina had lost the struggle and retreated to a quiet corner where she sat on the ground with her head hanging down.

The doctor stood before Victoria with a grim smile. "Still full of good intentions, madam?" Do you feel any responsibility toward *them*?"

She forced herself to ask, "Who are they?"

"Women of the regiments," was the crushing answer. "A lot are wives of the men in hospital. They cannot be accommodated there, and no provision has been made for them by the army authorities. A great number are widows of those who died from cholera in Varna or were killed at the Alma. A small number are deserters—women who quit their husbands and regiments when they landed here on

their way out from England. It is they who first occupied
these cellars and have attracted the others. They roam the
place at night and entice the soldiers from the unit sta-
tioned here, but the money they earn is spent on hard liquor made locally. I would not go down there when they
have been drinking for fear of my life."

"What do you think *we* could do with such creatures?"
It burst out of her like a swarm of angry bees.

He remained cool. "Putting your mind to the problem
might stop you interfering with my patients." He sketched
a salute and began walking away. "I do not give a damn
for these trollops, madam. I just want an end to their activities, since they spread disease and fever among men that
are fit. Otherwise we shall have no army left."

That night the weather turned bitterly cold, and frost
lay upon the ground in the early morning, with a severe
wind keeping temperatures low. All through her breakfast
Victoria thought about the wounded who would be left
lying out in such weather, and she thought about her vow
to give Hugo's life to someone who still had a chance to
live it. That doctor had told her she must not give the men
food, but he could not prevent her from making them more
comfortable—he could not prevent her from *caring*.

In a trice she was at her writing table making lists, and
very soon Letty and Zarina were being swept along in her
wake. By mid-morning the little party was crossing the
choppy Bosphorus with parcels and baskets filled with their
purchases. Victoria led them straight to the landing stage
where she knew there would be men in a pitiful condition.
When Letty and Zarina hung back with strange reluctance,
Victoria urged them on, and soon they were following her.

There, exposed to a punishing wind off the sea, victims
of the Crimea were trying to struggle unaided up the steep
incline from the pier, on weak emaciated legs, protected
only by thin uniforms torn and falling apart at the seams—
stiff with mud and blood. No man had a cloak or great-
coat—some had no jackets—and nearly all were wearing
boots held together with strips of rag over bare feet. There
were those with no boots at all, yet they trod over the frost-
hard ground, so sunk in their own wretchedness that one
pain was lost beneath all the others. Those who could not

walk were unloaded from the caiques and laid upon the ground to await their turn for a stretcher, but anyone with two feet was expected to make his own way, leaning on his comrades, stumbling, clawing and often falling with a scream of pain. The Turkish navvies and boatmen did not care, but Victoria suffered with them.

Seeing an infantryman go down on his knees from exhaustion, she dropped her basket and ran to his aid, gathering her woolen skirts in one hand as she ran and calling to Letty. Her friend did not go, and it was Zarina who took the man's other arm to raise him up and help him across the stony approach to the hospital. The smell of his body was revolting, and his face was blank with the horror he had been through. Any lady should have shrunk from him, but Victoria had seen so much in that valley at Kadikoi, the man could have been Hugo, so tenderly did she move with him.

It was natural to return to aid another, and, with the help of her maid, Victoria went back and forth with men leaning gratefully and heavily upon her slender shoulders. Letty, who could not bring herself to have such close contact with the filthy creatures, went around distributing socks they had bought, finding it as much as she could do to put them over the mud-caked feet of the wounded as they lay shivering on their stretchers.

As time passed Victoria became more and more possessed by the need to lessen the degradation of those she helped, and her brain was so busy with plans as she tramped back and forth, she did not notice her tiredness. When Letty departed to visit Jack, she and Zarina worked together, kneeling beside the helpless until someone fetched them and talking in quiet voices that occasionally broke through the blankness of their resignation.

Their efforts had at least one small reward, when Victoria came to a young officer who knew her and smiled through his beard. She had been busily putting a sock on his left foot, and then found her hands frozen as a closer look revealed a right leg that ended at the ankle.

"There is certain to be another like me who needs only one, Mrs. Stanford," he said faintly.

Looking closely at him for any recognizable signs, Victoria said, "You have the advantage of me, sir."

"Beneath this beard, ma'am, is the honest face of William Carpenter. I had the honor of dining with you in Captain Jenson's tent on the night you arrived in Varna without equipment or dinner."

Immediately, the memory of a laughing young lieutenant who claimed to read palms leaped into her mind to present a harsh, unbelievable contrast with the man before her.

He told her of the fearful storm at Balaclava and how the hospital tents had been blown away, so that all the sick and wounded had to be sent down to Scutari. He told of the state of the army and the general feeling of hopelessness among the men condemned to spend the winter in front of Sebastopol. He told her, in effect, that anything *anyone* could do for the Army of the Crimea was desperately needed, and her resolution strengthened.

During the following ten days she went to the pier, laden with boxes and baskets. The Turks grew used to seeing her and even allowed themselves to give a little more assistance to the soldiers who were fighting a war on their behalf. She distributed socks, put rugs over those who were left lying in the December cold, cleaned their faces with warmed rosewater, gave them news of comrades who had come down several days before and told them of great loads of supplies that would be on their way from England shortly. She did not mention the horrors inside the hospital, the mass burials each sunset and the complete breakdown of the commissariat department which could no longer supply anything for the sick and wounded. The situation inside the Barrack Hospital was completely out of control.

Every night she sat writing letters—dozens of them—to the relatives of those who could give her addresses. Each one was individual, referring to the man she remembered quite clearly as belonging to each name and address on her list and assuring his relations that he was receiving attention. She passed on personal messages from the patients and gave the address to which to reply, although she doubted letters would ever reach the patients in time. She had heard that men lay in wards for a fortnight before anyone had time to come near them, and half were so ill they could not give their names. Mass burials saved the necessity for uninscribed wooden crosses.

Letty knew her friend was urged on by some powerful

drive that could not supply her with super-strength forever but made no attempt to curb the daily activities. Victoria was amazingly immune to dirt and blood, Letty noted, and felt a little ashamed of her own sensitivity. However, she had enough to worry her. Jack's thigh wound, which had only just started to heal, had broken open again and started festering. Medical attention was spasmodic, and she knew her husband was in constant pain. Apart from that, a new fatal fever had broken out in the Barrack Hospital due to the breakdown of all sanity arrangements, and patients suffering from other complaints were dying at the rate of sixty or seventy a day as the fever spread. Letty lived in fear of it spreading to the smaller hospital before Jack was discharged.

Three weeks after arriving in Scutari, Charles was declared fit for duty again and assigned to one of the transports plying to and from Balaclava. He arrived at the hotel in Constantinople one evening unexpectedly while Victoria was engaged in a pile of letters and went up to the room she occupied. Entering without knocking, he stood watching his wife, who was too absorbed to hear his entrance.

Her hair was drawn back into a severe style, and the harsh light from the oil lamp on her writing desk made her look older as she bent over the paper. The dress she wore was hardly suitable for dining in the select hotel restaurant—it even looked muddy around the hem—and she had no shawl around her shoulders, despite the chill of early December. He sighed. Had this woman ever danced down the stairs of Wychbourne in a silver-green dress that turned her into a dark desirable rose to be crushed against him until the heady perfume overwhelmed him with desire?

"Good evening, Victoria."

She spun around, dropping her pen as her hands flew to her throat. "Charles!" There was dismay in the utterance of his name. She made no attempt to go to him.

"I am sorry to have alarmed you," he said.

"No . . . . no, it was just that I thought you were still in the hospital." With a glance at her desk she said, "Have you dined?"

He twisted his mouth. "We do not 'dine' in hospital, Victoria. I have nothing to eat since this morning. Will you

kindly dress in something suitable so that we may go down
to the dining room?"

She rose immediately. "I have been in the habit of taking
a tray in my room at night. I will not keep you long."

He walked across to the writing table and sifted through
what appeared to be letters of condolence and medical bul-
letins on a host of soldiers. Here and there was one concerning an officer, but the wording suggested the writer
had personal knowledge of each subject. He frowned. What
had his wife been doing that had prevented her from visiting him even once?

They went downstairs, exchanging generalities rather
stiffly until they were seated.

"You have no idea how it feels to be in a civilized room
again with carpets beneath one's feet, furniture and curtains . . . and even a small orchestra to soothe one's ear.
There were times when I believed I would never breathe
pure air again."

"There are many who will not" was her sharp answer.

He overlooked it. "I must thank you for the things you
sent in to me."

Her lovely sad eyes fixed themselves on him. "I would
have done the same for many others, but the authorities
would have none of it. It is very hard to know the men are
starving and be refused the chance to help."

"There are people especially trained to do that," he told
her, and she closed her lips on any reply she had been
about to make. After a moment or two he said, "I sail on
tomorrow's transport for Balaclava. Will you have your
things packed and ready by nine o'clock?"

"I cannot go with you, Charles."

The cold finality she used tightened his mouth and put
him on his mettle. "*Cannot?*"

Quietly she told him what had occupied her time in Constantinople, as though she saw nothing degrading in a
woman of quality mingling with lice-ridden malodorous
soldiers who were well used to dirt and squalor from childhood. She made no mention of her neglect of him in comparison. He grew angry as she spoke and full of self-disgust.
There had been plenty of time for thinking in hospital, and
such thoughts returned to him now.

What a tragic mistake it had all been! A naïve child-

woman had promised him something she was incapable of
giving, then turned to a man who had called himself his
brother. Together, they had robbed him of his rightful future—nothing would persuade him they had not—and betrayed his pride. What kind of weak fool was he that, after
all that had happened, these past months had beguiled him
into a new kind of admiration and dependence on the
woman sitting across the table? Since she had fulfilled the
regimental duties of a wife so admirably, it had been easy
to slip into a belief that she had also valued the bond that
kept them together.

Just how wrong he had been hit him now. Hugo was
gone, as he predicted—probably by a rash disregard for
discipline, since his body had been found by French troops
operating way out on the left flank of that valley—but,
even in death, he had dragged Victoria away from him.
Alive, Hugo could eventually have been blotted from her
mind; dead, he had assumed a heroic quality he did not
deserve. To be betrayed once should have been enough for
any man; to receive a hysterical outburst of rejection from
his wife over a man who no longer lived was the ultimate
insult.

All that remained intact was the outward image of their
marriage. Not a soul knew of the curse of her childless-
ness; not a soul would believe Victoria was not a devoted
wife. She was highly regarded in the best circles—even
Lord Cardigan had expressed his admiration for her. She
could be useful to him, and he had every intention that she
should be. Charles knew he held the trump card. Now he
produced it.

"Praiseworthy though your motives undoubtedly are, I
cannot have my wife behaving like a camp follower," he
said smoothly, watching for her change of expression.
There was none. "Your duty lies with me, in Balaclava."

"I am sorry, Charles, but I shall not go." It was said
quietly but with absolute firmness.

"You will do as you are told, madam," he snapped, conscious that she was using the safety of a public room to her
advantage.

There was undisguised loathing in her study of him.
"What an overbearing phrase that is! Little Victoria Castle-

don would have obeyed you, but she had a lot to learn. It has all been learned now. When I am no longer needed here, I shall come back to Balaclava. You claimed to have no further use for me, Charles. I have found many who have."

"You refuse to do as I say?"

"For the moment, yes."

"Very well." He dipped into the pack and came out with his ace. "I shall make arrangements for you to return to England, where you will do your best to comfort my father at Wychbourne." Ah, he knew that would hit her hard, and his chin went up triumphantly. "You have no choice, Victoria. I shall issue instructions to the bank not to meet any hotel expenses or bills from tradespeople incurred by my wife, and I can have your luggage sent on in advance. You could hardly remain here in those circumstances."

She resorted to pleading, which was more to his taste. "For once, will you not put selfishness aside? Is it beyond your humanity to see that what I am doing is in the interest of this army and our country? Charles, from what I hear daily from these men we have lost this war if the Russians attack us. There are but a handful of men in the Crimea fit to hold a gun or ride a horse. Do you truly hold your own gratification above the pride of your heritage? Of what use will it be to have me as a dog at your heels when the Russians take you prisoner? Lieutenant-Colonel the Honorable Charles Stanford, heir to the Blythe title and second-in-command of the famous Hussars, having to bow the knee to some Russian princeling—that is what you will be doing if this appalling death rate is not stopped."

He did not like the picture. Amazed that she could know so much of what was happening in the Crimea and here in the hospital, he had to concede there was truth in what she said. Still he said, "Washing a man's face and putting socks on his feet is not going to cure him of cholera, nor prevent the loss of a limb. You are merely playing nursery games, Victoria."

"I am giving them back a little of their pride."

Bitter pain pierced him through at the soft, almost caressing, concern, and he blurted out, "You should be cossetting and succoring our son, not these gutterlings."

Very still suddenly, she fixed him with a long gaze. "You forget we have both lost the one thing we wanted above all else in this life."

He did not trust himself to reply to such a comment. If they had been alone in a room it would have been different.

She went on. "As you say, I have no choice, but will you agree to a compromise? Jack Markham has taken a turn for the worse, and I really should not leave Letty alone at such a time. If you allow me to stay with her, I give my word to return to Balaclava when Captain Porchester puts in at Scutari next."

He leaned back in his chair, tired and swept by the feeling of hopelessness he had experienced of late. Not yet forty-two, he felt the burden of years weighing on him as if he were gray and bowed. The sword cut in his arm was now only a scar, but his foot felt the raw air in its bones, and he had a slight drag on that leg. Balaclava was not much short of hell at the moment, from what he had heard, and he had no regiment of which to be second-in-command. The mere thirty who had survived the charge had no horses to ride and were probably down with fever or frostbite by now. Would the situation be any easier in the company of a woman who hated him?

"Stay here, if you must, Victoria," he told her tonelessly. "I cannot see that it matters where you are."

With Letty so preoccupied with Jack, Victoria found herself alone with Zarina in the daily task of meeting the wounded, and, despite the bitter winter weather that had now reached them, she continued to bring what little relief she could to the men. One day the red-haired doctor appeared before her with a cup of soup and said, "You never give up, do you? Drink this or you will be joining those poor devils."

She shook her head. "I would rather you offered it to one of your patients."

He began to shout at her above the wind. "If we all did that, no one would survive. The medical staff would be too ill to tend the patients." He took her arm and guided her up the slope. "If you are not selfish enough to drink it before their eyes, stay up here for a while."

Reluctantly she sipped the hot broth, and he surprised her by breaking into a grin. "Did you know you are acquiring a certain fame? We hear nothing from new arrivals but praise for 'the lady with the sad eyes.' They have even heard of you before they get here. Those who have recovered and returned to Balaclava give out the news to those on their way down."

"Some do recover, then?"

He sobered. "That was before winter hit them up there. I have never known anything like this in all my years as a doctor, and I hope to God I never experience it again."

She felt suddenly depressed. "I am doing so little."

He took the empty cup from her fingers. "If everyone in England did a fraction of what you do, I should not be needed here much longer." He gave another grin. "You are still an inveterate meddler, my dear madam, but I have no intention of stopping you."

He strode away, and Victoria felt warmed by his words. It was a long time since anyone had smiled at her like that. Picking her way back down the slope, she took up her pad and pencil to write down addresses for her letters and went among those waiting to be carried in. The first man was a Scot, and she always found it difficult to understand what they said. Bending low, she concentrated on the unfamiliar accent, writing what she hoped was the correct street name and assuring him the letter would go off to his mother that evening.

"God bless you, ma'am," said the man in the way most did, and she moved on. This one was full of bravado for her benefit, and she was in the midst of conversation with him when a hand caught at her skirt. Glancing around, she saw a figure lying a few feet away.

"I will be there in a moment," she said, then caught sight of a captain's insignia on the Hussar-blue sleeve and felt the blood drain from her. A step, and she was beside him, scarcely daring to look down at the man he could not be.

His chest was bound with vile bandages, the left sleeve of his jacket was cut away to reveal more bloody rags, the lower part of his face was covered with a matted brown beard, and running downward from above his left eye across his cheek was a deep puckered scar, crimson and raw, that hid his expression. But the blue-green eyes gazing at her were unmistakable.

The notepad fell from her hands; the pages were caught by the wind and tossed like autumn leaves all around her as she sank down beside him. Her fingers reached out to touch his stiff hair, his eyelids, then to trace the outline of his split left cheek with a trembling caress that came to rest on his mouth. He put up a hand to hers and she caught it up in agony to lay it against her wet face.

"Where did you go?" she whispered. "The world has been so cold without you."

CHAPTER THIRTEEN

The Turkish navvies listened dumfounded to the English lady's sudden inexplicable reversal of opinion, for it now appeared she was telling them they must *on no account* take that certain soldier into the hospital. Ever since she had begun her daily visits she had harangued them into getting the men *into* the hospital. One gave it as his opinion that the madness that sent an unveiled Christian female to do the work she had been undertaking had eventually taken possession of her completely and jabbed a finger in the direction of the hospital to which she was heading in a frenzy.

He was partially right. Victoria was possessed by something akin to madness, for nothing and nobody was going to take Hugo from her into that hospital. Her driving urge had been to save just one man, give Hugo a life for a life. Now she had a man to save. She could give Hugo his own life, and the only way it could be done was by keeping him out of the dreaded Barrack Hospital.

Reaching the doors, she brushed aside the orderly who would have prevented her entry and stepped into the corridor. It was only her state of single-minded frenzy that allowed her to walk about in this place blinded to its horrors. On either side of the corridor lay men without bedding or coverings of any sort, crammed closely together so that one could not turn without touching another and covered with lice that swarmed over the walls and floor.

Hurrying through the first corridor, Victoria entered a high barren room where the stench brought a terrible faintness and nausea that checked her for a moment. Seeing a young nun moving about at the far end of the room, she went in, lifting her skirts above the layer of muck and filth that covered the floor, grimly concentrating on the woman in gray and seeing nothing of the skeletal men piling the sides of the wards—mere lumps of misery with no pillow but their boots to raise their heads above the overflowings

from toilets unable to cope with several thousand more patients than they were meant to serve.

The nun was firm. Miss Nightingale was too busy to see
anyone, and the doctors were working almost without
sleep. The one with red hair was performing an operation
at the moment. Mrs. Stanford must leave immediately. The
nun was adamant, but Victoria was even more so. Brushing
past, she left the religious woman holding her bandages and
hurried through the doorway and up some steps to the upper floor. There, a ward similar to that she had left revealed the same pitiful story, but a small screen at the end
of the room drew her in the confidence of finding someone
in authority behind it.

Heedless of faint moans and voices calling for water, she
went the length of the room until she stepped around the
screen. There was no doctor, as she had imagined, but
something so utterly terrifying it forced its way into her
suspended awareness. Beside a rickety wooden table was a
basket full of limbs, some with uniform sleeves still upon
them or the worn remains of a boot. They stuck out at
angles, just as they had been thrown, the fingers on one
hand crooked as though beckoning to her.

Victoria uttered a shuddering cry before backing away,
then turned and ran blindly through the filthy chilled
room, knowing she must get away from the horror at the
far end. At the top of the stairs she ran into someone coming up and gave a small shriek before collapsing against
him in relief.

The red-haired doctor led her swiftly down the stairs and
through a ward to a side door that gave onto a courtyard.
The yard housed the two outbuildings used as mortuaries,
but there was only the smell, not the sight of death, here,
and the mere fact of being outside again made Victoria try
to steady herself. Tears streamed down her cheeks against
her will.

"Sister Thomalia said you were wandering about by
yourself. I hope the experience has cured your meddlesome
tendencies," he said savagely. "This is no place for females.
I told you that long ago."

"Please . . . do not use your wrath on me right now,"
she begged. "I am in the greatest need of help and you are
the only one to whom I can turn."

A surprising change came over him. The rough aggressive manner dropped away, and a droop of weariness aged him in a flash. "There is hardly a soul on this damned stretch of land who does not need my help right now," he told her in a tone filled with helplessness. "You have just been inside that place. It is not possible for a man to share himself between thousands, so it will not matter if I desert them in your cause for a short while. Please, calm yourself and tell me the reason for your distress."

"Will you walk with me to the beach?" she asked thickly. "There is down there . . . a friend whom all believed killed in the battle of Balaclava. I cannot tell how ill he may be." She put her hand on his arm to start walking beside her away from the hospital. "I do not ask you to tend him—only tell me his condition. It is my intention to move him to a hotel in Constantinople. Once there, I will engage a doctor to give him treatment for as long as there is hope . . . but nothing will induce me to let him enter here. He had just returned from the dead. I will not send him straight back."

He cast her a resigned look. "If he has been sent here, we have orders to take him in."

Fire flashed from her eyes. "Who will ever miss him, sir?"

Choosing not to answer that, he reached the spot where Zarina was standing guard over Hugo. He was covered with one of Victoria's rugs against the severe weather. "Is this the man?"

Victoria nodded. "Only tell me he will not suffer a setback if I arrange transportation across the Bosphorus."

"My dear madam, if he still lives after the journey from Balaclava, a trip on a ferry will do him no harm." He squatted down and pulled back the rug, then took scissors from his pocket to cut the bandages away from Hugo's chest wound.

Victoria found her teeth chattering with the cold. Uncontrollable shivering took possession of her limbs. Zarina put her own shawl across her mistress's shoulders. The girl looked ill enough herself, these days, and Victoria refused the attention in gentle tones.

The doctor stood up, shaking his head. "That chest wound is serious—very serious indeed. On top of that he has a touch of enteric fever and is suffering from the usual malnutrition."

"And if he goes to Constantinople?" asked Victoria through stiff lips.

"He has a good chance of recovery" was the surprising answer. "A nutritious diet will build up his resistance to the fever, and once that dies down the wound will have a chance of healing. Good food, constant care and clean, warm surroundings are all he needs."

"You have orders to take him in your charge," Victoria reminded him.

His frankness gave her her answer. "If I do, he will die."

She decided on equal frankness. "Have you any idea of trying to prevent my taking him with me?"

"Among thousands his absence will merely mean a few feet of extra space on the floor. He is an officer and will report himself fit when the time comes, I have no doubt. Take him, madam. I shall voice no objections."

"Thank you." It contained so much gratitude, that carelessly used phrase, but the doctor had one more thing to say before he left.

"You intend to devote yourself to this one man. What of your work here with all these poor wretches?"

She gazed at him long and helplessly. "Perhaps you are right. This is no place for a female . . . unless she is a Miss Nightingale."

After a few seconds his uncompromising features broke into a warm understanding smile. "Yes . . . unless she is a Miss Nightingale." He pointed to Hugo. "You must cover that chest wound with something. Your petticoat would do." He turned and walked back to the Barrack Hospital.

Victoria had Hugo carried into her own room at the hotel, then sent a note to the British Embassy asking for the name and address of the best doctor in Constantinople. While she waited in a fever of impatience for the information, her hands were busily employed in washing his face and hands, covered with ingrained dirt. It horrified her to see lice crawling through his hair and beard and the red weals on his skin where they had bitten him mercilessly.

Just when the tears began to flow she was not aware, but

as she cared for him with passionate tenderness she spoke of everything that had been locked inside her since she had seen the truth reflected in the Mirror Room. She spoke as a young girl to her first sweetheart, as a mistress to her lover, as a mature woman to the possessor of her soul. He heard none of it. The journey across the Bosphorus and the subsequent carriage ride had left him unconscious.

The doctor who answered the summons was French, courteous, very competent and susceptible to feminine charms. Taking the situation immediately in hand, he sent out for a young Turkish youth he trusted implicitly, saying he could do nothing for *le capitaine* until he was cleaned. Victoria left and went to Letty's room while Zarina took instructions down to the kitchens for invalid foods to be prepared.

With all this activity going on, it was hardly surprising that word reached the ear of the hotel proprietor, who presented his black-mustachioed countenance at the door of Letty's room to inform Madame that he could not allow his hotel to be used as a hospital; he could not allow guests to be exposed to infection; he could not allow special food to be cooked in his kitchens. Five minutes later, he was bowing himself out, clutching the list of special dietary requirements specified by the doctor and assuring Victoria that she had only to ask and he would be delighted to afford any assistance she might require. Wiping his brow with a silk handkerchief, he bustled down the stairs muttering under his breath about Madame Stanford, who looked so tiny and restful, yet had just flown at him like a she-wolf with cubs. Her husband was a lord, she said. They knew all the lords in England. They knew the British Ambassador *and* the French Ambassador. One word in the ears of all their friends that Yashul Ahmed was a disobliging man and this hotel would immediately empty and remain that way. Yashul Ahmed would be ruined.

Letty returned to find Victoria sitting with her head in her hands, overwhelmed by what had happened, now she had nothing to do but wait. Cast down by her own worries over Jack, Letty joined her friend in an outburst of tears. They sat together, holding hands and finding comfort in each other's presence until Victoria could speak the truth she hardly yet dared believe.

"He is in my room being attended by a doctor I have hired," she said fervently, "and do not say I should not have done it, because I could not bear to let him out of my sight again—I *could* not."

Letty hugged her and burst into tears again. "God is truly good, Victoria. I shall not entirely believe it until I see him with my own eyes." She drew away and wiped her eyes. "My dear, I understand your actions—but do you think it is wise to take his health into your own hands?"

"He is in the hands of an excellent doctor, Letty. I knew his life would be forfeit the minute he crossed the threshold of that hospital . . . oh, I am sorry . . . I did not mean . . ."

"I know," said Letty. "Jack is just suffering a setback at the moment. He is keeping cheerful, and this news will be like a tonic to him. I wish I could remove him here, but I doubt they would allow it."

"Perhaps in another week or so," suggested Victoria. "In the meantime, say I may share your room, for there is no other to be had that will allow me to be so near Hugo."

"Naturally you will share my room."

Victoria was quiet for a moment, then: "I have to offer you an apology."

The brown-haired girl was surprised. "I have no notion why."

"While we have been in Constantinople I believe I have behaved toward you with slight constraint on occasion. I beg your pardon. My own compassion has not stood the test. I am about to abandon my work for selfish motives."

"I see," said Letty, then smiled. "Victoria, why are you so afraid of emotion? When I first met you it was plain you were at your nerves' end—hardly the picture of a happy bride—yet you gave no hint of the reason. After you lost your child you changed dramatically, yet not one word did you speak to me of the experience. Then again, it was perfectly clear when we arrived in Varna that your husband was no longer speaking to his brother, nor Hugo to you. I still cannot guess why. I have known from the first that you loved Hugo and have watched you bear it in silence. He has also suffered from it and found no relief." She took her friend's hands. "You are here until Captain Porchester returns. Can you not let yourself be the weak, gentle creature

you were born to be? Can you not let yourself be a simple
woman? Until that ship arrives can you not forget duty,
sacrifice and longing . . . and just love him?"

The doctor knocked before leaving and said he had left
the Turkish boy watching over the patient, who was growing feverish. Madame could go in, if she wished, but should
do nothing to disturb him. In view of le capitaine's illness
he would call again that evening.

Both ladies went along immediately and stood looking
down at Hugo, who was extremely restless. He looked human once more in a striped nightshirt brought in by the
lad. His hair and beard had been trimmed and washed
clean; the terrible smell that had clung to him had been
replaced by antiseptic that seemed to drench the entire
room; there were clean bandages around his chest and left
shoulder; and the blueness of cold had left his lips.

The boy explained in halting English that the bedclothes
had been taken away and burned in case of infection, and
completely clean linen had been put on both bed and patient. Le capitaine's uniform had been put in a bag and
taken to a Turkish woman who would clean and mend it to
Madame's satisfaction. His own duties were to feed and attend the patient.

Content that everything possible was being done for
Hugo, Victoria collected her few belongings and, with Letty's help, took them along to the other room. They had a
quiet meal there, waiting for a further report from the doctor. When he tapped on the door it was to inform them
that the fever was mounting, and it might be as well for
Madame to remain by her husband's side during the night.

She did not feel disposed to correct the medical man's
error, and Letty just smiled with understanding when her
friend took a shawl and prepared for her vigil.

"Pray for him, Letty, as I shall for Jack," Victoria said
swiftly before departing.

The fever brought sweat glistening on his brow and heat
to his body. Already, he was turning his head on the pillow
in some torment of spirit, and, as the night began in earnest, his restlessness increased and wild muttering betrayed
the onset of delirium.

Soon after midnight he fought to cool himself by throwing off the bedclothes, and Victoria jumped from the rock-

ing chair to fetch a bowl of water and towels. Ordering the
boy to hold the patient down, she doused Hugo with cool
water to keep his temperature from rising. This much experience she had had in the sickroom at Aunt Almeira's when
her cousins had been feverish.

For an hour or more they both worked, holding him
down when he tried to throw himself from side to side,
keeping the blankets over his burning body and wringing
out towels to lay across his forehead. Shortly before dawn
the fever broke, and Hugo lay quietly, as if he had never
been the struggling maniac they had watched all night. Victoria leaned wearily against the bedpost and breathed a
prayer of thanks while the lad straightened up the room.

It was already growing faintly light when she made to
leave. The Turkish boy gave a small bow and said, "Many
thank-yous, Madame!"

She smiled wearily. "And many to you, young man."

He stared at the door after she had gone, wondering at
the strangeness of this English lady.

When Hugo awoke it was to a new world of warmth,
comfort and diminution of pain. He lay looking at strange
yellow flickerings on a white sky. Were the guns still firing?
No, he had come away from that valley. Could it be the
light from campfires dancing on the hospital tent? This ceiling was not sloping; it was too warm and pleasant here for
a tent. Of course, it had blown away while he lay beneath
it, and the wild drenching night had been all around him,
the shrieks of the wind mingling with the moans of his
companions who were left to lie on blankets in the mud.

Somnolence brought his eyelids down again, but the
sounds about him continued to feed the guessing game in
his head. There was a rhythmic squeaking of timbers such
as he heard on ships, but this bed was too steady and his
stomach was making no protest. A small groan broke from
him as the nightmare of that last voyage returned. An
eternity of retching, agony and degradation in putrid semi-
darkness that ended on a beach covered in ice. The wind
had bitten into his body like sharp knives, and the sky had
been stormy-dark, but it had been a complete release and
he had wanted to be left there forever. He remembered it
vividly now—the sharp stones beneath his head digging

into his skull, the blessed smell of fresh air and salt spray, the women moving around with shawls tightly wrapped across them . . . the *women!* He had seen Victoria there.

His eyes flew open as her name burst from him. He knew she had really been there that time—not another in the parade of ghosts that had passed before his eyes for so long.

"Victoria?"

By some miracle she was beside him, looking down as she had on that beach. This time she wore a dress of some bronze shimmering material, and her cheeks had the color of life in them.

"Hush, my dearest," she told him. "I am here."

He allowed himself the joy of a long look at her, not knowing nor caring how she came to be there.

"You were on a beach," he said at last. "What were you doing there?"

"So very little," she replied softly, "until I found you."

"Charles . . ." he began, but she said quickly, "He is back in Balaclava."

He said no more for a little while, trying to reason where he was and why Victoria was with him, but it was too much for his tired brain. Her hand closed over his on the bedclothes, and he looked down at it.

"All we ever seem to do is meet in unexpected places for a brief while. My whole life is spent imagining you to be around every corner. When we do come face to face, there is nothing we can say."

She lifted his hand to her cheek as she had on the beach, and he felt the wetness against his fingers. "To know you are here is all that matters. Words are not necessary."

"Neither are tears, Victoria. They have all been shed between us."

She sat on the side of the bed, holding his hand between her own as the weariness invaded him, closing his lids over the vision he saw. How different she was now from that questioning girl he had first seen by the glow of candles at Wychbourne. If she had been his . . .

When he next awoke there was sunshine flooding across the counterpane. There was still warmth and comfort around him, and he felt hungry. A French doctor came to dress his wounds and, after that painful business, told Hugo

he was pleased with his progress but he must remain in bed
for at least a week unless he wished his chest to burst open
again.

"You are very fortunate, Monsieur, that your friends
brought you to the hotel immediately." He smiled. "Madame is a very formidable lady. Monsieur's brother is even
more fortunate than yourself, I venture to suggest."

"Yes," said Hugo.

After the doctor departed, a dark-eyed Turkish youth
brought a tray with a bowl of broth, a soufflé and some
jelly. To finish, there was a glass of port wine. He ate it all
with less attention to manners than to getting it inside him
as quickly as possible.

Left alone, depression returned, to march a long line of
recollections before him and relight the pain that had lived
with him since October. He remembered the sun-washed
valley and the gasping shadows returning; he remembered
the wounded from Inkerman being carried in, half hysterical from the nightmare of bayonets in the fog; he remembered the mud and slime of the Crimea where frost bit into
hands and feet that projected beyond the one thin blanket
at night. He might be safe and warm here, but the Army
was slipping away as it sat before Sebastopol.

Victoria came to visit, and he felt ashamed of his own
gloom when he saw the joy light her face at the sight of
him.

"Your appearance is very timely," he confessed. "I have
become quite fractious and will most likely throw my basin
at you at the first sign of your crossing me."

She smiled. "Now I know you are better. You have always been an unruly patient, Hugo." Sinking into a rocking
chair before the fire, she provided the answer to the puzzle
of squeaking timbers and flickering yellow lights on the
ceiling. "The latest bulletin from the doctor is very encouraging."

He could just see her face from where he was lying.
"The doctor thinks Madame is a very formidable lady. I
would go further than that, Victoria."

"Letty is coming to see you just as soon as she returns
from the hospital," she said, cutting across his overture to
an expression of thanks.

"Letty is here?"

"Jack is in the General Hospital. I fear he has taken a turn for the worse. There is a bad wound in his thigh that will not heal. He was brought down to Scutari with Charles after that terrible day. There were so many—I will not allow myself to think how many. Harry Edmunds died in my arms. I have written to his family but could not give any last messages, for I truly believe he did not know it was the end. And poor Stokes just disappeared—like many others. His wife is over at Scutari every day in the belief that he will appear, as you did." She rose and came to stand at the end of the bed, and he drank in the beauty of her soft concern with greedy eyes. "Hugo, they brought me your . . . effects. They told me you were dead."

He knew they must speak of it sooner or later. "They believed I was. I am told two Frenchmen brought me in after coming across me way out on the left flank where they had been operating that day. I must have crawled at an angle, for I could not see where I was going. They threw me across a horse and delivered me to our own lines." He looked closely at her, but she appeared to be well in control of herself. "I was covered in blood and apparently lifeless. The orderlies accepted the Frenchmen's word, and I was put with a pile of our dead." He hastily reassured her, "I knew nothing of any of it. In fact, I knew nothing until several days later when I learned that it was only because an orderly noticed that I felt unusually warm that I was not interred that night. I was removed to the hospital tent, but they had very little hope of my survival. It hung in the balance for three weeks."

He sensed her anguish but continued. "Even when it appeared that I might live they would not send me to Scutari until I was strong enough to stand the journey." He gave a twisted smile. "They did not know that ships and I do not make a good partnership."

"I would not say you were fit to endure the voyage now," she protested. "What made them order it?"

He was beginning to feel tired again, yet did not want to close his eyes and blot out the picture of her in the sunshine that he treasured. "Conditions up there are unforgivable, Victoria. The soldiers in this army have been betrayed by their commanders and by the government in England. The fit men are ill; the sick are dying. There is no place for hospital patients since the great storm swept the tents away, so they are all being sent here. Those who are not wounded have fever; those who are not fever-ridden are starving; those who are not starving are dying of frostbite."

Victoria came around to him and sat on the edge of the bed. "Do they have no idea what it is like at Scutari?" she asked gently. "I understand the sick have more chance of remaining alive if they are *not* sent to the Barrack Hospital."

He watched the sun playing on the gold ring on her hand. It gleamed a warning at him. "Charles has become fit again, I take it?"

"Yes."

Dismayed at his lack of courage, he found it necessary to force the question through his lips, so that he must face the answer she would give. "He must also have believed I had not survived that day. Did he . . . write to his father of the news?"

She made no answer, and he was forced to swallow his pride. "Did he show no sign of . . . I left a letter to be delivered if I should . . ." His words trailed off at the expression on her face.

"Charles did not once inquire after you that day and, when I broke the news to him, showed no interest, apart from a certain sense of resignation—as if he had expected it."

He winced. She had spared him nothing. Why should this truth touch him so deeply? "Charles is not a man who forgives easily."

"He had nothing to forgive," she cried with emotion that thickened her voice and deepened the brown of her eyes. "Hugo, I have done something you would condemn in a man. When I have told you, you will have to decide whether you are a man who easily forgives."

His heart quickened. "I told you once never to apologize to me. There is no need."

She put her hand to her throat where it played with a large brooch, the wedding ring taking his attention the whole time.

"Because Charles was in the hands of the surgeons your—" she plainly found the word difficult to say— "*effects* were handed to me. I read the letter and tore it up."

Swiftly he knew it was not easy to forgive that. The letter had been written after his mother's death when he was feeling the loss of his family and was meant for his brother's eyes only. He felt somehow diminished before her in the knowledge that she had read the words he had hoped would save his soul from damnation. It was an effort to remain silent.

"You *are* angry," she said sadly, "but it can be nothing to the anger I felt when the truth became known to me. Hugo, that letter did not belong to Charles. No action of yours robbed him of his son, nor put my life in danger."

After Victoria left him, Hugo lay staring at the reflection of flames dancing on the walls. Overwhelming tiredness seeped through every nerve and fiber of his body. It was easy to understand her actions when she was handed a few keepsakes that she believed were all that remained of him. He now understood and tried to excuse, the reading of a private letter, but it did not prevent his feeling humbled in her eyes. Yet, if she had given it to Charles, how much more humiliated would he now feel? He winced inwardly, remembering the cold words in which she had told him of Charles's indifference to the news of his supposed death. He would not have believed hatred could extend beyond the grave. Charles was a Christian; forgiveness of the soul was part of the creed.

Closing his eyes brought no sleep, neither did it ease his thoughts. The lifting of the burden of guilt he had carried for so long was no relief, for the weight of his brother's deliberate vengeance for that day more than compensated. He was the perfect whipping boy. Eyes flying open again, he thought of the future. Brotherhood was a bond that could never be broken. For them, the love and loyalty had turned into revenge and distrust, yet they were as firmly tied together as before. Charles would always need to punish him for something he truly believed had robbed him of the sons he should have had. Did he also hate him for not being a blood brother—a Stanford who could continue the line in his stead?

As for himself, the desire he had always had to be just that—a blood brother and true part of the family—would keep him striving to attain the standards Charles had always set him. It was that that had kept him crawling up that valley, had sustained him as he lay in the mud of Balaclava, had kept him sane during the voyage down to Scutari. From now on it would drive him even harder. The campaign in the Criméa was not yet over. He would be there at the end, as he had vowed.

It was the end of another day, and his stamina was low. Pain always crept in with the dusk, and too many ghosts raised their heads in the gathering twilight. He wished the boy would come in and light a lamp to chase them away. Turning restlessly, he wondered how long it would be before the *Sirocco* returned and Victoria went back to Charles. How could he make her return to such conditions? It was hell enough for men—no female should be exposed to it.

As soon as he was fit, he would return himself . . . and the game would begin again. He, striving to stay alive, while Charles waited for him to go to pieces. How in God's name would it all end?

For Victoria the days glowed with joyfulness. The doctor had been too optimistic in his estimate of one week in bed, for Hugo was still there after ten days. It made no difference to Victoria. He was getting stronger and would recover—and she could be with him. She still awoke in the night, panic-stricken in the belief that she had only dreamed his return, but it happened less often as time passed.

Letty still went each day to visit Jack and returned to tell Victoria how much better he was in a voice that was optimistic but wistful. Zarina Stokes still haunted the beach at Scutari, believing that if one man could return from the dead, so could another, though she never found the one she sought. Victoria made no attempt to stop her; she was too absorbed in her own happiness.

Two days before Christmas she hurried along the corridor on her morning visit to find Hugo sitting out on a chaise longue looking very pleased with himself.

"Ha!" he cried when she appeared. "I shall soon be filling you with admiration at my elegant bow when you enter. Ladies have been known to faint away with delight as I bend over their fingers."

"You will be the one to faint away if you try such elegance too soon," she laughed, coming around to stand before him. "I am glad you have taken off that beard at last. Now I know you again."

"Even with this?" He touched his cheek.

"It is- an honorable scar. It is part of you," she said softly.

"Oh yes, it is part of me forever." His vivid eyes suddenly held turquoise fire. "We were sent to charge the wrong guns that day, Victoria. It was the most tragic blunder in this campaign."

"I know." She sat in the rocking chair. "I was on the hill with many others. We could not believe what we saw. At the outset it was naturally assumed you were going to recapture the guns lost that morning, but you rode right past the smaller valley."

"Do I not know it! There is the most heated battle going on up there over it—everyone anxious to avoid taking the blame. The commander-in-chief insists that his order referred to the guns we had lost to the Russians that morning—they were dragged into Sebastopol that night, I am told, amid much rejoicing. Cardigan insists that he was told to charge the guns at the end of the valley and that his protest was met with a reminder that orders must be met without question. The brigade-commander insists that the written order was ambiguous, that he could not see the guns other than those we attacked and that Captain Nolan, who brought the order and was in a state of extreme excitement and insubordination, pointed to the end of the valley when asked what the order meant." He ran a hand through his hair in anger. "It was plain to us all that what we were ordered to do was deplorable madness, but I have to admit we could *not* see the captured guns from our position in the valley. Also, in fairness to Nolan, he did gallop out in the most inexplicable way, waving his sword and shouting at Cardigan, so it could be that he realized the order had been misinterpreted. We shall never know. The poor fellow was the first to fall. Whatever the truth of the matter, it was still unforgivable for commanders to send men so needlessly to their deaths." He leaned back wearily. "What we did was against all principles of cavalry tactics, was contrary to the ethics of warfare. Lord Cardigan appears to be the only

commander who raised objections to what he was told to
do. It is that fact that leaves me so disturbed, Victoria."

"They have been trained to obey orders. Is that not the
duty of any soldier?" she asked tentatively.

"Oh yes," he flung back, lost in his own anger, "but .
those men were not *any* soldiers. If an order is ambiguous,
no commander should take the word of a staff captain to
persuade him to send an entire brigade to destruction unless any good would come from such an act. It was not
as if we were being threatened by those cannon." He
banged his fist down on the chaise longue. "Orders
or not, if an enemy was sitting quietly several miles off
I would take the time to acquaint the commander-in-chief
of the position from where I was and request more explicit
orders before I would allow such a thing to happen. No
one would be more willing to fight to the last man against
overwhelming odds if we were defending a strategic position, but there was no sign of an attack being made upon
us at that point, was there?"

Suddenly he came out of his anger and broke into a
smile that warmed her after the chill of his words. "My
tongue ran away with me. I think you are the only woman
to whom I could speak in such a way. Is there no end to
your virtues?"

"Indeed, yes. I can be extremely disagreeable, as you
will now witness. Unless you cease plaguing yourself with
thoughts that have made you quite agitated, I shall ensure
that you remain in bed tomorrow."

He sighed. "Mmm . . . *extremely* disagreeable! You
have ceased to be the angel I imagined you." His slow
smile broke through once more. "You should be drenching
my head with cologne and feeding me with broth."

She felt a sudden lurch inside her as his words brought a
picture of golden-fair braids wound around a face of clear
classical beauty. Looking down at her hands, she said,
"That duty should more properly belong to another, I believe."

"Oh . . . who?" It was said with a tinge of amusement
that increased her disquiet.

Her head came up. "Has Miss Verewood been informed
of your safety?"

"Miss Verewood?" He looked calm enough. "I should
not imagine she knows I was ever reported lost. If my . . .
if Lord Blythe did not know of it, she would . . ."

"I wrote to your father, Hugo. The news would have
brought him great grief, but he would wish to know. Three
days ago I sent the glad tidings of your survival."

For several seconds nothing passed between them save a
look of painful understanding, but all he said was "Thank
you for that."

She remained sitting very upright in her rocking chair.
"Hugo . . . why did you do it? Charity Verewood will
drag on you like an anchor. You cannot wed her!"

He looked taken aback. "I have not said that I would."

"Have not . . . but she told me that you were promised—that you had asked her to wait for your return. On
the night of the Farewell Ball she said we were to be sisters
very shortly. Hugo, there was a letter from her among
your . . . effects."

"She wrote to tell me of Mama's death. It was that letter
I kept." He seemed bewildered. "I cannot understand this.
Sister? Why would she say such a thing?"

"You must have given her some reason to believe it."

"Certainly we both knew my parents hoped I would
make a decision at the ball, but I did not ask for her hand."

"Did you ask her to wait for you?"

"No . . . at least, I cannot remember precisely what I
said. You passed while I was telling her the difficulties of a
man going away to war, and my whole mind was filled
with distress at how I was obliged to treat you." He gave
her a look of dismay. "I could not have promised myself to
someone without knowing it, could I?"

Being together and trying to avoid any kind of deep
emotion was a strain on them both. The only relief was to
indulge in lighthearted teasing, and Victoria now found
herself saying, "If she is Miss Verewood anything is possible. Has she not referred to the matter in her letters?"

"I was not looking for such things in her words. She
wrote of my family and Wychbourne, of places and people
I knew. The letters meant a lot to me for that reason. Victoria, was she absolutely *certain?*"

He looked so comically tragic she burst into laughter.

The memory of that angelic face asking her to be a sister increased her merriment. If only she could be there when the girl learned the truth!

Hugo was still in a masculine daze. "What am I to do?"

Through her chuckles she said, "There is only one answer. You must remain in exile all your life. That way you will never return to be claimed by her."

He scowled. "I cannot see any humor in the situation."

He was still scowling when the door opened and Letty walked in. Slowly, the laughter went out of Victoria, and the chair ceased its rocking. Her friend was white and blank-eyed, her shawl trailing from her hand. She looked in Victoria's direction.

"I was wrong. It is *not* possible to accept the wisdom of the Almighty."

Immediately Victoria went to her, but her hands stopped in mid-air.

"They took off his leg last night. He had the fever, and the shock was too great. He is dead, Victoria, and I cannot accept it. You know what it is like. For the sake of my sanity, support me now, or I shall be lost."

CHAPTER FOURTEEN

By the middle of January Hugo was sitting in a chair every day. The wound in his chest was gradually healing enough to allow him to move without his breathing becoming too labored, that on his shoulder was clean and comfortable and the pains in his skull came less regularly. All signs of fever and starvation had gone long ago.

It had become routine for the two ladies to spend the greater part of the day with him, reading the newspapers, playing chess or just conversing. Strangely, it seemed to Victoria that Letty found more strength in Hugo's company than in hers. She had been beyond comfort for a week but had gradually steadied in the constant company of the two people who had been closest to herself and Jack.

In order to try to come to terms with the Almighty over the blow he had dealt her Letty found a great need to attend church daily, and Victoria willingly accompanied her. She had things to say to the Lord, too.

These days with Hugo were the sweetest she had ever known, and her love, although it could hardly grow deeper, broadened into a new landscape of emotions that increased her capacity for understanding, sympathy and passion. Although he had not so much as touched her hand since his first day with her, she knew as she sat watching him that he was a man completely unlike Charles. Her eyes lingered on his hands while her skin burned for the touch of them. She studied his mouth as he spoke, knowing that if it should seek hers it would start her trembling. When he was not aware of her scrutiny her eyes drank in every detail of the fine muscular body and recognized the ache in her thighs for what it was—that which she had found degrading and painful with Charles could be heady surrender in Hugo's arms. As she sat playing chess or talking in quiet friendship, her body cried out for him. Nights became torment as time passed. Stronger than her will, the erotic pain of imagining him beside her in the bed made her toss and turn feverishly.

Gradually, she found him doing the same. Looking up quickly, she would catch his eyes watching her. There were times when he would grow quiet, others when he hardly stopped talking long enough for anyone else to speak. He began to look hollow-eyed through lack of sleep. Both were afraid of being left alone without Letty, and both knew the reason.

Things came to a head at last. For five days there had been a traveling circus pitched within sight of Hugo's window, providing them all with a means of entertainment as they watched and commented on the procession of people passing on their way to the large marquee. They were doing the same one late January afternoon when Victoria suddenly found herself quarreling fiercely with Hugo. It was over nothing that mattered, yet she defended her statements as if her life depended on them. Hugo was equally aggressive. She felt her cheeks growing flushed, and his eyes were glittering as their voices rose.

"Hugo, I have seen the man in the ticket box every day this week," she cried. "Allow me to know that he is wearing a different jacket today."

"May I remind you that this is my room, Victoria, and therefore I have had a greater opportunity of watching what goes on outside its windows."

"May I remind you, sir, that your sight cannot be relied upon since you blew yourself up in a military exercise," she retorted, her bosom starting to rise and fall quickly. "And you are in this room only because of my generosity."

She was sorry the minute it had been said, and Hugo fell silent.

Letty got to her feet. "When Jack and I began to argue he always took me on his knee to kiss and make up." She walked to the door. "You two need to do the same. No, do not rush out after me, Victoria. You are neither of you in need of a chaperone every minute of the day."

The door closed behind her friend, and Victoria felt every nerve tighten. Suddenly, the room seemed too small and Hugo too near. With dismay she heard her heartbeat banging a drum that resounded between these walls, and the unbearable ache of desire flowed through her. Meeting his eyes, she saw her own thoughts reflected there. Weak and melting, she was thrilled but frightened to know she would this moment surrender body and soul to him if he should ask. Her lips would part beneath his mouth in an ecstasy of invitation, her bare limbs would burn with pulsating fulfillment as they twined around his. Her body would take his as greedily as his would take hers. The fusion of their passions would be a glorious expression of life and immortality that would make all else dim by comparison.

Unable to draw her gaze away from his white face and the blaze of possession in his eyes, she whispered, "I did not mean what I said to you."

"I know . . . *I know,*" he said savagely. "We were not fighting over the color of a man's jacket. If that were all we had between us do you think I would sit here day after day devouring you with my eyes against the time when you are no longer here? Do you think I would count the wide-eyed night hours away until you return? Do you think I would pound my conscience so mercilessly, tighten my control with such desperation?" He thumped his fist on his knee. "By God, do you think I would lose my brother, my family and my past, yet have no regrets each time I look at you?" He angled his gaze away and looked through the window. "I have some idea what you suffer at his hands, but have you any notion what it does to me each time I think of it? No woman will ever understand the fierce pride of a man when he takes possession of a woman he loves; when another has the privilege it is almost beyond endurance."

She sat still, held in thrall by the moment. He was disarmed and laying his devotion at her feet.

"You know why I left Wychbourne so hastily—all to no avail. You also know why I was so insufferable at the Farewell Ball. After what happened that night I told myself I could forget you, that it was just a matter of time." He turned back to her. "I shall never imagine such a thing again. You are part of my life forever . . . *but you are my brother's wife.*" His eyes closed in pain. "To see you beside him is almost more than I can stand. To watch his arrogant possessiveness builds great fires inside me. To know you are lying in his arms at night drives me from my bed in a fever." His eyes were clouded when he reopened them. "He accused me of coveting you. Dear God in heaven, if there was any way we could be together I would take you from him . . . but the only way I can love you is with honor, Victoria. All the time Charles stands between us it must remain the way it has been."

There was only the ticking of the clock, the crackle of logs in the grate when he stopped speaking. Even her very breathing seemed suspended. Their love had been consummated by his honesty. With his words he had given her his immortal soul. Through his denial of her he had possessed her more completely than Charles had ever done on his wildest night.

With her body afire and trembling with the response he had aroused in it, she sank down beside his chair. "You are the most honorable man I know," she told him softly, "but women are less exacting in their codes of behavior, my dearest love."

Placing her hands against his upper arms, she leaned forward to touch her lips against his, meaning only to ease the longing with a butterfly caress. The physical contact was so sweet, so ecstatic after the months of denial, that what began as a mere brushing of his lips took complete control of her. Rising like flood waters came the surrender, total and absolute, that Charles had never commanded, and her mouth began to tease and entice with submissive insistence—an invitation, a plea, to take what it offered.

Hugo began to tremble. His hands came up to pull hers away from his shoulders, but when she angled her head so that he must bend over her to continue the kiss, he followed the soft temptation with growing demand. Swept by the heady need to drive away the remainder of his restraint, she slid her arms around his neck so that he could not escape her by lifting his head—but it was not necessary.

There was hunger, despair, anger in the way he lifted her against him with arms grown suddenly strong. Her head spun as he drew out of her the almost wanton excitement and replaced it with a joy that swirled through her senses at the complete reversal taking place. Hugo's hands held her prisoner, and she was now the captive in the chair while his mouth teased and enticed in a way she had not dreamed was possible.

Then, suddenly, he was thrusting her away from him, putting back his head as if in torment. He was trembling still, and Victoria watched him, bemused by the glory of that kiss. Neither spoke for a moment or two, then his hands dropped, releasing her arms.

"Why did you do it, Victoria? It was madness," he said wildly.

"My whole life is touched with madness at the moment," she cried with passion. "Am I to die when you die, then live again when you are reborn . . . and have no more of you than that?"

"There *can* be nothing between us. By God, did you not understand what I said just now?"

"Yes," she said bitterly, "I understand very well, but it is there whether we acknowledge it or not." She got slowly to her feet. "You also said you would never try to pretend I was not part of your life."

His eyes were still blazing. "If I could only move from this damned chair!"

Shaken by the storm that had invaded her at his touch, she matched his anger with her own. "You do not care to be at a disadvantage? No, you are a man, strong and sensible to what the world expects of you, but I am one of those weak creatures who must comfort the strong and weep over them. We are always at a disadvantage. We must wait, we must pray, and we must always depend upon the whims of those who control our lives. It is not always easy to be a woman."

She turned and hurried toward the door, but he stopped her when she reached it.

"Victoria . . . where are you going?" It was said with weary regret.

Looking back at him, she saw how pinched and ill he appeared once more, and her passion turned to pity. It was not always easy to be strong she now realized, and she understood the pain of his rigid code of values. Calmer in that instant, she smiled across the length of the room.

"All we did was kiss and make up, Hugo. Do not blame yourself because I am weaker than you." The door closed softly behind her.

She walked slowly back to the room she shared with Letty. Her friend was not there, but a note lay on the table and, after Victoria read it, she went to stand by the window to gaze out at a now blurred circus tent. Letty was downstairs talking to Byron Porchester, who had brought the *Sirocco* into Scutari that morning.

The *Sirocco* was due to head back to Balaclava on February 5, and the week that passed before that date was full of heights and depths for Victoria. She knew she must go as she had promised. The time she spent with Hugo was lit by the love he had confessed, yet shadowed by the coming parting. She found herself selecting every word with care so that it would not be wasted. She listened to his voice so that she would not forget its richness when she was gone, watched him as though through a telescope so that everything about him leaped at her from a distance and imprinted itself on her mind forever.

Captain Porchester impressed upon the two ladies that Balaclava was a place of ice, fever and starvation when he left it, although supplies of warm clothing, food and wooden huts were reputedly only a day's voyage away. After Jack's death Letty had avowed her intention of going back as Victoria's companion, hoping to find, as she had, some comfort in helping another man back to health in the hospital tents there. Both ladies went shopping for provisions, rugs and warm coats. They bought as many as they could manage to take, knowing the officers would be grateful for the chance to purchase them. Socks joined the coats and even waistcoats, quite exotically embroidered but warm and strong.

On the third morning of that week Victoria awoke to find it light. Letty was still sleeping, and there was no sound of rattling cups from the tiny room Zarina occupied. She waited fifteen minutes, then slipped from her bed to discover why the girl was not preparing the tea. The room was empty. The tray stood ready, but no kettle heated on the tiny stove. Victoria shivered in the chill. Zarina Stokes had not slept in the trundle bed; the few trinkets and possessions normally laid out on the box beside it were gone.

Sinking down on the rickety bed, Victoria touched the coarse blankets in sadness. Zarina had been more than a maid. The girl had worked unstintingly for her, both in domestic duties and with the wounded. She had been growing quieter every day, Victoria now realized, ever since the doctor had shown them the doomed women in the cellars

beneath the Barrack Hospital. Since they had found Hugo
so dramatically, the girl's hopes had been disappointed day
by day, week by week, for she had haunted the beach
throughout the bitter weather. She must eventually have
accepted the truth.

Heavy at heart, Victoria got up and went back to her
room. Where had the girl gone? What would become of
her? Why had she chosen this place in which to vanish?
The answer lay on her dressing table when she went to
brush her hair. Zarina was illiterate, but her message could
not have been plainer. The treasured poster she had carried
everywhere with her lay on the polished wood as a gift of
apology and explanation. Quickly Victoria went to the window. The circus tent and its accompanying wagons had
gone—moved on during the night.

Inquiries of everyone she knew produced no other maid-
servant who would be willing to go up to the Crimea. The
stories had gone around Constantinople; there was no one
who did not possess a vivid imaginative picture of an icy
purgatory.

Resigning herself to failure, Victoria returned to the hotel on the day before the *Sirocco* was due to sail and said to
Letty, who had complained of a headache and remained by
her fireside, "There is nothing for it, I fear, but that we
must fend for ourselves until we can find some clean, honest woman already at Balaclava. Have you a talent for
making tea, Letty?" She smiled at the girl as she sat to
warm her hands before the flames. "You look so much better for remaining indoors today. The color in your cheeks
is most encouraging."

Letty did not smile in return. In fact, she seemed ill at
ease.

"Is something wrong?" Victoria asked with sudden foreboding. "It is not Hugo?"

"No, my dear. Hugo is suffering from nothing more than
having to say goodbye to you tomorrow . . . as I am."
She left her chair and went to sink down beside the other
girl, taking her hands in warm emotion. There was the
brightness of unshed tears in her eyes, yet something
seemed to have put life back into them. "I cannot come
with you to Balaclava."

"You have changed your mind and will return to your papa?"

"Yes . . . for the very best of reasons. Victoria, I am to have Jack's child. I thought it could not be so, but the symptoms were so insistent I called on the doctor this afternoon."

Victoria could do no more than gaze at her friend in astonishment, as all the implications of such news filled her mind.

"We had such a short time together in Balaclava before that terrible day," said Letty softly. "We always wanted a child. It is very poignant that one afternoon in the tent on a battlefield should have brought us our desire."

"But . . . how will you manage?" asked Victoria, still bewildered.

"Papa is a doctor, as you know. I shall be in good hands. I have spent the afternoon coming to terms with this and see quite clearly the overall pattern. Jack was taken from me, but I still have part of him. As he lay dying he was reborn in our child. I shall have someone who loves and needs me. Is that not all any woman wants?"

"Yes," said Victoria bleakly.

Her baggage and boxes were collected by two of the ship's crew the following morning and, soon after breakfast, Victoria went to say goodbye to Hugo. She got as far as the door then her spirits failed her. How could she say the only word that should never pass between them? How could she find the courage to walk away from all she had ever wanted in her life and go back to the man who had started by terrifying her and now filled her with a hatred that was even harder to bear?

For a moment she leaned back against the door, reliving the kiss that had been such a riotous, anguished, ecstatic mistake, for it had proved her dreams of a passion that was as much a joy to a woman as a man. While it had been only a dream it had been containable, but that she had heard the overture, her senses craved the crashing chords and the soaring final crescendo. Driven by that need, she turned and knocked on the door of the room that had become so familiar.

Hugo was dressed and shaved, and got to his feet when

she appeared. "See how fit I am," he greeted her, with the ghost of a smile. "Soon, I shall be taking a turn about the square outside."

She could not smile back. "No one would recognize you for the ruffian who arrived seven weeks ago. I am certain my reputation was quite lost when word flew around parlors and public-rooms."

"For your husband's brother, society allows you to do all that humanity demands."

She searched his face with her eyes. "But you are not his brother, are you?"

Seconds passed, then in a voice grown husky, he said, "I have never said thank you."

"And I have never asked if you forgive me for reading your letter to Charles."

"There are things that do not have to be said between us, Victoria. We both know that."

"Yes."

He walked with great care in her direction, but halted several feet away from her—too far for her to reach out and touch him, as she ached to do.

"Well you mind too much when I am forced to give you no more than a cool nod when I return to Balaclava?"

She looked at him appalled. "Hugo, they *cannot* order you back to duty!"

"No . . . but I shall go."

"You are too ill. You can scarcely walk. You are . . . "

"I am lucky to be alive. The minute I can sit on a horse without falling off I intend to return to the regiment. I have to see out this campaign."

She looked down, unable to face the swell of bandages beneath his coat, and the scar that cut so deeply into his cheek. All at once, the crashing chords were too near, and she had an overpowering urge to hear the full sound. Trying to steady herself with quick indrawn breaths she said, "Have you any notion what it will do to me to know you are in danger once more—that it could all happen again?"

Tension was suddenly between them with dangerous force, and his voice showed that he knew it.

"Have you any notion what it does to *me* to see you go off to that place today?"

It was impossible to remain strong. With her throat thick with tears for their parting she brought up her head and challenged him. "No, I have not. Everything you have ever said to me has been something unsaid. *You know that . . . I do not have to tell you . . . some things do not have to be said between us.*" She felt the tears well at the back of her eyes, and the pain catch at her breast. "I do *not* know . . . you *do* have to tell me. It is time some things *were* said between us. Hugo," she begged desperately, "I want to hear you say what it will do to you when I leave here. For seven weeks we have been loving each other in silence. This might be the only moment in all our lives that you can speak of what really lies beneath that armor of honor. You died once without leaving me any token of what is within your heart. I could not live if you died a second time with the words still unspoken."

He turned away, as if by doing so he would be immune from her challenge. When he answered, it was with difficulty. "I . . . there have been moments of such blazing . . . understanding between us, it seemed to me that words would be pale, in comparison. Dear God . . . Victoria, these seven weeks have been a mixture of heaven and the fires of hell, you know that."

"No . . . I do not know! I have heard so much from you of honor, duty, and loyalty, but nothing about love—a love that can be so strong yet remain hidden even through seven weeks as we have just spent. Tell me about that kind of love, Hugo. *Show me!*" she cried. "Put it into words that I shall never forget."

He had gone white, and his eyes were brilliant in the scarred face. "What is it you want of me, Victoria? Is it a man who can see only you and his passion? Do you want a man who would take you into his bed at every possible opportunity, and have the hotel servants reporting of Madame naked beneath her brother-in-law's sheets when they took in breakfast? Do you want someone who will sit toying with his mistress on his knee while the salons, drinking-parlors and mess-halls resound with her name and coarse laughter? Is it your wish that I should take you under my protection, cut us both off from families and friends, live in countries that harbor rogues and outcasts from society? Do you want no more from me than I have given countless women in the past? If that is so I will take you here and now. I will put into words you will never forget and I will show you with a vigor that will set you moaning just what I have been wanting these seven weeks . . . but I will leave you crying on my bed for all that was between us that has been lost in that one act of passion." He stood fighting for command of his voice, but it remained unsteady. "That is not the way I love you, Victoria. You are my soul, my very life. Words are nothing when they can be used by the whole world; passion is easily spent. I believed . . . I believed . . . "

She could stand no more. She put up a hand to cover his mouth, but he snatched it away and covered it with kisses. Then, he reached out with his other hand and followed one of her tears as it rolled down her cheek. "It breaks me to let you go, but only remember this. Every time our eyes meet, I love you. Each time I salute and pass by, I love you. When you feel you can go on no longer, *I love you.* That is my token for you."

Knowing she would never leave if she did not go at once, Victoria drew her hand away and turned blindly for the door. Without turning to look at him, she asked, "How . . . how shall I know when you are returning to Balaclava?"

The answer was a long time coming. "It will be the same as it always is. One day you will look up, and I shall be there."

She opened the door quickly and went out, knowing the pain she felt was his also, but she had to ride it out for ten minutes before she felt sufficiently able to face anyone.

Letty was waiting with Captain Porchester in the public-room, and their farewell was less of a strain. All the same, when the carriage pulled away from the hotel leaving Letty waving until they were out of sight, Victoria felt quite desolate. Behind her was warmth, friendship, and love; ahead lay a frozen world.

The sea-captain was astute enough not to attempt to cheer his guest and merely made the normal polite remarks on the way to the ship, then left her to settle in her cabin until they sailed.

"The officers and I hope you will honor us with your company at dinner, ma'am," he said at the door. "They have been looking forward to renewing your acquaintance,

and, to make you feel at home, there will be two military
officers joining us. As you know, we are taking a batch of
new recruits up to Balaclava and two officers traveling with
them, Surgeon-Major Prescott and Lieutenant Marshall of
the artillery." His pale eyes twinkled. "I have taken the
liberty of informing them that you are an old campaigner
who can give them some advice on conditions before the
enemy." He chuckled. "The younger one is no more than a
boy who will, no doubt, turn pale and tremble at the knees
when he hears one of his own guns firing. When he hears
from your own lips what you have witnessed, it might put
some courage into him."

Reluctant to mix with company, Victoria nevertheless
found her depression vanishing as the evening wore on. She
liked the doctor immediately. Gray-haired and dignified,
with a ready wit that flashed when least expected, he was
intensely interested in all she had to say, and if his expression betrayed the belief that no lady should be asked to
return to such hardship, he did not say so. The young lieutenant was fresh-faced and fair, with beautiful manners and
an obvious pedigree that set the seafaring men against him
unfairly. Though his extreme courtesy and air of grandness
did seem out of place in the tiny cabin, he did not deserve
the ragging he received, and Victoria retired in the firm
belief that the young man was doomed to be carried back
to his cabin as drunk as a lord before the night was half
over.

She expressed her fear to Major Prescott, who escorted
her back to her cabin. "I beg you to take pity on Mr. Marshall, sir. The ship's officers have a gleam in their eyes that
bodes no good for him."

The major laughed. "Rest assured, ma'am. Mr. Marshall
can take care of himself. If anything suffers, it will only be
his surplus of dignity."

She turned at her door. "I have seen men reduced to
creatures, Major Prescott. Where he is going he will need
every scrap of dignity he can muster. Good night, sir."

"Good night, ma'am," said the major thoughtfully.

That was the start of a bond of understanding between
them. Every day they could be found taking a stroll around
the deck, muffled in rugs and thick gloves, deep in conversation. The doctor questioned her ceaselessly on the land-

scape and climate of the area before Sebastopol, where the
army was still holding a siege enforced more by the
weather than their strength. In turn, Victoria asked him
searching questions about the prevention of such cata-
strophes as she had seen at Scutari. On one occasion she
put to him the advisibility of fighting cholera by remaining
on one's feet and walking back and forth.

He raised his eyebrows a little. "Anything that prevents
the patient from simply giving himself up to the grave from
the first symptom is beneficial, ma'am. What you suggest is
rather drastic, however. Only a man with great courage or
fanatical determination could carry it off." He cast a sideways glance at her profile. "That alone would not cure him
if the disease took complete hold. Only the Almighty could
save him, then."

She smiled faintly. "I think the Almighty is on his side,
sir."

He stopped and faced her frankly. "Mrs. Stanford, you
are quite remarkable. I would say I know of no other
woman with whom I could have such a conversation. Even
my own very dear wife prefers to speak to me of bonnets
and morning calls."

Victoria laughed quite gaily. "How very fortunate for
you, sir. Imagine how dull it would be to spend each evening by your fireside speaking of nothing but boils and amputations."

Reluctantly he smiled back. "Ma'am, I see now why you
have survived so much and can return to it. I shall write of
your courage to my wife, with your permission."

"If you wish, Major. I hope that you will become one of
our frequent visitors when we reach Balaclava. I fear all
my former friends are gone."

"I shall be honored and delighted to become one of your
new friends." He gave her a wry look. "I very much fear
Captain Porchester feels I monopolize too much of your
time already."

Victoria took the news calmly. "I am sorry for that. He
has been so very kind to us and our friends. To make
amends, shall we take a cup of tea with him? I have been
invited at any time I wish. We can collect Mr. Marshall on
our way."

The major laughed. "Much better not, ma'am. The

young man is already contemplating blowing out his brains whenever you smile at another."

"Then I must smile at him more often," she said quietly, lost in memories of Harry Edmunds and a valley washed in sunlight.

To Victoria the sight of Balaclava was dismaying. Although the sun was making mockery of all the tales of a bitter winter, the warm yellow light only served to clarify the shambles the little town had become. The beach was littered for as far as the eye could see with debris, planks, masts and tangled rigging—all that remained of the ships that were pounded to pieces and sunk during the hurricane of November. Victoria was very moved by evidence of such a disaster, remembering how the harbor had looked when shs first entered it with Letty beside her on this same ship four months before.

The little row of houses where they had made their home had gone—pulled down to make way for a railway line running up from the harbor toward Kadikoi. Captain Porchester deplored the fact that it had not been laid before winter set in, to prevent the terrible inability, caused by the winter wind, to reach the vast number of camps. Victoria went further and condemned the authorities for having no foresight in any aspect of the war and was borne out in her judgment by the ghastly presence in the harbor of floating human limbs thrown into the sea from hospital wagons after battlefield amputations, with no thought that the tide would not carry them out to sea. In such a land-locked port, flotsam remained where it was tipped, to rot and putrefy the air for months.

Each jetty was crowded with wagons and carts of every description, taking off the great sacks, boxes, baskets and crates of provisions, the wooden walls and roofs of stout huts, the medical packages with a cross on the side, bales of warm clothing, barrels of grain for man and beast, and the inevitable and desperately needed round shot and shell for the constant bombardment of Sebastopol.

To counterbalance the inland flow of supplies there was a thin, constant stream of sick and wounded coming down from the trenches, some of which were now only a mile or so from the Russian defenses, where men stood thigh-deep

in mud for twenty-four-hour watches or had their hands
and feet eaten by frostbite as they manned the guns.

Hugo had spoken of the scarcity of pack animals, but
there was evidence of an influx to replace those poor
starved creatures. Everywhere were oxen and white bullocks, patient-faced mules—even dromedaries—and great
sturdy dray horses. But what could be seen of the troop
horses of the Dragoons and Lancers, in Balaclava on various errands, suggested that regiments were still suffering
from lack of healthy mounts.

Despite the sunshine, a freezing wind blew through the
gap in the hills, and those who came aboard when they
hove to spoke of snow several inches deep up in the camps.
As it was still a labor of patience to ride past Kadikoi over
a road that melted to sticky slime when the sun shone Victoria was obliged to remain on the *Sirocco* for the night.
She had no horse and must wait until Charles came down
from the cavalry camp to make arrangements for her residence. Major Prescott came to bid her farewell and promised to get a message to Colonel Stanford as he went up the
road.

"As soon as you are settled, ma'am, send me word. We
shall then see about accepting your help in my hospital—
wherever it might be." He smiled. "I mean to put you
straight to work, you see."

"Thank you, Major. I cannot tell you how glad I am that
fortune decreed we should travel together. When I felt
Constantinople I thought I had seen an end to my useful-
ness, but you have given me a new lease of life." She
laughed. "Dear me, this war has made me a creature who
must be busy all the time. Whatever shall I do back in
England, needed no longer?"

He kissed her fingers in salute. "I cannot imagine a time
when someone will not need you, ma'am. Au revoir. I trust
you will find your husband fit and in good spirits."

"Oh, thank you," she said, having forgotten Charles in
the subject of her hospital work. "Au revoir, Major."

Lieutenant Marshall bade her a sadly ardent goodbye.
She treated him with gentleness and cheered him with a
promise to ride over to the artillery camp to see how he
did just as soon as she could. She remained on deck after
they had gone, watching the new arrivals disembarking and

marching away across the mud. They were all pale and ill-assorted, their new uniforms mocking the ragged winter campaigners who stared at them, lost in the wonder of having once looked that way themselves.

"Show us these bloody Rooshians, mate," called one to men he thought were navvies. "We'll soon put a shot in their backsides."

"Get one of us to show you how to hold your gun, sonny" was the reply from one of the infantry veterans, "or you might end up never being a father." His villainous-looking companions joined in the raucous laughter. They had no sympathy for cocky recruits who had had several weeks of drill as training and thought they were crack troops. The backbone of England was buried beneath the mud here; these were merely gristle!

Having made the voyage without a maid, Victoria was accustomed to managing for herself, although she missed Zarina's talent for putting up hair with swift skilled fingers. She was engaged in this difficult task the next morning when Charles quietly entered the cabin and closed the door behind him. He said nothing, just stood looking at her as she waited for some kind of greeting. He had aged. The cold sharp light showed lines of strain on his face and a hollowness in his cheeks that pulled his mouth down into a curved line of resignation. The blue of his eyes was dulled by a film of hardship, yet their stare gave him an attraction that almost brought a shiver from her. He wore a sheepskin coat over his faded threadbare jacket and boots that would seem to have been fashioned, by anyone but a cobbler, from some kind of greasy felt. With his features honed down by hunger, Victoria thought that, but for his coloring, he could have been a wild nomad from the desert regions.

"You received Major Prescott's message?" she asked eventually.

"I should not have come otherwise. I hardly expected you to be on the ship."

She looked away and began pinning her hair into place. "I promised I would be."

It was not exactly a laugh, more a sharp outward breath. "I cannot imagine why you kept it. If you have tired of him it is of no use to run to me."

Victoria tightened her hold on the pins and lowered her arms, leaving a swath of hair across her shoulder. Dryness in her throat made her swallow. *Please let me remain dignified,* she prayed.

"You *have* been with him, have you not?" He said with arrogant contempt.

"I am surprised that you even concern yourself over the fact that Hugo is not dead," she said.

"That does not answer my question."

"Yes, I have done what I could for him. When you arrived here and heard he was on his way to Scutari, you must have known I would see him among those brought ashore."

"Naturally. I also realized why you were so determined to stay."

It took her breath away. "That is ridiculous! How could I possibly have known he was alive?"

"Through your searching conversations with those who had come down previously. How nobly you spoke to me of serving your country when all the time you dragged your petticoats on the beach like a camp follower for the purpose of hearing word of him. Have you no pride, Victoria?"

"I suppose I have not," she said steadily, "for I most certainly would have inquired of every man coherent enough had I not truly believed Hugo dead after the battle. He was, in fact, almost interred that night but for the sharpness of a soldier who noticed his warmth."

Normally quite contained in anger, Charles today appeared mastered by it. His hands shook and his jaw was working visibly.

"I see. You found time to visit *him* in hospital, it seems."

Knowing Byron Porchester might have told the whole story to Charles, thinking it would please him to know one of his officers had been pulled from the grave by the two ladies, she decided to tell the truth from the start.

"Hugo was barely alive when he arrived in Scutari. If he had entered the Barrack Hospital he would have died—a doctor confirmed the fact and gave his permission for me to take him to Constantinople. Hugo stayed in the hotel, where a French doctor attended him. When I left he was on the road to recovery." Swiftly she added, "You have

heard of poor Jack Markham? It was such a blow to us
all."

He ignored that. "Why have you come back?"

"I gave my promise that I would."

"Had you created such a stir that you were obliged to
leave Constantinople? It does not surprise me. A married
lady taking in a young officer to her hotel, setting the staff
on its ears over special diets and leaving her friend to go
out alone while she remains on the upper floor all day
long! It does not take much imagination on the part of the
guests to know that an intrigue is taking place." He moved
angrily about the cabin. "You wonder how I know about
this? Musgrave, of the Engineers, received letters from his
wife, who is wintering in Constantinople. He naturally assumed I knew of all this and rode across to express his
pleasure at my brother's recovery. He has, of course, written back to inform his gossip-loving lady that Captain Esterly is entitled to consideration from Mrs. Stanford . . .
but no one will believe such complete and utter devotion are
necessary to someone with no blood bond with my family."

Victoria clutched the hairpins even tighter. "Charles, I
do not care what Mrs. Musgrave believes—nor anyone
else, for that matter. It is a pity such people have not more
awareness of what else is going on around them, or I
should have had a large band of assistants on that beach,
and a few more might have been saved."

He swung around with uncharacteristic violence. "They,
ma'am, have some sense of their station in life. One does
not expect a lady to scramble all over a beach in search of
her lover, nor parade her amours before society."

"Unless you lower your voice, sir, you will be acquaint-
ing the entire ship's crew of your opinions," she told him
icily. "I should like an apology for that. You know quite
well I searched for no one on that beach. When you left
Constantinople, do you not think you would have read the
fact in my whole demeanor if I had known Hugo was still
alive?"

He leaned forward, resting one hand on the table before
which she sat. "Do you deny you turned the hotel upside
down for his sake?"

"Hardly that. I used harsh words on the proprietor to

persuade him to oblige some requests that were not in the least abnormal. I believe they inconvenienced no one."

"And you spent the greater part of each day with him?"

She took a deep breath. "Can you not even bring yourself to speak his name? Yes, I spent a great deal of time with Hugo . . . in company with Letty Markham. After Jack died, she benefitted as much from the company as Hugo."

"Do you expect me to believe you were never alone in his room—that you did not become lovers?"

She was starting to tremble. "No, Charles, because it is quite plain you will believe anything that will give you justification for continuing your campaign of hatred against Hugo. You will have guessed I told him the truth about the child, so now you must charge him with something new."

"Oh no, ma'am, this is not new," he said through his teeth. "On a previous occasion you both contrived to meet behind my back—with tragic results."

It was impossible to remain seated where he could tower so aggressively over her. Even standing she had to look up at him, but it gave her a greater sense of dignity to be on her feet. "I think you cannot conceive of a relationship that can survive without any kind of physical contact, Charles. But, even so, you would know how ridiculous your suspicions are if you could have seen him covered in blood, unable to speak and dressed in filthy rags."

"And you took him with you to a select hotel?" It was said with scandalized derision.

She looked steadily at his face. "Do you wish I had let him die?"

Halted at last, he stretched to his full height and took a grip on himself. "I wish he had been man enough to stand a little suffering without indulging in the pampering of a female. It is hardly the example to set. He has always been weak and unstable. It was plain from the outset he would not last out the campaign."

"That is not true. He intends returning as soon as he is fit."

Immediately Charles had fresh fuel for his fire. "So I have my answer at last," he said slowly, flicking his eyes over her body. "You will not continue your relationship here. I swear you will not! I have a hut in the camp that is relatively protected from the cold and bitter weather. You will live with me there and see to my comfort. You will give me all the care and consideration you lavished upon him. You will keep up a semblance of propriety that will persuade everyone that the gossip from Constantinople is false." He gripped the table. "When he returns you will have no contact with him whatsoever. If I so much as catch him . . . by God, I swear I shall make him pay for what he has done."

"He has done nothing," she cried.

"Does he also hide behind your skirt while you defend him?" he asked with searing contempt. "You should be coddling our son, not a grown man, Victoria."

She returned his contempt in her own look. "I think it might be as well that I cannot give you one, for I fear the poor child would never live up to your demands for perfection." Resuming her seat at the table, she finished pinning her hair with fingers that shook.

Within a few days Victoria had settled into her new routine and found several old friends at Kadikoi, who greeted her with such genuine pleasure it brought a lump to her throat. Lord Dovedale gave her an outrageously exaggerated account of how he had disposed of a dozen or more Russians during the charge and emerged with no more than a lance thrust in his upper arm, but Victoria detected a desperation in his lightheartedness that was to be found in all who had spent the entire winter in the Crimea. Colonel Rayne looked ill and worried. It was not an enviable task to command a regiment of fifteen old soldiers and two hundred new recruits who hardly knew one end of a horse from another and had no chance of learning because there were no animals to ride. The fifteen troopers who had ridden in the charge were ridiculously emotional at the sight of their second-in-command's wife back again with them— several had tears in their bloodshot eyes when she stopped to speak to them. So, despite all else, Victoria had a wonderful feeling of homecoming when she found herself surrounded by Hussar uniforms once more.

The hut was hardly spacious, but it kept out the cold more effectively than flapping canvas, especially since

Charles had stuck newspapers over the cracks in the walls. There was chopped straw on the floor to bind the mud, but once she set foot outside, Victoria found it necessary to lift her skirts high as she struggled through slush and snow to reach her destination. There was no horse for her, but any time she wanted to ride one of the officers willingly lent his own. In no time she had a host of new friends. They lost their hearts to her, but she was wise enough to know it was more what she represented than her own self they found fascinating. In this world of hardship, mud and constant bombardment, a reminder of heady pleasures, a soft voice and sweet perfume were a breath of spring and civilization to young men far from home.

She grew used to hearing the rumble of guns from Sebastopol and the thunder of their own artillery that went on day and night as both sides gradually slaughtered each other a few at a time. It was commonplace for the cavalry to be turned out at a moment's notice because of a sudden alarm that proved false. There was no doubt in anyone's mind, however, that the war was not going to end for a long time yet. Old campaigners grew resigned; new recruits fretted at doing nothing but drill. They had come out to finish it off, hadn't they—not tramp back and forth in the bloody mud being bawled at by the sergeant?

Major Prescott had been entertained to dinner and had no reason to be as surprised as Victoria when Charles appeared to approve the idea of his wife working in the hospital hut of which the major was head. On reflection, Victoria believed it must have been to allay gossip by being seen to tend other wounded men but was glad of the outcome, whatever Charles's reason. She lost no time in starting and found immense satisfaction and comfort in what she was doing, knowing that this time she had the approval and professional teaching of the doctor.

It was almost ten days before an opportunity presented itself to ride across to the artillery camp, but Victoria borrowed Major Prescott's spare pony late one afternoon and rode, with the doctor, to visit Lieutenant Marshall, as promised. A severe frost had made the ground iron-hard and easier to negotiate, but the two-mile ride left her numb with cold. The adjutant, a bearded, shabbily dressed man of indeterminate age, with cheery manners, invited them into his tent for a drink of half-roasted coffee when they inquired after the young subaltern.

"Marshall, you say?" he asked as he took the tin can from his portable stove and poured the hot concoction into two mugs. "We have no Lieutenant Marshall here, ma'am. There is a Captain Martin . . . or Ensign Carshalton."

"He traveled up with us on the *Sirocco* on the tenth," said Major Prescott helpfully. "Fair-haired . . . cousin of the Duke of Cumbria, or some such person."

"Ah, *Marshall*," said the adjutant, recollection coming to him. "Yes, of course." His dark eyes examined them curiously. "A particular friend of yours, was he?"

"Was?" repeated Victoria softly.

"His first day at the gun was his last, I fear. That is why I did not immediately recognize his name."

"Oh, how sad," she breathed with genuine sorrow. "Did he suffer?"

"I believe not. He had been five minutes at the front when a shot took him in the head, killing him instantly."

They rode back, touched by the poignant incident, yet it was not of the fair-haired young man Victoria thought but of a dear face scarred forever by a sword. Once he arrived back here she could lose him as brutally, as instantly, as Rupert Marshall.

It was growing dark very rapidly and the cavalry camp was still distant when a galloper dashed past shouting that Russian cavalry had been seen crossing the plain ahead, and they would be advised to go around by the French camps. It added a mile or two to their journey, but they turned and headed that way without hesitation; squadrons of Cossacks liked to roam at twilight in the hope of catching piquets off their guard.

Young Marshall forgotten in this new excitement, Victoria was not immediately aware of her surroundings, except to nod her head to those Frenchmen who greeted her with cheers and flamboyant salutes as she rode along the outskirts of their camps. However, in the half-light her eye was caught by the sight of a girl, one of the *cantinières* who served with the French regiments and were so admired by the soldiers. This one was attached to the Algerian Rifles and wore a dashing uniform of trousers, beneath a full skirt, and jacket to match those worn by the regiment.

Victoria had admired them since her days at Varna for their courage and their service to the soldiers, which extended far beyond provisioning the men. They thought nothing of galloping over the battlefield with a cask slung around their necks, to give drinks to the wounded lying helpless there. In the main, they were vivaciously attractive and somehow managed to retain their feminine dash even under such terrible conditions and so contrasted strongly with the drab slatterns who traveled with the British Army. The *cantinières* were the darlings of the regiments, from colonels down to the newest recruit, and this one was very obviously entertaining an officer at her wagon at the moment.

A seductive laugh rang out at what he had just whispered in her ear, and Victoria was about to look away when the man by the wagon turned his head slightly. Dressed in the uniform of the Crimea—forage cap, shaggy sheepskin coat and high boots—he looked like any other officer in the Anglo-French force, but his jacket beneath the sheepskin was Hussar-blue and the upward tilt up his chin held all the Stanford arrogance of which he was capable.

A quick glance at Major Prescott told Victoria he had also recognized Charles. Her cheeks flamed, and her entire body flushed.

CHAPTER FIFTEEN

Spring arrived early, carpeting the area before Sebastopol with crocuses, hyacinths and yellow iris, even snowdrops to remind the British soldiers of the countryside of their home villages. The valley that had witnessed the death of the Light Brigade was blue with larkspur and forget-me-nots that rooted around the skeletons, shot and shell that remained there still.

Blue skies allowed a warming sun to come through, to put new life into stiff limbs and raise the spirits of men with heads sunk too far into their shoulders. The mud began to harden; walking and riding became a pleasure again. Supplies flooded in from official and charitable sources in England, where William Russell's reports printed in *The Times* had aroused public outrage at the treatment of British soldiers in the Crimea. With temperatures going into the eighties once more, the men were inundated with thick socks, flannel drawers, scarves, sturdy boots and greatcoats—all the things they had lacked throughout the winter.

Huts went up in all the camps and new, stronger tents blossomed like mushrooms along the hillsides. Supplies of horses arrived to mount the cavalry that was now reinforced by two splendid regiments straight from India, both nearly seven hundred strong, each regiment containing more than the entire brigade on the day of the charge.

Despite the daily bombardment of the front-line trenches, the gentlemen officers felt the breath of spring in their bloodstreams, and it meant only one thing to them—racing! The spring meetings began in April and drew great crowds of spectators to cheer in their favorite as he thundered across the turf or cleared the jumps in true counties style. If the officers were more reckless than usual, who could not understand it? The younger and madder of the gentlemen indulged in dog hunts, in which the poor quarry was one or more of the half-wild dogs that roamed the hills and valleys. The hunt would return filthy and exhausted, but the war had been forgotten for a while.

For the rank-and-file there were foot races and competitions to liven the dullness and theatricals performed in store huts, large marquees, even in an amputating room of the hospital. All the parts were taken by soldiers, the Guards showing marked thespian talent, extending even to providing damsels of quite spectacular grace for their six feet three inches. Band concerts became very popular—those given by the Rifle Brigade being the favorites—and an influx of provisions of every description, sent by private philanthropists, meant that officers were able to give dinner parties once more.

These returning civilities of military life were not all-male functions by any means. Spring and public emotion in England had brought about the arrival of steamers full of visitors, sight-seers and officers' ladies who had spent the winter in Constantinople writing to their friends that they were "with the Army." The sight of crinolines among the tents was nothing unusual, and frilly parasols were to be seen protecting delicate heads in the vicinity of the big guns in forward positions of the British trenches.

Picnics were enthusiastically arranged for parties of ladies, who were escorted to the hills by lovelorn officers. They pointed out the principal Russian fortifications and offered their telescopes for the dear creatures to scrutinize the town of Sebastopol within its resistant walls. The favorite attraction, however, was that valley beyond Kadikoi where a brigade had galloped into a gray cloud of smoke and emerged as a handful of stumbling men. The visitors trod that same earth and gazed down the length of that sun-soaked vale, thrilling with excitement at an escapade that had taken on immortality with its bravado—so much so that it was now acclaimed as a victory, inasmuch as the Russians had been completely demoralized into instigating no further attacks on troops who displayed such discipline and heroism.

One lady not to be found in such places was Victoria Stanford. She, who remembered so vividly the horror of the charge, deplored the idea of arranging excursions into the valley and further held in contempt those females who gushed and exclaimed in frail tones designed to quicken the heartbeats of their escorts. At dinner parties in the huts and tents she was unusually silent among the fashionable ladies who appeared in décolleté dresses of muslins and silks, who captivated the officers with their white skins, floral perfumes and round admiring eyes. Colonel Stanford's wife, tanned by the sun, saddened by the truth and with hands that looked more like those of a kitchen maid, was too much of a comrade-in-arms now. Her stalwart friends succumbed to the general madness of spring and deserted her for a pair of innocent blue eyes beneath fluttering lashes or a white-gloved hand lying with such fragile helplessness upon their own battle-stained sleeves.

For Victoria, it was just another lesson in life. The men needed some lightness in their routine, heaven knew. Her work at the hospital more than occupied her. Major Prescott had become a valued friend since the night they had ridden through the French lines. He treated her with an immense respect and taught her the rudiments of nursing, so that by the end of May she was dispensing medicine, tying bandages and dressing wounds with expertise. Despite the social activities, the war continued. Men were being killed and wounded in the forward trenches night and day.

Her work was her salvation. Charles was difficult to live with, day in, day out. Changes in temperature set his wounded foot aching, and the drag in that leg was more pronounced on such days. His temper became sharper. Inconveniences he had experienced without complaint for months suddenly became intolerable. The hut became an oven in the early summer heat, and he took off all the newspaper lining the walls. Then he complained of drafts at night. Some days he ignored her completely, on others he made jibes at her lack of conversation apart from amputations and dysentery. He compared her unfavorably with the new arrivals, found fault with her clothes and the air of illness that hung around her.

She always knew when he had been over to the French lines, for the smell of brandy was on his breath when he came in. It was then he was at his most contemptuous. Yet, strangely, there was a reverse side of the coin—times when he had an air of resignation, of hopelessness, and spoke bitterly of wasted years. Lord Cardigan had gone back to England along with other officers who used ill-health to retire from the lists, and Charles spoke of an army being abandoned to its fate when the glorious dream had faded. He spoke of his inner feelings quite frankly but almost as if Victoria were not there—lost in some faraway world of his own. She listened and said nothing—and watched the distant road whenever a ship came in.

Fate was not to be cheated. On a breathless morning in early June, Victoria rode her new mare along the track leading to the encampment of the 3rd Division, where the major tended the regiments' sick. She pulled to one side to allow a column to pass. They were not recruits, for their uniforms were faded to pink or gray, and, as they plodded sweating past her, a strange strong pain began to possess her every nerve.

He was there, riding beside the column with six other officers. There was no smile between them, but his eyes said *I told you how it would be.* Drawing alongside, he saluted and bade her good morning. With less than three feet between their saddles she longed to put out a hand to him, but they both sat upright and impersonal beneath the watching eyes of those around them.

"I had not heard of a ship arriving," she told him breathlessly.

"We did not disembark at Balaclava but at Kamiesh. We have marched from there this morning." While his vivid glance almost consumed her with the fire it held, he spoke of ordinary things. "You will be pleased to know I saw Letty safely installed on a ship for England. I bring a letter for you from her."

"Thank you." The words were automatic while she studied him in detail. The scar on his face had paled, and his hair now hid the deepest part of it high on his skull. The gold-laced jacket fitted smoothly across his chest with no bandages to swell it, and there was some return of the sturdiness he had once possessed.

"Perhaps you would send a messenger with it to the hospital of the Third Division. I am there most days."

His eyes narrowed with speculation. "I see. If that is what you wish."

She tried to tell him by her expression that it was anything but what she wished. "I cannot expect you to play postman."

"But you are playing nurse."

She caught her breath. "Yes. News of my talent in that direction preceded me. It was already spoken of among the officers when I returned to Balaclava, and Charles was most particular to hear all details from me."

He stiffened. "He raised no objections, I hope?"

"Charles never raises objections," she said meaningfully. "As you know, he is a man of extreme opinions. That I am able to continue my useful work is due to his insistence that what I do for one should be seen to be done for others."

Restricted by the proximity of the trooper who accompanied Victoria, Hugo controlled himself with difficulty, rasping in a low voice, "By God, if he has . . ."

"No," she breathed quickly. "There is no need for your concern. He can only hurt me by hurting you." Uneasy at the danger of having so private a conversation with him in public, she tried to smile and appear less intense. "The situation has changed. I believe you have a hard time ahead. Please . . . be on your guard."

His mouth tightened. "I believe I can handle it." Then, in a softer tone: "It cannot be worse than the past three months."

With her bones melting she tried to think of some way to tell him that life had been suspended for her also since last February, but the column had passed and he was obliged to go.

"The world is a different place all of a sudden, Victoria" was his soft farewell.

"So different that I hardly recognize it," she whispered after him and watched as he trotted off beside a major of the Highland Regiment. From this moment she would resume the sweet torture of seeing him every day while Charles stood by, watching them; would relive the anguish of a war in which he was a living target.

All that day she saw Hugo's face on every pillow, read his name on every card. As new patients were carried in the feeling of tension increased. Would she look up one day and see his broken body once more? A week later she did look up and find her heart missing a beat, but it was not Hugo she saw.

Nurses had been arriving in the Crimea under the super-

vision of titled ladies, who became more obsessed with their
own standing in relation to Miss Nightingale than in healing the sick. A great number of these were Roman Catholic
nuns, and a storm broke out when the army medical authorities and a large number of politicians in England maintained that the Holy Sisters were going from bed to bed
converting men to Catholicism when they were too weak
to know what they were doing.

Victoria had heard there was similar trouble in Scutari
and, although not in a position to support the theory, did
believe that the nuns of all denominations probably spent
time listening to deathbed confessions they could have
been better spent lessening another man's pain. Personally,
she tended the men's bodies and left their souls to God.

These nurses all worked in the General Hospital down in
Balaclava, so Victoria saw little of them except when one
of the ladies brought parties of visitors to the small regimental hospitals in the camps, to the annoyance of the medical
men who were obliged to allow such things for the sake of
showing British civilians that conditions were now extremely good in the Crimea. Victoria had no time for such
people, feeling that they were staring at her patients as if
they were exhibits at a fairground. The men, however, were
very cheered by the sight of elegant ladies drifting through
the dim stifling hut and saw their vague smiles as concern
for them.

A party entered the hospital one oppressive afternoon
while Victoria was desperately combating a fever that
seemed likely to take off her patient by nightfall. She heard
a small expression of annoyance from the young doctor
examining a hip wound at the next bed but did not allow
the disturbance to hinder her own work until the rustle of
silk skirts ceased beside her. Glancing up through a gauzy
curtain of hair that had escaped its pins, she met a pair of
doll-blue eyes in a face of calm purity framed with flaxen
braids.

Charity Verewood wore a gown of blue plaid taffeta that
looked bright and fresh with its white bib front and cuffs.
Sapphires glowed in her ears, but they were nothing to the
fiery contempt with which she treated the girl in drab cotton beside the bed. Victoria saw the fractional shock sustained by the other girl before a glance swept her from

head to toe. In that moment, Victoria's cheeks turned crimson.

The party moved on, Charity having made no sign of acknowledgment, and Victoria turned back to her patient in turmoil. The flood of color in her face had nothing to do with embarrassment; she knew just why Charity had come to the Crimea and wondered if Hugo had already entertained her.

The fever broke at four-twenty. Victoria rose wearily from beside the bed and made her way to Major Prescott's office, to which was attached a small washroom. It was usual for her to drink a cup of tea with her friend before leaving, and the kettle was already on the boil. Going through to the washroom, she tidied herself and buttoned her sleeves with great thoughtfulness. Her own face was browned by the sun until she looked like a woman of Turkey. The fresh supplies of gowns she had brought from Constantinople were purchased with the battlefield more in mind than picnics and ballrooms, and without the services of a maid her glossy hair had been twisted into a large chignon. She had seen others beguiled by dainty damsels from England. Would any man be proof against a lavender-scented ministering angel with clinging determination and the freedom to devote all her attention to him?

Hugo knew the new members of number-one squadron were consigning him to the devil—and worse—but the drill movements had to be learned and there was no easy way. He had been hard at his squadron since he returned, with some result, for they were improving daily. On the first day he sensed some resentment from men who had been commanded by a subaltern as newly arrived as they, but he had heard his sergeant telling the recruits, "The captain was in the Charge, see. He knows how important it is to move quick, believe me, and he can ride a horse better than you lot can walk." After that, there had been a noticeable alertness—even in Lieutenant Selby, who had commanded rather languidly in Hugo's absence.

Sitting his gray stallion, Ash, that he had brought from Constantinople, Hugo felt his strength being sapped by the stifling afternoon heat and decided it was time to finish with a short résumé of his own particular field movements that his men had used to such effect in Ireland. The few remaining of them were enthusiastic in encouraging the recruits to perfect them quickly, and the sergeant began giving his orders.

One or two blunders ruined the first attempt at change of formation, but the second time it was executed well enough for Hugo to request that it be repeated at the trot. It was a little ragged, but they completed it in good order and had just trotted back to formation when Hugo heard a voice behind him saying, "Are you quite mad?"

Charles had ridden up unnoticed and had stopped beside him. "I cannot think what Rayne would say if he knew of this. Unfortunately, he seems no better today." His chin lifted. "What do you mean by teaching the men this damned nonsense? By what right do you decide to teach squadron maneuvers that are not in the book of cavalry drill, are practiced by no other British cavalrymen and are designed to make them appear more like a fox hunt than a military formation?"

With determination, Hugo restrained himself. Charles had been after his blood from the moment they had come face to face the week before, but the past months had forced patience upon him and he bit back the quick retort he would once have made.

"I am sorry to hear about the colonel. This heat does not make his condition any easier, of course."

"You know his views on your irregular methods. To continue them amounts to insubordination," his brother snapped. "I suggest you now spend half an hour drilling your men in the correct manner."

"They have been doing so for an hour already."

"Really? It was not the impression I received."

"You have only been here a few minutes," said Hugo pointedly, feeling his temper rise.

"Long enough to see the whole squadron is inefficient, lazy and badly handled. Half an hour, I said."

"Dammit, sir, in this heat . . ."

"Dammit, sir, you will do as I say!" Charles brought his riding crop down with such force it broke across the pommel, the end flying away across the head of Hugo's horse.

With a frown the younger man looked at his brother who was usually so controlled. "I assure you the man have had the correct instruction for one hour. Another thirty minutes in this heat will not improve them."

Charles, who was looking at the broken crop with absorbed irritation, murmured, "You should have thought of that before you put them through your circus tricks. Sergeant Cairns!" he called, and the man came across with a smart salute. "Captain Esterly is not satisfied with the wheeling in column, the advance at the canter and the front form. These movements will be drilled until four o'clock. Captain Esterly will remain to see that they are done to his satisfaction."

"Yessir." The sergeant answered without batting an eyelid, but Hugo had known the man for seven years and could read his thoughts faultlessly. He fancied he could read those of his troopers during the next half hour. It was as well they could not read his.

Hot and angry, he returned to his tent and called his servant to bring water. The fortunes of war had sent him up the seniority scale quite startlingly, so that he now commanded a squadron in his own right, but an incident such as this did not help bind together two troops of men and the officer commanding them. Personal persecution by Charles he could handle, but when it extended into professional matters he could not stand by and accept it without protest. When an opportunity presented itself he would tackle his brother. Kicking a box out of the way, he unhooked the tight collar of his jacket and tugged it open.

"Jessop!" he roared until the man appeared with a water jug.

"Yes, Cap'n, I'm jest coming."

"Jessop, how many times have I told you not to address me as *Cap'n*? I am not in command of a pirate frigate," Hugo told him irritably.

"Oh aye, sir," said Jessop peaceably in his Hampshire dialect, making the whole thing sound more nautical than ever.

"Why did you not join the Navy, Jessop?"

The sarcasm was lost on this new recruit. "I didn't fancy it, sir. They goes too far away from 'ome for my liking."

Hugo gave up and missed Stokes for the hundredth time since he got back. He emptied the jug into a tin bowl.

"What culinary delight have you prepared for me this evening, Jessop?"

"Beg pardon, sir?"

"Dinner, man."

"Oh aye . . . oh *dinner*," he said with a slight spark of life. "You've 'ad an invite out for tonight, so I didn't bother gettin' nothing. One of them staff swells comes up—all in 'is cocked 'at and feathers—and gives me this. And 'e says in 'is grand voice *this 'ere's a hinvitation to dinnah for Captain Esterly, my good man*, then 'is 'orse wets hisself all over my overalls."

Hugo, with his head in the bowl of water, began to laugh and came up spluttering, feeling around for the towel. "How very inconsiderate of the horse," he said when his breath had returned. "Where is the invitation?"

There was neither mirth nor his former anger in him when he read the note, but he had to sit on his bed and read it again before he could take it all in. That Charity Verewood was aboard a pleasure steamer anchored outside Balaclava harbor was difficult enough to believe, but that she had a letter from his father revived such a parade of memories he felt a little sick within the stifling canvas walls.

Deeply thoughtful, he plunged his head into the bowl of water again, then looked at his pocket watch. Four forty-five already. There was not a lot of time if he was to present himself at the harbor with other officers at seven, when a small boat would take them out to the steamer.

He climbed the Jacob's ladder that evening with more pleasurable anticipation that he had felt for months. His letter to his father after learning of his mother's death had gone unanswered—at least, a reply had never reached him—and he could not wait to read the words Lord Blythe had entrusted to Charity. Now he knew he was not responsible for the tragedy of the child, he was entitled to face his family with a clear conscience. Was that what his father had written to him?

A member of the ship's crew welcomed them aboard and conducted them to the saloon where they were to be received. After the darkness outside, the bright glow of lamps and a civilized evening party dazzled Hugo for a few moments until he spotted Charity with several ladies in the far corner.

Everything about her was pale and fragile. The white shoulders rising from a shimmering fondant-green dress drew his eyes immediately, and the soft gleam of spun-gold around a perfect face reminded him so vividly of evenings at Wychbourne that his surroundings fell away and he was lost in the past. It was only when he was halfway across the saloon that he realized she had gone deathly white and was staring at him in shock. His steps slowed. She was looking for the first time at a familiar face scarred and hardened by battle.

She left the group and came toward him, her hand at her throat. His bow was brief. "It is good to see you again. In such a place I had not expected such a pleasure." She was still overcome, so he put his hand beneath her elbow. "This cabin is very stuffy. Let us take a little fresh air."

Out on the deck she put her hand on his arm and let him support her as they walked, the sound of the sea faintly audible above the chatter from the saloon. Her scent of lavender reminded him of days in Buckinghamshire, and the quiet swish of satin skirts was infinitely nostalgic.

She stopped and turned to face him. "Forgive me. After so long . . . I did not know."

Her voice was soft and sweet. He had forgotten her coolness and her clean, delicate lavender scent; the serene quality of her beauty that typified English ladies of wealth and breeding; the paleness of a complexion that had never been exposed to sleet and burning sun. In that moment he felt an overwhelming urge for the release he had not had for well over a year. In that moment she filled him with the excitement of physical desire aroused by fragile, submissive femininity. He took her hand and lifted it to his lips.

"It is I who should ask forgiveness for not informing you of everything that happened, but I was quite ill for some time. When one is here, in the midst of war, it is easy to forget that those in England cannot imagine the difficulties of exchanging letters."

She turned her face away to mask her distress. "I believed you were dead . . . as did your papa." Her small hand moved in his. "The minute the news arrived to contradict our sorrow, I resolved to come here. There was so

little information on your situation. I could not rest until I
had seen you." The round blue eyes ventured to meet his
again, and he caught his breath as she added, "Can you
imagine my feelings as I waited for you tonight?"

"You made this journey purely on my account?" His
voice was husky with emotion that was almost mastering
him. "I cannot believe it is really you. Out of all this—" his
hand waved in the direction of the shore—"you appear,
looking exactly as if we were in the drawing room at
Wychbourne." He was not good with words. She brought
the freshness of Wychbourne's meadows, the quiet of summer twilights and the warmth of England and home so very
near, yet he was unable to tell her so. "You do not know
how it feels to see you so unexpectedly."

Her eyes grew rounder and more luminous. "I wrote to
inform you of my arrival."

"The letter did not reach me. I have had no news of
home for some months." He drew closer. Her nearness was
heady, and his pulse began to pound.

The hand held in his tried to escape. "Hugo, I think we
should return to the saloon. Our absence will have been
remarked, and Lady Cullingham, who so kindly invited me
to travel with her, will be looking everywhere for us."

"Then she will eventually find us," he said softly. "We
are standing in sight of the saloon."

"Have you no thought for propriety?" she begged breathlessly.

"I have no thought for anything but the pleasure of this
moment," he told her impulsively. "Let us hope Lady Cullingham searches the entire ship before she comes on
deck."

"I beg you to collect yourself." Her reply was arch. "We
have been but ten minutes together, and I am to be here
for three weeks. The June evening has plainly made away
with your senses."

Her very proper concern for being alone in the moonlight with a gentleman, plus the soft surrender in her eyes,
incited him further.

"My senses have indeed flown . . . but it is not the
June evening I hold to blame for the fact."

She stepped back from his advance. "Please . . . the
other guests," she whispered. "We must return to them."

Moving away along the deck, Hugo followed, completely dazzled by the prize she held just beyond his reach.

The evening was intoxicating in every way. Wine flowed freely throughout a meal such as he had forgotten could be produced. The atmosphere was cultured and civilized. The ladies were all inclined to flirtation, the gentlemen flatteringly complimentary. The officer guests were feted and treated like heroes. With each glass of wine, Charity appeared to Hugo even more desirable, yet more elusive. She talked to him of his home and family, gave him letters from his father and Aunt Sophy, assured him Lady Blythe had suffered no pain before she died. She gave him news of his dogs and horses who were thriving in the country air. She spoke of riding across old familiar haunts and of country matters concerning people he had known since childhood.

He said nothing to her of pain, mud, fever and hatred. It was all forgotten under the spell she cast around him. When the small boat pulled alongside to take the guests ashore he bade her good night with some ardor and finished by offering to conduct her around the camp at Kadikoi the following day. At eleven-thirty he would ride down to Balaclava with his spare horse for her. He watched until she was a pale, distant figure in the moonlight who had returned him to the happiness of the past.

The present overtook him the minute he arrived at the cavalry camp. Although half asleep and hazy with wine, he sensed immediately that something was afoot. Tents were open and vacated; the horse lines were empty. Quickly sobering, he spurred his horse to a gallop and thudded through the neat lines of tents until he reached the open plain beyond. There he found the several thousand men in their saddles in battle order, silent and watchful in the moonlight.

Searching out his regiment, he saw Lieutenant Yates-Fawcett at the head of No. 1 Squadron and rode up to him.

"What is it, Desmond?" he asked in low voice.

The subaltern looked relieved. "By George, am I glad to see you! There is a rumor afoot that we are to end it at last. We turned out two hours ago. The assault on Sebastopol is set for tomorrow, but, suddenly, the piquets reported movements of enemy cavalry, and we thought we had a fight on our hands. Skirmishers went out but saw nothing of them. They must have turned away."

Hugo felt elated. "Sebastopol to be taken tomorrow? How true is it, do you think?"

"True enough. Chiltern says the Guards have orders to move down at dawn, as have the Highlanders."

"After so long, it is hard to believe it will be finished within the week."

The young man made a face. "Sorry, old fellow, but I have to say that you are very likely to be finished very shortly. Colonel Stanford flew into one of his rages when he knew you were not here."

"I left word where I could be found."

"On a pleasure steamer outside Balaclava harbor? Hugo, the battle could have been over by the time a message reached you."

Hugo had the following two hours during which to reflect upon the coming confrontation with Charles and knew it would be fatal to lose his temper this time. In a purely military matter, Charles was his senior officer and must receive respect and obedience. Anything else would amount to insubordination, and his brother would use his rank without hesitation.

Just before dawn the cavalrymen were told to stand down, except No. 1 squadron of the Hussars. They remained in their saddles while their commander was called to receive orders from their acting colonel, who had returned to his hut. Hugo rode through the camp, his blood fired with wine, trying to fight down his anger at being made to face Charles in his living quarters. His brother was using uncharacteristic misjudgment in trying to break him, for it only increased Hugo's determination to complete the campaign. When Sebastopol fell tomorrow the war would be virtually won. Just one more day. After so much, he must hold out for one more day!

With that thought he went into the hut where Charles was sitting at a table. The sleeping quarters were separated only by a blanket nailed to the roof and dangling to within a foot of the floor. Behind that blanket Victoria would be lying wide-eyed, he felt sure.

"Where were you at midnight?" Charles asked, opening the contest.

"I left word with the adjutant of my whereabouts."

Charles leaned back. "I asked where you were."

"Aboard the steamer *Norvic* anchored outside Balaclava harbor."

"You did not apply for permission to put yourself so far beyond reach of orders."

"I sent to Colonel Rayne, who saw no reason why I should not go," he replied, trying not to sound smug.

He knew he had not succeeded when Charles narrowed his eyes. "The colonel is ill and should not be worried with trivia. It so happened that you were needed. You must be aware of growing tension in the situation here. It is hardly the time to abandon your responsibilities for pleasure."

"I did not choose the time. Miss Verewood is visiting the Crimea and sent to tell me she had some letters from my family."

Charles flushed dark red. "Do you tell me you deserted camp merely to collect letters? If I did not know you, I would say you were simply irresponsible, but, of course, I might have guessed there was a female tied up in this. It used to be milkmaids until you turned to other men's wives. Tired of that, I suppose you think to use Miss Verewood for your ends."

Hugo wanted one thing straight before he went any further. "Is this a private matter between two men or a regimental interview? If it is the first, I shall leave now; if the second, I have every right to protest at my private life being slandered when I have no chance of redress."

Charles hesitated, then said, "In future, you will apply to me whenever you wish to leave camp. Meanwhile, you will take your squadron on reconnaisance patrol until sundown. The storming of Sebastopol will begin at dawn tomorrow, and the commander-in-chief wants accurate information on the position of the enemy outside the fortress. You had better be certain your report is accurate. Men's lives will depend on your word."

It was Hugo's turn to flush. "If you feel I cannot be relied upon, you had best send another of your commanders."

"They have been through a winter up here—a winter you spent in luxury at a Constantinople hotel. I think it is only fair you take your share of the duties for once. If I

recall correctly, you were unable to stand on your feet during the storm at sea when so many horses were lost; you
surrendered your troop to McKay for several weeks
through sickness at Varna and left Yates-Fawcett in command of an entire squadron last night. Hardly an impressive record of devoted service."

"Is that all, sir?" asked Hugo with difficulty.

"Yes. The adjutant will give you details of the area to be
covered by the reconnaisance. Just one more thing," he
added when Hugo was at the door. "You will not use
troopers to deliver your letters to my wife at the hospital."

He swung around. "McPhaden was going that way. He
took a letter from Mrs. Markham, that is all."

"Really?"

It was said with such insulting incredulity that Hugo
took a step back into the hut. "You know there has never
been any justification for your accusations—and I know it
now. You cannot hurt someone with nothing on his conscience. Take a grip on yourself, Charles, or it will be you
who does not last out this campaign."

"Get out!" Charles brought his fist down on the table.

Victoria wiped her cheeks quickly before Charles pushed
aside the blanket and went to sit on his bed.

"Sebastopol will be ours by tomorrow night," he mused,
more to himself than to her. "The Army can expect to be
back in England by Christmas."

She made no comment. These days he made no demands
on her other than to run the tiny wooden hut to his satisfaction and to entertain guests he chose to invite. For sexual satisfaction he had the French girl, and fellow officers
provided the conversation. His complete disinterest in her
hospital work kept Victoria silent in his company, but he
spoke his thoughts aloud to her as she had to Glencoe, so
very long ago.

She was the recipient of all his sudden outbursts against
the inefficiency of the commissariat, the ever-lasting delay
of the assault on the besieged town that had held out far
longer than anyone had dreamed possible and the bizarre
fact that the besiegers were in worse straits than the besieged. He would sit gazing into space for long minutes sunk
in gloom, then recite his doubts they would ever storm the

fortresses. On occasion he lost his temper in uncharacteristic style with his servant or over foolishness on the part of one of his officers. When he had been to the French lines or after an evening in company with friends who had complimented Victoria, he fell to baiting her. Once, when she had refused to be drawn, he had gripped her arm and said, "Damn you, if you think so highly of him, why do you not leap to his defense and protect him, as you did in Constantinople?" Her continued silence closed the subject.

Now, lying in her bed, wakeful with the pain of Hugo's admission of being with Charity until well after midnight, she could think only of the approaching end to the war. The battle tomorrow could take him from her forever, yet, if he lived, what would her future in England be without him?

All that day the regiments moved up to the front. The roads were full of troops marching with a swing in their steps and a smile on their faces. They knew what lay ahead, but they were there to fight, not sit around looking foolish while the Russians jeered at them from the walls of the town. Every man of them would rather die fighting than rot away month after month in his tent.

The air of excitement spread throughout the British and French lines, and the big guns intensified their bombardment until there was no pause in the shattering salvos that left a pall of smoke over the area between the Allied trenches and the fortifications before the town.

For Victoria, nervous and tightly strung after the interview between Charles and Hugo, the prebattle clamor and activity were almost unbearable. Hugo was out on patrol—always dangerous in these hills where bodies of cavalry could come face to face over a slight rise—and after a sleepless night his reactions would be slowed. The sudden crashes of gunfire made her jump, and Major Prescott soon noticed the state she was in.

"My dear Mrs. Stanford, why not take a rest from this today?" he suggested. "You look very tired. It will be no help to make yourself ill."

She shook her head. "You need me most particularly today. One would think I should be immune to the sound of guns after all this time, but they never seem to cease."

They were preparing for new casualties by returning to

his tent any man who could leave the hospital without risk to his health. They would need all their beds and space, they were certain.

June 18 dawned amid the din of a bombardment that shook the very hills. Victoria offered up prayers for those who were taking part in the storming of the defenses and thanked God the Light Cavalry was only providing a cordon around the outskirts in order to keep civilians away from the battle. The horsemen themselves were disgusted at being given such an undignified duty, while the infantry earned the glory of bringing the enemy to its knees.

One lady not to be found among the throng who had gathered on surrounding hills with picnic baskets and parasols to keep the sun's injurious rays from delicate complexions was a petite dark-haired girl in a plain cotton gown. Victoria had seen something so terrible that day in October, nothing would induce her again to watch tiny figures stumble and fall beneath puffs of smoke, as if it were a game with toy soldiers. Her concern was with the reality of pain.

The first casualties began to come in by midday and spoke of walking through a solid wall of fire that took down entire ranks of men without leaving one alive. They were all shocked and shaken. Redcoats were lying upon the ground before the great earthworks, so thickly that others were walking over them as they lay screaming in agony.

Soon the hut was full, and orderlies began laying the wounded outside in rows beneath the broiling sun, where flies descended in droves, crawling in the open wounds to torment the men. Hardened to the sight of gaping wounds and unrelieved suffering, Victoria kept on her feet until it began to grow dark, when an uncontrollable shivering overcame her. The dish she was holding dropped to the floor with a clatter, and a nearby orderly reached for her as she felt the sky descending.

Major Prescott, sweating and exhausted, detailed a young ensign with a mere broken wrist to escort Victoria back to Kadikoi, and she mounted her mare wearily. All along the road they passed a dragging trail of mule carts piled with wounded and shell-torn soldiers making their tortured way back to their lines on foot. Every face was gray and haunted.

Victoria was as silent as her escort. There were so many! They filled the roads and beyond. They were blackened with smoke and glaze-eyed. They were in tattered uniforms, and many were hatless. They were separate—each man lost in his own world. They were all coming *away* from Sebastopol.

The cavalry camp was empty. Victoria absently thanked the ensign and assured him she would be all right before going into the silent hut. She sat motionless in a chair without lighting the lamp and was still there when the Hussars returned, hoofs clattering on the dust-dry ground and voices floating on the still air. Charles entered and walked slowly past her to push aside the blanket screen. She heard the creak as he sat on his bed.

Dragging herself to her feet, she lit the lamp and went into the sleeping end of their hut. He was sitting with his head in his hands but raised it with an effort at her approach. He looked haggard and a hundred years old.

"The French broke through but will never hold it. We were repulsed," he said through a dry throat. "Sebastopol is impregnable, and we shall be here for another winter."

CHAPTER SIXTEEN

Six days after the terrible failure of the assault on Sebastopol, James Escort, Adjutant-General of the Army, died from cholera very suddenly and was followed to the grave four days later by Lord Raglan, commander-in-chief of the British force in the Crimea. Raglan's symptoms were of a choleric nature, but many maintained the disaster of the previous week broke a stout heart that was already cracked. This was the man who had held back the cavalry at Alma when the Russians could have been routed. This same man settled his army neatly around Sebastopol when it should have marched straight into the town the previous September. Lord Raglan it was who sent the ambiguous message that sent the Light Brigade to its destruction. Yet, he was mourned as a kindhearted man—a gentlemanly old warrior who had been given a task for which he was too old and unfit.

Seeing the row of tragedies as a sign of doom, the besiegers' morale plummeted. With the insupportable heat of high summer came a vicious return of cholera, which left the men undecided whether it was better to succumb immediately or face another winter that would take them off in the end. There were no signs that another attempt would be made to capture the fortifications; indeed, many officers were packing up and going home on one pretext or another. They earned no condemnation from their fellows, rather their wry congratulations on doing something they themselves would be only too pleased to do, given half a chance. One fact that did arouse their fury was that, back in England, Lord Cardigan was being feted as the hero of Balaclava and was traveling the country with a boastful story of his part in the charge that had aroused such fervor in patriotic breasts. To men like Hugo Esterly it seemed the devil looked after his own.

As deeply despondent as everyone else, Hugo found himself seeking Charity Verewood's company more and more. When he was with her it was possible to put aside present

problems. Not once did she ask about the battle of Balaclava nor show any interest in the renowned charge; it was
as if she sensed that talk of home and horses was balm to a
man who had seen the face of God and returned. Since he
had no intention of applying to Charles for permission to
leave Kadikoi, Hugo always arranged with any fellow officer he knew was going into Balaclava to accompany Charity back to the camp, where they spent many pleasant
hours riding in the nearby hills in company with other officers. It became a regular sight—the golden-haired girl so
immaculate in severe habit and correct hat, surrounded by
young men who felt the pulse of youth and health returning
merely by standing within the bright aura cast by this vision from a world they had almost forgotten.

Hugo's delight in her company was enhanced by the
words in Lord Blythe's letter. For the first time since he
had made that terrible journey down Mexford Heights
Hugo felt free to speak about and feel part of Wychbourne.
Not knowing if Charity had any knowledge of the rift between Charles and himself, he carefully avoided mentioning
his brother, and the girl followed his example until the afternoon before the steamer *Norvic* was due to leave for
England.

A small party was making an excursion to St. George's
monastery—a favorite picnic spot for tourists—and on setting out had passed a petite dark-haired young woman riding a chestnut mare. The officers had greeted her gaily, but
she appeared to have none of their high spirits. The two
women exchanged glances but nothing more.

Hugo felt his usual distress at Victoria's lifelessness, a
lifelessness emphasized by the dazzling creature beside him.
Only now did he realize how full of resignation the once
vivid face had become, how frail her slender body had
grown, how infinitely introspective her beautiful brown
eyes appeared these days. There was no smile from him;
his look told her once more that he was forced to be a
stranger and must pass by on the other side.

The encounter made him silent for most of the journey,
but they had no sooner dismounted at the monastery and
begun to explore than he found himself alone with Charity
some distance behind the others. The building stood on a
rock right above the sea, with an impressive view of the

cliffs below that dropped precipitously into the inky-blue water. The aim of visitors was to climb to a vantage point before wandering about the gardens. Charity took the climb slowly, and Hugo automatically remained by her side.

She stopped to rest on a ledge cut in the rocky ascent and smiled up at her escort. "So thoughtful on a truly lovely day? You have scarcely said a word to me since we set out, Hugo."

"I beg your pardon." The eyes he saw were suddenly blue and the face tranquil. Shaking himself alert, he smiled back. "What, has Lord Dovedale left your side at last?"

The eyes widened. "I am hardly flattered that you have only now noticed we are alone, when we have been so for at least ten minutes."

He made a rueful face. "I am not excelling myself in gallantry today, am I? Truth to tell, you are so often surrounded by admirers I give up all hope of a tête-à-tête with you."

Her eyelashes lowered. "Let me renew your hope. Lady Cullingham, with whom I travel, has decided to remain in the Crimea for a while. Her husband was fortunate enough to obtain permission for her to live aboard his ship while it is in harbor. She has invited me to stay in her company. I am to give my answer tonight."

He had still not retreated far enough from his thoughts to understand. "Remain in the Crimea? I cannot believe that is what you wish to do."

She looked at him with such cool appraisal he began to feel resentment. "You certainly are not excelling in gallantry today!"

"I am sorry for that," he replied stiffly. Suddenly he wished he had not come on this excursion. "Perhaps we should join the others."

She put out a hand and caught his sleeve. "Hugo, I can remain silent no longer. It is against my better judgment that I speak of so painful a subject, but I cannot hold back from giving the comfort I am able to offer."

Taken by surprise, he let his polished riding boot slide off the edge of the step he had intended climbing and turned back to her. She was so very close to him that he could not help noticing her flawless complexion that bloomed in the perfect July day like a pink-tinted magnolia. How very different it was from that small sun-browned face that had challenged him an hour before. Deep inside him a protest swelled. Would it be like this for the rest of his life?

When he thought of Victoria he was back again in that valley, crawling agonizingly foot by foot toward the sunlit happiness of having her, and knowing he would never reach it. As he had then measured every foot he covered with some familiar comparison, so he now counted his life in days when he saw her against those when he did not. Where was he hoping to go? Victoria remained as unreachable as ever and he had only two choices—to change direction and perhaps chance upon an unexpected release from his pain or to turn back into the smoke pall and be swallowed up forever. In silence he stood looking down into Charity's smooth, uncomplicated face and knew himself at the crossroad.

He was all Charles had said—a conceited sentimental weakling. His conceit led him to believe he could continue this campaign despite his weakened physical condition. The wound in his skull often gave him terrible headaches in the oppressive heat, and the long patrols, on which he was sent so often because he knew the hills better than the newly arrived officers, left him more exhausted than he should be. Could he survive another winter like the last?

Sentimental he plainly was, because Charity's presence had shown him how much he valued his home, family and everything that had made his life what it was. And the last part? Was he a weakling to acknowledge that he would never master his love for Victoria? Charles had challenged him to last out the campaign and control his passion for a woman he could never have. Why did he cede victory to his brother and go home with Charity? Those cool blue eyes promised him rest from the burning fires of amber-brown ones. The slender white-skinned body offered peaceful release without demanding his heart and soul. Charity would never remind him of a frozen beach at Scutari where he had looked up from the yawning grave to see his whole life kneeling beside him with wet cheeks.

"Hugo, are you all right?"

He came out of his trance to focus on Charity once

more. Against the incredible blueness of the sky, her clear-
cut beauty shone in the sunlight, suggesting clean refreshing escape. Desire flared, and he reached for her hungrily.
"You look so lovely it is not surprising that I am not in
possession of my senses today," he breathed.

She turned away from his grasp with great dignity. "We
are in full view of our friends, I beg you to remember. I
find it difficult to understand you this afternoon." She went
across to lean against a rocky overgrown bank. Its cool
shade gave her a remote beauty.

He followed quickly, imprisoning her against the bank
with an arm at each side of her. "Perhaps you will understand this more readily." The flame inside him rose to set
his head on fire as he bent over her soft body, lured by the
English perfume of sweet lavender. For perhaps five seconds the leaping pleasure of mastery inspired the strength
of his hold. His kiss was passionate, but it was short-lived.
His lips searched and found nothing; his hands touched
only whale-boned stiffness; his body pressed against a pas-
sionless doll. Drawing back, he looked at the calm face untouched by love or even physical excitement, and the foolish plan vanished.

"I do not know whether to be flattered or not," she said,
smoothing her hair instinctively. "The situation in the Crimea is so unusual that I suppose I cannot judge you by
home standards." A faint indulgent smile appeared on lips
that seemed completely unaffected by his burning kiss.
"Then again, you have always been impetuous, Hugo."

The flame died, while the memory of another kiss—one
had not sought but could not forget—transformed his passion to anger.

Pointing up the steps with his riding whip, he said, "If
we do not join the rest we shall have to return without
having seen the view . . . and that is our reason for coming, is it not?"

Before she could answer he began to ascend. They remained with the group until the end of the return journey,
when Hugo found her beside him at the head of the party.

"Are you more yourself now?" she asked calmly.

He gave her a sideways glance. "I believe so."

"I am so glad. My experience with those suffering in all

kinds of ways led me to allow you to recover before speaking further to you."

"That was most considerate of you."

"Not at all. A person under stress should be allowed to ride out his moods. It is of no use to cross him when his mind is set in one direction."

He said nothing, for there did not appear to be any reasonable comment he could make, and she continued, "As I said earlier this afternoon, I have shrunk from speaking on such a topic, but when I see it ruling your health and well-being I cannot stand by without offering comfort."

He rode on looking straight ahead. "I am not clear on your meaning."

"Hugo." She said his name persuasively. "I admire your loyalty, but your mama confided everything to me. Before she died it troubled her beyond suppression, and I was able to give her what heart's ease I could by promising to do everything in my power to bring about a reconciliation between you and Colonel Stanford."

He turned and looked at her then. "She told *you?*"

"Why should she not? I have been like a daughter to her and she knew it would not be long before I . . ." She broke off delicately. "Who else would she turn to in her sorrow but the one who had your interests most at heart? Certainly it was of no use appealing to she who brought tragedy to the whole family."

His hand began tightening on the reins. "Is that your opinion or Mama's?" he asked through stiff lips.

Unaware of any change in him, she went on. "It is not an opinion, it is a fact. I cannot tell you how much it angers me nor how greatly I feel for you." She flicked at a fly on her horse's ear with a riding crop. "You might think you are hiding the way you regard her, but to one who knows you as I do it is all too plain that her presence here is a constant reminder. Do you truly believe I do not know what has made you fractious today?"

Suddenly he remembered sitting in blindfolded darkness listening to this same sweet voice telling him he should not be bothered with items from newspapers in case the strain was too much for him. He also recalled a lively voice retaliating—a voice without substance, a girl he had never seen. Dear God, if only he had not! A rush of longing as strong as he had ever felt beset him, making him flinch beneath its onslaught. He had left behind a beloved brown face. How could he have imagined escape lay in this beautiful cold creature who humored him like a difficult child?

"I saw from the start that she was not content with the prize she had won but must needs draw all attention. Her youth persuaded me that I was, perhaps, misjudging her, but her lack of years did not prevent an excess of guile. Knowing you would find it difficult to think ill of her, I decided to speak to her on the dangers of playing on your too easy nature to the displeasure of your brother." Her voice sharpened. "Nothing would induce me to describe her manner to me when there were no gentlemen around to impress, but I knew at once she would cause grave disharmony in the family that had honored her with its name." A sigh was faintly audible above the birdsong and gentle sounds of horses moving through grass. "My only regret is that I did not know the full extent of the tragedy when you left England. I could have eased your distress so much more effectively." She cast him a searching glance that he did not acknowledge and would not meet. "When I heard the full story I realized why you did not ask anything too definite of me at the Farewell Ball. Your scruples are much to be admired, but you should have known I would not let such a thing alter my feelings for you." Her tone became softer and more persuasive. "With me beside you she would not dare to continue to persecute you, and Colonel Stanford would see the truth in no time. He has, I believe, been completely influenced by her, for nothing else would have led to such a reversal of character. To turn upon a brother he loved from childhood could only be brought about by shock or some other strong force beyond his control."

At that point Hugo ceased to hear her voice or any of the nonsense of which she spoke. He was back in the study of a house in Brighton's Brunswick Square, facing Charles across a room. The words they had exchanged were still etched in his mind after all this time. He could still hear his brother's tone of voice and the contempt with which he had addressed him. For a while he rode automatically, unaware of anything else as he felt strength and determination flood back into him. So, he might be back in that valley clawing his way to his goal, but he would not give it up. *He would not give it up!*

Nothing was different today—the usual cases lay in the hospital hut, the camps had their accustomed busy look, the guns fired spasmodically between trench and fortification and Hugo had gone riding with Charity Verewood—yet Victoria felt that everything had come to an end. The sights in the hospital sickened her and held back her usual ready smile. She left it, wishing never to return. Wherever she looked on her ride back to Kadikoi were tents, soldiers and piled arms. If it were all swept away, what a beautiful place this could be.

Men in uniform swarmed over the hills. How she hated the everlasting scarlet jackets and cavalry blue, the riflemen in green and staff officers with their cocked hats. Reaching the cavalry camp, she had a ridiculous urge to continue right on through it until she came to the sea. How beautiful it had looked from the distance, sparkling and constant despite the conflict on land. Did it really cleanse body and spirit? Would complete immersion in it leave her as untouched and bland as Victoria Castledon had been?

Riding through the officers' lines brought the real reason for her mood to the fore. Since Charity had arrived in the Crimea life had become shadowed, not as it was shadowed by death and suffering, because they were clear-cut and visible, but by some uneasy foreboding of disaster. This morning had started well. Byron Porchester had been to dinner last night and the pleasure of the evening had lasted while she had her breakfast. Then the mail had arrived, bringing a letter from Letty, who was contentedly awaiting the birth of her child at her new home with her father. Victoria had been glad. Letty had come with the regiment only because Jack had been part of it. Once he had left the ranks she had no link with this life. Jack's child would be enough for her.

The letter had lifted Victoria's spirits until she had encountered the picnic party. She had seen the look in Hugo's eyes, the apology, the sympathy, the *comparison.* Then he had ridden off with Charity, as had the young officers who now clustered around the bright English flame. To be fair, Victoria knew part of the reason for the young men's desertion of her was Charles's growing unpopularity with his officers. As acting colonel, his attempts to improve on Colonel Rayne's impersonal command of the regiment waxed and waned. In some respects he extracted greater efficiency from the men, but his control over his temper diminished as the weeks passed, making unreasonable demands on men who were either as war-weary as himself or were excusably new to the situation. His personal campaign against Hugo could no longer pass unnoticed, and where there was resentment, respect began to suffer.

She dismounted and handed her mare to a groom before going into the hut. No one knew better than she how much Charles was losing his grip on himself. Day by day she watched him dragging his foot as he walked, knowing it gave him pain as he lay in bed at night. When she offered him a little laudanum he always refused, on one occasion knocking the cup from her hand with sudden violence. She had not made the offer since. The failure of the assault on Sebastopol had depressed him, so that he was obsessed with the winter to come. But then, who was not?

By the time Charles came in, Victoria had washed and changed into a fresh dress, full of the knowledge that Hugo could be as easily distracted by the Divine Huntress as any other man. Did he also visit the French lines or some house in Kamiesh? She closed her eyes against the image, just as Charles pushed aside the blanket and limped toward her.

"Rayne is dead," he said harshly. "I am now in command of this regiment."

Her eyes flew open. "Poor man. He fought if off for so long."

"There is no rhyme or reason in a valuable man like Rayne being lost while others appear to have nine lives," he cried savagely. "I begin to believe Satan himself has put his deadly grip around this army."

Ignoring the inference in his first sentence, she said, "The regiment must be thankful it has such an experienced and capable man to step into Colonel Rayne's shoes."

"Must it?" He swung around, eyes blazing. "How little you know of the situation here. You think a few hours spent mopping the brows of the sick qualifies you to comment on a disaster such as this. You are here to see to my comfort, that is all. You can forget all this nonsense of hospitals." He was shaking convulsively by now. "I will tell you what this means. My whole time will be spent fighting the authorities. Do you know, ma'am, that I have been attempting to get adequate stabling for the horses of Number Three Squadron for four months? *Four months!*" He put out on arm with finger pointing. "The wood is down there in the dockyard rotting away from disuse, yet I am told there is none available. Half the regiment's saddles are falling to pieces, and yet my repeated requests to send an officer to Kemiesh in search of replacements have been continually turned down. A shipload is on its way from Scutari, I am told, but where is it?" He raised his voice. "Where is it? Oh no, Victoria, you know nothing of where Rayne's death places me."

"I thought you always wanted to be colonel of the regiment, Charles."

He sagged and put his hand to his forehead. "Yes . . . colonel of a regiment such as we had in England. What have I now? Five hundred recruits, half of whom cannot ride in a straight line, led by officers who laugh at the word *duty* and prance around like lovesick poodles behind any female in sight." He swept her full-length with a pitying glance. "I see why you returned from Constantinople. In the company of ladies of undoubted breeding and beauty, he was unable to resist his nature. It was not you who tired of him, but he who washed his hands of a drab creature who can speak of nothing but cholera and bandages. How does it feel to see him jumping through hoops at her command?"

She drew in her breath. "About the same as it feels to see you at the feet of a French wanton."

His hand caught her across the left cheek, the power of the blow sending her backward a pace or two. The shock was comparable to that on her wedding night when he had used violence against her. This time he was quite as horrified as she, for it showed in his expression just before she turned and fled from the hut.

"Victoria . . ."

His cry floated into the approaching dusk, but the devil was on her heels now and nothing would have halted her. Seizing the bridle of Charles's horse as it was being led away, she ordered the trooper to assist her into the saddle, then set off at a gallop through the lines, scattering soldiers as she went.

The horse was fresh and flew like the wind across the open hillside. Something inside Victoria had snapped with that blow. Reason had been swept aside. As she let the great creature take her where he would, the wildness that comes with a complete breakdown set her crying with great racking sobs until the sound of it filled her head.

She leaned forward to ease the agony in her stomach brought on by her sobs. "God have mercy on me. God have mercy on us all," she shouted to the wind, in a voice that echoed the cries of all those she had watched through their death throes.

On and on she rushed, the thudding hooves reminding her of that October day when she had seen all the glory and obscenity of battle. A long wail left her as she despaired for all those who had gone—Harry Edmunds, Cornet McKay, Trooper Pitchley and cheerful friendly Stokes. Her cheeks were drenched with tears for all those who had dragged themselves up the beach at Scutari to enter the indescribable horror of the hospital; for poor Jack Markham and brokenhearted Letty; for Zarina Stokes, who could not face the thought of those abandoned women in the cellars; and for the fresh-faced Rupert Marshall, who had seen only five minutes of the war in the trenches before surrendering his life. She sobbed for Hugo, her one eternal love, who had suffered so deeply and still suffered from one night when he had removed a blindfold and saw her standing before him.

But her most anguished tears were for herself. For her own humiliation and pain; for her dearly bought dignity that had been demolished in an instant by a man who had struck her as he would strike a slut. Had compassion debased her? Had humanity so low a value that those who practiced it were thought to be of no account? Her friends had drifted away to those pale useless creatures who demanded all and gave nothing. Visitors looked askance at Colonel Stanford's wife when they heard she spent most of her time bandaging the limbs of common soldiers and writing letters for those who were illiterate, and they turned their well-bred attention elsewhere.

Her husband had been contemptuous of her fear of his

love-making, had considered her useless because she could
not produce children, and now, when she had achieved so
much that was worthy, he showed that the work she did
reduced her to the lowest of creatures—lower than the one
he had defended with that blow.

In near darkness she galloped on, knowing nothing would
make her return and nothing would stop the spring that
was welling up inside her and flowing from her eyes. The
wind rushing past her ears was cold with approaching
night, and the grayness ahead was studded with stars. If she
could only reach one of those she need never come back to
earth. It should be possible. Alone out here with the great
striding creature beneath her, why should she not leap
from the summit of this hill right up to one of those beckoning lights? They were almost on the summit, she noticed,
and urged the horse on with a fevered cry. With her eyes
on the stars she was not aware of anything but her desire to
escape. She did not hear a sharp challenge from several
yards ahead.

"Who goes there? Who goes there, I say? *Halt!*"

Victoria gathered herself for the tremendous leap into
the sky as the horse took off. There was a deafening report
and the animal stumbled as it landed on the other side of a
small water course, then continued on its way in a broken
halting rhythm that gradually slowed until it stopped,
flanks heaving and whinnying with pain. For a few moments Victoria sat motionless, then slid from the saddle to
bury her face in the warm glossy neck in despair. She
would never get away now.

Hooves thundered up and someone catapulted to the
ground behind her.

"Victoria, you are not hurt? *Tell me you are not hurt!*"
He seized her shoulders and forced her around to face him.
He was white, and the hands that held her shook.

She gazed at him while her heart cried out against this
cruelest of blows. Of all people to be here at this moment
of her complete humiliation! With a moan she pulled free
and began stumbling over the grass turned emerald by the
enchanting glow of dusk, but he was after her in a second,
pulling her to a halt and raising his voice from the depth of
his fright.

"What do you mean by riding out here beyond our lines?

Dear God, do you realize my trooper could have killed you?"

Shaking off his restraining hand, she turned away again. When she spoke it was in a defeated monotone. "It would not have mattered. I am nothing. I have always been nothing."

"How dare you say that when, to me, you are *everything?*"

She spun back to face him, the memory of Charles's words raging through her. Her great need was to hurt—to break him on the wheel of her own love, to scourge him with the lash of her jealousy. He stood before her, tall and strong with the scar of courage upon his cheek, but she wanted to topple him in the dust beside her and witness his suffering. The thickness of tears in her throat forced the words out in jerky contempt.

"And what of her? Is she *everything* to you also? Your proud talk of love and honor has been trampled in the mud with her arrival. You are no better than all the rest who form her languishing retinue."

He covered the distance between them in two strides. Even in the gathering darkness it was clear he was ablaze with a passion she had never before seen in him.

"What do you want from me? What would you have me do? You will never be free, and I am only human."

"Then take her!" she cried. "Take her into your life and into your very soul. Let her diminish you day by day until your life is colorless and your soul is no longer your own. Trot in her shadow like a bondsman, if that is what you want." The wetness on her cheeks grew chilled by the night. "Your mama always held her above me, so do your duty and take her!"

"I cannot, Victoria," he said with an effort. "You are there between us all the time."

The very night held its breath as they exchanged their pain, their joy, their helplessness in a long glance.

"I . . . I am so sorry," she whispered.

He took her against him in a swift movement and held her there. "No . . . no," he murmured in anguish against her mouth. "Never apologize to me."

Sweet rioting pain beset every limb as she was drawn against him in the crashing surrender of all they had tried to fight for so long. His mouth touched her hair, cheeks, throat and closed her eyelids before returning to take her lips with gentle savagery. She moaned softly as the pain in her thighs overwhelmed her and her breasts burned beneath the pressure of his body. Her hand went up to twist in his hair, and the fur busby fell to the ground, where it rolled slowly down to the waiting horses.

His head was thrown back as he took in a great sighing breath, and Victoria found herself swung up in his arms while he began to walk into the darkness with the erratic steps of a man in a daze. Her fingers stroked the scar on his cheek and went on to trace the outline of his lips, until they parted and teeth bit gently against her flesh. Her hand dropped to tear open the gold-encrusted collar of his jacket to expose his throat. It was fever-warm beneath her kisses, and the pulsating thud of his heartbeat sent a wild message through her, to set her whole body throbbing in time to it.

With a groan he brought her face up to meet his once more, letting her feet slide to the ground, crushing her aginst him in an embrace that washed away her subjugation to Charles and put her very life into Hugo's keeping forever. There was so much of her that should belong to him, the weight of the burden brought small cries of pain that he tried to silence with his mouth, then with trembling fingers. Snatching his hand away she pressed it against her breast, arching backward in her agony and driving him deeper into the realms of passion.

Drugged with desire, he gathered her up in his arms once more and began walking away from the horses into the cloaking darkness. A shadow rose up ahead and broke his progress.

"Captain Esterly . . . is that you, sir? Is everything all right?"

"What . . . who is that?" he asked like a man coming out of sleep.

"Bramble, sir," said the trooper, and a hint of anxiety touched his voice when Hugo drew close enough to be visible in the darkness. "Oh lor', is Mrs. Stanford all right, sir? Did I hit her?"

Hugo barely heard him. "I shall have to take her back. She cannot go alone."

"Is she hurt bad?" he asked, voice unsteady.

"For God's sake stop behaving like a girl and pull your-self together." Vicious anger was his only outlet for an emotion he had been denied. "Thanks to your bloody atrocious marksmanship you have only hit the colonel's horse. Get down there and bring the beast up to the post with mine."

"Yes, sir. I . . . I'm sorry, sir."

"Get those damned horses!"

The man went, and Victoria began the long journey back to reality with Hugo as he carried her to the piquet post. Leaving his men under the command of a sergeant, he took her up in front of him on the gray horse and led the wounded charger by the rein for the half-hour ride back to camp. Neither spoke as the gray took them at a steady walk through the dark night toward the faint glow of campfires.

Victoria knew there would never be another night like this when a skyful of stars witnessed their love. She was reluctant to pull herself from the soft mood of submission as she leaned back against his solid strength, his left arm encircling her as he held the reins. She was still wrapped in the joy of surrender. She could feel Hugo's tenseness in the way he held himself in the saddle. She longed to turn her face up to his and caress his mouth with hers; she dared not. Did he blame her for forcing a surrender that had made a mockery of his sense of honor? After tonight, how could they go back to nodding acquaintances? He would find it either impossible to forgive her or resist her.

At the outskirts of the camp Hugo suddenly pulled the horse to a standstill, where it shook its head restlessly and fidgeted from leg to leg.

"How can I take you back to him?" he demanded in despair. "It was something he did that drove you out there in such distress, I am certain."

She said nothing, only pressed closer against him.

"Did he hurt you?"

Against the blue cloth of his jacket she said, "It was nothing to what I felt when I saw you with . . . that girl."

He put back his head in an impotent gesture while his breath came out in a long sigh, then he set the horse forward again in silence.

Outside Charles's hut Hugo lifted Victoria down and

held her still for a moment. In the starlit darkness his face
was a rigid shadow.

"How can I take you back to him?" he repeated in a soft
groan. "It is too much to ask of any man."

She knew he was asking the question more of himself
than of her. "How can you *not* take me back to him?"

The gleam in his eyes vanished as he closed them mo-
mentarily. "Dear God in heaven, how will this all end?"

The groom appeared from the shadows and took the
reins of the two horses. Victoria began to move into the
hut, forcing Hugo to accompany her.

Charles was sitting in a chair by the light from a lamp,
but he stood up when they entered side by side, a flush
dyeing his face darker in the pale glow. For a moment
there was silence, then he said to Victoria, "So you ran to
him. Have you no pride whatsoever?"

"Are you inhuman that you can sit here while Victoria is
exposed to all kinds of danger?" Hugo blazed. "She could
have been killed, but the bullet ended in your horse's
rump."

"Get out of here!"

"By God, Charles, if I had not been commanding the
piquet and recognized your charger, she could have been
fired upon by every guard along the Tchernaya River. Do
you care nothing for her safety?"

"I told you to get out."

Victoria began to tremble. She could only guess what
had passed between the brothers in the past; it frightened
her to see such naked aggression now. The air inside the
hut was full of tension as they stood, two powerful men,
ready to spring at each other's throats. It occurred to her
that love and hatred were conceived in the same womb,
that a caress could destroy as surely as the sword. Putting
a hand on Hugo's sleeve, she said, "Please go," but he was
past listening and was as white as Charles was flushed.

"You had a right to order me out of Wychbourne,
Charles, but this hut is not your legal property."

"My wife is . . . and you have been ordered to stay
away from her."

"Victoria is a woman . . . a warm human creature who
is entitled to your care and protection. She is not part of
your legal property."

Charles gripped the table to steady himself. *"She is my wife!"* He was shouting now. "If you still refuse to accept that she is, I shall have to drive the lesson home in such a way that you will . . . and I shall break you in the process, Hugo, I swear it. Do you think I shall tolerate your dragging my name through the mud? Everyone was buzzing with the sordid facts when you flaunted your amor in the face of Constantinople society. My wife was discussed in every mess and cookhouse in the Crimea."

"That is a damned lie," roared Hugo. "She commands nothing but the deepest respect from every man who knows her."

"Then, by thunder, it is about time you joined their ranks. This is a little out of your style tonight, is it not?"

Hugo clenched the hilt of his sword until the sinews stood out in his hand. "What do you mean by that?"

Up went Charles's chin in the Stanford gesture. "You normally avail yourself of my wife's generosity when I am safely distant."

There was a paralyzing moment while Hugo took the full force of the words in his face, then Charles burst into a flood of abuse. "You dare to lay down the law to me when you have been amusing yourself in the hills with Victoria! I have been right all along. You have no strength of character, no sense of duty, no sense of honor. I have no need to ask what happened out there, for it is written all over you." He was fighting unsuccessfully for command of himself. "You shall pay for it this time, believe me."

Victoria watched him take two steps toward Hugo and ran between the two men. "No, Charles. *No!*"

He pushed her aside so roughly that her foot twisted and she fell across the table with a sharp cry. It grew unnaturally quiet, and she just had time to see the brothers staring in horror at her as she lay there, before Charles said, *"Now* will you get out?"

Victoria felt she had reached the limit of her endurance. "Please, for all our sakes, go," she begged Hugo through a torrent of tears.

He gave her a long look from a face grown haggard, then turned to Charles. "I swear, if you ever harm her again, in any way whatever, I shall take her from you. I shall forfeit my future, my profession, my honor . . . but I shall take her as surely as if she had never borne your name." He spun on his heel and strode out, his sword swinging against his leg.

CHAPTER SEVENTEEN

It was not until the first week of August that Victoria felt well enough to move about the camp once more. The events of that one night had left her defenseless against the notorious Crimean fever that moved in to take possession of her exhausted body and kept it tossing and turning.

Major Prescott called every day and those friends she believed had deserted her during the last few months proved her wrong by showering her with gifts and good wishes. When she began her convalescence not a day passed when there were not two or three officers gathered around her chair in the shade to entertain her with anecdotes and easy conversation. Of Hugo she saw nothing and yearned for the sight of him.

No one mentioned the horse that had been shot by a jumpy sentry, and she wondered what explanation Charles had offered for his wife being in the hills alone at dusk. She remembered only too well what had driven her there and could not forget it or pretend it had never happened, as Charles appeared to have done. Nor could she forget the sight of two men flogging each other with words while every nerve strained to hold back their wilder instincts.

She knew there was no alternative but to return to England. Wychbourne was out of the question, but perhaps she could rent a small cottage near Letty or a modest house not far from Aunt Almeira in Brighton. It did not matter where she went so long as it was away from the Crimea.

The resolution was so strong in her she thought nothing would change her mind, yet when, on August 9, a general order went out to clear all regimental hospitals of walking sick and send to the General Hospital in Balaclava all patients who could be safely moved, Victoria sent word to Major Prescott that she would be ready when needed.

Rumors began to fly that another attack was to be made on the fortifications of Sebastopol, and when the medical officers were told to take in enormous quantities of drugs, lint, bandages and bedding, it seemed to everyone that a

bloodbath was expected before the prize was finally taken.
Spirits began to rise again but were doomed to be dashed
in the worst possible way when four nights later it became
known that the preparations were for defense, not attack.
Deserters from Sebastopol had provided information of
enormous Russian reinforcements arriving to support an attack on the British and French lines.

Liking the idea of spending another winter under bombardment no better than their enemies, the Russians had
decided to launch a tremendous attack finally to drive the
Allies from their positions and recapture Balaclava.

As the word spread, the British soldiers grew angry. Denied the opportunity to repeat the assault on Sebastopol,
were they now to be forced to defend themselves from an
enemy they had held under siege for nearly a year? Words
were bitter, and some memories were long. The Alma, Inkerman and the Charge of the Light Brigade were spoken
of by the survivors, who asked what it had all been for.

For several days the regiments were ordered forward before dawn, but, although large numbers of Russians were
seen massing in various areas, no attack came.

Hugo commanded the outlying piquet again on the night
of the fourteenth and spent a miserable time recalling the
last occasion he had done so. Since then he had avoided
seeing Victoria. By going out of his way he made certain
never to ride past Charles's hut; he shunned the company
of his fellows lest she should be among them; he spent his
free time on his bed with a book, for that was the only way
he could ensure isolation from her—although, unable to
concentrate, he did no reading. Unable to sleep, unable to
forget that he had lost all command of himself with her in
his arms, he tormented himself with memories. What devil
had taken him in tow? How could it have happened so
easily when he had fought it so hard for nearly three years?
Suppose that trooper had come upon them earlier, when he
had been weakening her with kisses, to spread Victoria's
name through the trenches with lewd suggestions. Hugo's
thoughts left him fevered and gaunt by day and wide-eyed
at night.

Piquet duty at least gave him something to occupy the
night hours. The situation was tense, and he was particularly alert that night. There were no alarms, but a thick

mist descended with a curtain of rain soon after midnight and cast doubts on any attack being made in such conditions—the lesson of Inkerman having been learned the hard way. At 5:30 A.M. they were relieved and rode back to Kadikoi wet to the skin, tired and stiff with chill and glad to leave the thick obscurity that could be hiding an ambush.

In the cavalry camp the Hussars were lined up in readiness, as they had been every dawn for the past week, and Hugo rode up to give his report to Major Mackintosh, an experienced man who had transferred from the 16th Lancers. While he was doing so, the attention of the mounted squadrons was attacked by the arrival of a staff officer at full gallop, who reined in and presented Charles with a message.

Excitement rippled through the ranks. Their commanding officer frowned. Watching, each man would have liked to have known what he said to the elegant, aristocratic staff captain and Major Mackintosh. Hugo heard and shared his brother's protestations.

"Does the general require absolute compliance with this order, Captain de Lacy?" Charles asked haughtily. "Am I to assume there is no fog at headquarters?"

The staff officer was a humorless man at the best of times and took his duty very seriously. "I believe he has marked the order *immediate*, sir."

"He has indeed, but is he aware that it is damned madness to send a cavalry patrol off in weather like this to locate a column of enemy horsemen *thought* to be moving along the Woronzoff Road toward Sebastopol? My men could be slaughtered. With no chance of seeing the enemy from a distance, they could ride slap bang into them . . . and if the force is larger than suspected, there will be no one able to return with the information."

The staff officer kept a wooden expression. "It is imperative that the general should know the strength of reinforcements flooding in, sir."

Charles grunted and showed the order to his second-in-command, taking his attention away from Hugo's report. "What do you think of this, Alistair?"

The major read it and frowned. "It is asking a great deal

of those who have to carry it out. Is it worth risking the loss of an entire troop for such information?"

"The general appears to believe it is." Under his breath Charles said, "It is painfully obvious he was never in the cavalry." He looked at the paper in his hand as if he hoped there might be some way of avoiding the order, decided there was not and sighed heavily.

"Tell the general we shall do as he asks."

The captain saluted and departed hell for leather. It was well known among soldiers that staff officers never moved at less than a gallop—even when simply going to the mess for breakfast.

Charles watched him go and said, "Alistair, steer clear of becoming commanding officer and you will never have to decide which of your men to send to possible destruction." He sighed again and closed his eyes. "Make it B Troop."

"Very well," said Major Mackintosh and called across to the troop commander, a youthful captain who had been in the Crimea for a mere three months.

Hugo decided his report would have to wait until those poor devils had been dispatched on their way and wearily began to dismount. His movement caught Charles's attention, and their eyes met across the top of Hugo's saddle. In that moment Charles said, "Just a minute, Alistair. Codrington is too newly arrived for this. Captain Esterly will lead the patrol."

Hugo's heart missed a beat. He was shaken to the core, but he was not the only one.

"Captain Esterly had only this minute returned from all-night piquet," the major protested quickly.

"He is the commander who knows the terrain most intimately," snapped Charles. "He will go."

Major Mackintosh was dumfounded; Captain Codrington was astonished; B Troop was uncomprehending. To send a man out on such a duty when he was red-eyed from staring into the darkness all night, wet through to the skin and drooping in the saddle was a completely irrational act. They all knew there was no love lost between the colonel and the man who had been reared as his brother, but he was risking the lives of an entire troop by choosing an exhausted man to lead them. Hugo Esterly was highly esteemed by the regiment, their best officer, but no man would be at his most efficient after piquet duty on a night such as they had just seen.

All eyes swung to the man concerned, waiting for some protest from him, but all he did was stare at his commanding officer as if he were mesmerized, then climb back into his saddle and move forward to the head of B Troop.

Hugo gave his commands without knowing what he did. It had come, after all—the sword thrust in the back that would solve the problem for him—only Charles was delivering it himself. Even after all that had passed between them, he was stunned to think that hatred would drive his brother to such lengths. Lost deep in the tangle of their relationship, he did not see the reflection of his own shock in Charles's eyes as he rode out into the blanket of mist in the direction of the Woronzoff Road.

Ten minutes later he was perfectly calm. It was done and nothing could undo it. He could not see where it would all end—maybe today for him—but what of Victoria? She would suffer whatever happened. For now he must leave the decision in the hands of God. He commanded twenty-five men who deserved the benefit of his skill and knowledge. Personal thoughts must be put aside for their sakes.

Looking around, he saw Lieutenant Marks and Cornet Fielding trotting behind him and knew they were reliable men. Right now they had very grim faces, so he smiled and said, "Cheer up, lads. Think of the advantage *we* have of knowing they are there. They'll have the shock of their lives when we appear out of the fog."

Colin Marks made a face. "It is more likely to be the *laugh* of their lives when they see our numbers."

"Nonsense" was Hugo's reply. "Ever since we charged their cannon last October they firmly believe British cavalrymen are a breed of madmen who will stop at nothing and go in fear of meeting any of us."

Young Philip Fielding, eager and overawed by this officer who had ridden in that famous charge, said, "I do not doubt your word on that, but I should be very glad if you would make yourself most conspicuous when we meet them. It might be that they are not so timorous of newly joined members."

They all laughed, but they had not gone much farther when Hugo sent back word for complete silence. The Woronzoff Road ran along the top of the hills, and they were climbing steeply through woodland. Hugo certainly knew the terrain intimately after a year of patrols and piquets, but in thick mist that was growing more opaque with daylight, even a native would have been uncertain of his whereabouts.

The wooded area stretched to within half a mile of the road; once they broke clear of the trees they would be in danger of bumping into the moving column at any time. Hugo had been given the position from where it had been sighted from a Turkish outpost—at least, there had been no sighting, just the sound of moving cavalry—and by estimating the speed of a column of horses he had a general idea where it might be found now. The difficulty was to get himself and his men to that point.

They had dropped to a walk and picked their way through the trees with great care, but Hugo had no landmark to guide him. It was eerie pushing through undergrowth and straining one's eyes into the grayness, wondering if a shadow was a tree or an enemy. The trees stopped and Hugo halted his men, saying quietly to Lieutenant Marks, "Stay here until I make a reconnaisance. There is a large knoll in the area that will give me my bearings once I know whether we are north or south of it. Philip, come with me."

The two men went out side by side, until the swirling mist came between them and the remainder of the patrol. The only sound was the liquid plod of hooves on wet grass and the faint chink of harness. The young cornet was plainly fighting a battle with his nerves, and Hugo grew angry. In this war they had not once been given the chance to fight a real cavalry action. Now in the worst possible weather conditions for mounted soldiers, they were playing Blind Man's Buff with an uncertain number of the enemy. What had happened to the *arme blanche* that had swept into the Crimea in a mass of glittering steel to scatter the enemy and chase them home with their tails between their legs? What he would give for just one heady clash of steel against steel before the conflict was over!

They came upon the knoll before five minutes had passed and returned as speedily as possible to those ghostly figures waiting among the trees.

Colin Marks looked distinctly relieved. "God, it's unnerving sitting here," he confessed softly. "I expected the ghost of Hamlet's father to appear at any moment."

"If that was all I was expecting I should feel a lot happier," said the cornet gloomily. "I saw half a hundred men out there in my imagination."

They moved off behind Hugo in a northeasterly direction and soon came to level ground, where he halted to listen. There was just a strange unnatural deadness of sound that increased their uneasiness. Hugo did not miss the quick swivel in the saddle, nor the rolling eyes that betrayed the troopers' edginess, and signaled them to move on. He understood it. They were brave men when they knew what they were fighting; this was not to their liking at all.

Five hundred yards farther on, he thought he heard the faint drumming of hooves and held up his hand to halt his men again. The fog was so thick here that the rear rank, unable to see his signal, walked into the body of the troop. Now they had stopped Hugo heard something that could be the plodding of horses way off to his left.

"Do you hear that, Colin?" he asked the lieutenant.

"I have been hearing things for the last half hour" was the reply. "That would be about the right position for the road, wouldn't it?"

"I want to move in closer. Instruct your men to follow without spoken comands." He looked keenly at the subaltern. "Can they do that?"

He grinned. "If not, I shall want to know why when we get back."

In completely unorthodox manner the patrol moved around to the left and headed for the road. Yet when Hugo halted them again ten minutes later, the noise of traveling cavalry, louder and more recognizable now, was coming from their right.

"Damn," he swore. "We must have crossed ahead of them in this fog."

The two younger officers exchanged a look, relieved at having crossed ahead of the enemy and not into them. They eased their horses forward when Hugo began a right-hand curve forward. They might think their leader very cool, but Hugo was every bit as keyed-up as they. With more luck than judgment he had located the enemy's position, but how was he to get near enough to see the enemy without being seen himself?

The rumble was louder now; he stopped to listen. In the sudden cessation of movement, the noise bounced back at him with significant intensity. There was undoubtedly a large force on the move. The creaking of wood and the rumble of wheels told him there was also horse artillery nearby. Worst of all, it was impossible to tell exactly where. The noise was swirled around in the fog so that it seemed to come from both sides at once.

Under his breath Hugo asked the two officers which side they thought the enemy was on, and both gave conflicting replies. "That was my impression," he said grimly. "Damned impossible to tell in this murk. It deadens sound and throws up an echo elsewhere." He sighed. "We must keep moving or we shall lose them. Take the men on at a steady walk while I go ahead to see if I can find the road."

"Hugo . . . take care," warned Colin Marks.

"If I encounter them I shall take *flight*," he said with a lightness he did not feel and urged his gray into a trot. As a man alone he felt even more nervous. He still could not decide whether the Russians were on his right or his left. Acutely tired after his all-night piquet and shivering in the dampness that chilled his soaked uniform, he blamed his physical condition for his dulled senses. So much so that when the fog appeared to be thinning up ahead he thought it a trick of his strained eyes and trotted on the same pace.

His eyes had not deceived him, though. The grayness broke up quite suddenly to leave one of those wispy clear patches found in hill areas. Slowed by weariness, Hugo could not take in what he saw for half a moment, then the blood drained out of him. On his left was a solid column of Russian Lancers extending into the mist ahead and pouring out from the mist behind him. They rode wearily, as if they had come a long way, their dark uniforms melting into the colorless atmosphere, the pennons at the end of their long lances hanging damply limp. Their horses made heavy going of it, their heads nodding in resignation as they covered yard after yard with their burdens.

Hugo swung his head to the right and saw an endless column of horse artillery plodding parallel to their comrades, the big horses straining at the traces, the guns shud-

dering and rumbling over the uneven surface and ammunition wagons creaking in protest against the load of round-
shot. His throat grew dry, his knees weakened. By some
fancy of the devil his patrol had wandered directly into an
entire brigade on the march, and they were now walking
between two enemy columns, hemmed in and completely
outnumbered.

Experience and military flair overcame physical tiredness to set his brain furiously deciding on the best action to
take. So far he had not been noticed—the soldiers were
used to having outriders on their flanks. But any minute
now his own troop would break out into the open, and they
would not go unremarked. Even as he thought it the two
subalterns appeared from the mist and the entire troop
could be seen behind them.

Everything happened at once then. A Russian officer
spotted the British Hussars but, fortunately, was so astonished he did nothing for almost half a minute. In that time
Hugo abandoned several ideas. To go on as they were
would be fatal. Instant retreat would lead them into safety
of fog, to be protected by the ignorance of those coming up
of their presence. But there was not enough room between
the enemy columns to perform the complicated maneuver,
and he cried out in spirit for his own squadron, who knew
the simple drill methods he had devised that would be so
useful at a time like this. If they were to survive they must
move now, when they could see the enemy. Any action in
the thick fog ahead would be doomed.

With the sweat of desperation breaking out all over him,
he wheeled and began galloping toward his patrol, which
was moving along with the columns, as mesmerized as the
Russians. When he was halfway back a shout went up and
he knew there was no time to give instructions. He prayed
to God those subalterns were as steady as he believed them
to be.

Still at the gallop, he veered to his left and drew his
pistol. Singling out a lead horse on the gun carriages as he
hurtled toward the enemy column, he fired. The beast
dropped immediately, pulling down his companion, the gun
carriage going up and over them, carried on by its own
momentum. Those ahead moved on; those behind walked
straight into the upended gun and struggling horses. Confu-

sion broke out. Horses gave shrill screams of fright, men shouted orders, the rear part of the column creaked and rattled to a standstill.

Ahead of the crashed gun carriage a gap had opened, and Hugo made for it, yelling to his men to follow, and heard with great thankfulness the calm English voice of Colin Marks giving orders. As he flew past the confused artillerymen, one brandished his sword. Hugo emptied the other barrel of his pistol into the man's chest.

Galvanized into action, the Russian officers let fly with their pistols, but the patrol was nearly through the gap and heading into the security of the fog. Hugo stood by until they had all passed him, then swung around behind them, grateful for the fog that he had just been cursing. He overtook the troopers, who were severely shaken but laughing with nervous excitement, and joined Lieutenant Marks at the head of the column. Only then did they realize Cornet Fielding was no longer with them.

With the memory of the boy's scared face before him, Hugo did not stop for second thoughts. Ordering the subaltern to return to camp, he jerked his horse around almost savagely and raced back the way he had come. Shooting out of the fog once more, he saw the boy lying just beyond the overturned gun and made straight for him. Jumping from his saddle, he knelt quickly, but Philip Fielding would be frightened no more. With great regret Hugo closed the sightless eyes, then became aware of hooves a few feet away and let his glance travel upward.

A Russian Lancer officer sat a huge black stallion—a handsome man with dark mustache and eyes that were almost black. There was an air of hauteur in his face and bearing. His sword was drawn.

Hugo got slowly to his feet and said in French, "I come only to collect my dead."

The Russian looked him over for a few moments, then answered in impeccable English, "You are an officer of the British Hussars, sir, and wear the mark of battle. Did you take part in the charge at Balaclava?"

"I did, sir."

The Russian put up his sword in salute. "I honor you, sir, and regret our acquaintance was made under such unhappy conditions. The fog produces strange fellow travelers, does it not?" He backed his horse a few paces. "Take your comrade. You will not be challenged."

"Thank you, sir."

Putting the boy over his horse's neck, he mounted and began walking the gray toward the gap-created by his own making, followed by the Russian a few paces behind. Once past the guns, he reined in and turned to salute the other officers, who had halted by his own soldiers.

"If we should meet in conflict I shall do my duty, but if we should chance to meet in peace I shall be honored to entertain you," said the Lancer with a smile. "Your name, Captain?"

"Hugo Esterly . . . and yours, sir?"

"Alexei, Prince Libinski."

"It is I who am honored, sir. I pray we do not meet in conflict, for our duty would be a sad thing, indeed."

The fog persisted until mid-morning, when the cavalry stood down. Charles entered the hut, where Victoria was reading letters that had come up to camp that morning. She looked up.

"I will instruct Brooks to prepare breakfast."

"Yes" was all his reply, but when the servant put the plate before him the eggs were left to congeal and the letters were left unopened while he sat staring out through the open door.

Victoria put the finishing touches to her own letters, for the mail would be collected that afternoon when the post officer returned on his way back to Balaclava. She was used to her husband's silences, and there was nothing they could say to each other now. He no longer went to the French lines, as far as she could tell, nor did he taunt her with comments about Charity Verewood. Since the girl appeared to have returned to England there was no occasion for him to do so, but she sensed an air of resignation about him that dulled his senses and stilled his tongue.

Even so, it eventually struck her that he was behaving strangely this particular morning, and she glanced at him curiously. He sat like a man in shock, arms resting on his knees, shoulders hunched, gazing at something beyond life and reality. In the blazing sunlight that threw harsh rays through the door she saw a stranger. His blond hair had

begun to turn silver at his temples, and the aristocratic features were not as finely-etched as they had once been.
Deep lines tugged down the corners of his mouth and gave
his eyes a recessed fierceness that added years to his appearance. The bowed shoulders, the foot that twisted
slightly, the privations of the war had all robbed him of his
proud stamp of breeding.

A trooper interrupted her thoughts with a smart salute
and a message that B Troop had returned from patrol with
only one casualty—Mr. Fielding shot dead. "Captain Esterly's compliments, sir. Do you wish to hear his report?"

Charles stared blankly at the man. "Eh? No . . . Major
Mackintosh can deal with it."

The man went out, and Victoria said, "How sad about
Mr. Fielding!"

Charles rose from his chair and walked past her behind
the blanket screen. He did not seem to see or hear her. His
face was gray and haunted, a mask of incalculable personal
anguish. She heard the creak of his bed and began sealing
her letters thoughtfully. A few minutes later she went out
into the full heat of noon to visit the adjutant and obtain
the address of Cornet Fielding's father so that she could
write her condolences, as she always did when one of the
regiment was lost.

That evening there was a party in the tent of Lieutenant
Marks for all the officers of the Hussars, and the merriment could be heard well into the night as the story of the
morning patrol was retold, embroidered by wine-charmed
tongues. Charles sat working at forms and strength returns
by the lamplight, but Victoria sat in her doorway listening
to the sounds of the camp and the young men's hearty
laughter. Young Philip Fielding had been buried just three
hours ago; the mourning was already over. That was how it
was now. A sad farewell, then drink and be merry, for tomorrow it might be one's own turn. She understood only
too well why they did it but held the memory of the dead
officer in her mind a little longer. It was as well she did not
know who had led the patrol that morning, nor under what
circumstances.

At dawn the following morning the alarm went up and
men tumbled from their tents to saddle up and form squad-

rons to ride out of camp. In the faint light Victoria watched them go and prayed for their safety. She could not see well enough to pick out Hugo, but her heart went with him wherever he was. There then began for her those terrible moments of waiting, listening for the sound of musketry and cannon in the distance that told her the Russians had made their attack.

Unable to remain still, she called for mare to be saddled and rode out of the camp in the direction of the hills, where she found the cavalry formed up, sabers and harness gleaming in the early sunshine, waiting to charge the enemy should they break through the French defenses at the top of the hills. Prepared for an attack on their lines, the Allies had been taken by surprise when the assault had come along the banks of the Tchernaya River instead.

From her position slightly uphill Victoria looked down on the rows of horses and riders with a sick feeling in her stomach. Would she ever be able to look at proud cavalry regiments without recalling that October day? Near the head of the Hussars was an officer on a gray horse. She looked at Hugo's distant figure and felt weakness flood through her at the memory of the night she had ridden the gray with his arm encircling her. Turning away, she drove her mare to the brow of the hill toward the hospital, where Major Prescott made her welcome and ordered tea for her.

By 10:00 A.M. it was all over. The Russians had been beaten back in such confusion the ground was littered with bodies, and the Tchernaya was piled with those who had died trying to force the bridges or who had fallen in while trying to retreat and had drowned in the swift waters. The French, Turks and Sardinians held the line along the river—held it so bravely the British cavalry had not been called into action. Victoria returned to camp thanking God once more but asking him to bless all those who had fallen.

The Lord was called upon by great numbers during the latter part of August, when it was obvious to everyone that some grand effort must be made by one side or the other before the Crimean winter swept down upon them again. The regiment were kept in constant readiness to meet a last desperate Russian attack along the whole Allied front, while the besiegers made contingency plans for a last-ditch assault on Sebastopol if the enemy showed no sign of making a move.

The tense wait for the rolling waves of Russians to come flooding out of predawn darkness, combined with the strain of standing by their arms and sleeping by their horses, began to tell on soldier and general alike. One side would have to break before long.

Victoria found relief in helping Major Prescott, but Charles's only outlet appeared to be in torrents of violent abuse of all those who had brought about the war, had led the armies, had mishandled the campaigns and now sat waiting when they should be attacking.

"We shall be here for another winter, Victoria, take my word," he said many times. "They will sit facing each other until they wake up one morning to snow on the ground and find it is too late. You do not know what it is like here in the winter. We shall never survive it."

He embarked on a fierce campaign of efficiency within the regiment, calling parades twice daily, drilling the troops incessantly to make sure the recruits were up to standard and clamping down on any excessive recreation. A request for a camp concert was immediately denied; the officers were refused drinking parties in their tents and were checked on in a way they had not experienced since Lord Cardigan left the Crimea. As for the soldiers, anyone caught in a condition unfit for duty was severely punished.

Victoria found herself the recipient of all his complaints and fears, needing to say nothing, so long as she sat still, yet he seemed to find no comfort in her presence at the end of it. He spent long minutes brooding in physical and mental isolation, especially at night when she knew he lay staring at the ceiling until the trumpet blew "Stand to Your Horses," at 4:00 A.M.

The last day of August was exceptionally hot. When the regiments stood down at 9:30 A.M. and returned to camp, Charles came in, red in the face and smelling strongly of sweat. He went straight through to wash and Victoria heard him talking to himself under his breath. She closed her eyes for a moment in a mixture of relief and despair. Hugo was safe for today, yet she knew it must come sooner or later. Until it did she must remain here, for there was no hope of a passage to England during this crisis. How much longer could she go on without seeing Hugo? How much longer could she bear to live under the same roof with Charles?

She told the servant to prepare breakfast for the colonel, then went behind the hanging blanket to collect her straw bonnet. Charles was holding a towel in his hands and staring at it as if there were some mark upon it. She took up the hat and was leaving again when he stopped her.

"Where are you going?"

"To the hospital." She did not turn to face him. When his hands took her shoulders in a light grip she flinched. Two steps, and she was free.

"Victoria."

This time she turned. "Yes?"

"I do not want you to go today."

"I have promised Major Prescott."

"I will send a trooper with a message."

"No," she said tonelessly. "I am needed there."

"You are needed here," he said in slurred tones. "*I* need you."

Her quick turn brought him after her, taking her arm and forcing her to stop.

"Let me go, Charles," she said in a quiet but unsteady voice.

For answer he turned her around to face him, looking down at her with eyes whose pale blue had faded into gray. His features were working with emotion, and his fingers dug into her arms convulsively.

"I thought I said once that you were not to go there any more. Why are you defying me?" Without waiting for a reply, he went on. "Do you know the date? Tomorrow is the first day of September. Autumn comes swiftly here, then it is winter. The cold creeps in everywhere. It eats into one's bones and the very marrow within. The eternal whiteness makes one dizzy and blinded. The horses freeze overnight, so that there is a long line of corpses with their legs in the air in the morning. Can you imagine that? You were not here and cannot know what it is like."

"No, Charles, I was not here."

"You were in Constantinople . . . with *him*. All the while I was trying just to keep alive you were devoting yourself to another man. Do you not think that a case of provocation beyond the bounds of acceptance? Do you not think *any* man would be bound to demand satisfaction for his wrongs? I only acted as any reasonable man would. He *was* the most experienced of my officers, and I had every right to send him. No one could accuse me of . . ." He broke off. "This will never end until we go back to England. We cannot stay here for another winter. You do not know what it was like."

She was trembling now. "I do not know what it was like because I was in Constantinople. There, day after day, I saw men who had been reduced to crawling bundles of rags and helped them go to slow and degrading death in Scutari Hospital. Each night I had to scrub myself to get clean, each morning I went back onto a bitterly cold beach to give what little comfort I could to those who *really* needed me—or needed anyone who had enough compassion to extend to them. You do not know what *that* was like, Charles." Trying to steady herself, she added through stiff lips, "However, everyone assures me we shall be home for Christmas. It will be over soon."

"It will never be over," he said in a strange, aloof voice. "Do you think it will ever be possible to forget what has happened here?"

"For those who have taken part, no, never. I wonder if those at home will lose their noble ideals with the coming of peace."

"Peace?" he echoed. "I think I have forgotten what that is." His attention seemed to have wandered away from her.

"I must go," she said, trying to move. But he held her steady.

"You must not. I want you here." He screwed up his eyes as if he could not focus on her. "If you go, there will be nothing."

Overcome by violent trembling, she began to struggle, but it only increased his agitation. He pulled her against him in a desperate embrace while he buried his face in her hair.

"I *beg* you not to go," he whispered hoarsely. "You give all those filthy, ignorant men your attention. Do you not think I need it more than they?"

Fighting against his closeness that filled her with revulsion, she pulled free and began to back away, wide-eyed and breathing fast, but he caught at her skirt and crushed the material in hands that shook.

"Victoria . . ." He fought for words. "Victoria . . . I have lost everything else. You are all I have left."

She took in the drooping shoulders, the grizzled face and clutching hand and wondered if this could be the same man who had taken her with such supreme brutal arrogance on her wedding night and who later told her she was of no further use to him. Had she ever been afraid of him? Had she ever let this man persuade her she was nothing? As she looked at him in that moment, the dam burst and swept her ahead of the great piling waters so long kept harnessed.

"If I am all that is left, then you have *nothing*," she cried. "You have never had me. There has not been one moment when you have. Not all your heritage, your noble name or your Stanford heirlooms bought me. Not all your strength or cruel possession of me took one single part. Not all your demands of me, nor your persecution of Hugo won one whit of me to your side. Even if our son had lived, he would have been all yours, not one part mine. From the moment you put that sapphire on my finger and made your ultimatum, you relinquished the hope of anything I might give you." She snatched the skirt from his hand. "If you have lost everything, it is by your own hand and your own choosing. You are left with nothing, Charles. *Nothing.*"

Shaking from head to foot, she ran from the hut to where her horse was waiting, ready-saddled.

Hugo was trying to compose a letter to Letty Markham on the subject of a collection that had been made among the officers of the regiment for her new son. The sum would be credited to a large London store so that she could choose whatever she wished for the boy as a gift from his dead father's fellow officers. Letter-writing was not one of his greater talents, and the task was not going well, especially in the suffocating heat of the tent. He crushed the paper in his hand.

Deciding to leave it for the moment, he lay on his bed with his arms beneath his head. Victoria could advise him exactly what to write, but he could not ask her. Off went his mind on thoughts better suppressed. He was far away when Brooks, Charles's servant, entered in half-uniform.

"Captain Esterly . . . sir, come quick . . . there's been an accident." The man looked white and shaken. "Sir, it's the colonel. I don't know what to do. It . . . it looks like he's dead."

In one moment Hugo was on his feet and out of the tent, running down the long line between the guy ropes until he reached his brother's hut. His thoughts as he ran were held in suspended animation. He stopped short in the doorway, then walked slowly in.

Charles was crumpled up in the sleeping end of the hut, his face on the dusty floor. Entangled in the fingers of his right hand was his pistol. His right temple was shattered and bloody.

"Dear God in heaven!" whispered Hugo. He sank slowly down on one knee to turn his brother's face around. The pale eyes stared at him in sightless accusation, the proud features cursed him with their marble stillness, the once bright hair frosted with gray spoke to him of a light now snuffed.

"Charles . . . *dear God, no!* Not like this," pleaded Hugo on a breath.

Nearly thirty years flew before his eyes as he held that head in his hands so that it would not rest in the dust. Two boys playing soldiers in the nursery, or hide-and-seek in the shrubbery, the bright golden hair of one betraying him to the smaller one. A youth and a small boy meeting eagerly in the school holidays, catching up on those things dearest to each other's hearts and racing across the paddock to show off new horses. A young man and a youth—the former arriving in all the splendor of a cornet's uniform that somehow made him more than mortal and earned the other's total envy and adulation. Two young men, laughing and vital, a captain and a cornet, shaking hands and clapping each other on the back in that bond of brotherhood and comradeship that stands all tests. Two mature officers in a loved and familiar room, one with a black band over his eyes and the other describing his happiness.

He put his hand over Charles's eyes and closed them forever. Then he put a hand over his own. He stayed there a long time, until there was a movement behind him as the blanket was pushed aside. He raised his head in a daze. Victoria stood there in a sprigged cotton dress and a chip-straw bonnet, distraught and clutching her skirt. It seemed to Hugo that she had ceased to breathe. He got to his feet a shocked and grieving man, unable to accept the truth.

"We have done this," he said hoarsely. "We robbed him of everything that was his by right. We broke his pride and betrayed his trust. I would have remained blinded forever rather than set eyes on you. I wish never to see you again."

CHAPTER EIGHTEEN

Lieutenant-Colonel the Honorable Charles Reginald Stanford, commanding officer of the Hussars, was buried with full military honors at the Crimea on September 1, 1855, after his tragic death in a shooting accident.

That was how the world was notified of the events of that last day in August. It was spoken of in the French and English camps for no more than a day. Death came as regularly as breakfast in the Crimea, and officers were notorious for playing with their pistols as a means of passing the time. Several had shot off their toes, one had put a hole in his forearm, yet another had wounded his brother as they sat admiring the decoration on the handle of the weapon.

By September 2 the incident was forgotten in a greater excitement, as spies gave evidence of an imminent attack by the Russians. The regiments stood to their arms. The British cavalry formed up in the plain beyond Kadikoi every day at 2:00 A.M. to counter any attempt to descend on Balaclava and remained there until it appeared an attack would not be launched that day. Meanwhile, on the 5th, the allies began a tremendous and earsplitting bombardment of Sebastopol, noting with some satisfaction that the bridge of boats leading from the port was never empty of Russian citizens, who appeared to be evacuating the town.

Amid the frantic and deadly preparations, Victoria carried out the sad duties of a widow with an air of desperation, as if she dared not leave herself nothing to do. Her friends rallied to her, but Hugo came nowhere near. Since that moment of death he had behaved as if she were not there. At the graveside he had stood like a lead soldier from a nursery toy box until he had stepped forward to lay Charles's sword on the coffin as a symbol of honor. His face had been gray; he knew there had been nothing honorable about his brother's death. After the earth had been tossed onto the crude coffin, he had walked away, never acknowledging the widow.

Over the past three years Victoria had faced so many of life's challenges and found the courage or compassion to live through them, but now her reserves had run out. She was a creature without purpose, a slender stem with no root, in need of the support she had given to so many in their despair. The one person who could provide it had turned against her. Never had she felt more lost and alone. In life Charles had kept them apart; in death he had made them strangers.

Since she was unable to stay in the cavalry camp, the best that could be done for her was a room in the quarters occupied by the nurses and Sisters of Mercy at Balaclava General Hospital, until the emergency was over and a passage could be arranged. Two nuns moved in together to allow the bereaved lady privacy, but Victoria found their attempts at Christian comfort only increased her plight.

Over and over again she suffered the guilt of not realizing the extent of Charles's need of her that morning, of not seeing that he was as ill as any of the men she had gone out to tend. Every time she closed her eyes she saw him again, hollow-eyed and haunted by the thought of another winter. Hour after hour she struggled to see the light through the darkness of Hugo's words.

Suicide was dishonorable. It offended against Christian principles and marked a man as a coward. That a man like Charles could contemplate taking his own life was beyond acceptance. The truth still would not penetrate the blanket of unreality wrapped around her, and she knew Hugo had come to terms with it only because he held himself responsible and saw her as the cause. *Is he right?* she prayed. *Dear Lord, are we to blame?*

In her strange room, surrounded by nuns and several of the high-born ladies who had always held aloof from her, Victoria tried desperately to face her future and found she could not. The little town of Balaclava reminded her sharply of the short time she had lived there with Letty last October, and she longed for her friend's support now. For the first time she realized the vulnerability of a woman alone.

The officers were kindness itself. Major Mackintosh had packed all Charles's belongings into boxes and sent them down to her new quarters. Lord Dovedale had seen to the

sale of the horses and equipment, and Captain Codrington
had dealt with the letters of condolence that came pouring
in. If he noticed that a great many of those from private
soldiers were promoted more by Victoria's past kindness
than any sadness at the passing of her husband, he did not
say so. Like all her friends, the youthful captain was solicitous to a point beyond friendship, but their sincere and
sometimes shy affection highlighted Hugo's renunciation
and shut her further within herself.

Byron Porchester called on her several times and made
no secret at his distress over her grief. Kind though he was,
she turned down his offers to be of service. Although he
was perfectly proper, she felt that too much dependence on
the sea captain now might lead to embarrassment later, and
she did not wish to hurt him.

The days seemed endless, the nights longer, and such
was her state of mind that when, on September 8, the Allied forces launched their final mammoth attack on the
Russian outer defenses, she cast aside convention and the
good opinion of others to return to Major Prescott's hospital. When one of the high-born ladies made a pointed comment, Victoria retorted that her husband was safely in the
hands of the Lord, but the wounded and dying still had
need of help.

How right her words were to prove only became plain as
the sun went down on that day. The French force had
stormed their objective at midday and captured it with
great élan, but the British had been beaten back with devastating losses. Yet another blundered battle fought in chaos
by untried lads who soon lost heart and discipline when all
around them began to fall in great bloody piles.

Seizing their opportunity, the Russians, who had retreated before the French, rushed across to reinforce their
comrades and caught the unfortunate troops, trapping them
in a bottleneck.

The ladders they had carried into battle to scale the
walls of the forifications were broken and useless, so the
retreating redcoats were obliged to hurl themselves from
the walls to escape, and it was not long before the Russians
found their way to the spot to bayonet them as they came
down. Within minutes, the ditch below was full of bodies,
the dead pouring down onto the wounded and burying

them, while the living trampled over them in their frenzied efforts to return to the comparative safety of the trenches. The surviving officers remained until last, in a vain attempt to take the position by sheer audacity, but they eventually fell or were taken prisoner. The British commander-in-chief was obliged to report to his French counterpart that his attack was a failure and to swallow the bitter fact that his allies had carried off a brilliant assault in a matter of minutes and had the tricolor fluttering above their prize.

Victoria worked hard in the hospital all day and, as she saw the long line of ambulance wagons winding their way up toward the camps, breathed a prayer of thanks that the cavalry had been employed only to provide a cordon around the area. She knew they hated the duty, but mounted troops could not be used to attack fortified walls, although she had heard Lord Dovedale suggest it would not surprise him to be ordered to charge the town of Sebastopol, since the entire campaign had been fought on absurd lines.

Before it grew dark, Major Prescott insisted that Victoria should return to Balaclava. Reluctantly she agreed to allowing a sergeant to accompany her back.

The roads were so familiar after a year, as were the camps filled with uniformed men going about various duties. The smell of horses, of meat boiling, of latrines, of the sweet grass, the tang of the sea, the cool freshness of evening, would she ever forget them? Would she ever be happy among petticoats and embroidery, drawing rooms and vinaigrettes, sedate strolls in the sunshine and women like Charity Verewood? Would she ever fit into a life where bugles did not wake her and the thud of hooves above the shout of men's voices accompanied her breakfast?

She had become part of the regiment and was unable to break away from it. With growing sadness she journeyed down to Balaclava past the camps that housed depressed, dispirited men, sharing their inglorious day and their trepidation of the morrow when they must renew their attack. She asked herself what must be their inner thoughts and feelings as the night hours ticked away, and she knew she would have no patience with drawing-room beaux. And when some fresh-faced squire tried to impress her with how he had galloped at a fence during the hunt, she would think

of glittering rows galloping at cannon. Long after peace
came she would remember those shuffling creatures on the
beach at Scutari and the ragged bearded men with staring
eyes who had lived through the winter and greeted her
when she arrived back. She would remember how an army
had died through neglect and stupidity, and it would be
impossible to hold her tongue on the subject. She would
want to tell the truth of it when she returned—how the
-defenders of their island had been sent off to do their honorable duty with no more regard once they left Britain's
shores than a cargo of animals would have been given.
They would not want to hear, but she would insist on their
hearing it.

On her arrival in England Lord Blythe would expect his
heir's widow to make her home at Wychbourne. That great
house with all its corridors and precious contents would
not compare with a tent on a spring morning; the elegant
dinner table would seem pretentious after an ammunition
box; the green acres would leave her lonely for the sight of
white pyramids, horse lines and scarlet and blue uniforms.

They reached Balaclava, and Victoria turned to the sergeant. He had respected her silence during the journey. He
had a face burned brown by the sun, clear green eyes, and a
mouse-colored mustache. He looked to be a simple honest
man of around thirty. His scarlet jacket had faded to pink.

"How long have you been in the Crimea, Sergeant?"

"Same time you have, ma'am. They might call us both
'old soldiers,' I suppose." He smiled gently.

"May God bless you tomorrow," she said with a lump in
her throat and went inside quickly.

Deep in thought, she sat on a chair and looked from her
window at the smoke hanging still in a great pall over Sebastapol. The sergeant had confirmed her own thoughts—
she was too much of a military wife to desert it now. For a
wild moment she wished she were a trooper's widow who
could marry another right away, but she was a lady who
must observe the conventions. The answer lay in that wish,
however. Marriage to another military officer was her solution—someone a little younger than Charles and with a
more yielding nature. A gentle, understanding man would
have a good wife in her, for she would devote herself to
him and his career, traveling with him wherever he went.

Affection could be between them, for he would surely make no worse demand of her body than Charles had done.

Her spirits dropped. No doubt she had all the qualities required to be a campaigning wife, but it had been hurtfully apparent that breathless, round-eyed admiration from dainty, delicate, *helpless* creatures was what appealed to the officers who now looked upon her as a friend but no more. Slowly she walked across to the mirror to stare at the woman she had become. Nearing twenty-one now, the echo of her experience could be plainly seen in too thin tanned features that were dominated by dark eyes that had lost all luster, and her hair that had once bounced in glossy curls added to her severe look with its present drab coils.

As she stared, another face peeped over her shoulder—a young, beautiful girl who saw in her myriad reflections the truth of a love destined never to die. She turned away and put her back to the mirror. The vision did not fade, so she put up her hands to cover her eyes. It was as futile a gesture as the other, and the numbness following Charles's death vanished completely as she broke into a paroxysm of sobbing for her lost love. Without Hugo she would have *no* future.

It was dark when Victoria became aware of her surroundings once more. Dragging herself to her feet, she lit the lamp. She was in the midst of attempting to arrange her hair in a more attractive style when one of the nuns came to tell her there was a man outside inquiring for her—a rough-looking man who looked as if he could easily become violent. His request would have been denied, except that he was in the uniform of the Hussars and might have some message for her.

Full of apprehension, she snatched up a shawl and stepped out onto the wooden veranda of the building. There was a soldier standing at the end beneath a lamp and, as she drew near, Victoria slowed her steps. His uniform was in the most appalling state—as if he had taken part in today's battle. His left trouser leg was missing and had been replaced by filthy bandages that stretched past his knee. The gold lacing on his jacket was torn and blackened by gun smoke; the fur busby was clotted with mud. His black mustache had merged into a flowing beard, yet, as changed as he was, Victoria knew him, and her hand went out to grip the rail.

"Stokes!"

He stepped forward quickly. "I'm sorry if I give you a fright, ma'am. I didn't ought to be here, by rights, but . . . well, I had to come, somehow." He peered closely at her. "Are you all right, ma'am?"

"I think I should like to sit down," she said faintly. "Perhaps you would sit beside me on the steps for a moment."

He helped her settle on the wooden veranda, then lowered himself carefully to the boards several feet away from her. As she recovered a little from her shock, the full import of his appearance hit Victoria.

"I am so sorry. You . . . you know your wife is no longer with me?"

He nodded. "The captain jest told me."

"She searched for you every day among the wounded, but nobody had seen you and so many had just vanished that day after the smoke cleared. She would not have gone, except that everything pointed to your never returning. Please believe that."

"I know," he said simply.

"She would never have been happy as a servant in England, and it seemed almost providential that there should have been some of her own kind of people in Constantinople when she was feeling so bewildered."

There was a short silence between them. Then he said, "If I could've got word to her I would have done. All I remember of that day was riding toward them guns and thinking how crazy we all was to obey such a command. I never got as far as the guns. My mare fell and tossed me over her head. Next thing I recall I was being marched along inside high walls and not knowing who I was or what I was doing there." A hand that was thin and sinewy scratched at his beard. "Time I got my senses back it was too late to send notification to our people, and the Russians weren't eager to put themselves out over a trooper."

Victoria leaned back against a post. "You have been a prisoner all this time in Sebastopol?"

"Some were taken into Russia, but they let all us out jest before dark today. I went straight to Captain Esterly when they told me about the colonel." He appeared awkward. "I know I shouldn't have disturbed a lady in mourning, but I had the feeling you wouldn't mind, ma'am. You've always been . . . well . . . *different* from other gentry—right from the start, you was. I'm real sorry about Colonel Stanford. This war takes men in all manner of ways, don't it?"

"Yes, Stokes. All manner of ways," she echoed thoughtfully.

They sat staring out across the bright starlit night toward the sea. "The captain has taken it real bad. Jessop says he sits in a trance all the time and snaps his head off if he's disturbed. Isn't there nothing you can do, ma'am?"

Victoria did not find it strange that he should think she should be the one to comfort Hugo. He and Zarina had always known the truth. She made no attempt to be coy.

"I only wish I could. Shock takes people in unusual ways, Stokes. As soon as you are fit enough to take over from Jessop I suggest that might be an excellent move. He has missed your friendship quite as much as your services, you know."

He made no direct answer to that. "So many are gone. I hardly recognize the old Hussars. Poor Mr. Markham, Mr. Edmunds, Colonel Rayne . . . I reckon the captain was lucky. I heard from the lads what you have done, ma'am, and I reckon you should get any medals that are handed out for this lot."

She smiled sadly. "Thank you, but Mrs. Stokes was quite as industrious as I at Scutari. Without her I do not know what I should have done. I felt I had lost more than a maid when she left so suddenly." Thinking about the day Zarina had vanished brought something to mind, and she got to her feet. "A moment, if you please. I have something you might be glad to keep."

When she returned from her room Stokes was standing beside a gray horse she recognized as Hugo's.

"Your wife left this because she could not write me a note. I have had it with me ever since, but you are the one who should keep it now."

Stokes took the circus poster and carefully unrolled it, tears coursing down the grimed cheeks—but Victoria had seen men cry often enough in this war.

She put her hand on his arm. "I am so glad you are back, Stokes. I have seen so many go, it is particularly joyful to see one return." He nodded and mumbled something before mounting the gray. "Perhaps you would tell Captain Esterly . . . tell him . . . tell him—" she knew her pride had gone a-begging, but did not care—"tell him I shall pray for his safety in the coming days."

Stokes saluted and rode slowly away into the darkness.

At 11:00 P.M. Victoria was awakened from an uneasy sleep by a tremendous explosion that shook the ground and set the water jug rattling in the bowl. She jumped from her bed and ran to the window. Over Sebastopol there was a red glow brighter than any sunset she had ever seen. She could only imagine that the guns had started up once more and hit a magazine. However, it could only have been a random shot, for all remained quiet after that. She had only just drifted back to sleep shortly before dawn when her heart began to thud heavily with fright as the whole of Balaclava shuddered yet again—and again and again.

The nuns rushed from their rooms onto the veranda, where Victoria joined them to witness an awesome sight. Over the beleaguered town was the vivid shifting light of enormous leaping flames. Black rolling clouds of smoke spiraled upward into the faintly lightening sky. As they watched, another tremendous roar preceded more smoke and additional red and yellow lights. Sebastopol appeared to be on fire from wall to wall!

So it was that after twelve months of misery, death and destruction on both sides, the Allies captured an empty, ruined town. The Russians, who had evacuated under cover of darkness, after mining the streets and blowing up all their supplies and equipment, were fast getting away across the bridge of boats into the interior. No one was ordered to pursue them. The cavalry watched them go from the top of a hill. The field officers raged, calling down curses on their generals' heads, and almost wept at their own impotence. Quite a few, Hugo Esterly among them, pressed their superiors to take unauthorized action and earned severe censure for their insubordinate conduct.

One newly arrived officer was heard to ask, "What did we want with Sebastopol, by the way?" None of those who had gone out with the first ships could remember the reason.

The soldiers sat in their tents or trenches and said nothing. A rather simple lad who had been in the previous day's assault and had escaped unscathed said, "Have we won the war, then?" and was told to shut his gabber before someone did it for him. Where was the glorious victory, the triumphant advance sweeping the enemy ahead of it, the prize? Sebastopol had not so much fallen as retired from the lists. The Allies were left in their maze of trenches and fortifications, their neat circle of camps, their well-stocked harbor, surrounding a useless ruin.

Quickly, the Russian town was invaded by camp followers, men from the Allied ships and adventurous French troops intent on plundering the houses before everything was reduced to cinders. There was a rush on the evacuated town, men returning with priceless silver, pictures, rich clothing, chairs and tables. One great Zouave staggered up from the walls with a piano across his shoulders.

Because the town was still heavily mined and dangerous, and because there was a great stock of liquor available to anyone who walked into the cellars and stores, the British cavalry was used once more to throw a cordon across the plain leading to Sebastopol with orders to prevent anyone who did not have an official pass from entering. They also patroled the streets of the town, but since their orders did not extend to the troops of their allies, there was a good deal of bad feeling in the British camps, where it was felt that the ban should extend to all or none.

Victoria was kept busy in the hospital, for the retreat of the Russians had enabled the wounded from the disastrous assault to be collected from inside the fortifications. The enemy had left their own wounded behind, and they were treated along with the others. A Rifles officer who could speak Russian was pressed into service as a translator, and he said the prisoners spoke of their relief at being in English hands rather than being put in the hospital in the town, where conditions were as bad, if not worse, than at Scutari. The doctors had fled with the retreating army, leaving the occupants of the hospital to their fate, it appeared. The tale brought much sympathy from the medical staff, but, when it appeared that among the patients were English officers and men who had been captured during the failed assault in June, it was apparent something would have to be done immediately.

Permission was granted for Major Prescott and two other medical officers, plus their staff and ambulance wagons to collect the Allied wounded stranded in the hospitals. Victoria was very quick to ask if she might be included in the party.

"I have watched this war from its beginning," she said. "Will you not allow me the privilege of entering the town for which my husband and so many of my friends died?" Who could resist such a plea?

From a distance the white-walled houses in Sebastopol looked untouched, but once through the cavalry cordon and into the town itself Victoria could see they were merely shells. Together with her three officer companions she appreciated the truth behind this campaign—the tremendous courage and loyalty with which both sides had clung to life and resisted defeat for an entire year. Evidence lay before them of privation, misery and death equal to that suffered by the besiegers, and the girl found herself admiring those who had withstood it only until it was senseless to continue into yet another winter.

There was something hauntingly tragic in riding through the abandoned town, knowing people had lived, shopped and entertained their friends there not so long before. All over the streets were fragments of shell and round-shot, chunks of masonry, smashed glass, wooden beams and torn curtains blackened by smoke. The horses had to pick their way through the rubble and rolled their eyes with nervousness at the pungent burning smell that still lingered.

Large mansions of elegant design had shattered roofs and shell holes in the walls; churches were hollow naves and not much else, the vessels and artifacts having long since been seized by the plunderers. The barracks with its heavy cannon pointing up at the British lines was an enormous place that suggested its occupants had vanished in an instant on the utterance of a magic spell, so alive was it with the ghosts of men who had sat at tables, lain in the iron beds, cleaned their equipment by the windows and fallen in to march to the trenches from its courtyard. The shops had been ransacked until there was not even a signboard outside to tell the nature of their trade, and the gardens and squares were all trampled to gain the fruit growing on the trees or the flowers rioting over low walls.

Victoria rode carefully through this vast fortress, greatly affected by all she saw. Wherever they turned were the dead that had not even been buried by the broken-spirited inhabitants. It was all too dreadfully apparent that hundreds of thousands had perished in the defense of something that was now of no use to anyone—so many that the Russians had been unable to inter them all. Great piles of decomposing bodies lay rotting in courtyards, ditches and huts, casting a nauseating stench over the whole area. The Allied troops had the dreadful task of collecting them all on carts and digging deep pits to contain them.

Victoria had seen death enough, but this was a nightmare of it. Bodies sat against walls with open eyes and arms stiffly extended in a last appeal; some lay naked where they had been stripped for their good uniforms and boots by the victors; others were shattered and unrecognizable. By one, a mere boy, sat a dog, thin and starved, howling for the touch of the hand that had offered it friendship.

The streets were full of military men, French and English, who went about the business of allocating and occupying sections of their prize of ruins, but Victoria rode along the streets seeing Sebastopol through different eyes. Suppose she were a Russian lady riding through a shattered, blackened Brighton, and here was Pavilion with no roof and crumbling walls, the hangings torn and the treasures carried off? What if the hundreds dead here were soldiers from the garrison and residents who had been slaughtered as they desperately defended the elegant seaside resort? What if that dog were Waterloo or Salamanca howling beside the decaying body of his master? A shiver ran through her.

They reached the hospital and encountered a small cavalry piquet. The officer challenged the party. For Victoria there was a smile.

"Good day, Mrs. Stanford. Might I suggest you wait here while these gentlemen enter? Remarkable lady though you are, I really would not recommend the sights to be seen inside."

For once, Victoria was quite happy to play the protected female and chat to the young subaltern while Major Prescott and his fellows set the ambulance orderlies about their grisly task.

"To tell the truth, I am glad the medical fellows have come to sort this out," the cavalryman confided as he sat his horse beside Victoria. "I deplore this duty; it gives me chills up the spine. On the first day our people came into the town they heard the most weird wails and cries coming from this place." He nodded his head at the hospital. "One fellow with a little extra courage entered and found one of our infantry officers lying trapped beneath a pile of dead, quite mad from his wounds and starvation. He must have been there for days."

"How terrible!" Victoria cried. "Poor man. What an unspeakable plight to be in."

"Yes, quite so. He might have recovered from the wound, but his mind could not stand what he saw around him. Sad when a fellow cracks up like that." Instantly a great tide of red flooded his face as he remembered to whom he was speaking, but Victoria just said, "Yes, Mr. Finchley, it is."

It was after midday when the ambulance wagons rumbled off with several English victims who had been found in the hospital and the medical officers emerged looking white and grim-faced. Victoria had been resting on a wall in a shady place, for the heat was quite as extreme as the cold had been the previous day, and her desire was now to return to familiar ground. A few hours in this town was quite enough, she discovered.

In company with the three officers she followed the main street, and could not help thinking of a circus. French, Sardinian, Turkish and British uniforms filled the town with color as the soldiers trotted their horses or marched hither and thither. Every so often they came upon Frenchmen emerging from premises with loot of every kind, many of them carrying bottles from the cellars and drinking as they went.

One French officer rode up to Victoria in gallant manner to present her with a bottle of perfume and a hand-embroidered altar cloth, which he took from his jacket. With Bacchus to inspire him, he insisted on presenting each of the gentlemen with a small token of his esteem and honored comradeship, then galloped away, reeling in his saddle.

Major Prescott smiled at her. "Those fellows have a way with them, have they not? While we sit glumly in camp, they make the best of the situation."

She smiled, the extravagant French gesture having amused her. "One cannot blame them, I suppose—and here are a few more, determined on making a victory out of this."

Around the corner had come a small group of Sardinians. Judging from the way they were singing and laughing they had concentrated their plundering on cellars and wine-stores. In their rather exotic costumes they made a comic picture, arms linked and dancing with intricate but uncertain steps through the cobbled streets. As the group of four riders drew level, the Sardinians greeted them with bows and elaborate gestures of friendship, clustering around them to pat the horses and rub at the polished boots of the officers with their sleeves amid much grinning and excited gabbling.

One of the men approached Victoria, rolling his eyes knowingly, and pulled from beneath his loose tunic a lady's petticoat, beribboned and covered in lace frills. Salaaming unsteadily, he offered it to her, dark eyes flashing and a grin revealing yellowed teeth.

Victoria drew back. The man pressed nearer, thrusting the garment at her with drunken determination and shouting something in angry tones.

Major Prescott said, "I think you had better accept it, ma'am. It might be the most diplomatic thing to do, under the circumstances."

Trying to look pleasant, Victoria took the crushed petticoat and nodded in acknowledgment, but her action aroused surprising emotion in the men, who gave a yell and became tremendously excited. The donor of the gift took hold of Victoria's skirt and shook it vigorously. The Sardinians crowded around the mounted group more closely, frightening the horses, who stamped and tossed their heads.

The ringleader was still tugging at Victoria's skirt and repeating the same phrase that brought a concerted yell from his henchmen. Then it dawned on her that the men wanted her to put the petticoat on, and the first stirrings of alarm began deep inside her. Major Prescott seemed to sense danger at the same time and said in a loud voice, "Stand away! Stand away and let us pass!" and when this met with no response brought his reins down like a whiplash on the man tormenting Victoria.

In that instant the mood of the drunken men changed. Three of them seized the major and dragged him from his horse. The other two officers drew their swords—an act that exploded the Sardinians into a fury of hatred—and Victoria watched appalled as the three British officers were hurled to the ground and attacked with knives. She just had time to see one run his sword through the arm of a burly Sardinian before they all went down, and disappeared beneath a mêlée of thrashing drunkards and shying horses.

Next minute, rough hands seized her legs and tumbled her from her mare, then her arms were taken and twisted behind her as the ringleader tore off the skirt of her riding habit. There was no time to cry out, for all her efforts were concentrated on her struggle. One of them ripped her petticoat from her. She kicked out frantically at him, but he only laughed in her face with a belching breath of sour liquor. Wild, terrible thoughts came to her as he seized her feet and she was carried toward a house by the two men. Conscious only of the sun beating down to blind her, the filthy animal smell of the Sardinians, and the savage sounds of the three officers being murdered by men driven crazy by drink, she cried aloud for someone to save her. Nothing could stop what they meant to do, and she moaned in growing dementia, praying to God to spare her from the horror to which they meant to subject her—praying that they would simply kill her as they had the men.

The house into which they staggered with her was entire except for the roof that was open to the sky and had once plainly been owned by a wealthy family. Her feet were dropped, and one of the men snatched a green cloth from a circular table, spreading it on the floor with a lewd flourish, before the other man forced her down upon it and began tearing at the brown cloth of her jacket.

During the next few moments her reason began to fade as she fought to hold them off. She sobbed to think this was going to be the terrible end to it all. She sobbed for all that was past—for the first time she had been ravished by

Charles, for the son who had lived for such a short time within her as a result of that union, for the steady impersonal submissions she had suffered since then, but mostly for Hugo, her dear beloved Hugo. Her body that he had respected with such honor was to be taken and destroyed by savage strangers who would leave her here to be found by some passing soldier. He would never know she had been thinking only of him at the end.

Her strength had gone now. *"No-o!"* she cried out in a terrible wail, knowing there was no one to hear her.

The day was stifling, the stench sickening and the duty onerous. Hugo was brooding and bad-tempered, moods reflected by his men, who watched the Allies plundering gleefully while they sat upon their mounts in the streets of Sebastopol. The rollicking, boisterous foreigners were making a fortune over their spoils, and the British soldier was a laughingstock in the Allied camps.

Slowly, they patroled the ravaged streets, the men sullen, Hugo lost in his own remorse and suppressed longing. It was a moment or two before the noise of a fracas reached the Hussar patrol and registered in the mind of its leader.

When it did, Hugo halted his men to listen for the direction, then set off at the canter. As they advanced down the street the hollow clopping of hooves raised a sound so deafening that when they turned a corner and into a milling mass of men and horses that Hugo judged to be a dangerous mob, he had to shout at the top of his voice an order to draw swords and advance.

Having his own men with him this time, he used his new methods to bring them speedily from their rigid formation into skirmishing order and led them straight into the pile of Sardinians who had gone completely crazy at the sight of blood and were now attacking each other quite as fiercely as they had their first victims.

Hugo began attacking with the flat of his sword until the group parted and he saw, to his horror, the uniforms of British officers somewhere among the tangle of arms and legs. Shouting to his men, he forced a gap with the gray horse, then began to lay about him in earnest. Within a few moments the Sardinians were begging for mercy and throwing their knives to the ground, many of them having sustained severe injuries to arms and heads as the Hussars surrounded them.

Hugo jumped to the ground and went down on one knee to assist Major Prescott. He was deathly white and his left sleeve was saturated with blood. The lieutenant lying beside him had several stab wounds in his chest and a swollen cheek where boots had kicked without mercy. The other subaltern was trying to drag himself to his feet but was held by the sword knot around his wrist that attached him to a weapon firmly fixed into a Sardinian right up to the hilt.

"I got one of them," he said faintly, then collapsed again.

Hugo tried to raise Major Prescott into a sitting position, but the man was too agitated to help himself.

"Mrs. Stanford," he whispered. "See to Mrs. Stanford."

Every part of Hugo stopped; for five seconds he died. "Victoria?" It came out as a croak. "Was Victoria with you? *Answer me, man*," he roared and shook the dazed doctor like one possessed. "*Where is she? For God's sake tell me where she is.*"

Major Prescott's look told him everything. The blood pounding through his head burst upward like a geyser to leave a red mist of madness. Unseeing, he mounted the gray and turned it, all in one movement, not knowing where to go but driven to go *somewhere*. Setting the beast into a gallop, he was a few yards away when, from a nearby house, came a crashing sound followed by an almost inhuman cry, "*No-o!*"

Turning the horse at the gallop, he set it at a tall window leading from a terrace outside the house. The creature never faltered, taking off in a valiant leap that took them onto the terrace and through the delicate empty window frame to crash into the room within. Hugo pulled up the beast savagely, but it collided with a circular table, slewed sideways and thumped against the opposite wall with a pained explosion of breath. He was out of the saddle like a madman, dragging the creature on the floor to his feet, killing him with a single sword thrust. The other, who had been standing by laughing, still had the look of bleary surprise on his face when the sword sliced across it. For several seconds Hugo stood swaying on his feet, fighting his way back to sanity. Then he dropped the sword and knelt to gather Victoria against him.

"My God, my God, what have they done to you?" he groaned, rocking her like a child while his hand cupped the back of her head with infinite tenderness as she lay against him, racked with weeping.

He held her tightly as the warmth began to flow back into his every vein and nerve, and the memory of. that starry night on the hillside showed him what a misguided fool he had been this past week. He closed his eyes against the pain of all that had been between them. He knew they would never be happy apart for as long as they lived. Holding her now was the sweetest thing he had ever done, for it was his true moment of union with her—free from guilt, free from passion, free from any barriers.

Her sobbing had almost ceased, and he drew the green tablecloth up for warmth against the aftermath of shivering that had beset her. Her head tilted back to look at him.

"How many times have I looked up and suddenly found you there?" she whispered.

When he saw the little brown face and deep brown eyes, the ache in his throat thickened his words. "I was wrong that day. Unforgivably wrong. I am so sorry."

Her finger went up over his mouth. "Never apologize to me—there is no need."

His kiss was gentle, but it told of the love of three years, the need he had of her and the honor so dearly paid for. When he drew away her face had become the same he had seen across the dinner table at Wychbourne so long ago—beautiful, sensitive and on the brink of womanhood, highlighted by eyes full of shy questions and the bronze reflection of candles. Then, as now, he had just had his eyes uncovered to reveal everything in dazzling clarity.

"I love you, Victoria. I shall always love you."

"I know," she said softly.

For the moment, the ruined town of Sebastopol, the anguish of the Crimea, the pride and the jealousies faded, leaving them lost in the world of each other.

Her eyes searched his face hungrily. "My dearest . . . I can never give you a son."

He drew her close to him again and said against her temple. "All I shall ever want is you, and a life where there are no tears, no hatred." He gave a deep sigh of exhaustion.

"The battle is over, my sweet love. Now we have all the time in the world."

With her face pressed against the faded blue cloth of his jacket Victoria remembered an October morning when the mist had just risen from a sun-washed valley. He was right. They had all the time in the world.

M 6 R